The Shadow
And
The Draw

The Shadow Drawn Series

Book 1

R D Baker

For Mark - every argument we had over this story was worth it. You're everything

For Skye - your love and cheers and tears were the only things that kept me going some days. Thank you for loving these characters as much as I do

Trigger Warnings

Please be aware of the following potential triggers within this book:

> *Explicit depictions of sex*
> *Graphic depictions of violence*
> *Sexual Assault*
> *Spousal Abuse/Domestic Violence*
> *Kidnapping*
> *Torture*
> *Suicidal Ideation*
> *Suicide discussed as a past event*
> *Occurrences of Trauma and PTSD*

Be Kind to Yourself, Always

Prologue

There was a time, many centuries ago now, when angels and demons lived within the Halls together. It was a peaceful existence, one ruled by a strict Blood Covenant. An inter-mingling of the species was not allowed. Each kept the to their own kin.

This unity was the lifeblood of the Old God, giving him strength and power over the dominion of the Halls and of the Earth Realm.

There did, however, come a day when an angel violated the Blood Covenant, and he and his demon lover fled the Halls, seeking shelter on the Earth Realm to await the birth of their child. Upon discovery, they were banished forever from the Halls, and their child taken from them.

The angels, against the wishes of the Old God, cast the demons out of the Halls, claiming they had corrupted the peace upon which their existence was built. The demons all fell, in one terrible night, to the Earth Realm.

The Old God grew weak, the broken bonds between his children robbing him of his power. The Line between the Earth and the Halls was severed, only restored once the demon-angel child chose to descend to the Earth Realm herself, rising to become the first Shadow Queen.

The archangels plotted to destroy her, wishing for the freedom and power they enjoyed when the Old God did not have his eyes on the Earth Realm.

She was buried deep underground, doomed to an eternity under the surface of the Earth she so loved. Legend abounded of a place called Hell, spoken as a threat, as a punishment.

But without the presence of the Shadow Queen, there was no need for the existence of a place such as Hell -

that was what the Earth was for.

1
Amryn

"This is the last time," I say, panting, grinding my cock into her hand. Fuck. "This is the last time." I say it again, like it means something.

"Yeah," she says with a sigh, her teeth nipping at my lower lip, her hand gripping me harder.

Fuck. Fuck. Fuck. My hand moves under her skirt, and my cock seeps against her palm as I feel she's not wearing any panties.

"This has to stop, Cora." My fingers dip inside her, and she sucks in a breath.

"Mmmm."

Is she agreeing, or does she just want me to shut up and fuck her? She answers my question pretty quickly, putting one of her feet against the wall behind me, opening up for me, guiding me to where she wants me.

"Oh fuck. Cora." I say it like I'm going to stop, like I'm going to pull back. We both know I won't. My cock slides inside her tight little pussy, and she sighs, her hands on my ass.

"Amryn," she says, her brown curls bouncing as I begin to fuck her, "Amryn, you feel so good."

"So do you, baby." Oh fuck, so do you.

This has to stop. She's not mine to take. She's 21 next month, and then the Ascension takes place, and she's Finn's. But right now, I'm inside her. Right now, she wants me. Right now. There's nothing else but right now.

There are voices and laughter outside the window, people passing by. Cora begins to moan, and I hold her face in my hand, my thumb straying over her lips. "Baby, you gotta be quiet," I say to her. She takes my thumb into her mouth, biting it, sucking on it, her lips vibrating around it as she moans.

She raises her other leg, wrapping it around my waist, and I sink even deeper into her, hot and wet right to the base of my cock. I groan, trying to stay quiet as the voices outside get louder, people right outside the damn window. Anyone would just have to peer in to the darkened room to see her wrapped around me on the counter. To see me buried deep inside her.

She whimpers against my hand, her brow crinkling as she clenches her green eyes shut. She's even tighter now, now that she's about to come. I grab her hands, pinning them above her head against the wall, grinding myself against her, my lips on hers. She tastes good. She feels good. She fucks good. Why does it have to be so good?

Her mouth escapes mine, and she moans loudly, and I feel her pussy contracting, her thighs shaking as she comes.

I don't have to hold back anymore, and slam myself into her as she pulsates around me. I groan into her hair as my cock twitches inside her, spilling more heat, more liquid between her thighs.

I'm breathing hard, trying to be quiet, straining to hear if the voices outside have changed, if anyone heard us and is listening, wondering what that noise was. I let go of Cora's hands, and she wraps her arms around my neck, nuzzling into me, sighing.

"Amryn," she whispers, "fuck."

"I know, baby." My hands cradle her ass, holding her to me.

"You're so good." She sighs, and her eyes look up at me, and I get that feeling in my belly that only she can give me. "I love -"

I kiss her, quickly. I can't hear that. I can't hear her say it. She needs to make it easier for me to stop. She needs to tell me it's the last time, just like every time. It needs to be the last time.

"I do, you know." She says when my mouth finally releases her.

"You can't, baby." My fingers stroke a curl out of her face.

"But I do."

I pull out of her, stepping out of her grasp. "This has to be the last time." I tell her, pulling my jeans back up.

"You always say that," she retorts, running a hand through her curls, which hang wildly around her shoulders.

"Well, I mean it this time."

"Do you?" She shakes her head.

"It's not going to get easier for us if this keeps going."

"It's not going to be easy now," she replies. "You're kidding yourself if you think it will be."

"I know that. But you're Finn's, and -"

"I'm mine," she tells me pointedly, climbing down off the counter, her chin sticking out at me as her eyes blaze into mine.

"Baby, of course you are," I say with a sigh.

"I get to decide," she says, "not Finn, not you, no one else." But even as she says it, her face drops, and we both know it's not true. She puts her cheek against my chest, wrapping her arms around my waist. Fuck. She's so beautiful, it makes me ache.

"Where the fuck is Amryn?" We both hear the voice outside the window.

"Time's up, baby." I say to her, kissing her mouth one more time, wanting her so badly, just wanting to go and find a place to be alone with her.

Cora sighs. "You go on ahead." She tells me.

I sneak out of the bathroom, checking the hallway of the cabin. It's dark. Everything's quiet. I walk outside, and the noise of the clan becomes louder, music playing. It's the last full moon before the Ascension. It's a big deal, like everything seems to be at the moment. I don't feel like being at a party, but everyone's here. And I'm expected to be here.

11

I cross the lawn quickly, trying to get as much distance between myself and the cabin as I can, so no one suspects anything. I'm still breathing heavy, and the hot night air isn't helping. Sweat prickles at the back of my neck, and I can still taste her, still smell her on me.

We've been saying it's the last time for years now. There never should have been a first time, we both knew it wasn't allowed. But I can't stay away from her.

"Amryn!" I hear Finn's voice, and turn to see him walking towards me. He's lost his shirt, determined to show off the new alpha ink he's so proud of, his arms covered in the symbols of the clan, and intricate knots and vines trailing down his back. He claps me on the shoulder, smiling widely. "Where were you, brother? We've been looking for you."

"Sorry, just needed to get some shit done before I could party," I reply, "how's the party going?"

"Everyone's here," Finn replies, gesturing to the bonfires ahead, "just can't find Cora."

"I'm here." The sweet voice behind us wrenches at my stomach. Cora pads barefoot across the grass to join us, her skirt swishing as she walks, the thigh-high split revealing her muscular legs. Finn puts his arm around her, kissing her temple. Her green eyes flicker to mine for a split second, and a flush rises on her cheeks. "Sorry, just had to use the bathroom." She says, smiling up at Finn.

"Not a problem, babe." Finn guides her towards the bonfires, turning to look over his shoulder at me. "Come on, brother. Let me buy my Draw a drink." He laughs, leaning down to talk to Cora as they walk.

I follow them wordlessly. His Draw. I'm just Finn's Draw. The loyal bodyguard.

"Hey, Runt!" Vale's voice rings out over the music, and he waves enthusiastically, gesturing for me to join him and the group of guys he's standing with. "Runt! Come here!"

"Really wish you wouldn't call me Runt, Vale." I say jovially as I reach him.

Vale chuckles, pulling up the brim of his trucker cap to reveal a brow already soaked in sweat from the fire and probably too much beer and whiskey. "Hey man, it's just a joke, right?"

I nod, crossing my arms over my chest. "Yeah, and it's real funny, every single time."

"I got someone for you to meet." Vale says to me, his beard twitching as he grins at me. He stands aside, and there's a pretty girl behind him. "This is Sass."

She looks up at me with big brown eyes, her shiny brown hair hanging down to her waist. She gives me a smile, and extends a hand. "It's Saskia, but everyone calls me Sass."

Vale and the others are snickering behind her. I try not to roll my eyes, I don't want to give them the satisfaction. They love doing this to me, every single chance they get.

"Nice to meet you, Sass, I'm Amryn." I say, taking her hand. It's so small in mine, warm. She's tiny, no bigger than 5 feet, and I tower over her. She's wearing jeans so tight that she'll probably need to be cut out of them, and a lacy purple tank top, her cleavage on full display.

"Amryn," she repeats, looking me up and down. "I sure like that name."

13

"Maybe you could go and get Sass a drink," Vale offers, snorting as he tries to suppress a laugh.

"Sure." I keep a hold of Sass's hand, pulling her along behind me towards the table laden with kegs and whiskey bottles. I hear the laughter of the other guys as we walk away. A lifetime of ignoring their taunts has trained me to ignore it, but I can't pretend it doesn't sting.

"What are you drinking?" I ask her as we reach the table.

"Just a beer," she purrs, watching as I pour her one. She takes the red plastic cup from my hands, her fingers brushing against mine. "So you're the Draw, huh?" She asks me. "I bet you're really strong." Her hand reaches out, her fingers tracing over the tattoos on my arm.

I give her a smile. "I guess I must be." I'm aware of eyes boring into me, and I look over Sass's shoulder to see Cora, under Finn's arm. She's glaring at me, her lips pulled down into a pout.

Sass takes a step closer to me. "What a life to be born into though." She says. "It would get so lonely."

I pour myself a whiskey. I want to feel a little numb. I can still feel the echo of Cora's heat on my body. And now I have a pretty girl in front of me. Being with her does this to me every time - a stoic reminder of everything I'm not allowed to have.

Sass stretches up and runs her hand along the sides of my head. "I love the feeling of a shaved head," she says, giggling. "Can I kiss it?"

I raise my eyebrows at her. "You want to kiss my head?"

14

She nods, biting her lip. "We can start with this one, and then, well, who knows?"

I down the whiskey. I fucking hate this. I never know if these girls just feel the thrill of me being off limits, or if they want to taunt me because they know I can't have them. I look back over at Vale and the others, and they all laugh heartily.

Fine. Fuck them.

"Go ahead, Darlin'." I lower my head, holding my long black hair to one side while putting an arm around Sass's waist.

She almost shrieks with delight, putting a hand on on either side of my face, and brushing her lips against the shaved sides of my scalp. "Oh, it feels so nice," she says with a sigh.

Desire shoots to my groin. She's not Cora. She's not Cora. No, exactly, she's not Cora, that's the fucking point. I raise my face to hers, and give her a grin.

"You're real cute," she says, and she strokes my cheek with her manicured finger. "Real fucking cute."

"You know you're not allowed to touch me, right?" I ask, my voice dropping to a low growl. I want to play this game as long as I can.

Sass bites her lip. "That just makes it all so much more fun." She murmurs, and plants a kiss on my mouth.

I suck in a breath through gritted teeth. "Now you're really pushing it, babe."

"Well maybe we could go somewhere and push a little further, huh?"

I hesitate for a moment, then pull her in, kissing her hungrily. Vale and the other guys cheer loudly, audible over the pounding bass of the music. I'm not allowed to do this. Someone will intervene in a moment. But fuck it, right now, she's throwing herself at me and I'm not going to say no.

"Hey." And there it is. The voice I knew I would hear. I release Sass's mouth, keeping her hand in mine, and turn to look into Lordain's face. "What do you think you're doing, son?" He asks.

"Just having some fun." I reply, pulling myself up to my full height. I'm taller than him now. The Alpha. Well, the Alpha for now. Only a few more weeks of his reign left before Finn takes over. Finn, and Cora.

Lordain's eyes narrow, his thick black eyebrows pulling together into a frown. He looks down at Sass and shakes his head. "You know the deal, Saskia. You get going now."

"But -" she begins to protest, stopping short as Lordain growls low in his throat. "Sorry." She lowers her eyes to the floor, releasing my hand and hurrying off into the crowd.

Lordain turns back to me. "You know the rules, Amryn."

I cross my arms over my chest. "Yeah, I do. No touching, no kissing, no hugging, no fucking, right?"

Lordain sighs, and narrows his eyes a little. "I don't quite remember putting it like that."

"That's the general idea, though, right?" I can't help but sneer a little.

16

"I don't pretend that this is easy for you, and I know those boneheads over there like to dangle the girls in front of you for their own entertainment." He casts a look over his shoulder at Vale's gang, and they all quickly turn their backs. Lordain shakes his head as he turns back to me. "You have to resist all temptation, Amryn. Even when it comes in a sweet little package like the one that was just all over you."

"Sorry, sir," I reply, "living like a monk just gets a little irritating sometimes."

Lordain nods. "I know. I know. But -"

"Do you know, sir?"

He frowns at me. "I beg your pardon?"

"Do you know?" I say it again. "I mean, you got a wife, and I imagine you wouldn't want to go too long without -"

"That's enough," he interjects, his face darkening, "I don't make the rules, our traditions are what they are. We all have our roles to play and -"

"I don't have a choice." I finish his sentence for him. We both know it's true. I walk away from him. I don't want anymore lectures. I pass Vale, and shoot a fireball at his feet with my hands. "Fuck you, man."

Vale laughs. "I don't think so, buddy."

Fuck. Fuck it all to hell. Fury burns in my veins, coursing through my body. I storm into the forest, into the darkness. I just want to be alone.

Alone. Exactly what I'm fated to be.

The stars twinkle overhead, clouds racing past the full moon. The wind is warm, and it smells like Summer. I take a deep breath, trying to calm myself, trying to stop the heat burning in my hands. I'm angry enough to set the whole forest on fire, and that would be - bad.

"Hey."

Oh fuck. "Not now, Cora." I keep walking,

"What the fuck was that?" She's moving fast to catch up to me.

"Nothing."

She grabs my arm. "Stop."

"Why?" I shrug her off and keep walking.

She puts herself in front of me, blocking my way, her hands against my chest. "Why were you kissing that girl?"

"Because I wanted to."

"You wanted to?" She sounds hurt. "Why?"

I jam my hands in my pockets, because I know if I touch her I'll be fucking her against the nearest tree before I know it. "Because for one second a girl was throwing herself at me and I didn't want to say no."

"Amryn -"

"Just leave me alone." I push past her.

"I don't want to leave you alone." She says, and I can hear the hurt in her voice. "Why would you kiss someone else when we just -" She trails off.

"Cora, I don't want to kiss anyone else, but sometimes, I just want to feel like I'm a regular guy, who can do those things, you know?" I can feel the sneer on my face, and I don't want to be cruel, but I'm hurting. "I have to watch you, with Finn, all the time. You think that's easy?"

18

"You know I don't feel that way about him."

"And?" I say with a laugh. "What does that change? I'm still just the Draw, still just your dirty secret -"

"You are *not* my dirty secret!" She cries.

"No?" I scoff. "Then what am I?"

She shakes her head. "You know exactly what you are, Amryn, you've always known that."

"Yeah well, I can't be that. And this -" I gesture back and forth between the two of us. "It stops, now."

"Amryn -" She takes a step towards me.

"Go back to the party." I point over her shoulder. "Your fiance's waiting for you." I turn on my heel.

"I want to be with you." But she doesn't follow me. She knows there's no point.

I keep walking, through the forest, away from her. The night is warm, and the moon is bright.

Only four weeks until she's his.

Tonight was the last time.

2
Cora

It takes me a while to realise the drumming I can hear is rain against my window, and not the thumping in my head. I pull my pillow over my head. I'm an idiot. I shouldn't have had so much whiskey last night. It does this to me every time. But seeing Amryn with that girl, and then having a stupid fight with him...

I don't have a right to be angry. He's not mine. I know that. Even though he's been my first, my only. I've never been with anyone else. I never want to be with anyone else. But I don't have a choice. None of us do.

I roll onto my back, throwing my arms out. I hate this. I'll never forget the look on Amryn's face the day we were summoned to the council and told what the Fates had decided - that I was destined for Finn, and Amryn was destined to be alone, to be the Draw.

It still didn't stop us, of course. I've loved Amryn ever since I can remember. It's always been him. I close my eyes, breathing in deeply, allowing myself a small smile. I think back to that first time, and all the times since then, remembering the feeling of Amryn's mouth on mine, his hands on me, his -

"Cora!" My mother calls from the kitchen. I can smell bacon, and coffee. She's been doing this a lot lately, putting in a lot of effort to make every meal, every moment we have together special. I think she's scared. I think she's realising that soon her little girl will be a married woman, and won't be at home anymore.

I push back the comforter and swing my legs over the side of the bed, my head hammering hard. I clutch a hand to my temple, and swear to never drink again. This is bullshit.

"Cora!" My mother calls again.

"Coming!" I stumble to the bathroom, pulling on my white robe with the wide kimono sleeves as I go. As I fold it over my chest, I look down and see the love bite on my breast. Shit. We're not being careful enough. Not that it matters. It was the last time. Right?

My mother's standing by the stove serving up bacon and eggs when I walk into the kitchen. She gives me a big grin. "How's the head?"

I grimace as I sit down at the white table under the window. "I hate whiskey."

My mother laughs, placing a plate in front of me. "Come on, eat up. It'll make you feel better." She pours me a coffee, stirring in the oat milk she insists is better for me than regular, and places that down too. "So." She fixes me with a stare as she sits down with her own coffee. "How are things with Finn?"

21

I shove a forkful of bacon and eggs into my mouth so I don't have to answer right away. Finn's fine, I guess. He's tall and blonde and muscular and all the shit the girls love. He's a good kisser. He's strong. He'll be a good alpha.

I look up to see my mother still waiting expectantly. I shrug. "Things are fine. He's very - affectionate." I choose the word carefully.

My mother frowns. "He's not overstepping any bounds, is he?"

"Oh no." I shake my head quickly. "No, nothing like that."

"Because Lordain and Morgan have been very adamant about the both of you keeping that until after the wedding," my mother says sternly.

"I know, Mom," I assure her, trying to keep my tone light. "It's nothing like that. He just - I dunno. He wants to kiss me all the time, he touches me a lot, tells me how beautiful I am all the time." I stab my fork into my bacon.

"Because you are beautiful, sweetie," my mother says indulgently. "I mean just look at you. Curly hair and that golden skin and your beautiful green eyes, of course he wants to look at you all day."

I smile. Mothers always think their children are beautiful. "Yeah well, he seems very pleased to have such a pretty fiancee."

"And rightly so." My mother sighs as she leans on the table. "I heard Lordain had to pull Amryn into line. That boy -" She shakes her head. "I don't know. I have a feeling he's going to be trouble for you and Finn."

"No he won't." I don't mean to snap, but I do. "And he's not a boy anymore, Mom."

"I know you're fond of him, sweetie -"

"And you're not?" I ask her incredulously. "I mean, you practically raised him after Elspeth died."

"Of course I am," she replies quickly, "he was always a good kid. But now, I mean, he needs to know when to fall in line."

"It's not easy for him, you know." I say. "I mean, imagine not even being able to touch another person? No kissing , no hugging, never holding anyone's hand? That's awful."

"Those are the rules, Cora."

"Well, the rules are stupid." I throw my fork onto my plate, the pounding in my head returning as anger swells within me. "Why can't the Draw do their duty if they're in love? The Striker is allowed to have a regular life, have a family and -"

"That's just Fate, sweetheart." My mother interjects. "We demons know how important the Draw is, and it's a role that should be respected. Especially by the Draw himself. Look at Lordain. His Striker died in the last war, so now he relies fully on Roche to protect him."

"And what if Roche dies?" I ask dryly.

"The Fates will choose a new Draw for him," my mother replies, "because the Draw is the one that is important. The most important of all. And that burden brings strict requirements with it"

I shake my head. "Amryn didn't ask for this." I say quietly. None of us did. I don't say that part out loud.

My mother reaches across the table and takes my hand. "Come on now, I didn't mean to upset you. Eat your breakfast and we'll plan your birthday party."

I raise my eyebrows. "My birthday party? I'm not seven years old anymore."

My mother laughs. "No, but you'll be 21, and since you can't have a party on your birthday because of the ascension, I thought it would be nice to celebrate before it. A 21st birthday is a big deal, honey."

It sure is. Adulthood. Responsibility. Crossing a threshold there's no coming back from.

"I wish your Dad was here."

The words catch me off guard. My mother never talks about my father anymore, she stopped years ago. She really must be feeling nostalgic, with my birthday and the Ascension coming up. "He'd probably love the party." I say quietly.

My mother chuckles, but her eyes look sad as she gazes out the window at the falling rain. "Yes he would."

We sit in silence for a while, and I drink the disgusting oat milk coffee, swearing to never touch the stuff again once I have my own house. Oh fuck. My own house. With Finn. The impressive log cabin Lordain had built for us - where Amryn fucked me in the bathroom last night. My face burns at the memory.

"Oh," my mother says suddenly, "your wedding dress arrived." She gets up from the table, rushing in the direction of her bedroom.

24

It had taken us a long time to pick out a dress. I didn't want to get married in white, but everyone insisted. It felt wrong to me. Not because of the stupid "virgin" thing - no, I think I was just determined to push away the idea of being a bride. I wanted black or pink or red, under the premise that I wanted something fun. Something different. But different wasn't OK.

My mother carries out the garment bag, holding it up and unzipping it, revealing the flowing white gown with thin straps. It's simple at least. "And we can do your hair with the white flowers," my mother says, gazing adoringly at the gown.

"Sounds great, Mom." It doesn't sound great at all, but I don't want to ruin her mood. "Well, thanks for breakfast." I get up from my chair and clear my plate.

"Where are you going?" She asks, zipping the dress back into its bag.

"I need to go train," I reply, stretching my back. "A workout will be good for my hangover."

My mother looks out the window. "But it's raining."

"I don't care!" I leave the kitchen quickly, and head back to my bedroom to change into black leggings and a neon pink crop top. Yes, a workout is definitely what I need. I pile my curls on top of my head and secure them with a black scrunchie.

The rain is invigorating, and the compound is quiet as I make my way across the grass towards the training yards. The windows of the log cabins are dark, and smoke curls from some the chimneys even though it's summer. Everyone's sleeping off a hangover it seems.

There's about 400 of us living here, on these acres and acres of land in the valley. It used to be a much smaller clan, but now Lordain is the head of the biggest one. Ever since my father died, and our home was destroyed. Lordain took the survivors in. I should be grateful I guess. Some days it doesn't feel like much of a blessing.

I look up at the wooded hillsides, watching the mist roll down off them, wondering if Amryn is still out there, or if he returned last night. I shouldn't have followed him. I have to be so careful not to arouse suspicion. It would put Amryn in danger.

I grab a bo staff as I enter the training yard, swinging it absently in my hand, twirling it across my palm. I approach the wooden dummy with the swinging arms, and slam the bo staff into its body, sending the arms flying into rotation. I easily hit them all back, alternating the bo staff back and forth.

"You've gotten real good at that."

I stop, smiling to myself. I turn around, and Amryn's standing there, in the rain. He's not wearing a shirt, and his tattooed arms are crossed over his chest, and everything's muscly and bulging and so fucking hot. His black hair hangs over one shoulder, his hazel eyes fixed on me. And he's smiling at me, our fight from last night forgotten.

I hold the staff out to him. "You want to have a turn?"

He shakes his head. "I like watching you."

"Oh come on." I grin at him. "Show me your moves, Runt."

He raises an eyebrow. "Don't call me that."

26

I bite my lip. I don't even know why I said that. It's cruel. I shouldn't call him that.

He steps forward, grabbing the bo staff from me. I stand back, and watch as he spins the staff in front of him, behind his back, seemingly not even touching his hands as it whirls around him. With a deft movement, he swings it at the dummy and shatters the top of it clean off in a shower of wood splinters.

He throws the staff to the ground and stalks past me.

"Amryn, I'm sorry."

He stops, turning back towards me. Oh god, he's so beautiful.

"Don't call me runt."

"I know. I know. I'm so sorry."

He points a finger back towards the houses of the compound. "They all talk to me like that. But not you." His finger points at me. "Not you. Ever."

I shake my head. "I'm sorry, Amryn."

He nods and looks away, unmoving.

"Did you like that girl?" I ask him.

He looks back at me and scoffs, smiling. "Seriously?"

"Yes seriously." I pick at one of my fingers. "I mean, she was pretty."

"She was." He looks up at the rain falling. "You're prettier though."

"Did you want to fuck her?"

He shakes his head, grinning crookedly. "Not allowed, baby, you know that."

"But if it was -"

"Cora." He interjects, his expression suddenly earnest. "Leave it."

He's right. This is a pointless conversation. I'm jealous and that's all there is to it. "Where did you go last night?"

"Up into the mountains," he replies, looking up into the green hills, now shrouded in mist. "I just needed to -" He shakes his head. "It doesn't matter." He goes to one of the wooden stores, opening it and pulling out two boxing pads, putting them over his hands. "Come on, Alpha Queen. Let's see what you got." He drops into a lunge, the pads in front of him.

We've been training together for years - or rather, Amryn's been training me for years. He's the born warrior. We know each other's moves, almost like we know what the other person is thinking, but lately I've been able to surprise him, and it's a thrill every time.

I smirk, then rush at him, swinging to the left, raising my right knee at the same time, smashing my fist into the pad and catching him in the ribs with my knee. Amryn stumbles backwards, chuckling. "Is that all you got? You really did drink too much last night."

I spin and kick backwards, Amryn dodging me easily. He backs up along the yard, and I follow him, my right fist shooting out and connecting with the pad.

"Oh come ON," he jeers, "that's all the Alpha Queen can throw at me?"

"Why you hiding behind those pads, Amryn?" I tease, and stick out my tongue. "Afraid I'm going to hurt you?"

He straightens up and raises his eyebrows. "Oh, it's hand-to-hand combat you want, huh?" He throws the pads aside, and raises his bare hands. "Come and get me then."

I rush at him, and as he raises his hands I drop into a spin kick, taking out his legs, and he falls flat on his back. He laughs, and launches himself back up on to his feet and tries to grab me, but I duck out of his grasp and spin behind him, jumping on his back, getting his neck in a vice grip.

"Look at you," he says, then grabs on to my arm, flinging me ass end up, and I land on my back in the mud. He leans on his knees over me, and grins. "What are you doing down there?"

"You should watch out." I turn over and crawl away in a low crouch. "I'll get you when you least expect it."

Amryn throws his head back and laughs, then launches himself at me again, landing on top of me, hands either side of my head. He looks down, and sees my feet planted against his stomach, giving me a crooked grin when he looks back at me. "Nice one."

I push with all my might and while he doesn't fly as far as I would like, it's far enough. As usual though, his recovery is lightning fast, and he's back on his feet.

"You can do better than this, Cora," he says, putting his hands on his hips. I can't help but notice how low his jeans are hanging, the rain and sweat mingling on his body and running down his abs. "Eyes up, soldier." He barks, grinning.

I roll my eyes. "I can do way better than that, just depends on how much pain you're prepared for."

He bares his teeth at me and spreads his arms wide. "We both know you can't hurt me, baby."

"You sure about that?"

"Haven't managed to so far." He cocks an eyebrow. "Not anything I didn't want to have hurt anyway."

My mouth twitches into a self-assured smirk. "Maybe today's the day your luck runs out, huh?" My veins glow white as I summon my flames.

Amryn laughs. "I dare you." He flexes his outstretched arms, his tattoos rippling. "I double dare you."

I throw myself at him, the white bolts of my flames leaping from my fingers and striking him like lightning, sending him flying, flat onto his back in the mud. I laugh. "You shouldn't dare me, Amryn." He lies completely still. I roll my eyes. "Come on, get up." I say. He's still not moving. "Amryn, this isn't funny."

Oh fuck. Oh no. He's the only one who can withstand my flames, he's right I can't hurt him. But he's lying there and he's still not moving.

He wasn't ready. I hit him too hard. Shit shit shit.

"Amryn!" I hurtle to his side. His eyes are closed, and he's still not fucking moving. I grab his chest, shaking him. Is he breathing? "Oh my god, Amryn, Amryn, oh shit."

His chest shakes as he begins to laugh, squinting at me in the falling rain. "Gotcha."

"You fucking asshole." I slap him hard across the face. "You scared the shit out of me!" He grabs my hand and

30

rolls me over onto my back, pinning me down in the sodden mud. "Ugh!" I cry out as the mud seeps into my clothes, and all through my hair. "Amryn, let me up!"

"Do you yield?" He's grinning at me, laughing as I sink further into the filthy mud.

I spit in his face. "Fuck you."

His eyes flame, and then he crushes my mouth with his. This is dangerous. We're out here in the open, anyone could see us. But his mouth on mine is so electric and so fucking delicious and all I want is for him to tear my clothes off and fuck me right then and there.

He pulls back from me and grins. "You need a shower, Cora, you're disgusting."

I buck underneath him. "So let me up."

He presses his hips between my thighs, and I can feel his cock swelling against me through his jeans, and oh my fucking god I'm dripping wet in every possible way. "Do. You. Yield?" He asks me again, his lips nipping at mine.

"Yes," I say with a sigh. Oh fuck, I want him so bad.

"Yes?" He's still holding me down, tracing the tip of his nose along my jawline.

I nod, my eyes fluttering shut as he presses himself harder between my thighs. "Yeah."

He gets up and pulls me to my feet. "Come on, let's get you all clean." He takes my hand, leading me across the yard. We're headed towards his cabin, just beyond the copse of trees, the small one with the red roof and the crooked chimney.

We almost reach it when he suddenly drops my hand and turns around, his face apprehensive. He's looking past me, and I turn to see Lordain walking straight towards us. Oh shit. His fists are balled at his sides, his eyes fixed on us. I can see his beard twitching, probably muttering to himself.

"What's this?" He asks us, his eyes darting from me to Amryn and back again.

"Just training," Amryn answers, his arms crossing over his chest.

Lordain looks me up and down. "In the mud?" He asks incredulously.

"It's raining, sir." I reply, meeting his gaze.

"And what were you doing going to Amryn's cabin?" Lordain asks

"He offered to let me clean up," I reply flatly. "My poor Mom would have a heart attack if I came in and sullied up her pretty bathroom with all this mud."

"I have an outdoor shower," Amryn interjects, smiling amicably. "Makes things so much easier."

Lordain looks from me to Amryn again, and shakes his head. "I don't need to tell the two of you what this looks like."

"What does it look like?" I'm on dangerous ground. I'm challenging the alpha, and my future father-in-law. But I gaze at him as innocently as possible, my hands clasped behind my back like a good little schoolgirl. I even raise my eyebrows. "I just want to get this mud out of my hair, sir."

Lordain exhales heavily. "I've got my eye on you." He points a finger at Amryn. "You are my son's Draw, and I expect you to honour that."

A muscle in Amryn's jaw feathers. "Yes sir."

"And you -" He darts his finger in my direction, "you behave yourself in a manner that befits an Alpha Queen, do you hear me?"

I nod curtly. "Yes, sir. Always."

I can see Lordain wants to say more, but he won't make an outright accusation out here. Not against me, not against Amryn. Finn loves us both too much. The thought makes my stomach twinge with guilt for a split second, and I almost feel bad for betraying Finn.

Lordain spins on his heel and storms away as the rain begins to fall harder.

Amryn exhales heavily next to me. "Well, fuck," he says quietly.

"That could have gone a lot worse." I say, looking up at him. "You can't do that in public."

"I won't." He replies. "I told you, it was the last time last night."

I swallow hard. "Sure. I know that. Anyway, maybe I should just go back to my place."

He grunts and turns, heading back to his cabin. "Don't be ridiculous, you can shower here."

I hesitate, watching his retreating back. He stops, and I see his shoulders heave as he sighs, his head tipping back. "Are you coming?" He's not really asking me.

I hurry after him, the feeling of mud in my hair and my ears just too much. I'm desperate to be clean, and warm. I cast one last glance around the compound before following Amryn through the tall wooden gate at the back of his cabin.

The outdoor shower is in the corner of the small courtyard, a rain-shower head in the wooden ceiling. I hug myself as Amryn turns on the water, and I feel cold. I know what I'm doing is dangerous. It's stupid. I should have gone home. But I don't want to leave...

"OK." Amryn says, putting his hand under the stream of water, "it's nice and hot now." Steam rises, furling across the courtyard. "Get under and you can rinse those clothes." He stands back, leaning against the wall, his arms crossed over his chest.

I step under the stream fully dressed, undoing my hair, running my hands through it, trying to shift all the grit. The mud washes off my clothes, and I try to take off my crop top, almost impossible because it's soaking wet.

"Amryn, I can't -" I look at him helplessly. "Can you help me?"

He steps forward without hesitation, putting his hand under the band of the top, and yanks it up over my head. And of course now I'm fucking topless in front of him. He drops to his knees and peels my leggings off, and I rest my hand on his shoulder for balance as I step out of each leg.

We both pause like that, for what feels like a long time, and he holds onto my leg, bent over his arm, staring at it. He brings his lips closer, brushing along my inner thigh, and I gasp, my fingers digging into his shoulder. He

34

presses his lips into my flesh, his other hand on my ass, kneading my skin.

"Amryn, you said -"

"I know what I said." His eyes look up at me. "And I'm a fucking liar." He dives back between my thighs, his tongue pushing the lips of my pussy apart, finding my clit.

I throw my head back. Oh fuck. No no no. We can't do this. But his tongue swirls around me, and he puts my leg over his shoulder, so he can open me up wider, his mouth exploring more of me. Oh it feels so fucking good.

I jam a fist against my mouth to suppress my moans. Shit. His hand moves between my legs and he pushes two fingers inside me. I'm sure I'm about to explode. His mouth is locked on my clit, his tongue rolling up and down, up and down, and I don't think I can stand, I'm going to fall over, my legs are shaking so hard.

"Amryn," I gasp. I know he won't stop. He won't stop til I come, and I don't want him to stop.

He curls his fingers inside me, his tongue working me harder, and my head flushes with heat, my orgasm rising. That sweet pressure in my belly pushes out, out, out, until my body contracts and I fold in on myself, biting into my hand to stop myself crying out. I whimper as I subside, tasting blood, and seeing I've broken the skin on my hand.

Amryn rises before me undoing his jeans and kicking them off as they fall down his legs. I know he's not done with me yet. I've seen that look so many times.

"Amryn," I say weakly, putting my hands against his chest, "someone's going to hear us."

He backs me up against the wall of the shower, his hand on my throat, his mouth pressing into the soft flesh behind my ear. Oh fuck. I quiver as his lips move. I can't resist this. His other hand is on my breast, catching my nipple between his fingers, pulling and teasing it.

The heat between my legs from my climax is rising again, and it's unbearable. I groan. Fuck it. "I want you inside me." I know I shouldn't do it. I shouldn't encourage this. We said it was the last time. It's always the last time. It's always the last time with us.

Amryn hoists me up around his waist, and I know he's not going to take his time, his thrusts almost jaw-shattering. I love it when he's like this. I wrap my arms around his neck, holding him close to me. He's out for his climax now, and I want him to have it, I want him to have it inside me. Fuck, he feels so good.

He grunts, trying to keep his mouth closed, trying to suppress the sounds he really wants to make. "Fuck." He gasps. "Oh fuck." He shudders, his arms tensing around me. Then with a rush he releases, coming inside me, his breathing rapid. I nuzzle into the crook of his neck, breathing him in, feeling his warmth and his skin, and fucking hell I love him.

He pulls back, breathless, and I smile at him. He doesn't return my smile. "What's wrong?" I ask him.

"I want more time," he says with a sigh. I unfurl myself from him, putting my feet down on the floor of the shower. "I want more time," he says again, leaning against the wall, leaning over me. His hand moves up to my cheek, stroking it gently. "I fucking hate this. Always having to be quick, be quiet, be -" His mouth sets in a hard line, and he

36

shakes his head. "Guess we won't have to worry about that soon. We're out of time." He pushes himself off the wall, away from me, running a hand through his hair under the water.

"I want more time too." I press myself against his back, laying my cheek against his skin, wrapping my arms around his waist. "I just - I wish for it too."

"I go in to Isolation next week." He sighs heavily. "Alone. Again. I'm always fucking alone."

I grip him tighter. "You're not alone. I'm here."

He laughs bitterly. "You're not mine."

Yes I am. I can't say it. I can't do that to him. That would be cruel.

He turns around and looks down at me, his eyes full of sadness. "That girl?" He says, shaking his head. "I kissed her to feel something, something different. I wanted to push away everything I feel when I'm with you, because when we're together it's perfect, and then afterwards, I mourn you. I grieve for every single moment I know we'll never have." He points towards his cabin. "I lie in that bed at night and I ache for you. It kills me, every single time."

I feel tears burning my eyes. "I know." I don't know what else to say.

"You should go." He says. "Lordain will be watching the cabin and if you stay here too long, he'll get suspicious."

"Ok." I reply quietly. I struggle into my soaking wet clothes, which feel absolutely terrible, and make me feel even worse. I look up at him, and his face crumples as he gazes back at me.

"Don't look at me like that."

"Like what?" I ask.

"Like you need me." He replies.

I do. I do need you.

I avert my eyes, and clear my throat, willing the lump that's formed there to dissolve. "I'll see you at the Table then." I don't know why I say it. I guess I'm always waiting for the next time I see him. It doesn't matter when or where. I just need to see him.

He's silent as I leave, and the wooden gate thumps shut behind me. The rain is falling harder now, beating down from the bruised sky. I let it wash over me, make me feel cold, chill me to the bone. I don't want to be warm. Amryn is warmth.

"How was your workout, honey?" My mom calls out as I walk into the house.

"It was fine!" I call back, and my voice cracks. I flee to the bathroom, locking the door behind me. I turn on the hot water, and I stand under the shower and cry and cry, until my mother starts banging on the door, asking if I'm OK, and if I could please stop wasting water.

"What happened to your hand?" Finn points at the bite mark on the heel of my hand.

I look down at it, my mind racing. "Uh, it was one of the dogs."

Finn takes my hand, inspecting the small wound and the bruised marks around it more closely. "That doesn't look like a dog bite."

I pull my hand away, and smile at him. "Well it is, so -" I shrug. "I guess I got too close when I was feeding him, and he nipped me." We're sitting on the hood of his truck, watching the sun set over the canyon. The sky is purple and orange and pink above us. I lean back against the windshield, one hand behind my head. "I can't believe we're getting married in 3 weeks."

"I know," Finn replies. "I can't wait."

I can.

I smile at him. I've become really good at playing the part. I've had to. Finn's gorgeous, long blonde hair and tanned skin and big muscles. At least he's attractive. It could be so much worse. The thought makes me cringe at myself, as though being forced to be with someone handsome makes this whole situation any better.

"You're so beautiful," Finn says, lying on his side and gazing at me. His hand reaches out, tracing down the deep neckline of the black shirt I'm wearing. "It's so hard not to just fuck you now."

I force a giggle. "Having to wait sucks, doesn't it?"

"Yeah." Finn turns his head, looking up at the sky. "Too bad our first time will have an audience."

My head snaps over to look at him. "What?"

His eyes languidly make their way back to mine, and he frowns when he looks at me. "What?" He rises up on one hand. "You didn't know?"

I sit up, feeling my heart hammering in my chest. "What do you mean, an audience?"

"The Ascension ceremony, it's public." He shakes his head, smiling at me like I'm an idiot. "It's just a part of the old rites, they have to make sure we really, you know."

I shake my head. "That we really what?" I need to hear him say it. Because the thought makes me feel so dizzy I want to tear my skin off. "Finn, that we really *what?*"

"Cora, come on, you know what I mean."

"You mean you'll fuck me in front of the whole clan?" I feel nausea sweep over me. He cannot be fucking serious. He nods, his calm demeanour making me want to throw him off the cliff we're parked on. "Finn, please. Tell me you're joking."

He laughs out loud. "No, babe, I mean it. It's OK. You don't have to be afraid." He reaches out and strokes my cheek. "It's just our first time, and then we can have time to do it properly afterwards."

"In front of my mother?" I ask. "In front of your parents? In front of -" Amryn. In front of Amryn. My new husband is going to fuck me in front of Amryn.

Amryn's going to kill him. Oh my god, Amryn is going to fucking *murder him.*

I lurch off the car, breathing in deeply through my nose. This cannot be happening. This cannot be real. As if things weren't bad enough. I look out over the canyon, and hear Finn jump down off the hood, his footsteps crunching in the stony ground as he walks up behind me.

40

"It's OK, babe." He puts his arms around my waist, pressing his cheek to mine. "I know it's a bit strange, but it'll be OK. I'll be gentle. I promise."

"But in front of everyone?" I ask weakly. There's no point questioning it. That's how the clan works. That's just how it works. "I wanted our first time to be special."

"And it will be." He turns me around to face him, his hands stroking my face gently. "Look, it's a weird tradition. It'll be awkward. I know it's not a girl's dream for it to be like this. But afterwards, I'll take my time." He kisses the corner of my mouth.

He'll take his time. He'll have what Amryn's never had. Finn will be able to take his time and savour the experience. I don't want our first time to be special, I don't even want to think about that. But I expected it to at least be *private*.

"We should get back." I say as he leans his forehead against mine. "We need to be at the Table, the council meeting starts soon."

Finn sighs. "You're right." He kisses me, softly, gently. Like he has time.

We bump along the road, back down to the compound, the sun disappearing behind the mountains. Finn makes small talk, but I'm barely listening.

In front of the whole clan. The *whole fucking clan*.

Finn pulls up out the front of my mother's house, and leans over to brush a kiss on my lips. "I'll see you at the Table," he says to me, smiling.

I barely smile back before I stumble out of his truck, stalking across the front yard towards my mother's house. No one told me. How could no one tell me this?

"Mom!" I throw the front door open. "Mom!"

She comes hurrying out of the kitchen, frowning. "Honey, is something -"

"Did you know?" I ask. Of course she knew. She's been part of this. She knows what it entails. "You knew and you didn't tell me?"

She shakes her head. "Tell you what, honey?"

"About the Ascension." I can barely say it, the thought makes my breath freeze in my chest. How fucking humiliating. "You never told me that Finn, and me -" I gasp, trying to get the words out, panic seizing my stomach. "In front of everyone. Everyone?"

She approaches me, her face breaking into a look of sympathy and understanding. "Oh honey, I thought you understood." She takes my hands in hers. "It's not as bad as you think."

"So you, and Dad, when he became Alpha..." I trail off.

She nods. "Yes. It's a requirement of the Ascension."

I can't look at her for a moment. "Mom, I don't think I can do that." I shake my head emphatically. "I know it, I know I can't do that."

"Now, now, it's OK." She gives me a reassuring smile. "It's not as bad as you think. The room is dark, you won't be able to see anybody. Just Finn. It'll be like no one else is there."

"But they'll be able to see me?" I ask. "You'll be able to see me, like that."

She takes a deep breath. "It's just a ritual. It would be no different than if you told me you were pregnant, then I'd know you and Finn had had sex too."

"Knowing and seeing are two different things." I shake my head. "I can't do this."

"Yes you can."

"Mom, it's barbaric!" I cry.

"Cora, it's tradition." Her voice changes, and her expression darkens a little. "Now stop getting yourself all het up over nothing. You're going to be a Queen, and this is what we go through when we become Queens. Finn has to claim you, that is simply how it works." She drops my hand. "Now go and get ready for the Table, you can't be late."

She leaves me standing in the lounge room, and I hear thunder rumbling in the distance. I want to scream, or run. But I can't. I'm trapped.

I'm so fucking trapped.

3
Amryn

"Looking good, Runt." Vale approaches me, his bald head shining under a layer of raindrops. He looks me up and down and whistles. "Very sexy. All in black. Bet the girls love it."

"Do you ever get tired of being a complete asshole, Vale?" I ask. I'm standing outside the Council building, where we convene at the Table, and I really don't have patience for Vale's bullshit today.

My arm stings from the new Draw ink I was subjected to earlier, an 8-pointed knot on my forearm, the sign of my status. My servitude, more accurately. Because we demons heal quick, the ink has silver nitrate in it. We're allergic to it and it halts the healing process, to give the ink time to settle under our skin. I have tattoos over both shoulders and down both arms, they've never bothered me before.

This one fucking does. It hurt and it burned and now it just fucking itches. My sleep has gone to shit so I'm tired, and right now I just don't want to deal with Vale being an ass.

But instead of continuing to be a fucking jerk, Vale laughs and claps me on the shoulder. "Hey, no look, I'm sorry. We gotta stop this shit. We're not kids anymore."

No. We sure as hell aren't. "So you gonna stop calling me Runt?" I ask.

"Yeah. Come on, we got jobs to do now, right?" He leans his back against the wall beside me on the porch, his hands in his pockets, looking out at the falling rain. "I'm sorry for the stunt I pulled with Sass the other night." He looks over at me, and I'm pleased to see he's a little sheepish. "I mean it, man. That was a dick move."

"Hey, whatever, right?" I don't need his apologies.

"No, not whatever. " He shifts on his feet and sighs. "I guess - I dunno. All this ascension shit has made me realise, like... You have a real bum deal in all of this." He glances over at me, rubbing the back of his neck. "I mean, you're just a guy, you know? You have urges and needs and all that, and you can't -" He breaks off, shrugging. "We all gave you shit for it for years, called you Runt, sent girls after you when we knew you couldn't do anything and - well, I'm sorry. You didn't deserve that."

I nod. "I appreciate that, man."

Vale extends a hand, clapping it to mine and putting one arm around my shoulder. "We gotta work together now."

I force a laugh. "Yeah, we do." He's trying, the least I can do is appreciate it.

A shiny black car pulls up, and Vale and I stand to attention. "And here comes the royal family." Vale says quietly, chuckling.

The back door of the car opens, and Lordain climbs out, his greying hair smoothed back over his head. He looks so old all of a sudden, and I wonder if it's because his reign is over. Is that how it works? His Queen, Morgan, climbs out of the other side, her hair the colour of fire, unnaturally red. I wonder if she dyes it now, if she's noticed her ageing like her husband's now, and is determined to hold on to her youth.

They walk up on to the porch, and Lordain nods at me. "Is my son here yet?"

I shake my head. "I haven't seen him."

At that moment, Finn's truck pulls up, and he and Cora climb out of it. I try not to look at her, but I bite my lower lip and I remember her taste and FUCK. This is not the time. She's wearing a long black dress, with thin straps that cross over the low back. Her olive skin is on show, her shiny curls cascading over her shoulder. She's perfect and she's beautiful.

Her eyes find me as Finn takes her hand, and she smiles and my stomach wrenches, butterflies erupting in my chest. I nod in their direction, trying to keep my eyes on Finn.

"You're late!" Lordain says.

Finn shrugs, a wide smile breaking across his face. "Hasn't started yet, has it?"

Lordain shakes his head and stalks up the porch steps, Morgan following him wordlessly. She looks in my face as

46

she passes me, then casts a quick glance over her shoulder in Cora's direction. She gazes back at me with an expression that I can't quite read. Then she's past me, and I guess I must be imagining things.

Guilt does that to you.

Finn and Cora walk past us, and Cora's eyes flash to mine for the briefest second. Fuck.

Vale and I follow them in, and the council's all assembled, the old and the new. It feels like stepping into a new life. It's really happening. The moment we all joked about for so long. It's actually happening.

I take my place at the Table, to Finn's right, Vale sitting beside me. I dare a glance in Cora's direction, to Finn's left. She's looking straight ahead, biting her lip, and I wonder what she's thinking. I guess it's all dawning on her now too.

Roche, Lordain's Draw, stands, and the room falls silent. "I welcome you all to this first meeting of the Old and the New." He gestures around the room. "It's an exciting but sobering time for our Clan. Since the angels cast us out of the Halls, we've had to hold on to our traditions, and the Ascension is vital for the continuation of the demon race. The Old God set down these Blood Covenants thousands of years ago, and we continue them proudly." He takes his seat again.

"Now," Lordain speaks up, "the order of the rituals for the Ascension are very important, and we must be clear on how the next three weeks will transpire." He nods at me. "Amryn, you are leaving for your Isolation tomorrow, is that right?"

I nod. "Yes, sir." Two weeks in the mountains. So I can learn to be alone. As if I needed any practice.

"It's essential for you to harness your powers in this time," Lordain tells me, "Roche, could you go on?"

Roche nods and fixes me with an earnest gaze. "This time of isolation will help you hone your ability to focus on the Alpha and the Alpha alone. You need to clear your mind of all distraction. Protecting Finn is the most pivotal position, and it comes with an immense burden of responsibility. And a great deal of respect from the Clan."

Cora laughs. "Is that why they all call him Runt?"

All eyes turn to her.

"What's that?" Lordain snaps.

"You're here talking about the Draw being an important position," Cora goes on, "how it's respected by the Clan. And yet, everyone knows what the clan does to Amryn. They tease him and they taunt him and they tempt him with women."

Lordain's eyes move to me. "I know, and I've spoken to Amryn about this."

"And the others?" Cora asks indignantly. My hands ball into fists on my thighs. She's being too brash. This could land her in trouble. "Have you spoken to them?"

"Cora -" Finn takes her hand, and Cora shakes him off.

"No, this isn't OK." She says, rising to her feet. "Amryn has a duty to perform, and you deny him every normal interaction, every closeness to another demon -"

"He's not denied anything," Roche interjects, smiling at Cora indulgently, like she's a fucking idiot.

Cora scoffs. "Oh, a life without being allowed to so much as touch someone else isn't one of denial is it?"

"I seem to have managed just fine." Roche retorts.

"I haven't seen anyone bully you either, Roche, how lucky for you." Cora sneers.

"Now listen here young lady -" Lordain's eyes darken. Shit.

"Cora, it's OK." I say quickly. She has to stop, this isn't going to end well.

She looks down at me, her green eyes blazing. "No, it's not." The veins in her arms are glowing white as she looks back at Lordain. "You always say the Clan is only as strong as the bonds between its members. This is strength? Calling the Draw of the Alpha a runt?"

"What is this runt bullshit?" Lordain asks, exasperated.

"The runt of the litter," Morgan answers, putting a hand on Lordain's arm. Her eyes move to me, and she gives me a soft smile. "The one that no one wants."

"That's what you all think the Draw is?" Lordain's eyes blaze as he looks at Vale and the rest of the new council. "He's in the position because he's unwanted?" He throws his hands up. "You young folks, you're all idiots. You know nothing."

"It has to stop," Cora says, "and you're still the Alpha. You need to make it clear to the Clan that the Draw is a position of respect. Amryn needs, no! He *deserves* the support of the clan, not their fucking ridicule."

Lordain slams his fist on the table, but Cora doesn't stop.

"And you can start with him." She points at Vale. "Vale is the one who encourages the others the most, and he's the Striker. If he can't respect the other council positions I have to question whether he can be trusted to fulfill his own."

Vale jumps to his feet and bows his head. "She's absolutely right, and I offer my sincerest apologies to the council and to Amryn. I've apologised to him personally and I apologise to him again now." He turns to me. "I'm sorry, brother. I really am."

"Do you accept this apology?" Lordain asks me.

I nod, and look up at Vale. "Yes, I have, and I do."

"Anyone who treats you that way again will answer to me personally." Vale says. "I won't have it." He sits back down.

Morgan looks at Cora with admiration. "Well done, sweetheart." She says. "We Queens have to keep an eye on these things." She turns to Lordain, stroking his arm. "The men focus so much on fighting, but we Queens have to focus on family."

Lordain nods and looks up at Cora. "You'll be a good Queen. The Fates chose well."

Cora sits back down, and Finn takes her hand, raising it to his lips. She smiles at him, and for a second her eyes dart past him, to me. And that feeling's back. The feeling only she can give me. That look she only gives me. Air rushes out of my lungs.

"Now, let's move on," Lordain says. "The day of the Ascension, we will have the wedding ceremony in the afternoon. And then at the peak of the Full Moon, the Ascension will take place in the Great Hall."

Morgan taps Lordain's arm, clearing her throat. "Darling, most of these young folks have never experienced an Ascension Ceremony before, maybe you should be a little clearer on what it actually is."

Lordain pats her hand. "Of course, you're right." He clears his throat, shifting in his chair. "The clan will assemble in the Great Hall at the peak of the Moon, and Finn and Cora will complete the Ascension there, with us as their witnesses."

What? I feel ice run down my back. They don't mean... They can't mean...

Morgan looks at us sweetly, her eyes grazing back and forth along the new council. "It's not as awkward as it seems, it's actually quite a lovely thing to witness."

What. The. Fuck?

"I'm sorry, ma'am," Vale speaks up, and I'm so grateful he does because I've suddenly lost the ability to talk, "I just want to know what to expect, so when you say they'll complete the ascension in front of the clan, you mean -"

"Cora and I have sex, Vale," Finn says, and laughs. "How does no one know about this? I knew about this."

Don't look at her. Don't fucking look at her. Don't do it. This isn't the place. My hands become hot, and I have to calm down. I have to watch, I have to watch him, with her. Fuck. Fuck. Blood roars in my ears.

Vale guffaws. "There's a side of you I never thought I'd see, brother."

51

"Gotta show you fellas how it's done properly," Finn says, with a snide chuckle that makes my stomach turn.

"Enough." Lordain snaps. "This isn't a joke. It's an important part of the ritual. The Alpha has to claim his Queen, that's how this works. I'm not going to sit here and listen to you all snigger like fucking children over our traditions. Show some respect."

Everyone falls silent again. My fingers dig into my thighs. This is barbaric. I feel eyes on me, and Morgan's there across the table, and that expression's back. It's almost like curiosity, like she's trying to get a rise out of me. I try to smile at her, prove that I'm fine, that this is just nothing, just another council meeting. But I can't move my face. Her eyes flicker over me, and she raises an eyebrow.

The meeting goes on, and there's talk of the wedding ceremony and the visiting clans, and I don't hear hardly any of it. I feel sick. After an hour, Lordain finally, mercifully rises from his chair, calling the meeting to an end. At the next meeting, Finn will take that seat. At the next meeting, Cora will sit where Morgan is sitting now. And I'll take Roche's place.

When Cora is his. After I've watched him claim her.

"Amryn." I hear Roche call out to me as I scramble to leave, to get the fuck out of that room, and I really wish he'd just go away. But I stop, and turn, my hands clasped behind my back to hide the fact that I'm shaking, and try to keep my face as neutral as possible. "Amryn, about the Isolation, I wanted to have a quick word with you, do you have a moment for me?"

"Sure," I say, trying not to look in Cora's direction as she passes me on her way out, hand in hand with Finn. I

52

wonder where they're going now. Is he just going to take her home? Are they going to go off for a drive and make out somewhere? It's none of my business. None of my damn business.

"Son?" Roche raises his eyebrows at me, and I realise he's been talking and I haven't been listening.

"Sorry, sir," I say, "just a lot to take in, you know?"

"I understand," Roche replies. "It's a big transition, for all of us."

Yeah, it sure fucking is. "Yes, sir."

"Now, the Isolation is an important time for you, we've gone over that." Roche says, leaning on the back of the chair beside me. He seems so small, as though he's shrunk in on himself now, his thick grey hair thinning at the top of his head. I wonder if, like Lordain, he's ageing suddenly, shrinking, the loss of their status taking their stature with them.

I'm still not listening. My head is roaring.

"...and the cave ritual is the final step, in the Isolation period," Roche is saying, tracing his fingers absently back and forth along the studs in the leather of the chair. "You have to make an offering of hair and blood, and leave these on the altar. The Fidelis Stone will throw up Finn's flame to confirm your position as his Draw, and then," he smiles at me and shrugs, "it's done, and you can come back home."

"That's all it takes, huh?" I ask.

"It's that simple," he says with a chuckle.

"So, sorry, I must have missed it, where did you say this cave is?"

"On the Grayson Peak," he replies.

"Great, I think I got all that." I just want to go, stop talking, stop fucking telling me all this meaningless shit.

"You'll be OK?" He asks, and his concern makes me angry.

I shrug, crossing my arms over my chest. "I don't need any practice being alone, sir." I reply.

Roche gives me a sad smile, and puts his hand on my shoulder. "I know it's not easy sometimes, but it really is a rewarding position, you'll see."

"Sure." Just stop talking and let me go home. But he just keeps giving me that smile, that look like he cares. I shift on my feet, itching to get out of here. "Well, sir, I have to pack and get ready for tomorrow, so if there's nothing else?"

Roche steps back, holding up his hands. "Of course, Amryn, you go on ahead. Safe travels."

I nod and stalk out of the room. He calls something after me, something about looking forward to seeing me when I get back, but my head is full and every sound is like I'm underwater. Like I'm drowning. Like I'm under the ice, and air is inches away, but I can't reach it.

I slam the door to my cabin shut behind me, leaning back against it, sliding down on to the floor. I stare at my shoes for minutes or hours, I'm not sure which. The light changes as it shines softly through my window, the shadows fading as the sun sinks behind the mountains.

Finally I'm sitting in the dark, alone, and my hands stop shaking.

I ache for her. And I hope she doesn't feel me, and I hope she doesn't come to me. Because I don't know what to fucking do if she does.

The knock comes at my window at 2am. She's here. Because of course she is. I haven't slept. I haven't been able to. Because as much as I hoped she wouldn't come, I knew she would.

I go to the door, and she's standing there in blue shorts and a white tank top, picking at her nails, her eyes wide.

"Hi," she says in a small voice. She launches herself at me, and I push the door shut behind her as my arms encircle her. It takes me a second to realise that she's crying. Her shoulders are quaking as she struggles to breathe. "I didn't know." She sobs. "I didn't know. And then Finn told me -" She buries her face in my chest.

I hold her close, letting her cry. There's nothing for me to say.

She looks up at me, her face red and tear-streaked. "I'll pretend it's you." She says, trying to smile. "I'm going to close my eyes and pretend it's you, not him."

I inhale sharply. My heart hurts. "Don't do that."

"Do what?"

I step away from her. "Don't tell me you'll think of me while your husband fucks you."

She flinches. "Why not?"

"Because I don't want to know that he - that you'll -" I punch the wall, and she jumps. "Fuck!"

She covers her face with her hands, and she's crying again, and I feel like an asshole. I sweep her back into my arms. "I'm sorry." I tell her. She has to try and get through it, and I'm thinking about myself. I have to watch but she has to be watched. By everyone. Fuck this. I just want to make it all go away.

"I don't want you to go up into the mountains." She whispers. "I can't be away from you for two weeks."

I don't want to go either. "I know, baby. But I don't have a choice."

"Two weeks, and then, at the end of it..." She trails off.

"I know. I know."

"Maybe we should just run away," she whispers against my chest.

I suck in a breath. We've talked about it before. Years ago, after the Council told us our Fate. She cried and cried, and she crawled into my bed, and I held her as she said we should just run away. But we were kids, we didn't know how the world worked, where would we even go? Where could we go where they wouldn't find us?

But we're grown now.

As quickly as the thought forms in my head, I push it away. We're not kids anymore, but they'll still find us. The clan will never let us go. They'll track us and haul us back. I'll be killed, and while they'll let Cora live, they'll make her life hell.

"Don't talk like that, baby." I stroke her hair. "It's no use. You'll make yourself crazy."

"I already am crazy." She says, her fingers clawing into me. "Crazy thinking about all this shit. Crazy thinking that I'll never be alone with you again."

"Cora, stop." I hold her closer, wishing that anything I said made a fucking difference. "We can't keep doing this to ourselves."

She sighs. "You'll be back for my birthday party," she says, her voice small, hopeful. She's holding on to anything she can.

"Yes, baby. I will be."

Suddenly her mouth is on my chest, her tongue flicking over my nipple, and her hand is moving down my stomach, over my crotch, rubbing me. I tense for a second, feeling myself swell under her hand. If someone saw her come in here, if one of the guards was watching -

She backs away from me, pushing down her shorts and tearing her tank top off over her head. She shakes out her hair, and moves back onto my bed, spreading her legs for me. A growl escapes me.

I take off my pants and crawl onto the bed over her. I push my face into the crook of her neck, and she smells so sweet. Her legs wrap around my waist, her hands moving my face to hers. Her green eyes gaze up at me, and her mouth opens a little, gasping as I sink my cock into her.

It's never the last time. It's just never the last fucking time. I blink away the thought of watching her with Finn, watching him fuck her, watching her mouth fall open in ecstasy for him. No. No. That's for me. That's only for me.

She moans underneath me, her hands on my back, her nails digging in to my skin. She sighs my name, my name. Not his. Mine. The only name that she's ever sighed like this. The only voice I ever want to hear say it.

Her breath hitches a little as I thrust harder. I lock my arms in under her, and she turns her head, her mouth seeking out mine. She opens up under my lips, her tongue soft. I slow down for a moment, just tasting her, pretending I could do this all night, that I could just reach across the bed and pull her to me.

"I love you." She says it against my mouth, and I can't breathe.

I fuck her harder, trying to push the ache away. I love you. I love you so much my heart isn't even in my body anymore, it's in yours.

But I can't love her, and she can't love me.

"Say you love me," she whispers against my neck. "Please."

No. Stop it. I shake my head, grunting as I feel myself rising.

"I need to hear you say it." She's pleading with me.

I can't. If I say it, it's over. Please, please just come. Please let me finish this. Please let this be the last time. I can go to the mountains and have two weeks to forget the feeling of her arms wrapped around me, and her lips on mine, and the taste of her on my tongue.

She pushes one of her hands between us, snaking it up to touch my cheek, pressing my face to hers. "Please tell me you love me." She's crying again.

58

With a roar I push myself off her, scrambling for the edge of the bed. I can't fucking breathe. "Cora, don't ask me to do that. Please, just, please don't fucking ask me to say that."

She sits up, looking at me, small, scared. "But why? Why can't you just say it?"

"Because I can't."

"Why?"

"Because it fucking hurts!" I put my head in my hands. "You need to go."

"But you love me don't you?" Her voice cracks, and my heart shatters into a million fucking pieces.

"Go." I can't do this. "I need you to go, Cora. This - it can't happen anymore."

She shuffles across the bed, sniffling quietly. Hearing her cry tears me apart, but she needs to go. I can't do this. She pulls her clothes back on, and I hear her pause at the door.

"I'm sorry." She says. "I can't help it." She closes the door behind her.

I throw myself back on the bed and stare at the ceiling. I just lie there, not moving, for hours, unable to sleep, watching the light slowly, slowly begin to change as the dawn breaks. I have to go up into the mountains.

I get dressed, the hollow ache in my chest slowing me down, tying me down. I don't want to leave her. I can't leave her.

I scale the mountainside, the morning mist lying over the canyon as the sky above me turns a million shades of pink. I look back down over the compound, hazy in the summer dawn. She's down there, is she sleeping? Did she lie awake all night, crying?

Enough. I keep walking, keep moving. The ache doesn't go away. The sun peers over the horizon, and it still doesn't stop the ache.

Two weeks. I'm an idiot. Two hundred years wouldn't be enough time to forget her.

Fuck it all to hell.

I pull the door of the cabin shut behind me, and take a deep breath of morning air. I look out over the sprawling valley below, the snow-capped mountains all around, and I'm glad it's not raining for my hike back. I finally get to go home, back to Nilau, and get the fuck off this damn mountain. The past two weeks have been boring. I did nothing but read and work out - all day. I read five books while I was here then re-read two because I got bored.

But I'm bigger and stronger and whatever else Roche was talking about. The usual bullshit they want from me. To be as big and buff as I can be so I can beat the ass of anyone who threatens Finn. Like a good little fucking guard dog.

It's Cora's birthday party today.

And two weeks haven't been enough.

I've tried not to think about her, but the very thought of trying not to think about her makes me fucking think about her. I miss her. I dreamed of her constantly, of her with Finn, of her getting married and going in to the Great Hall for the Ascension, seeing Finn kiss her and touch all the places only I've touched her. I'd wake up bathed in sweat and overcome with nausea, determined to tear him to shreds if he so much as fucking breathed near her.

But then there were the other dreams.

Where she was beside me, warm and soft and mine. Her body against my body, naked and beautiful, hot and sweaty and pulsating with wild breaths as she moaned.

And somehow those dreams hurt even more.

I make my way across the mountaintop, along the narrow, winding path. The sun is shining, and it's cool up here, but I know down in the valley it'll be warm, and humid, and maybe a storm will roll in later on.

I grasp the hunting knife at my waist. Roche said I have to leave an offering of hair and blood to the Fidelis Stone. All these rituals, and traditions. All these years we were being prepared for all this shit, and yet it feels like no one really talked to us about anything. No one really told us what would happen. Especially Cora.

Anger rises in my chest as I try to imagine the moment she found out, the moment Finn told her, probably casually, as he does. Big stupid Finn, who doesn't take anything seriously, looking at her with his stupid fucking face, telling her he's going to fuck her in the Great Hall as though that's totally normal. Like it's no big deal. Like it's nothing to fuck your new wife in front of a room full of people including your parents.

I should have told her I loved her that night.

I shake my head at myself. I'm an idiot. Like it would have changed anything. It would have made it worse. I've never said it to her.

I look up to see two eagles soaring overhead. They mate for life, don't they? That must be nice.

I remember when I was a kid, I was maybe 12 years old, one of the women in the village had a baby. She came to visit Anya with him, and Cora and I were just entranced. He was so sweet, tiny little hands with mother-of-pearl fingernails, and soft blonde hair.

I carried that baby around so proudly, asleep in my arms, and everyone talked about how sweet it was that the baby loved me, and what a good father I'd make one day. And I knew in that moment, I knew I really wanted that one day - my own family, kids, a beautiful wife. Well, not just a wife. Cora.

We'd lie in bed at night when either she had snuck to my room or I'd snuck to hers, and we'd hold hands and talk about our future. About our babies, about what we'd call them, about the house we'd build together.

And then, when I was 16, the day of the Council Gathering came. When Cora was promised to Finn. I grimace as I remember the feeling. The dread, the deep icy dread that overtook me that day. Morgan and Lordain had been so pleased, and Finn had been fucking thrilled. Of course he had been. The most beautiful demon to fucking exist, and he was getting her. She was going to be his wife.

I couldn't make sense of it, what the Fates had seen in me to make me a good Draw. What the Fates had seen in me that they had decided I was to live and die alone. But

I'd had to stand there and watch Finn be so happy over his pretty little betrothed. The girl I loved more than anything.

All I ever do is watch. On the outside. Never a part of it.

The path veers off steeply downwards, and the colour of the stone changes, from grey to pale limestone. The cave has to be here somewhere. I pick my way across the path that is now pretty close to the cliff's edge, and my backpack catches on the crumbing limestone as I pass.

The limestone gives way to my left, and I'm at the entrance to the cave, which is really little more than a low alcove in the cliff face. An altar stands in the middle, a pointed blue stone standing in the centre of it, like a spearhead. A stone bench has been carved out in the rock underneath it, and two shelves have been chipped out on either side.

I put my backpack down by the cave entrance, and kneel on the stone bench. Hair and blood, right? I reach underneath my hair at the back of my head, and slice a strand of my black hair off, wrapping it around my fingers and trying it in a knot. I place it on the small stone shelf on the left of the blue spearhead.

Blood. OK. I hold out my hand, and slice open my right palm. Roche didn't say how much blood, but I don't want to do this wrong. I squeeze my hand together over the cup beside the blue stone, and a stream of blood pours into it.

I put the knife down and pull out the bandage I'd put in my pocket. I wrap up my hand, knowing I'll heal fast. I always have.

I sit and wait. How long does this take? Roche probably told me, but I wasn't listening. Dammit. I should have paid attention. Nothing's happening. Did I do something wrong? Was I meant to do something else? Shit shit shit. Lordain's going to kick my ass. I'm sure he'll have some secret way of knowing I fucked up.

Suddenly the stone begins to hum. As I watch, it starts to glow. Right. Finn's flame will spring up, and I'll be bound to him as the Draw. I remember that part. I breathe a sigh of relief. I did it right after all.

A white flame shoots up out of the blue stone, sparks bouncing off the cave roof. White. I don't understand. Finn's flames are red... Fuck.

With a sigh I get up off the bench. I grab my backpack and make my way down the mountain, trying not to look up at the eagles that are still circling above me. Go and enjoy your lives together. Be happy.

I told myself I'd not think about her for two weeks. That two weeks would be enough to forget her. To forget how she felt against me, around me, on my mouth, on my tongue.

But even the fucking Fidelis Stone is taunting me. Throwing up a white flame.

Cora's flames are white.

I fucking hate this.

4
Cora

I open the door to Morgan standing on our front stoop, her red hair hanging down her back in big curls, a purple dress hugging her tiny frame. She smiles at me, flicking ash from her cigarette on to the white decking.

"Hello sweetheart," she purrs, giving me a sweet smile, "I thought it might be time to have a talk about your queenly duties, hmm?"

My what? I laugh awkwardly. "Oh, I think we have plenty of time for that another day," I say, "with the party tonight I have a lot to get done, you know?"

"It won't take a minute, sweetie, come on now." Morgan insists, rolling her eyes jovially.

I gesture over my shoulder. "I mean, my Mom was an Alpha queen too, you know. I'm sure she can tell me everything I need to know."

Morgan's expression is unreadable for a moment, and she quickly pastes a wide smile on her red lips. "Oh sweetie, with everything that happened when Ocario fell, I wouldn't want your Momma worrying about reliving all that."

She's being weird. Why is she being weird?

I shrug. There's probably no point arguing. "Uh, well, I guess I could spare a half hour." I say. "Mom!" I call over my shoulder. "I'm just out with Morgan, I'll be back really soon!"

"OK!" The response comes from inside the house somewhere, and Morgan grabs my hand, leading me down the stairs and giggling like she's my friend who's dragging me off for a night of dancing.

The party preparations are underway, fairy lights being strung up everywhere, bonfires being built up. Morgan pulls me past it all, and I wonder where we're going. My stomach turns a little as I realise we're headed for the Great Hall.

Morgan looks at me and pulls her shoulders up as though she's really excited. "So, the dress is all ready, yes?"

I nod. "Yeah, it came last month, it's gorgeous."

"You're going to be such a beautiful bride," Morgan gushes, gazing up at the trees overhead as we walk. "And to see my only child married, I mean, one day you'll understand what that means, how important it is."

"Yeah." I try to keep my tone light. "It must be exciting for you and Lordain."

"Oh we're thrilled, sweetie," Morgan says as we reach the Great Hall, and she pushes open the door, standing aside so I can go in ahead of her.

There's a bed in the middle of it. They've already set it up. My stomach feels icy as I look at it, as I look around the enormous room, where the clan will assemble and -

"Now, I know what you're thinking," Morgan says as she sits on the bed, leaning back on her manicured hands. She tilts her head and smiles at me sympathetically. "Trust me, sweetie, it will be so lovely for you. Finn's so handsome, and that body, well, I know he's my son, but -" She raises her eyebrows and chuckles. "I've seen him naked and I can tell you the package won't disappoint."

Yeah, he is your son and this conversation is gross. "Yeah, he's really handsome," I say, nodding, trying not to acknowledge that Morgan was just talking about her own son's dick. I walk around the bed, looking at the linen sheets, the candles standing at each corner. I guess it really will be dark, just like my Mom said. I swallow hard.

Morgan follows me as I walk. "What are you thinking, sweetie?" She asks me.

I shrug. "I don't know, I guess, it feels like a lot, you know? Being a queen and being responsible and all that."

"It'll be a change, of course, but don't you worry, you and Finn are going to be so happy, and soon you'll be holding a little baby in your arms, and oh, you've never felt a love like it." She says, putting a hand to her chest.

"You're pretty eager for Finn and I to have a baby aren't you?" I ask.

Morgan regards me with confusion. "You don't want a baby?" She asks me.

"Oh no, I do," I say quickly, "I do. I really want to be a Mom someday."

"Someday?" She repeats the word slowly, and I feel like I'm edging on to dangerous ground.

I laugh and shrug. "I'm just nervous about it, you know?" I point to the bed. "All... this. It's all new to me." God I'm a good liar. Oh yes, the nervous virgin who had a demon balls deep in her two weeks ago.

And there he is. The very one I've been trying not to think about for two weeks. And now all I can think of as I stand in front of my future mother-in-law is Amryn - his hands on me and his mouth on me. My cheeks burn violently.

"Sweetie!" Morgan exclaims, jumping to her feet, thankfully mistaking my blushing for the apprehension of a new bride. She clutches me in a tight hug, and sways me back and forth gently. "Now don't worry about it. It doesn't feel any different the first time than it does any other time. It'll be beautiful and you'll love it."

"I'm sure I will." Is this really all she wanted to talk to me about? Having sex with her son? Making babies?

She pulls back from me, keeping a hold of my hands, and gazes at me intently. "You'll be so happy. A handsome husband, a beautiful home, and then -"

"Babies." I say it for her. It's freaking me out. I don't want to think about babies anymore. "Anyway, Morgan, I appreciate you talking to me about all this, but I really need to go back to my Mom and get ready for tonight."

"Ah yes, the party, of course," she says, waving her hands. "Go, go. You need to get ready."

"Thanks." I turn to go, and hear her footsteps clacking behind me, high heels on wood.

68

"Oh Cora," she says lightly.

Fuck. "Yes, Morgan?" I try to keep my expression friendly as I turn back to face her.

"You and Amryn are very close, aren't you?" She asks, examining her nails intently.

My mind races, and I claw my fingernails into my palms. Two weeks without him. It's been enough time to forget. It has to have been.

"Yeah we are," I answer, kicking my foot into the ground and shrugging, trying to remain nonchalant. "We were best friends growing up, my Mom basically raised him, you know?"

Her brow furrows. "Oh yes, after his own mother took her life, of course. How sweet of your mother to be so kind to him."

"Yeah, my Mom is pretty great." I reply.

"He is so handsome, isn't he?" Her eyes are fucking terrifying as they meet mine. Like a snake about to strike. "Those muscles, that long black hair, ooh he's just - delicious."

"Sure." I nod, feeling a thin layer of sweat break out on my top lip. "I guess, not that it matters. Anyway, I really have to go." I push outside and turn left to head back to my Mom's house.

"He's coming back today, isn't he?" She calls after me, her voice high, and I know she's taunting me.

"I don't know!" I call back, over my shoulder, and storm away across the compound. My hands won't stop fucking shaking.

Of course he's coming back tonight, I know he is. But it doesn't matter. If I see him tonight, it'll be fine. Because it's been enough time to forget. It has to have been. Morgan has me fucking spooked. No one can suspect anything, because they're all waiting for Amryn to fuck up.

Get it together, Cora.

"Oh honey, you look gorgeous!" My mother says as I emerge into the kitchen, her hands clasped together to her chest.

I give a little twirl, laughing. "And it's pink!" It's also scandalously short, and the sweetheart neckline shows off more cleavage than Lordain would approve of. But I feel incredible and I'm determined to have a good night. It's my birthday party after all.

"Hey girl!" Ceili pushes through the kitchen door, in a tight blue dress, her pale blonde hair hanging down her back. "Happy birthday, cuz! You look so adorable!" She wraps me in a hug, and hands me a bottle of pink gin.

"Keeping me off the whiskey tonight?" I ask.

She nods. "We all know what you get like on whiskey."

My mother makes a noise behind us, and we all laugh. It's going to be a good night, I can feel it.

"One hell of a setup they got going on out there," Ceili says, perching up on the kitchen counter, her long tan legs swinging back and forth. "Finn has gone all out for you, cuz."

I smile. "And so he should, right?"

70

Ceili snorts as she laughs. "Whatever you say, princess."

My mother pours us all a drink, sparkling, pink and sweet, and we toast to me in the kitchen. We down them quickly, because they taste like fucking lemonade, and Mom pours us all a second round as Ceili tells us all about the latest guy she's been dating, my Mom blushing profusely at all the details. The second drink goes down even easier than the first, and I feel so damn good.

"Hey!" Finn knocks on the door frame, grinning through the screen. "Is this a girls only club?"

Music begins playing in the distance as he walks into the kitchen, and I don't know if it's the alcohol in my system, but he looks so delicious tonight, his hair tied back, his jeans hanging from his hips, his muscles bulging in a black tshirt.

"Hey babe," I say to him, and he looks me up and down.

"Holy shit." He sees my mother and grins crookedly. "Sorry, ma'am. She just looks, I mean-"

"Your fiancee looks stunning," my mother agrees. "Now how about you all go get started with the festivities."

Ceili and Finn practically drag me out of the house, and the compound looks amazing, fairy lights hanging everywhere, bonfires burning around the edge of the clearing. A DJ has his setup there by the grass, and there's a table absolutely creaking under the weight of all the food and booze.

There's so many people everywhere, clan neighbours who came early to celebrate their new Queen's birthday before the Ascension on Saturday, as well as our clan who are all drinking and laughing together. My mood dips a tiny bit as the date dawns on me - only five days to go. But I quickly push it away. Tonight it's my night and my birthday and I'm going to have fun. I coast on the buzz of the pink gin, and nuzzle in to Finn, who smells so good.

Calls of Happy Birthday ring out as I walk past, Finn's arm around me proudly, and I know he's loving showing me off. A true trophy Queen.

"What are you drinking, babe?" He asks me, his hand straying down over my back to touch my ass.

"Anything but whiskey or beer." I tell him. I'm light-headed already but I'm not an idiot. He returns with a bottle of something pink and fruity, and I down it way too quickly.

Ceili laughs. "Oh you are going to be hurting in the morning," she says, flicking her hair over her shoulder.

I shrug. "That's what parties are for, right?" I don't care. I want to have fun. I look out over the compound, over the teeming, laughing crowd, and my stomach drops. I nearly drop the bottle I'm holding, and I wobble on my high heels. Shit shit shit.

Amryn's moving through the crowd, tall and broad, his silky black hair hanging over his shoulder. He's wearing a tight white t-shirt and black jeans, and he somehow looks even bigger than he did when he left 2 weeks ago. His shirt strains around his biceps, and I can see his abs through the fabric. *Fuck.*

"Amryn!" Finn's voice sounds right behind me, and I jump. "You're back!"

72

Amryn walks over to us, his eyes flashing to mine for just a split second. "Hey, yeah I'm back."

"When did you get in?" Finn asks.

"A few hours ago."

"You all ready to be the Draw now?" Ceili asks. She looks him up and down. "You sure as hell look it."

Amryn laughs abashedly. "Not much to do up there but work out, so you know." His eyes settle on me. "Happy birthday."

"Thanks." I can't stop staring at him. The pep talk I gave myself this afternoon was all for nothing. Yeah, two weeks would be enough, right? Two weeks would be plenty of time to forget about him, right? Two weeks would give me the time I needed to move on and accept what's going to happen.

Two weeks hasn't done shit.

"I didn't get you a present, sorry." He says, his hazel eyes not moving from my face. "Not many places to shop up there."

I shake my head. "You don't need to get me a present, don't worry about it." I look him up and down for a split second, and I feel my cheeks flush. He notices, he must, because he looks away quickly, crossing his arms over his chest, clearing his throat.

The music gets louder, and people are starting to dance, the hot summer night and the free flowing alcohol clearly lowering plenty of inhibitions.

"Come on, let's dance," Ceili says, and seizes Amryn's hand.

He laughs uncertainly, pulling his hand back. "Oh I don't think that's allowed, honey."

Ceili looks at Finn with exasperation. "The Draw can't even dance?"

Finn claps Amryn on the shoulder. "My father is so drunk he doesn't even know his own name, you go on ahead and have fun tonight." He clears his throat theatrically. "I command it as your Alpha."

Ceili grins up at Amryn and drags him off to the dance floor, and I'm deeply ashamed of the pang of jealousy I feel. He looks over his shoulder at me as they disappear into the crowd.

I take hold of Finn's hand and follow them. "Come on, I want to dance too."

The music is so loud, pulsating through the ground under our feet. Everything is sweaty and heady and the summer night is almost oppressive, feeling like a storm might come. I move my hips to the music, grinding against Finn behind me, his arm around my waist.

Ceili and Amryn are dancing face to face, and I see her run a finger along his jawline, and she's laughing. Amryn smiles at her, and I turn around, grabbing Finn and kissing him. I'm being ridiculous, I'm jealous and ridiculous and I want to shut this feeling out. Finn doesn't seem to notice nor does he seem to mind, kissing me back freely. The music seems to be getting constantly louder and louder, and the pleasant floaty feeling comes back.

I turn and put my back against Finn again, and his hands are all over me, his mouth on my neck. I tell myself it feels nice. It should feel nice. I open my eyes, and see

Ceili putting her arms around Amryn's neck. He hesitates for a second, and I can see she's trying to talk him into something. "Oh come on." I see her mouth make the words. She pushes her face closer to his, and his shoulders tense.

Don't do it. I don't want him to. I don't want anyone else touching him. I tell myself I'm just trying to avoid trouble for him, but I know that's not it at all. I'm jealous. He's mine. And that's unfair. But he's mine.

Without thinking about what I'm doing, I grab Ceili and shove her at Finn. "Swap!" I say, laughing, trying to act like this is a perfectly normal thing to do and not completely fueled by my intoxicated jealousy. Finn laughs too and Ceili just looks at me with confusion. But then Finn spins her into a dance, and her face breaks into a smile, just going with the vibe of the party and not noticing what the fuck I'm doing.

I throw myself at Amryn, into his arms, against his rock hard chest, and we're face to face. He shakes his head, tensing for a moment. But then a small smile breaks across his face, and he begins to relax. His arms go around my waist, and we move together to the music.

He's so fucking close, I can feel all of him against me. I put my hands on his chest, and his heart's beating right there against my fingers, and his hazel eyes are fixed on me. He smells good. I'm drunk and I want him so bad, it's killing me. My hands stray down his stomach towards his waistband for a split second, and his eyes widen with alarm.

"Cora," he murmurs, pulling me close so my hands are jammed between us, unable to move any further. "Cora, what the fuck are you doing?"

"I don't know," I reply, my mouth close to his ear.

"Stop it." He says urgently, and my stomach wrenches a little. "You're drunk."

I turn my head, and his face is right there. We gaze at each other like that, the crowd pulsating around us, and then it's like it's just us, no one else is there. I'm drowning in his eyes, his eyes that are fixed on mine. Then he looks at my mouth, and heat floods between my thighs. His lips are so close, oh my god why did I do this?

Suddenly two pairs of hands grab him away from me, hauling him off through the crowd. I stumble for a second, trying to make sense of what just happened. Ceili and Finn stop dancing, and Ceili's hand flies to her mouth in shock, her eyes wide as she looks at me.

Finn's face is full of fury as he charges after them, and I rush to follow them, wobbling across the grass in my high heels. The music is still so loud, but I can see Finn calling something out to the men dragging Amryn away, gesticulating wildly with his hands.

"What are you doing?" I can hear his voice now, the music of the party fading away behind us.

Amryn is stumbling as the two men keep dragging him away from the party. He's not saying a word, and he's not fighting back.

"Where the fuck are you taking him, huh?" Finn calls.

"To the Alpha, where the fuck else?" Comes the reply, and they continue to shove Amryn along the path.

76

My heart is in my throat, and I kick my stupid high heels off, so I can run after them, they're moving fast.

The two men head for one of the bonfires near the lake, and I see Lordain and a few other clan elders standing there, watching sternly as Amryn is dragged towards them. Finn reaches the group just as Amryn is thrown to the ground in front of Lordain.

"What the fuck is going on?" Finn demands.

Amryn gets to his feet, and Lordain's leg shoots out, knocking Amryn back down to his knees. "You get up when I say you can get up." His gaze moves to me, and he gestures to me to come to him. "You, here, now."

I'm too drunk to protest, and I walk over. I cast a look at Finn as I move, who just shakes his head in confusion, his brow furrowed.

"What do you want with me?" I ask as I reach Lordain. The slap sends my head snapping to the side, and heat explodes in my face. I stumble and nearly lose my footing.

"You want to tell me what the fuck you're playing at?" Lordain is standing right over me, and he reeks of alcohol.

I look up at him, holding my face, my mouth agape. "You hit me."

"What the fuck, Dad?" Finn is suddenly by my side.

"Ey ey. Calm down!" Roche's call diverts everyone's attention, and we look down at Amryn, whose hands have exploded into flames. His eyes are fixed on Lordain, narrowed and filled with fury.

Lordain stands over him, grabbing his hair and pulling his head back. "You behave yourself you fucking little shit." He shoves Amryn's head away and turns back to me. "Now, you want to tell me what kind of behaviour you're displaying here?"

"Dad, it's a party, we're just dancing." Finn says. "She wasn't doing -"

"You call that dancing?" Lordain roars. "Did you see what they were doing?"

"Oh come on." Finn throws his hands up.

Lordain points his finger at Finn's face. "You need to get smart, son. That's your Queen, and this is your Draw. They need to be kept apart."

"Kept apart?" Finn yells at his father. "They're friends, Dad. They were just fucking dancing, having a good time. What is wrong with you?"

"There's something going on here, and I don't like it." Lordain insists.

"There's nothing going on," Amryn replies.

Lordain leans down into his face. "I didn't ask you."

"No, and you never do ask, you just accuse." Amryn spits back.

Lordain's fist goes up, and Roche rushes at him, holding him back. "Lordain, you need to stop this," he says, his brow furrowed. "This isn't the time or the place."

Lordain's eyes are wild as he looks down at Roche. "I told you not to let him train her, didn't I?" He snarls in Roche's face. "And you insisted their bond would -"

"Lordain, shut up." Roche's voice drops to a low hiss and he turns to face me, his expression shadowed by the dancing light of the fire.

"What are you talking about?" I ask, shaking my head.

Finn scoffs. "They're talking shit, Cora. All this shit," he gestures at the clan elders, "all of this, it's just old men realising they're irrelevant."

Lordain's eyes flame as they snap to his son. "How dare you!" He struggles against Roche's grip. "You owe me everything you little shit, I found you the best wife, picked you the most powerful draw and -"

Roche shakes Lordain by the collar. "Shut up!" He looks over his shoulder at Finn, jerking his head in Amryn's direction. "Get your Draw and your Queen, and get the fuck out of here, now."

"What's wrong, Roche?" Finn jeers. "You worry I'll pulverise my Dad for hitting my Queen?" Finn looks over Roche's head at his father. "You touch my Queen like that again, and we can battle it out, Pops. See who wins now, huh?"

Two more elders rush forward to hold Lordain back as he explodes at Finn's word, and I step back out of instinct. He's almost frothing at the mouth, he's so mad. An angry drunk. "You ungrateful little fuck!" He cries. "I'm trying to protect your clan, your legacy and -"

"No, you don't want to give up your status." Finn fires back at him. "You're so desperate to stay Alpha that you're just looking for a reason. You want to take my Queen away, you want to take my Draw away, it's pathetic!"

"I'm telling you -"

"What are you telling me, Dad?" Finn asks, crossing his arms over his chest. "Why don't you just say it straight?" He raises his eyebrows expectantly, and Lordain's gaze goes back to Roche. Lordain's mouth sets in a firm line, and he seems to lose some of his fight, shaking his head. He can't say it, he can't make the accusation outright. "Yeah, that's what I thought." Finn says. He walks to Amryn's side and helps him to his feet. "Come on, let's get the fuck of here." He puts his arm around me, and guides me away, Amryn following us.

"Are you OK?"

I look over my shoulder. The question came from Amryn. His hands are still glowing, the flames slowly subsiding. His eyes are fixed on me.

"I'm fine." I reply. It's a lie. I'm not fine at all. My cheek is burning and my head is throbbing and the panic that gripped me is making me feel like I'm about to pass out.

"Fucking asshole." Finn says. "Fucking stupid old man."

"Are you OK?" I ask Amryn.

He nods.

"All he can think about is being fucking Alpha." Finn rages. "I mean, can you believe him?" He shakes his head, squeezing my shoulders. "You two, dancing together, and the fucking deranged old fucker loses his mind. I knew he was paranoid, but fuck."

I swallow hard. Holy shit. My heart's beating so loud I'm sure Finn can feel it reverberating through my body.

Fuck. Fuck. Fuck. Lordain knows. Morgan knows. they're baiting us. They're waiting for us to fuck up. And I had to go and get handsy on the dancefloor and get us beaten up. Stupid, stupid, *stupid.*

"I can't believe him." Finn goes on. "Challenging me like that, hitting my queen. He's asking for a beatdown." He laughs maniacally. "He knows I'd beat him to a pulp now, he fucking knows I'm stronger than him, fucking geriatric old fuck." He stops suddenly. "Can you look after her?" He asks, shoving me into Amryn's arms. "I need to go back and finish this, it's bullshit." He stalks off through the trees back towards the bonfire, back to the lake.

I gaze up at Amryn, and he sighs. "Well, that could have gone sideways pretty fast."

"I'm sorry." I say, shaking my head. "I'm such a fucking idiot."

"No, hey come on." He puts a hand on my shoulder. "It's my fault, I shouldn't have danced with you or Ceili."

"I shouldn't have touched you like that, I'm so sorry." I rub my cheek, which still stings from the slap.

Amryn's brow furrows, and he moves his hand from my shoulder to my cheek. "Does it still hurt?"

I gaze at him, and shake my head. His eyes on me are too much. I want to be away from people. Away from crowds, and far, far away from the duelling fucking Alphas near the lake. I can hear Finn and Lordain raging at each other, even from here.

"Can you get me out of here?" I plead. "I can't handle this anymore."

Amryn guides me across the lawn, away from the party, the music becoming nothing but a dull thud, the voices and cheers and laughter of the partygoers fading away. He's taking me to Finn's house, my house. We take the steps up onto the covered porch, the storm door swinging closed behind us. It's mostly dark, the only light coming from the distant bonfires and the lamps that light the walkway. There's no one around. It's quiet.

"Are you sure you're OK?" Amryn asks me. He's standing in front of me, and he raises his hand to my cheek again.

"Yeah." I put my hand over his hand on my face.

"I wanted to kill him." He says. "I was ready to set that fucker on fire, and if he does that again, I'll kill him."

"Amryn, come on, don't talk like that." I sigh, and look into his eyes. "He knows. About us."

"No he doesn't." Amryn shakes his head. "Finn's right, Lordain just wants to hold on to his status. He's looking for excuses to kick my ass, that's all."

I know he's wrong, I know Lordain knows. But I don't want to think about it right now. "How was it, up in the mountains?" I ask instead.

Amryn scoffs. "Boring. Stupid." He pauses. "Lonely." His hand is still on my cheek. "I - I missed you." He knows he shouldn't say it. He knows what will happen. But he says it anyway.

And I can't stop myself.

I throw myself into his arms, my lips on his, and he reacts immediately, his hands in my hair, his mouth opening for mine, and he tastes sweet.

82

"I missed you so much." I'm crying, clutching on to him. "Oh god, I missed you."

"It was fucking torture." He says, his forehead against mine.

"I thought I could get over it." I shake my head. "I thought I could let you go, I thought it would help."

"Me too." He clutches me to him. "I spent all this time trying not to think about you and then I'd fucking dream about you, every single night." He shakes his head. "I don't know what to do, Cora."

Neither do I. There's nothing to do.

The alcohol is giving me courage I shouldn't have, not here, not now, especially not after what just happened. But I want him.

I push him down onto one of the chairs, straddling him, kissing him deeply.

"Cora, stop, wait." He says against my lips, but his hands are under the hemline of my dress as it rides up my thighs. "Someone might see us." He's breathing hard, and my hand moves down between us, rubbing him through his pants. "Oh fuck." He sucks in a breath.

"I need you." I tell him. Because I do. I fucking do, so bad. I pull my dress up, and I feel him undo his pants, and then his cock is rubbing against my thigh. His mouth is on my neck, his hands gripping the back of my head. I pull my panties aside, and he exhales heavily against my skin as I lower myself onto him.

The sheer ecstasy of having him inside me sends electricity coursing down my back. He feels so good, too good, too good to never feel this way again. He throws his head back as I ride him, and he moans, and it's because of me, because of how good this feels. He's mine. He's only mine.

This is so stupid. This is so dangerous. I'm addicted to him. I wrap my arms around his neck, working myself up and down his cock, my nerves firing, the alcohol making everything even warmer and hazier. He says my name, his hands on my hips, moving me faster.

"Cora!" Finn's voice echoes across the yard.

"Shit." Amryn pushes me off him. "Get inside, quick." He adjusts his clothing, and I pull my dress back down around my thighs as I hurry into the house.

I run to the bathroom, slamming the door behind me, leaning against it, panting. Fuck, that was so stupid. That was so so stupid. We nearly got caught.

I hear their voices outside, hear Finn going on and on about his father, his stupid father, the jealous Alpha. He's angry. Amryn's trying to calm him down, trying to tell him everything's going to be OK, but Finn won't stop raging. And he nearly caught his Queen fucking the Draw.

Finn would kill him. Me loving Amryn will get him killed. Lordain suspects. No, he knows. Amryn can kid himself all he wants, it's not about power. Lordain said it - we have to be kept apart. He knows. He fucking knows.

Tears spring to my eyes. This has to stop. It just has to. It doesn't matter how we feel about each other, it doesn't matter that I love him.

The Ascension is in five days, and then I'll be Finn's. There'll be no going back.

Tonight was the last time.

5
Amryn

The day is here.

I sit on my bed in my black suit, staring at the floor. I should get out there. The afternoon light streams into my window, and it's gold and warm, and everyone has been saying how great the day will be, what a perfect day for a wedding.

I didn't sleep last night. Every time I closed my eyes I saw Finn on Cora, and it made me sick. He's going to take what's mine today. He's going to destroy what's hers. And he has no idea. No one has any idea. Except maybe Lordain.

I shouldn't be surprised that he knows, he has his ways of finding out everything that goes on in this compound. And Cora and I have been irresponsible way too many times, just like we were on the night of her party, when she fucked me on the porch of her new house. We're idiots. We're reckless. It's almost like we want to get caught. They would kill me. And yet I can't stay away. I can't say no to her. I need her.

But I haven't seen her since that night. Well, that's not true - I have. We had to sit through the fucking rehearsal dinner two nights ago, and I pretended she wasn't there. It hurt her, I'm sure, because it fucking hurt me.

I put my hand to my chest, and run my fingers over the medallion I'm wearing, the one she gave me for my 18th birthday. The first night we slept together. I know I shouldn't surrender to the memory, but I do. I close my eyes and remember everything about that night; Cora putting her arms around me, whispering in my ear, telling me to come to her room once everyone was asleep.

I snuck in quietly, and she was waiting for me. I crawled into her bed, just like I had so many nights for years, but this time she was naked. She was warm and sweet, wanting me, just me, and I knew I wasn't allowed to do it, I knew she wasn't mine, but she gave herself to me anyway. And she claimed me for herself. There's no one else for me. She said there was no one else for her.

Except now, there is, because now everything changes. Because she'll be his. She'll be the Queen. There'll be no more sneaking around, no more stolen moments. I'll never see her again, not alone, not like that. It was finally the last time.

And it's killing me.

I get up off the bed, forcing myself outside, into the cruel fucking golden sunshine. There's no point delaying it any further.

Everyone's here, hundreds of people, all here to celebrate the wedding, and the Ascension. It only happens every 25 years or so, so everyone's put in a lot of effort, dressed up and dripping in gold and silver. There's white flowers everywhere, their scent carried by the heady summer breeze.

I'm the Draw, so I have to be Finn's best man. Front seat to seeing him marry Cora. Fucking amazing.

I make my way to Finn's house, pasting a smile on my face as I pass everyone. Happy, so happy. Everyone's happy.

Morgan is on the porch of the log cabin, in a floor-length red gown, her red hair pinned up on her head. She's smoking a cigarette, and smiles appreciatively as I walk up the porch steps. "Well hello there," she says, running a finger down the lapel of my jacket. "You look great, Amryn." She opens her silver cigarette case and offers me one.

Fuck it.

"Thanks," I say as I take it, and she lights it for me. I inhale deeply, and it feels better than it should.

"What a beautiful day, huh?" Morgan says, casting her eyes out across the compound. "Such a special day. My only son getting married." She takes another drag of her cigarette, and eyes me carefully. "The Summer Solstice is a pretty special day in so many ways, you know."

I nod. "Yeah it is." I don't know what she's talking about.

"Between the wedding and the peak of the moon, there aren't really any rules." She laughs, flicking the ash from her cigarette. "It's almost like the Clan is sort of -" She gazes at the sky, as though trying to find the right word. "Like the Clan is suspended in a sort of limbo. No roles, no rules. No status. Like the world is taking a deep breath."

I suck on the cigarette. "OK." I still don't know what she's talking about.

She grins. "You should have seen Roche after our wedding." She raises her eyebrows and chuckles. "Fucking every girl he could get his hands on." She covers her mouth abashedly for a moment and eyes me sheepishly. "Sorry, I know I shouldn't talk like that to a young man like you."

I feel an icy sensation wash over my shoulders. "You mean -"

"Oh yes, sweetheart." Morgan nods her head, laughing. "After the wedding, it's a free for all." She stamps the cigarette out in the ash tray, and gives me a shy smile. "I'm sure you'll have a fantastic night. So many pretty girls here."

I take a deep drag on the cigarette as she walks back into the house. Fuck. Nervous tension builds in my chest, and the butterflies storming in there make it almost impossible to breathe. I put the cigarette out, the taste of smoke lingering on my tongue. My eyes stray to the chair next to the table, and - fuck.

"Brother!" Finn comes out of the cabin, dressed in a black suit with silver embroidery down the sleeves. He grabs me in a bear hug. "Day's finally here!"

I give him a wide smile. "I'm happy for you." I say. I hope I sound sincere.

Lordain comes out of the cabin, with Morgan following. She gives me a conspiratorial wink. The butterflies keep storming.

"Well, let's go." Lordain says, leading the way with Morgan clutching his arm. "Luckily it's not raining."

I'd prefer that. Rain and mud and sodden and will anything not remind me of her? Shit.

The clans are assembled on the clearing, all standing and watching as the four of us make our way down the aisle. People reach out to clap Finn on the shoulder, to shake his hand. Everyone is happy.

There's a bough covered in flowers standing at the front, and Lordain stands underneath it, ready to perform the ceremony. Finn and I stand beside him, waiting for the bride, waiting for Cora to emerge.

"Nervous?" Lordain asks his son with a smile.

Finn shakes his head. "Nah. I can't wait."

Lordain nods his approval. "You're a lucky man."

Music starts playing, some sweet country song I recognise from somewhere, and the crowd turns to see Cora. I dig my fingernails into the palm of my hand. I don't want to see her. She's going to be beautiful.

And there she is, on the arm of her mother. She's in a long white flowing dress, her curls hanging loose down her back, white flowers in her hair. Her olive skin is glowing and her eyes are bright green in the warm summer light. She's smiling as she walks. She looks happy. Her mother keeps putting a hand to her face, and I see she's crying. Such a happy day. Everyone's happy.

They reach the bough. And Cora's mother kisses her daughter's cheek, smiling at Finn through her tears as he reaches out to take Cora's hand. They face each other, and I'm standing right behind Finn. Her eyes are fixed on him.

"You're so beautiful." He whispers.

"Thank you." She replies.

"We are here to celebrate the wedding of Cora to my son Finn!" Lordain announces loudly. "These two people have come here willingly to join their hands as husband and wife, and as Alpha and Queen of this clan!"

Willingly. I dig my nails harder into my palm, sure I'm about to draw blood. Fated isn't willingly. I know who'd be standing there looking down at her, smiling at her, telling her she's beautiful, taking these vows, if she had a choice.

I'm making this worse for myself. I'm addicted to feeling like shit.

The ceremony goes on. They say their vows. Promise to love each other, forsaking all others. Cora's eyes stay on Finn the entire time, and I try not stare at her face. It won't make this any easier for her.

The vows come to an end, and Lordain steps forward, rolling up his sleeve, revealing the knot tattoo on his forearm. He puts a hand on Finn's shoulder. "I relinquish my power to you, my son." Lordain says.

Finn nods and puts a hand over the tattoo. The veins in his hand glow bright red, and I see Lordain's fingers clench into Finn's shoulder, his mouth set into a hard line. There's a sickening smell of burning flesh. Finn pulls his hand away, and the tattoo is gone, a patch of burnt, red-raw skin in its place. Roche steps forward and his hands glow as he heals the burn, his powers as Lordain's Draw granting him the ability to heal Lordain quickly.

"It is done!" Lordain exclaims, and everyone bursts into applause and cheers. His eyes settle on me, and the smug smile on the old bastard's face sets my teeth on edge.

Finn turns to Cora, holding her face in his hands, and kisses her. She closes her eyes as he does, and she's smiling.

She's happy.

Let her be happy.

Just let it go.

"Great party, huh?" Vale sidles up to me, his face bright red from too much drinking, whiskey in hand.

I'm drunk as fuck. I've been downing tequila and beer and it's a fucking bad combination. I've managed to avoid Cora and Finn, their smiles and their embraces and the kisses I keep hearing everyone calling out for. I've stayed right away and gotten stupid drunk instead, and everything is hazy and hilarious. I don't feel connected to my body anymore. In the midst of it all, someone handed me a joint. Because there are no rules right now.

The full moon is rising above us. It'll reach its peak in a few hours. I try not to think about what that means.

Vale looks at me and laughs. "You gotta sober up a bit before the ceremony, brother. Come on." He pulls me to my feet. "Walk it off."

Ceili appears at his side, wearing a red dress. She looks pretty. Her big blue eyes look up at me. "Oh jeez, you look like you need some air." She turns to Vale, and waves him away. "It's OK sweetie, you go on ahead, back to the party."

"You sure?" Vale asks, his lip curling as he looks at me. "He's pretty fucking wasted."

"It's fine, we'll go for a walk and sober up." She smiles at him sweetly. "Really, we'll be OK. You go have fun."

"Yeah, go have fun," I tell Vale. Just fuck off. Leave me alone with her.

Vale shrugs and wipes a hand over his sweaty brow. "Just don't drink any more, you two!" He leaves with a wave, heading back towards the bonfire and noise.

"Finally," Ceili says, "I thought he'd never fucking leave."

"Vale," I slur, "is dense as fuck." I put my arm around her, and we walk towards the forest. It's dark over here.

Ceili giggles quietly as she nuzzles in to me. "I've never seen you like this, Amryn."

"I'm pretty sure you've seen me drunk before, babe." The words roll off my tongue, which feels thick, foreign in my mouth.

"Not this drunk." She says.

"You're drunk too," I chide, "don't even pretend you're not." I pull her in closer, and she feels nice under my arm.

"Well maybe a little." She tips her face up to look at me. She has full pink lips. Her eyes are glowing.

"A little a little, or a little a lot?" I ask, grinning.

She reaches up and runs a hand through my hair. "A little enough, I guess."

"Hey, so I found out something pretty fucking interesting today." I tell her. I put my hands on her waist, and back her against a tree slowly. I'm towering over her, and her face is lit up with anticipation. "You want to know what Morgan told me, babe?"

"What did Morgan tell you?" Ceili asks, smiling as her back meets the tree trunk.

"That Roche fucked every girl he could after Lordain and her got married."

Ceili bites her lip as she gazes up at me. "Is that so?"

"Yeah." I lower my mouth to hers. She's so pretty. She's so fucking hot. She has an amazing body, full breasts that are almost spilling out of her dress. And fuck I'm so hard. "No rules until the peak of the full moon."

She raises an eyebrow at me. "And what would you like to do while there's no rules?" She's waiting for me to move.

She's not Cora. She's not Cora.

My mouth crushes hers, and then her tongue is in my mouth. She tastes like strawberries and vodka. Her arms wrap around me. No one tells us to stop. No one is getting her off me. No one is pulling me away to be lectured, or beaten. I push my body against hers, and she feels incredible.

She pulls away from me and drops to her knees, undoing my belt. My pants open under her fingers and she pulls out my cock. She grips the base, gazing up at me with those big blue eyes, and then she takes me in her mouth.

I brace myself against the tree with one hand, the other in her hair as her head bobs up and down, her tongue swirling over me. I try not to thrust, but her mouth is hot and wet and her tongue feels amazing. My head is already swimming and now everything she's doing to me is making it even hazier, everything's warm and wrong and hot and tight.

I suck in a breath through gritted teeth as she draws me down further into her throat. Her eyes stay on me, watching me as I moan and gasp, and I can see she's loving it. She's loving what she's doing to me.

I want to fuck her. I just want to be inside her. I pull away from her, kneeling down in front of her. "Turn around." I say to her. She grins at me and obeys, puts both hands on the ground, pressing her ass towards me. I push her dress up around her waist, and yank her panties down her thighs. Holy fuck, her ass is perfect.

I grip her hips and slide my cock into her, and she moans, arching her back. No one is stopping me. I don't have to stop myself. I can fuck her for hours.

There are no rules.

"Amryn." She gasps as I thrust into her. "Oh fuck."

I grab her hair in my fist, holding her head up. "You like that?" I ask.

She whimpers. "Oh fuck. Yes. Harder."

I slam into her, and her pussy gets wetter, everything's getting hotter. Sweat prickles on my scalp and runs down my back, soaking my shirt.

"Amryn." She sighs.

Fuck. That's not her voice. I clench my eyes shut. She's not Cora. She's Ceili. I'm allowed to have her. It's OK. I want this. I want her.

She presses herself back against me, bouncing her ass on me, meeting each one of my thrusts greedily, like she can't get enough of me. "You feel so good." She moans. "I've wanted you to do this for so long."

"Yeah?" I ask, putting my hand around her throat, leaning over her to press my lips to hers. "You been thinking of me like this?"

"Yes," she breathes against my mouth, "I wanted you so bad." She quivers as I thrust again. "You can put it anywhere." She says suddenly. My stomach does a flip. She looks into my eyes and grins. "Anywhere, baby."

I've never done that. I'll never be able to do that after tonight. I feel her hand go between her legs, swirling over her clit. Fuck it. I'm drunk enough to not care, to do whatever's offered to me. She wants me. I'm not saying no tonight.

I pull my cock out of her pussy, dripping with her juices, and position myself over her. I push gently at first, feeling resistance as just my tip dips inside her. She pushes herself back against me, carefully, and I ease into her ass.

She whimpers loudly, her fingers moving faster over her clit.

Her ass is so tight I feel like I'm going to come immediately. I breathe in heavily through my mouth, gasping the thick summer air into my lungs. Oh fuck, *fuuuuuuuck*. I thrust into her, and her body holds on to me, hard. I am, I'm going to fucking come right away. I try to hold back as her thighs shake, trying to move gently even though it feels fucking amazing, waiting for her orgasm before I let go. I bite my lip to distract myself, the aching heat in my groin almost unbearable.

She tenses, her moans high-pitched as her fingers circle her clit furiously."Do it harder." She gasps. "Fuck me harder."

I thrust into her, and she cries out. I keep going, her hand clawing into the ground beneath her. Her breath catches for a second, and then her whole body quivers, and I feel the pulse against my cock, deep inside her. I groan as I come hard, filling her up.

My whole body's trembling, I can't fucking breathe, and my heart is hammering in my chest. My head isn't swimming anymore, it's screaming at me, asking me what the fuck I just did.

I pull out of her, and she laughs breathlessly. "You're amazing." She says. She straightens in front of me, pulling her panties back up her thighs. "You're really fucking good." She smiles at me over her shoulder, her eyes hooded with satisfaction.

I'm breathing heavily as I do up my belt. "That was fun." I say. I don't know what else to say. My climax has made me stone-cold sober.

96

"Bet you've never done that before." She says with a grin.

I shake my head. "No, I haven't."

"I could tell, you were gentle. Most guys aren't like that."

"I didn't want to hurt you." My fucking head is throbbing now. I get to my feet, and offer her a hand to help her up. I'm soaked in sweat, my whole body feels sticky with heat. "Well, after all that fun I need a shower."

Ceili wraps her arms around my waist. "Can I join you?"

I should say no. I should say I want to be alone. I should say that this was a mistake.

But I don't, because it's not a mistake. Because this is my one chance to get this all off my chest, to fuck who I want where I want when I want. I finally have time. Just not with her. Not like how I always wanted to.

"Sure." I reply, and she leans up to kiss me again.

We head back to my cabin. The next few hours are going to fly by. And if I'm with Ceili, I don't have to think about what happens next.

It's 2am.

The peak of the full moon is in half an hour.

Ceili and I didn't stop fucking after we left the wedding. She moaned and screamed and marvelled at the fact that I could just keep going, with barely a break. I fucked her in all the places in my cabin where I ever fucked Cora, some insane desire to erase the memories, to make new ones, like that would ever work.

Ceili and I walk hand in hand to the Great Hall. I feel a pang at knowing this night was the last night I'll ever touch someone like this, the last time I'll ever be intimate with another demon, but that gives way pretty quickly to an overwhelming feeling of nausea as we approach the bonfire outside the Great Hall. I keep telling myself it'll be fine. It'll be OK. It won't be a big deal. I can look away.

We walk in, and Ceili lets go of my hand to stand at the back. I have to stand at the front, with the council, beside Cora's mother. This is so fucking weird. Anya doesn't acknowledge me as I take my place beside her, and I know it's probably because she's just caught up in the ceremony of it all, but I'm just grateful, because I really don't want to look at anyone's face right now.

There's a large bed in the middle of the hall, covered in white sheets. No pillows. No blankets. No privacy. Four large pillar candles stand at each corner of the bed, unlit. No one is talking, the only sound the collective breathing of the clan. It's a little eerie, just breathing and shuffling and barely any movement.

A woman steps forward to lights the four candles. The lights go out, and all I can see is the bed dimly illuminated by the candlelight. There's the sound of wood scraping somewhere, and I look up to see a panel in the roof being pulled back, and the light of the full moon floods the Hall.

A figure begins to move towards the bed, wearing a long white robe. As they reach the bed, I see it's Cora. I can't see her face properly, it's too dark for that. But her

98

whole body is tense, and her hands shake as she takes off the white robe. She shakes out her curls hesitantly and lies down on her back, looking up at the ceiling. Her chest rises and falls with each shaky breath. Her hands are flat on the bed, her fingers flexing slightly into the bedsheets, no doubt to stop herself from trembling.

Fuck. This is so wrong.

Another figure approaches, and it's Finn. He pulls his robe off over his head, and looks down at Cora with a smile. He's running his hand up and down his cock, trying to get hard. I almost feel sorry for him. Almost.

He climbs onto the bed over her, and Cora's hands go to his shoulders, tentatively. He whispers something to her, and kisses her. Her legs open up for him, and he lays his hips between them, his hand on his cock, looking down as he guides himself inside her. I look away. I can't do this. I can't watch this. Listening is bad enough. The bed creaks quietly as Finn fucks her, and he groans. My stomach is a pit of ice.

Why is this taking so long? The minutes stretch on and on, and I shift on my feet. Come on. Get this over with. Let Cora get out from under everyone's eyes. This is fucking barbaric. She moans, and I think I'm going to be sick.

My jaw begins to ache from the tension. The air in the Hall is thick despite the open panel in the roof, only humid summer air pouring in. Sweat trickles down my temple, and I can feel my hair sticking to the back of my neck.

Then I hear another sound. Finn's grunting, sounding frustrated. The creaking of the bed changes, stopping, starting. I dare a look back at the bed. He's thrusting into her hard, rough. He stops, then starts again. Stops again. He runs a hand over his face, pushing his hair aside.

"Fuck." He grits his teeth, thrusting again.

Cora is looking up at him, her hands on his chest. Her lips move, but I can't hear what she's saying. Her fingers flex, moving up to his shoulders, as though trying to comfort him, pull him down to her. He pushes her away.

What is he doing?

Finn pulls out of her, rising up on to his knees, breathing heavily. His jaw is set as he looks down at her, a look of sheer frustration, then he grabs her hips, forcing her over on to her stomach. Cora cries out in surprise, and Finn throws himself onto her back, pushing her cheek against the mattress.

He thrusts into her hard, and Cora whimpers. "Ow!" She cries.

I'm going to explode. My heart wrenches in my chest.

"Ow!" She cries again. She grits her teeth. "Finn! You're hurting me!"

He's not stopping. My head snaps to the others, the elders who are just watching this happen. Lordain and Morgan stand motionless. I look at Cora's mother, and see she's clutched a hand to her mouth. Her chest is quivering. She's crying. She's watching her daughter being raped. They're all just standing here watching.

I look back at the bed, and Cora fights her head free of Finn's grip, looking straight ahead. She's looking right at me. Fuck. Fuck. I'm going to kill him. Tears are running

100

down her cheeks. She's crying. Someone stop this. Someone fucking stop this.

"Finn, please," she whimpers, "please stop." Her eyes are fixed on me, pleading.

I take a step forward, and a hand shoots out to stop me. I look down at Cora's mother, her eyes filled with tears, shining in the moonlight. She shakes her head. "They'll kill you." She mouths.

I don't care. I try to step forward again, and both her arms wrap around mine. "Amryn, they'll kill you." She whispers desperately.

Finn groans loudly and collapses on Cora. She's gone limp. Her face has disappeared in the mass of her hair. Cora's mother presses her face against my arm, and she sobs quietly.

"It is done." Lordain announces, stepping forward with his hands raised to the full moon. "We welcome our new Alpha, and his Queen." The clan bursts into some weird murmuring, a chant we're supposed to know, and maybe I do, but my brain isn't functioning right now.

Finn rises back up to his knees, his chest heaving, and the smug smile on his face makes me want to tear his fucking head off. He runs a hand down Cora's back, and I see her ribcage quivering as she sobs.

I can't take it anymore.

I storm out of the Hall, and break into a run out in the night air. I run until my lungs feel like they're going to burst. I run until my heartbeat is so violent I double over and throw up. All the tequila and misery and anger spill out of me. Tears are running down my face.

I just let that happen. I just stood there and watched that happen. I watched the woman I love be raped and did nothing. No one did anything. A roar escapes me, echoing through the empty forest around me.

I'm going to kill him. I'm going to fucking kill him.

6
Cora

It's raining again. It beats loudly against the window, and I watch the drops chase each other down the glass, gathering in one after another as they go, growing bigger and bigger as they race to the bottom.

I tried so hard to be happy yesterday. I did. I felt pretty and it was meant to be a special day. I told myself I love Finn. I have to, right? We're fated. There has to be something there. Even as I stood there, with Amryn right behind him, I told myself that Finn is the one for me now. We'll get married and have babies, and we'll be happy.

Happiness is a choice, right?

A storm rolled in last night after the Ascension, and everyone talked about what a good sign it was, that the Old God was pleased, was sending his blessing. Morgan told me how beautiful the ceremony was, asked me how I felt now that I was no longer a virgin. I don't know what I said. I was too dazed. Finn had to carry me to bed. I blacked out after that.

I woke up this morning and wondered if it was all a bad dream.

But now Finn is stirring in the bed behind me, and reaches a hand out to touch my back. "Good morning, babe." He says, shuffling closer to me. He kisses the back of my neck, nuzzling his face into the crook of my neck. "Or should I say, wife?"

I keep staring at the window. I feel numb, and hollow. I'm his wife. He claimed me. He did that to me, to claim me as his.

"You OK?" Finn asks.

"I'm fine." I reply. I sound like a robot.

"You sure?" He rolls me onto my back, frowning with concern. "Babe, what's wrong?"

I shake my head. "Nothing." But tears spring to my eyes, and I press a hand to my face.

"Babe, why are you crying?" He takes me in his arms. "What happened?"

What happened. Like he doesn't know.

"You hurt me." I whisper. I can't look at him. I roll away from him, sitting up on the bed, wincing as pain shoots through my groin.

"Oh babe, I'm sorry." He puts an arm around me. "I didn't mean to, I promise. It was nerves. I'm so sorry. I would never want to hurt you, babe."

"I said it hurt." I wrap my arms around myself. I don't want him to hug me. "I said it hurt and I begged you to stop and you didn't."

"Cora, come on, I had to finish it. You can't just stop an Ascension ceremony like that." Finn says, as though this is a completely reasonable excuse for what he just did to me. "And it was hard for me too, you know, having to perform in front of everyone like that."

"Hard for you?" I look at him, scorn narrowing my eyes. "Hard for *you*?" I get up off the bed. "You have to hurt me to get off, is that how it is?"

Finn jumps to his feet. "No!"

"No?" I scoff incredulously. "So holding my head down so I couldn't move or breathe, that was all just a part of it, was it? That was just what sex is to you? 'Don't worry, I'll be gentle', remember? That was gentle was it?"

He takes my hand in his, his eyes pleading. "Babe, I'm so sorry. Come on, come back to bed. I want to show you how good it can be. I'll be gentle, and I'll make you come, and we can forget all about the stupid Ascension ceremony. It'll be like our first time."

I wrench my hand away from his. "I'm sore, OK? I need to heal first." I storm out of the bedroom, down the hallway into the bathroom, slamming the door behind me so hard the window shakes in its frame. I collapse onto the edge of the bathtub, sobs racking through me. Everything hurts. Everything is sore.

Amryn never did this to me. It was never like this with him. He never hurt me.

I cry harder. I want him so badly. I want him to take me in his arms and hold me while I cry. I wanted him to rescue me last night. I couldn't see him, but I knew he was there. I could feel him. Every part of me was crying out for him to come and get me. But he couldn't do anything. They'd have killed him.

There's a soft knock at the door. "Babe, do you want some breakfast?" Finn asks.

"No." I snap, jumping up to turn the lock on the bathroom door before he gets any stupid ideas. "Go away." There's silence for a moment, and then I hear his footsteps retreat, slowly, down the hallway.

I turn and lean against the door, taking a deep, shuddering breath. There's a sudden rush from between my legs. I look down at my crotch, and red seeps through the fabric of my white shorts. Fuck. It's started. I cry harder. I can have a baby now. I'm a Queen and the Ascension started the process for the next generation of demons to be born. Mine and Finn's children.

I turn on the shower, washing myself clean. I put my hand to my belly, and try to imagine it swelling, holding a baby. Finn's baby. I lean my forehead against the shower wall and sob, because I want it to hold Amryn's baby. I want him to kiss my belly and sing to our baby and press his hands against me to feel our baby kick.

It's no use. That life was never meant for us.

Once I'm dried off, I go to the bedroom to pull on sweatpants and a t-shirt, and head into the kitchen, past Finn, ignoring his gaze.

"Where are you going?" Finn calls after me.

"For a walk." I reply as I walk out on to the porch, the storm door slamming behind me.

I tip my face up to the rain outside, breathing in deeply. It's quiet in the compound, everyone sleeping off
106

their hangovers and the late night. I press my hands to my face. They all saw it. They all watched. They're all fine with all of this.

If I ever have a child, please don't let it be a girl. Please don't let her be subjected to this. Please don't let any child of mine ever be trapped like me.

I walk towards the lake, the mountaintops around me shrouded in mist. It's the wettest summer we've had in forever. Endless rain. It suits my mood.

The lake is grey under the drab sky, lapping gently at the pebbly shore. My footsteps crunch over the rocks, and I pause at the water's edge. Maybe I could just walk into the lake and drown myself. Just walk in, and sink underneath the grey surface, and never come back up. Never breathe again. That's one way out.

Then I have a horrible image in my head, of Amryn racing into the lake, screaming my name. He pulls my body up out of the water, weeping. He clutches me to his chest, sobbing, screaming. Cora. Cora. No.

His mother killed herself. He found her dead in the tub. I can't do that to him.

I press my fists to my eyes, tears falling again.

There's movement in the water, and I jump. I hurriedly wipe my eyes, and see Amryn rising from the grey depths, wearing only a pair of black shorts, his wet hair stuck to his back, his chest heaving. He spots me, staring at him, and frowns. He shakes his head, and continues to walk out of the water, away from me.

"Amryn." I call out. I don't move towards him.

He pauses, his hands flexing on either side of him. Slowly, he raises his head to look at me. His face is pulled taut with pain. "Are you OK?" He asks.

I shake my head.

His face crumples, and he breathes through gritted teeth. "I'm sorry." He says. "I'm so sorry."

"Please don't apologise."

He walks towards me. "I should have stopped him."

I shake my head. "They would have killed you."

"And? So what? I would have died, I should have died for you, to stop that from happening to you."

I cover my face with my hands and start crying again. Don't say that. Don't talk about dying. "I don't want anything to happen to you."

"I can't do this." He says to me, and I move my hands to look at him. He looks like he's about to burst into tears. "I can't watch this happen to you."

"My bleeding started." I don't know why I tell him. But he'll understand.

His face contorts, and he gasps for air. "So soon you'll be pregnant with his baby." He shakes his head and runs a hand through his wet hair. "I'll have to watch you growing _"

"You'll have to *watch* me?" I cry. "You think watching is hard? Try living it!"

He holds out a hand. "Cora, I'm so sorry."

"You think I want to have his baby?" I clutch a hand to my stomach. "You think I want him to touch me, to come anywhere near close enough to get me pregnant? You think I want to lie in that bed with him every night knowing I don't have a fucking choice?"

He clenches his lips together as they quiver. "I'm sorry." He swallows hard. "I would take you away from it all, if I could. If we could run away, I'd take you right now, and I'd kill anyone who tried to stop me." His eyes are full of anguish. "But -"

"We're both trapped." I say simply.

He steps closer, and puts a hand on my shoulder. "He hurt you, didn't he?"

I nod. "I'm sore. He was rough." I reach up and touch his cheek. "He's nothing like you."

He scoffs, shaking his head. "The guy who let you get raped, yeah what a star."

I grab his face in my hands. "Stop it!"

"I should have stopped him!" A tear runs down his cheek as he cries out, and then his arms crush me to him, against his cold, wet body. I nuzzle into him, sobbing. He holds me tight, and I wonder if maybe we should both just drown ourselves, and escape our misery that way. Or maybe someone will see us now, like this, and then they'll just kill us both, and it'll all be over.

"I don't want to go back to that house." I whisper, my fingers clinging to his chest.

"I know, baby." He raises my face to his, and I can see him hesitate, see that he wants to kiss me. His eyes clench shut, and he presses his forehead to mine. "I know."

"Can I come to your house later?" I ask. "Finn's got to meet with the Astala clan elders. I can sneak out of the house."

Amryn's eyes open and he flinches, straightening up. "I don't know if that's a good idea. You're Queen now, the guards will be watching you."

"I'll make sure no one follows me, they won't even notice I'm gone." I start crying again, and I wonder if I'm ever going to fucking stop. "Please, don't push me away. I just - I don't want to - to do anything. I just want to be close to you. Just for a little while."

He sighs heavily, and presses a kiss against my forehead. His lips are so warm. "OK. Come by later. Just be careful."

I'm sitting alone at the kitchen table, staring mindlessly at the wood grain. Finn was very concerned about me, fussing over me when I got back from the lake. He had the good grace not to ask why my clothes were wet. He almost cancelled the meeting with the Astala's but I pushed him out of the door, insisting he couldn't miss it. Because I want to see Amryn.

There's a knock at the door, and I look up to see Ceili on the porch, smiling widely at me. "Hi cuz!" She lets herself in. "How's married life?"

I smile weakly. "Only been 24 hours," I reply as she sits down opposite me. "Probably a bit early to say."

"Where's Finn?" She asks, tossing her pale hair over her shoulder.

110

I rub my temple, feeling a headache coming on. "He's with the Astalas, having a big Alpha meeting so they can beat their chests together."

Ceili laughs, then eyes me carefully when I don't join in. "You OK?"

I wave my hand dismissively, and lean back in my chair. "I don't wanna talk about it."

"Oh, so not OK?" She nods. "Ok sorry, never mind. Let's talk about something else." She claps her hands together and smiles brightly. "So the wedding was amazing, what a party, huh?"

I smile weakly. "Yeah, I guess it was. Did you have a good time?" I ask, jamming my hands into the pockets of me sweater. "Last time I saw you, you were on your fourth tequila shot and going strong."

She bites her lip and examines her fingernails. "Oh I had a great night."

I laugh. "Breaking hearts again, huh? Who was it this time?"

Ceili shrugs, feigning innocence. "Just someone I've had my eye on for a while, and I finally had the opportunity to pursue." She leans back in her chair. "A big, strong, handsome someone with the most beautiful cock I think I've ever seen."

I raise my eyebrows. "So no one I know huh?" I say with a short laugh.

"Oh you know him alright." Ceili looks around conspiratorially, leaning over the table. "Did you know," she drops her voice low, even though we're alone, "that between the hours of the wedding and the ascension the rules of the blood covenant are lifted?"

I frown. "What are you talking about?"

"Yep." She nods emphatically. "No rules, sweetie."

"So what does that have to do with anything?" I'm confused.

"The Draw?" She bites her lip. "Mhmm. Him being off limits? Uh-uh. Not off limits anymore."

I can't breathe as what she's saying dawns on me. "You fucked Amryn?"

Ceili laughs. "I think it'd probably be more accurate to say he fucked me."

My stomach seizes up. "You're not joking."

"Why would I be joking?" She leans back in her chair, rolling her eyes to the ceiling as she sighs. "He was amazing. And also, he is *huge*."

"Where did you do it?" I ask, willing my voice not to dissolve into a squeak.

"In the woods, the first time." She grins, twirling her hair around her finger.

"The first time?" I ask weakly.

Ceili nods. "Yeah, and then we went back to his house. And then it was the shower and the bed room and then the floor because we fell off the bed." She laughs out loud. "Oh my god, and his *stamina*. He just kept going and going, it was crazy. I don't even know how many times I came. I could barely walk when I got up this morning." She sighs, throwing her hands behind her head and gazing

112

at the ceiling. "I can't believe I only got the one night with him. I am going to be suffering withdrawals from him for a *long* time."

I lurch to the kitchen and fill a glass with water, gulping it down. My hands are shaking.

"Are you OK?" Ceili asks me. "Are you hungover?"

I shake my head, leaning on the counter. "No, I think - I'm just a bit lightheaded, my bleeding started."

Ceili frowns. "Oh you poor thing, what a way to start married life, huh?"

"Yeah, it sucks." I fill my glass again, sure I'm going to be sick from too much water and the nausea that won't stop washing over me.

"You're not angry that I slept with Amryn, are you?" Ceili asks, rising from the table to lean on the counter beside me.

I shake my head. "Why would I be angry? He's not my - my - anything."

"No I know," Ceili says quickly. "I just know you two were close growing up, I didn't want it to be weird or whatever."

"It's not weird, Ceili, really." I reach over and take her hand, forcing myself to look at her face, forcing myself to smile. "It's fine. I'm glad you had such a good time with him. He - he deserved one good night like that."

Ceili pouts. "Why does it have to be only one night? Can you and Finn get married again?" She laughs and puts a hand on my shoulder.

"Yeah, why not?" I try to laugh too, try to show this isn't bothering me, but instead the floor tips away from me, and I put a hand to my head as everything around me sways.

"Cora, holy shit." Ceili grasps my hand. "Sweetie, you look awful. Maybe you should go to bed."

I nod. "Yeah, I think I might do that."

She nods, her brow crinkling with concern. "OK, you go on and lie down, I'll leave you to rest. I just wanted to check that you were OK. You know, after -" She shakes her head. "We'll talk about that another time."

"Yeah, sure." I smile weakly. I never want to talk about that, ever again.

"Bye sweetie!" She heads out the door, and I hear her footsteps down the porch stairs, crossing the gravel drive.

Once I'm sure she's gone, I stalk out the door, across the yard, keeping behind the tree line so the guards don't see me. My head's spinning. I feel sick. I'm going to fucking throw up. I circle around behind Amryn's cabin, pushing through the wooden gate, checking before I close it that no one has followed me.

I knock on the door quietly, and wait. Nothing. I knock again, a little louder, and I hear movement. The door opens, and Amryn's standing there, a small smile on his lips.

"You fucked my cousin?" I can feel tears in my eyes.

His face drops. "Shit." He pulls me inside, closing the door behind me.

114

"You fucked Ceili?" I ask him. "On my wedding night?"

"Cora, I was drunk, and -"

"You fucked my cousin in the woods, and then you brought her here?" I dash my tears away with my wrist. "How could you?"

"How could I?" He asks incredulously. "How could I what?"

"Sleep with somebody!" I cry. "How could you sleep with somebody that wasn't me?"

"What do you want from me, Cora?" He asks, holding his hands out in front of him. "I had one night, one fucking night to be like everyone else, one night to just not have to think and watch and wait to have the shit kicked out of me for looking at a pretty girl, and you're mad?"

"Why didn't you come find me?" I ask, stupidly.

He looks at me wide-eyed. "Are you fucking high?" He catches himself, takes a deep breath, running a hand over his face. "It was your wedding, Cora. You'd just married Finn. And we've said a million times it's the last time, the last fucking time, and we keep on running back to each other and making it worse."

"Was she good?" I ask.

"Oh, come on." He turns away from me.

"Because she couldn't stop telling me about how good you were!"

"Well great!" He throws his arms out. "What am I meant to say to that, huh?"

"She said she couldn't walk this morning, because -"
My voice catches in my throat, and I dash away the tears
from my eyes with the back of my hand. "Because you did
it, so many times."

"Cora, it was just sex." He shakes his head and shrugs.
"It was sex, that's all."

"But it was good sex, right?" My stomach won't stop
churning. "You had a good time, and you came, and -"

"You want to know if sex with her was better than sex
with you, right? That's what you're asking me, isn't it?"

"Well, was it?" I ask, not wanting to hear the answer,
because I might not like it.

"Of course it wasn't!" His hands claw on either side of
his face. "God fucking dammit, Cora. I just wanted - I
wanted it to be you, OK?" He looks at me helplessly. "I
wanted it to be you, and it wasn't. So I fucked her, I
fucked the next person who threw themselves at me, and it
was Ceili, and I'm sorry OK?"

"But you enjoyed it?"

He growls at the ceiling. "Why are you doing this?"

"Because -" I swallow hard. "Because you're mine."

His eyes flash as he looks at me, a combination of pain
and disbelief. "And who's mine, Cora? Who belongs to
me?" He shakes his head. "It's ironic that I'm the Runt,
but everyone seems to think they fucking own me."

I step towards him. "That's not what I meant."

He holds his hand out, stopping me. "I'm just the
fucking Runt, the disgraced son of the striker that couldn't
protect your father."

116

"Amryn, no -"

"No, that's how it is." He hangs his head, his hair falling over his face. "That's all they see. My father, failing. The clan falling apart, losing their home, losing everything, because of my father. My mother couldn't even stay around for me." He puts his hands to his face. "No, she had to go and kill herself and leave me alone, and I'm just alone, fucking alone."

I rush to him, putting my arms around him. "No, you're not alone, I'm here, with you."

"No you're not." He pushes me away. "You're someone else's wife. You're sneaking away and hiding and if we get caught I die."

I clutch a hand to my mouth. "I'm sorry, Amryn."

"I just wanted to feel normal." He sighs, throwing himself down into a chair by the window. "I just wanted to have one night of being like everyone else before I sit by and watch you all live your lives and have babies and -" He breaks off, running a hand through his hand.

"Amryn -"

His head shoots up suddenly, and he looks out the window. "Cora, get down."

"What?"

He launches himself at me. "DOWN!" He throws himself on me as a hail of bullets shatters the windows. He holds himself over me, shielding me as the gunfire continues.

I cower underneath him, my hands flat on the ground, and I hear an explosion in the distance, feel it reverberate through the floor. The gunfire stops, and we hear voices outside.

Amryn gets up in a low crouch, going towards the window. He turns and gestures to me to hide under the bed. I shuffle underneath it, my heart beating out of my chest. He makes his way to the window, and slowly, carefully looks outside. He drops back down again instantly, and his hands begin to glow.

"Stay here." He whispers. "Whatever happens, stay right there and don't come out."

"Amryn, what's happening?"

"Just stay there."

We hear another explosion, and he jumps out of the broken window. There's a yell, and running footsteps. Amryn calls out to someone, and a fireball explodes right outside the cabin. My heart is in my throat as I wait for Amryn's voice to sound again, so I know he's OK.

I hear him call out, is it to Vale? I clench my eyes shut. What the hell is happening?

Someone screams in the distance, a woman. It could my Mom. It could be Ceili. There's another explosion and more gunfire. I have to help. I can't hide down here under the bed while they're being attacked out there. I have powers, and Amryn's been training me for years. I can fight.

I crawl out from under the bed, and over to the window Amryn jumped out of. More gunfire. I duck back down, and wait for it to stop. Silence. Three seconds. Four. I get up and spring out into the yard and sprint for a tree, taking cover behind it. The sun is setting, and the cloud cover is making the compound prematurely dark. The power has been cut, and the only light is coming from the houses burning at the far end of the compound.

Something swoops above me, above the foliage of the tree, and my stomach drops.

Angels. We're being attacked by Angels.

I step out and summon my flames, looking up at the sky to see the winged figure circling Amryn's cabin. I send a fireball straight up at them, and they cry out in surprise as it catches one of their wings. They plummet to the ground, not far from me, and I send another bolt at them as they raise themselves up on their arms. There's an explosion of light, and when the flash clears, they're flat on the ground, unmoving.

"There!" I hear the cry, and see figures on foot rushing towards me.

They're not angels. These are demons. I can see their arms glowing in the growing night. One of them fires at me, bright orange flames, and I shield myself with my own flames, rushing straight at them. Once I'm close enough, I detonate a fireball. My flames overwhelm theirs easily, sending them running, screaming as they burn.

"Cora!" Someone calls out to me. It's Vale. I can't see him for smoke and flames. "Cora, where are you?"

I don't respond. I don't want to draw attention to myself. There's more gunfire, and I run in the direction of my mother's house. Please let her be OK. I feel like I'm moving through fucking molasses, and my eyes keep scanning the sky above me, which is hidden behind a thick layer of smoke.

Something swoops down behind me, landing heavily on the ground. I spin to face an angel, towering over me. He's at least 7 feet tall. He leers at me, his eyes pitch black in a blank white face.

"You must be the Alpha Queen," he says, pulling his lips back to reveal a mouth of sharp teeth that glint in the firelight.

I summon a flame in my hand. "Yeah I am, and I'm going to fucking burn you alive." I send my flame at him, and a red shield flies up in front of him, shimmering, iridescent in the darkness. The flame is swallowed up by it. What the fuck is this? I stumble backwards as the angel begins to laugh.

"What the fuck are you?" I ask.

"Oh majesty," he says, clasping his hands before him, "your powers are truly impressive. And yet -"

Suddenly there's arms around me, and Amryn pushes me behind him. He holds out a hand at the angel, flames leaping high. "What do you want?" Amryn asks.

"Your Queen of course." The angel says, his voice heavy with amusement. "The Alpha is of no use to me, but this one, the Shadow Queen, what a prize."

The - the what?

"What did you call me?" I ask.

The angel steps closer, tutting. "Oh dear, she doesn't know, does she?"

Amryn hesitates. "I don't know what you're talking about."

The angel laughs. "Of course, Lordain has done an excellent job keeping you all in the dark. Shame your father couldn't protect Rodelth. All this could have been avoided."

I bristle at the mention of my father's name. "You're going to die tonight." I say, stepping out from behind Amryn and throwing everything I have at this fucker, a fireball of white exploding in front of us.

The red shield flies back up, and Amryn throws an arm in front of me. "What the fuck was that?" He asks, watching it blink and then die away.

"Times have changed, demon," the angel replies. "Now, it's sadly time for you to die, and the Queen shall come with us."

"Cora, run!" Amryn cries, pushing me away from him.

I stumble backwards, and see the angel raise his hands, a shimmering silver dart appearing between them. With one swift movement, he fires it at Amryn. Amryn throws up his flames to shield himself, but the dart passes straight through them with a loud hiss, parting them like waves.

Amryn's eyes widen as the dart lands right in the centre of his chest, and he's thrown backwards from the force of its impact.

"Amryn!" I throw myself down beside him, my hands grasping uselessly at the dart, which is embedded in his skin. "Oh shit, no, no, no. Amryn! Amryn?" A dark stain begins to spread around the dart, like ink spilling over his skin. He starts to convulse, his eyes staring at the sky. "Amryn!" I hold his face in my hands. No no no. This can't be happening.

I hear the angel laughing behind me, and I turn to shoot a flame at him again. He steps aside and claps his hands together. "Bravo, majesty, that's the spirit!"

"Amryn?" He's going still in my arms. Blood is running out of his mouth. His eyes turn to me, his chest heaving as his breath slows. "Baby? No, please, stay with me." I feel tears running down my face as I cradle his head in my arms. "Please, no no no. You can't die, please, stay with me, baby you have to stay with me." His hand reaches up to touch my face, but doesn't quite make it. He breathes one last time, and his hand drops. His eyes go blank.

"No!" I'm screaming, clutching him to me. Amryn. Amryn. No no no no. Please no.

"Interesting." I hear the angel say. "What a display of emotions from a Queen towards the Draw." He's standing right beside me, and I glare up at him. "I have a feeling not all is as it is meant to be in the clan."

"Fuck you." I hiss. I hold Amryn to me, holding out my flames, shielding his body with mine. "I'm going to fucking tear you to pieces."

The angel laughs. "Ah, your majesty. We mustn't be rude." He opens his palm, and a small green flame forms in the middle of it. "Now, do forgive me, but this is going to hurt." He leans down over me. "A lot."

He presses his hand to my head, and I feel like my skull is going to shatter. There's a screaming in my head - or am I screaming? - pure electricity coursing through my brain, burning and shattering everything. I flail at his hand, trying to get away, but my vision goes dark, the pain coursing down my back, and I can't move.

I hear the angel laughing again, and suddenly air is rushing past me.

They're taking me away.

And they killed Amryn. Amryn's dead. Amryn's dead. He died in my arms.

I try to scream, but nothing works anymore.

"Just go to sleep." The angel says to me.

Amryn's dead. The thought echoes through my head as I lose consciousness, as I slump in the angels' arms, and all sound is drowned out.

Amryn's dead. I felt his heart stop. He died in my arms.

7
Amryn

ora. I can't touch her.

She's screaming.

She's begging me not to die.

She's pleading for me to stay with her, just stay with her.

I sit bolt upright, flames exploding from my hands. "Cora!"

"Hey brother, calm down." Vale is at my side. Where the fuck am I? I look around me, and I'm in the Great Hall. There's people everywhere, wounded, bleeding, crying.

I grab Vale's shirt. "Where's Cora?"

"Amryn , you need to calm down. You're hurt bad."

I was hurt, of course I was, the angel threw something at me. I put a hand to my chest, and there's silver dart, burning in my skin. I look down to see a black mark spread over my chest. "Where's Cora?" I ask Vale again. "She was there, with me, she was screaming."

Vale shakes his head. "They took her." Fuck. No no no. "Brother, you need to lie down, the healers need to look you over." His eyes flicker to the dart in my chest. "I've never seen weapons like this. They annihilated us. We didn't even hear them. They didn't trigger the alarms."

I try to get to my feet. "Fuck this, I need to find Cora." I stand and the pain in my chest doubles me over. My lungs are filled with acid, and I feel it burning up into my mouth, and my nose. My eyes water as my vision goes blurry, and Vale catches me before I fall, helping me lie back down.

"Amryn, you're not going to be any good to her if you fucking keel over right now." He says. "We'll find her, don't worry. It'll be OK."

I try to breathe, try to remember what happened, try to remember. "This angel had a shield." I say to Vale, my skull vibrating. I can taste blood. "It was red, shimmering and it absorbed Cora's flames. Like they were nothing."

Vale shakes his head. "Angels and demons fighting together. They've come up with some new tech, and they kicked our asses."

I clench my eyes shut, trying to remember. There was something else, Something else the angel said. My head fucking hurts and I can't see straight. The angel said something to Cora, about her father. About my father not saving him. He knew who we were.

One of the healers comes rushing over and kneels at my side, inspecting the wound. Her eyes are mournful.

"I've never seen anything like this before." She says. "This is dark magic."

"How many dead?" I ask.

She shakes her head. "So many. It's hard to tell. Last count was at 20." She looks up at me hesitantly. "This is going to hurt. Brace yourself." Her hands light up, and she grips the dart in my chest. She starts to pull it out, and my fingers dig into the bed underneath me. It feels like she's tearing my heart out through my ribcage. "I'm sorry." She says.

I shake my head. It's not her fault.

She's fighting it, and it feels like the fucking thing is burrowing into my ribs, trying to claw itself further into my body. "I can't hold on to it." She says, gritting her teeth, pulling at it again. Her brow furrows as she strains against it. "I just- I can't get it out. Oh god, what is this?"

I push her hands away, and grab onto it myself. I pull hard, and blood rushes into my mouth. I roll onto my side, coughing it up, watching it stream down the side of the bed and onto the floor.

"Holy shit." Vale looks at me in horror. "Amryn that thing's going to kill you." He tries to intervene, tries to stop me, but I push him away. I need to get this thing out of me, and find Cora. She needs me. She was screaming.

I grip it again, and take a deep breath, steeling myself. I pull hard, and I think I hear one of my ribs crack. The healer puts a hand to her forehead and winces as more blood pours out of my mouth. I suck in another breath, pulling again, and with a loud snap the dart comes out of my chest. My hands are shaking as I drop it on the floor, and the healer springs forward, putting her glowing hand on the wound that seeps and seeps blood.

I lie back, gasping for air. I feel the wound close up slowly, the needling, burning sensation of healing skin. All I can taste is blood. All I can smell is blood. My hands are covered in it.

Roche appears at Vale's side, a gash on his forehead, his face covered in soot. "35 dead." He says grimly. The healer suppresses a sob as she continues to heal my wound.

Roche looks down at me. "They attacked your cabin first," he says, "do you know why?"

They were after Cora.

The Shadow Queen.

I remember now. But how did they know where she was? They must have followed her, had angels scouting, watching her sneak to my cabin. They knew where to find her. I clench my eyes shut. I should have stayed with her, I should have fucking protected her.

"Amryn nearly died, he's lost a lot of blood, I don't think this is the time." I hear Vale say. I open my eyes to see Vale holding up his hands, trying to wave Roche away. "Roche, come on, this isn't the time."

"We need to know -" Roche breaks off as Vale squares up to him.

"I said, this man nearly died. We're not questioning him now." Vale crosses his arms over his chest. "Anything you need to know will have to wait until he's not coughing up his entrails, do you understand me?"

"The Queen is missing." Roche says impatiently, his eyes crinkling as he glares at Vale. "We don't have time for -"

"They fired with guns first," I say. My voice is thick. It doesn't sound like me. Roche drops to his knees beside me, his eyebrows raised expectantly. I try to breathe. My chest burns. "They fired on my cabin."

"Were you alone?" He asks,

I hesitate. "No."

"Who was with you?" Roche frowns.

Vale sighs with exasperation. "This isn't important right now."

"They fired on us, and then -" I try to remember. Blinking at the lights overhead. She was there, under me. Glass shattered. "I jumped outside and an angel tried to shoot me. I took him out. I tried to find Finn." I grit my teeth. I tried to find Finn instead of staying with Cora. I was so bound to duty that I abandoned her, and now she's gone.

The healer puts a hand on my ribs and a strangled cry comes out of my throat, the sensation of the bones knitting back together burning my insides. The blood is rushing out of my mouth again, and I spit it out on the floor. Fuck. I feel like I'm dying. I am dying. No, wait, I already did that. Am I dying again?

Vale puts his hands on Roche's shoulders, trying to guide him away from me. "Ok, that's enough, this man -"

"No!" I put my hand out. "We need to find Cora, now." I can't die now. She needs me.

"Did you see who took her?" Roche asks me.

I nod. "An angel, he was tall, white face, black eyes." He'd leered at me. "Sharp teeth. Had a red shield he could throw up to absorb Cora's fire." I breathe in deeply. It doesn't hurt as much now. "No one can take her fire." No one except me. I'd never seen it before.

Roche shakes his head, a hand on his chin. "Blood magic. They're using blood magic."

Vale looks at him quizzically. "What's that?"

"Old magic, it's been forbidden for a long time." Roche says with a sigh. "The angels used it against us to cast us out of the Halls, and now with the demons they've been able to weaponise it using new technology."

The doors to the Great Hall fly open, and Finn comes storming in. Blood is spattered across his face, and his hair is caked with it. He rushes to my side, skidding to his knees. "Did you see who took her?" He asks. "Did you see them?" His voice is cracking, and he looks like he's about to cry.

Vale puts a hand on his shoulder. "He's told us."

"It's Zadkiel." Roche says, and Finn looks up at him with wide eyes.

"Why the fuck would an archangel want Cora?"

"He called her the Shadow Queen." I say. I watch Roche's face carefully. Something else the angel said to me tells me this is important. I need to see how they react. *Lordain did a good job keeping you all in the dark.*

Roche's eyes widen for just a split second, his lip twitching. He clears his throat, and squares his shoulders.

"What a strange thing to say, there hasn't been a Shadow Queen since the Old Ways." He hurries away, his hands clutched behind his back.

Amryn! I clench my eyes shut. A woman's voice calls to me. She has long black hair, in a braid. She's got a baby on her hip. She looks like my mother, but she's not my mother. She waves, smiling. *Amryn!*

"Hey, you OK, brother?" Vale puts a hand on my shoulder.

"W-water." I gasp. I can't stand the taste of fucking blood anymore. I watch him rush across the Hall, filled with weeping, the heavy smell of blood and burning.

"I've done all I can," the healer says, and she looks pale. She's used a lot of her power. "I'm not sure - I just don't know with this magic -" She breaks off, looking around her, clutching a hand to her mouth.

"Thank you." I put a hand on her arm. "You saved my life."

She nods, and rises to her feet, hurrying away to help the next demon.

Vale returns with a full cup of water. He helps me sit up, and I drink. It tastes fucking disgusting, coppery, like metal shavings. But the blood washes down, down, and I can breathe easier now. I look down at my chest, and the black mark from the dart has stained my skin. I run a hand over it, and it doesn't budge.

Finn is shaking his head. "Where the fuck would they take her?" He looks down at me. "Where was she when all this started? The guards said she wasn't at home."

Fuck. "She must have gone for a walk." I say, my shoulders heaving.

"No one saw her, they said she just disappeared." His eyes narrow slightly as he looks at me. "Roche said they attacked your cabin first."

I meet his gaze. "She was with me."

His face becomes menacing. "What the fuck was she doing with you?"

My mind races. "I slept with Ceili." It's the first thing that comes to mind, and it's fucking ridiculous, but Finn's face relaxes. "I wanted to know that Ceili was OK."

Finn nods and waves dismissively. "Yeah OK, fine." He puts a hand to his forehead, and he looks tortured. "Where the fuck could she be? Where the fuck would they take her?"

I put a hand on Vale's shoulder. "Help me up, man."

But he shakes his head and pushes back against my chest. "Brother, you need to rest."

"We need to find Cora." I grit my teeth. "Help me up, please. She's in danger."

"You need to rest." Vale insists. "I mean it. You get up now and you'll be of no use to anyone."

I grunt and push him away, pulling myself into a crouch and trying to rise to my feet. My head spins, and my stomach lurches. My chest burns as I move. I take a deep breath, and blood rushes out of my mouth again.

"Fucking hell, Amryn." Vale grabs me. "I will tie you down if I need to, now lie the fuck down before you bleed out."

I collapse back onto the bed, and close my eyes. I'm afraid to sleep. I don't want to die. Vale, finally satisfied that I'm staying put, leaves my side. Finn sits beside me for a few more minutes, then I hear him leave too.

They've taken her, and I couldn't save her. Who knows where she is now. She's alone, and terrified, and what if they're hurting her? Tears sting my eyes as I remember the last thought I had, as Cora held me, crying, screaming my name, begging me not to die.

I never told her I love her. And now I don't know if I'll ever have the chance.

Amryn! The woman with the black hair smiles at me as the sounds of the hall around me drown out, as I fall asleep. *Amryn, come on!* She's got a baby on her hip. And Cora walks beside her, tucking a hand under the baby's chin. *Say, come on Daddy.* My stomach wrenches, and I hear a sob before I finally fall asleep.

Alone. Is she alone?

Rain patters against the canvas of the tent. I put a hand behind my head, staring at the shadows the candle casts above me. My cabin's destroyed, burnt out. Half the compound burned down. Now we're all in tents. Under the rain.

Cora's been gone 47 hours. 18 minutes. 37 seconds.

I put a hand to my chest. The black mark is still there, and while it aches, it's fading away slowly. I'm almost back at my full strength. The healers are amazed I came back at

132

all. No one else survived the blood magic strikes those bastards subjected the clan to.

The scouts can't find Cora. The clans are all out looking for her. Finn is going out of his mind. He paces and yells and punches things. Useless, stupid Finn. Spoiled fucking brat, acting like a kid who's lost his toys.

I have to keep it all inside, all my grief and my fear. No one can know. Even though it's killing me.

I close my eyes. I should sleep. I can't sleep.

Amryn. The woman's face is right in front of me. *Amryn, I know you can hear me.*

I sit up, throwing my hands out in front of me. But there's no one there. What the fuck is this? I run a hand over my head. It must be the poison, the blood magic from that fucking dart. It's making me hear things.

Amryn. She whispers right in my fucking ear, and I jump.

"Who the fuck are you?" I whisper to the candlelight. I wait. There's no response, just the steady beating of the rain overhead.

I give myself a shake. I'm hallucinating. I'm going insane. That shit's messed with my head.

Amryn, Cora needs you. The voice is soft but urgent. It seems to echo around me, bouncing off the walls around me.

I get up on my knees, my eyes darting around the tent. "Do you know where she is?"

"No, but you do."

I shake my head. "No, I don't. How can I know that?"

"Listen. Listen to me. You do. You need to listen for her."

"What are you talking about?" No response. I sigh. I'm fucking crazy now. I sit back, hanging my head. It's desperation, that's all. I want to find Cora so bad I'm imagining there's a way.

"LISTEN FOR HER." The voice is screaming in my head, and my hands fly to my ears. "SHE'S CALLING FOR YOU. LISTEN FOR HER. LISTEN FOR HER VOICE."

"Wha- what do you mean?" I ask, wincing.

"You're the Queen's Draw. Listen for her. Her heart is yours and yours is hers. You've always known this."

I clench my eyes shut. And she's there. Right in front of me. She looks like my mother. But she's not my mother.

"Listen for her. Listen for her. She's calling for you."

"Who are you?"

She shakes her head. "Listen for her. She needs you."

I open my eyes, and she's gone. I take a deep breath, and put my hand over my chest. I can feel my heart beating. My heart. No. Her heart. I close my eyes again. Listen to my breath. Listen to her breath.

Baby, tell me where you are.

I conjure up her face, her green eyes. Her scent, fresh and sweet. Her curly hair. Her smile. Her heartbeat against my hand. Her heart.

Come on, Cora. Tell me where you are.

The ground under me is hard, stone, no, concrete. I can smell salt. The ocean. There's the sound of a horn. A boat, nearby. I see her, curled up against a wall in a barren room, only walls and windows. She's scared. Her eyes are closed. She puts a hand to her chest. "Amryn."

My breath catches in my throat, and my eyes fly open. I scramble out of the tent and sprint across the yard, towards Finn's house, through the darkness. The guards see me coming and are instantly on alert.

"I know where she is!" I shout. "I know where Cora is!"

I pelt past the guards, throwing open the door of Finn's house. They're all sitting around a table, poring over a map, and everyone looks up at me as I burst in.

"I know where she is." I tell them.

Finn jumps to his feet. "Where?"

"Sfayder. In a warehouse. By the harbour."

Lordain and Roche exchange a surprised look, and I want to punch them both. I look back at Finn. "Finn," I say urgently. "Come on, we gotta move. Now."

"How do you know?" Lordain asks me, and his face is filled with - dread?

"That doesn't matter right now," Finn says, jumping to his feet. "Call the council. Let's move."

8
Cora

The sun sets again. The second time since I've been locked in this room.

My bones ache from sleeping on the hard, concrete floor, from sitting here curled up against the cold walls around me. Just walls, and windows. Nowhere to sit, nowhere to sleep. Just a barren room for me to lie in and cry in. I feel like I haven't slept, even though the nightmares that keep waking me tell me I've managed to drift off at least a few times.

I put my hand to my chest. I can feel my heart beating. A horn sounds nearby, the ferry crossing the bay. People so close. But I'm locked up here, and no one knows.

"Amryn." I lean my head back against the wall, and the tears start falling again. The hollow ache in my chest takes my breath away. I can still feel him in my arms, limp, lifeless, his beautiful eyes just staring at the sky. I hug myself, wanting nothing more than to feel his arms around me. And I'll never feel them again.

I dreamed of him last night. We were walking with a woman who looked like him, like his mother. She had a baby on her hip, a baby with soft black curls and big green eyes. Amryn was walking behind us. He was smiling. It was so peaceful. And then I woke up, and I was back in this fucking room, and Amryn was dead again, and that beautiful little baby, our baby, would never exist.

The door opens, and it's probably more disgusting food I can barely choke down. I turn away, huddling against the wall. I just want them to leave me alone. I don't want to look at anyone. These guards just leer at me, like I'm a piece of meat, like I'm here for their entertainment.

"Well hello there," a voice drawls.

My brow furrows as the tall man with the half-shaved head sidles across the room. I get to my feet, wiping the tears from my face, staying close to the wall. He's dressed in some kind of wannabe military costume, camo and straps and buckles everywhere, a khaki t-shirt stretched across his chest.

"I hope you've been comfortable enough," he says, his hands behind his back.

"It's actually kind of shitty," I reply.

He laughs, his lip ring shifting as his lips curl. "Why don't you say what you really think, princess?"

My eyes narrow. I've seen him before. "I know you."

"Yes you do, Cora." He stops, putting his hands in the pockets of his obnoxious cargo pants, leaning against the wall. "We've met, a few times actually." His eyebrows raise, and then fall again, disappointed. "Heath. My name is Heath. I'm Ragnar's son."

Ragnar. The Hjoldep Alpha. The rival clan.

I nod slowly. "Yes, I remember you. Last time I saw you Lordain was casting your father and his clan out of the forest."

Heath smirks. "And that was his first big mistake. We've found a whole new purpose out here."

"Become your own little militia, have you?" I ask, looking his pathetic uniform up and down.

"Something like that." He laughs. "The advances in tech are amazing." He turns and looks out the window. "While you all stayed up in the mountains with your motion sensors and barbed wire, the rest of the world evolved, and now we have weapons unlike any we ever had before."

"Are you preparing for war?" I ask cynically.

He looks over his shoulder at me. "War is always possible. And in this case, it's actually kind of inevitable."

"So what do I have to do with all of this?" I ask.

Heath turns and observes me pensively, walking across the room towards me. "Well, you're pretty extraordinary." He stands right in front of me, and looks down at my arms. "Those flames of yours, they really are something."

I shake my head. "They're just flames. We all have them."

"My soldiers told me what you did," he says, his lip curling into a grin, "they told me how easily you took us out. You never think why you can do that?"

"Maybe your soldiers are just fucking weak?" I retort.

He raises an eyebrow. "You ever see someone else with white flames. Cora? You see red, orange, yellow." He lowers his face to mine a little. "Never white, though."

I shrug, pressing myself against the wall, desperate to get away from him. "So what?"

Heath laughs heartily, leaning one hand against the wall next to me. "Lordain really has you all brainwashed up there, doesn't he?" He raises a hand to my cheek, and I slap him away, which elicits another laugh from him. "Ooh, you're feisty, I like it."

"Don't fucking touch me," I warn him. I back along the wall, away from him.

He holds his hands up, smirking. "Just relax, Cora."

"So what do you want with my flames?" I ask. "What, you want to stick an IV in me and suck them out?"

"Something like that." He tilts his head. "You're the daughter of an alpha, you know that, right?"

"Of course." I spit back at him. "I know who my father was."

"Anyway, that makes you kinda powerful." He rubs his hands together. "And power is something I would really like to have a little more of."

"You want to make me your Queen or something?"

"Oh I'd love to," he says, his eyes roving over my body. "But you're more than just a pretty piece of ass."

"Is that meant to be a compliment?" I'm ready to tear his head off if he tries to touch me. If my hands would stop fucking shaking long enough, that is.

"You know," he says, rubbing his chin, "my father wanted to have you killed, way back when you were a little baby." He pulls something from his pocket, a small satchel, unzipping it, slowly, deliberately. He retrieves a needle from it, filled with some black stubstance. His eyes flicker up to me and he chuckles. "Oh this isn't for you, princess. This is for me."

"What the fuck is that?" I ask, shrinking further against the wall.

"Chimera blood," he replies, flicking the needle then pushing it into his veins. "Fucking on this stuff is incredible by the way, you should try it some time."

"I'll keep that in mind." I wince as he injects the black shit into his veins, and the heavy sigh that leaves his lips makes my skin crawl. "So why did your dad want baby me dead?"

"Because my Dad has no vision," Heath replies, his eyes closed. He withdraws the needle from his arm slowly. "I'm not like him though."

"You have vision, do you?"

His eyes open, fixed on me, and he runs his tongue over his lips. "I sure do, sweetheart."

"Are you done playing the movie villain?" I hiss. "Just fucking tell me what you want."

He throws his head back and laughs. "Wow, you're not afraid of me at all, are you?" He rolls his head in a circle, his eyes closed, and takes a deep breath. When his eyes fix on me again, my stomach turns to ice. They're black. Like the angel's. "How about I teach you some manners, Shadow Queen?"

140

He stalks towards me, and I can't even scream. Before I can summon my flames he's torn me from the wall and thrown me on the ground, pinning me down with his body.

"I wonder what it's like to fuck a queen," he says, and his tongue darts out between his pale lips, licking the side of my face. "What's Finn been enjoying, huh?"

"Get off me!" I try to buck him off, but he's so heavy. His black eyes are terrifying. It's like he's possessed. It must be the chimera blood. It's making him strong.

"I'll get off you once I've gotten off, princess." He says with a throaty laugh. He holds my hands down with one of his, and I hear the clink of his belt. He puts his hands in the waistband of my sweatpants, trying to tear them down.

"Get off me!" I writhe under his hands, bucking hard. But he won't fucking shift. My whole body becomes hot, and I scream again as his lips press against my neck. Something is hammering in my chest, clawing from deep inside. My veins are glowing as my teeth snap into his cheek, tearing through flesh, but he doesn't seem to feel a fucking thing.

"Come on, princess." His breath is hot as he speaks against my ear. "I can show you a good time."

I scream again as his hands tear through the fabric of my shirt, and the force in my chest bursts out of me. There's an explosion of light, and I feel Heath's weight lift off me instantly. I lie there for a moment, astounded. What the fuck did I just do? The light fades slowly, and I can hear groaning from the other side of the room.

I sit up slowly, and Heath is lying a few feet away, flat on his back. My stomach turns, and I clutch a hand to my mouth so I don't throw up. His torso is ripped open, his rib cage visible. I get to my feet slowly, edging towards him. He looks up at me, his eyes wide, gasping for air. I can see his fucking lungs expanding inside his body. I can see his heart, squelching in the middle of the soupy mess that was once his internal organs. Oh my god. Oh my fucking god.

"Wh- what the fuck?" He stammers.

The door behind me swings open, and I summon my flames, armed, ready to strike.

The angel from two nights ago walks in, looks at me, then at Heath, and shakes his head. "I knew this wouldn't go well, never send an idiot demon to do diplomatic work, they have no head for it." He walks over to Heath, and tuts disapprovingly. "I told you to behave yourself."

Blood bubbles from Heath's mouth. "Hel - help me." He pleads.

"Help you?" The angel asks cynically. "Gladly." He leans down over Heath. "Here's some useful advice. Next life, don't rape anyone. And certainly not someone powerful enough to disembowel you."

Heath gurgles sickeningly, crimson red foam spilling from his lips, and then his head lolls to the side. He's dead. I killed an Alpha heir. Shit. Shit. Shit.

"Idiot." The angel turns to look at me, his eyes rolling to the ceiling, and an exasperated sigh escapes him. "I tell you, majesty, your kind are a rare breed these days. Most

142

of the time I know exactly why we cast the demons out of the Halls. Goodness me."

"I killed him." I say, breathing heavily, looking down at Heath's inert body. "How did I do that?"

"You've not killed before?" The angel asks.

I shake my head. "Not like this. With flames, from my hands, yeah. But not -" I put my hand to my chest, remembering the feeling I had, deep, burning, electric.

The angel smiles at me, like a proud father. "You're coming in to your power, majesty. Not even Lordain's witch can erase everything."

I frown at him. "What are you talking about?"

"Perhaps it would be helpful to know who I am first," the angel says, and does a bow. "I'm Zadkiel."

I feel rage swelling in my chest as the shock of my kill wears off. "You murdered Amryn."

He gives me a sheepish look. "Ah yes, I do apologise for that, majesty. That was rude of me."

Tears sting my eyes. "Rude? You fucking murdered him. Right in front of me. He was -" I sob. "He was right there, and I couldn't save him."

"Yes, yes, I know, and I am very sorry." He sighs, and smiles softly. "It probably wasn't the best way to endear myself to you."

"What do you want from me?" I ask, wiping my face angrily. "Why am I here?"

Zadkiel looks around him, his eyes coming to settle on me again as he takes a deep breath. "Majesty, your power will build, powers you aren't even aware of yet and do not fully understand. And whoever you ally yourself with will decide what the outcome of the War will be."

"What war?"

"The war between the Halls and the Earth Realm."

I shake my head, putting my hands to my temples. "I don't - I don't understand."

"I know it's a lot to take in. But you must understand that I have no interest in letting the Halls or their supporters here in the Earth Realm win."

"What?" I stare at him in disbelief. "You're pitting yourself against the Halls? Why would you do that?"

Zadkiel shrugs. "Because down here I mean something. Down here I am an ethereal being who commands the respect of demons and humans alike. People cower before me." He holds his head high. "Down here, they write books about me. They credit me with immaculate conceptions." He winks at me. "Can you imagine? It's bliss." His face falls, and he casts his eyes upwards. "Up there, I'm just the last archangel, the one that saved the son of that fool up on the mountain. The nice one." He shakes his head, pouting. "I hate being known as the nice one."

"So you just want to be admired?" I ask incredulously. "That's why you want the Earth Realm to win? So you can feel special?"

"It's much more than that, majesty." Zadkiel says. "There are some things not even I can overlook, and the Realm has become corrupted by it. Things must be set right once more, or -" He cocks his head to the side, and sighs. "Unfortunately we have to cut this short. Your people have discovered your location and are on their way."

My heart leaps into my throat. They've found me. "You're just letting me go?" I ask him. "Just like that?"

He looks at me blankly. "Well, I can rough you up a little if you feel this was all a waste of your time, dear."

"I mean - what do you want?" I stammer, shaking my head. "What was the point of all this?"

Zadkiel steps forward, and his black eyes gaze down at me. "You have an interest in keeping this realm safe too, majesty. And you will have to ask the right questions of the right people to find out how."

"What people?" I ask. "Why won't you just tell me what's going on?"

Zadkiel extends an enormous hand with long, sharp talons. When I don't react immediately, he gives me a warm smile. I tentatively offer my hand in return. I don't know why. His skin is icy, and clammy, all at the same time.

"Majesty, what was forgotten must be remembered." He lowers his mouth of sharp teeth to my ear. "Ask them what happened to your father." He steps back, and bows to me deeply, giving me one last toothy smile. "We'll see each other again soon, I'm sure." He walks to the window, opens it, and lets himself fall. There's a rushing sound, and I see his black wings spread, carrying him swiftly away into the darkening sky.

I listen, for any sign of movement, any hint of rescue. Heavy footsteps sound outside. I look onto the courtyard below me, and I can see guards running, wearing the same ridiculous get-up Heath was wearing. They raise their guns in the direction of the gate, but someone flies over it, raining down on them with fire. Bullets start flying, and I drop down to the floor.

They're here. And they're flying, their smoky wings unfurling behind them. We don't do that anymore, we haven't done it in years. I haven't flown since I was a child. I don't even know if I would still know how.

Cora, get down from there!

I clench my eyes shut. What the fuck was that? I take a deep breath, open my eyes and look out the window again. That was my father's voice.

Would you come and look at your daughter?

Pcholka, how did you get up there? Come down from there right now!

I shake my head. I must be hallucinating. Lack of sleep, lack of food. I need to focus. They're here. I need to get out of this room and find them.

I scooch across the floor, and reach up to the door handle, testing to see if it's locked. It gives way under my hand, and I edge out into the corridor in a low crouch. I summon up a flame, and get to my feet, sprinting along the concrete. A guard rounds the corner ahead of me, and raises his gun at me. I fire my flames at him, and there's a flash of light as he's obliterated, disappearing into an ashy print against the wall.

I've never killed like that before, but I don't have time to think about that right now. I don't have time to wonder what's happening to me. I just need to get out of here. I need to reach the others.

I hear more gunfire outside, and there's an explosion. I reach another doorway, pushing through it, to find a staircase. I make my way down, my flame illuminating the darkness, and there's yet another door, heavy, iron, bolted. I put my hands against it, push, it doesn't give way.

I close my eyes, reaching inside of myself, down into my chest, trying to find that same electric rush that shattered Heath's body apart. I feel the heat rise, and I open my eyes. I tell it to come out. I tell my heart to let it go. Explode. Blow this fucking door out. I flex my fingers, and the door explodes from the frame in a flash of white light.

The flash subsides, and I run through the smoke and sparks, straight into something - someone - hard. I cry out, summoning my flames, and push the figure away.

"Cora, it's me!" I see hands extending to me, and I look up into Finn's face. "Babe, it's me, oh my god, you're OK." He pulls me into his arms as I extinguish my flames. "You're OK."

"Finn." My hands clasp on to him. "Finn, you found me."

"We've got her!" I hear Vale call. I look up, and I see them all there, the council and the soldiers.

"It's OK," Finn says, stroking my hair. "You're safe now. I'm here, it's OK." He turns. "Let's move out." He scoops me up in his arms, and I nuzzle my face into his chest.

"You heard him, let's go."

I hear the voice, and my chest fills with ice, the hollow ache crushing my lungs. I know it's not him. I'm imagining it. He died in my arms. I just want that to be his voice, because I can't accept that he's dead. The tears start falling again.

Finn launches himself into the air, and I feel sick as I remember the sensation of Zadkiel taking me away, my body screaming in pain.

"It's OK, babe," Finn murmurs to me as we fly. "It's going to be OK. We'll be home in no time."

The sky darkens around us, and it's night. I put my arms around Finn's neck, and allow myself to be carried back to the compound, back to Nilau.

Zadkiel's words echo through my mind.

What was forgotten must be remembered.

The air changes around me, and I look out, seeing the familiar trees and the mountain mist in the moonlight. Finn lands outside our house, and hugs me to him. "It's OK, Cora, you're home now." He gently puts me on my feet.

The others land around us, laying down their weapons. I look around the compound, smoke still rising from the burnt out houses. I turn to Finn, grabbing on to his jacket. "My Mom? Ceili? Are they OK?"

"They're fine, they're both fine." He assures me. "They're safe." He looks over my shoulder. "We all OK?"

"Yeah, everyone made it back."

My heart skips a beat. I'm not imagining it. I can feel it's him. I turn around slowly, and I don't trust myself. He died in my arms.

But no. He's standing there, right there, his shoulders heaving, his hazel eyes fixed on me, and I see his lip quiver. He gives me a small smile.

Amryn. My very core screams for him. I want to throw myself into his arms.

"I saw you die." I say. Tears fill my eyes, blurring my vision, and I blink them away. I don't want to lose sight of him.

He takes half a step towards me, and falters. We can't. But I want him to. I just want to feel his skin under my fingers, warm, alive, moving. I put a hand to my chest, and his hand splays across his own, spreading over his heart - his heart, the one I felt stop, the one that's beating now.

"Are you OK?" He asks. His expression is tortured as his eyes move over me, taking in the blood that's drenched my clothes. His hand claws into his chest. "Did they hurt you?"

I try to shake my head, but I'm frozen. "N-No." I stammer. "Are you -"

"Come on." Finn interjects, ushering me towards the house. I gasp, straining to look over my shoulder, at Amryn watching us walk away. His eyes stay on me, his hand still on his chest. "Come on, babe," Finn says quietly, opening the door to our cabin for me. "Let's get you inside."

Lordain and Morgan jump up from the table as we walk in. "Oh Cora, my god," Lordain says, rushing towards us. "What have they done to you?"

I nod, and sink into a chair. "I'm fine, I'm OK."

Morgan comes over and tuts as she looks over me, her nose wrinkling with disgust as the smell of blood rises from my clothing. "Barbarians, absolute barbarians." She kneels down beside me and takes my hand, looking up at me with her violet eyes. "It's OK, sweetheart. They'll pay for what they did."

"Whose blood is that?" Lordain asks.

"I killed one of them," I say, nausea gripping me as I remember the sight of Heath's broken body. "I killed him."

Finn turns to Lordain. "Heath, Ragnar's son."

Lordain's eyes flash to me. "You killed an Alpha heir?"

I frown. "He was trying to rape me."

Finn's jaw clenches. "Good. Of course you had to kill him."

Lordain shakes his head. "This is going to start a war."

"Dad," Finn says, shaking his head, "not now."

"Should I have just let him do it?" I ask, rising to my feet. "Is that what I should have done?"

"You cannot kill an Alpha Heir without serious consequences, Cora." Lordain says to me.

"Consequences?" I scoff, my mouth open in outrage. "Is this some sort of joke? What the fuck is wrong with you?"

"Excuse me?" His voice is low as his expression darkens. "Watch your tone, young lady."

"I'm not a young lady, I'm your Queen, you fucking asshole."

He raises a hand to me, and I brace myself for the slap, but he stops and looks over his shoulder in surprise.

Amryn has a hold of his arm, and smoke is rising from the sleeve of Lordain's shirt. "You hit the Queen and I have to tear your fucking head off." He growls. His eyes are filled with fury.

Lordain yanks his arm away before it bursts into flames. "Get your hands off me you little shit." He squares up to Amryn. "How dare you touch me?"

Amryn's gaze becomes lethal. "It's my duty to protect her. From anyone. That includes you, you decrepit old fuck."

Lordain raises his fist just as Amryn bares his teeth, and Finn quickly pushes himself between the two of them "Hey, enough! What the fuck, Dad?" He's in Lordain's face, his expression menacing. "You don't hit the Queen, ever. And after what she's just been through?" He shakes his head, and taps his temple. "You're fucking crazy, Lordain."

Morgan takes her husband's arm. "Come on, darling. This has been a stressful night for everyone. I think we should let them all get some rest."

Lordain shakes her off. "We need to know what happened." He says, turning back to me. "Did they tell you anything? Why they took you?"

Finn slams a fist on the table. "We're not doing this right now."

"I'm the -" Lordain begins.

Finn towers over him, his eyes blazing. "No, *I'm* the fucking Alpha. And right now, you need to step the fuck down."

"They told me to ask you what happened to my father." I say, and all eyes turn to me. I meet Lordain's gaze, and hold it. "They told me to ask the right people about it. Are you the right people?"

He scoffs, a puzzled smile breaking across his face. "Your father was killed, because his father -" He turns to point a finger at Amryn, "- failed in his duty, and couldn't protect the Alpha."

Amryn's face darkens, and his eyes move to me.

"Don't look at her, you little shit," Lordain spits, "you look at me."

Amryn's eyes move back him, and he sneers, taking a step forward. He grits his teeth, and his hands start glowing again. "Or what?"

"Enough!" Finn puts a hand on Amryn's chest, pushing him back. "You, you need to go. Go walk it off." He turns to Lordain. "And you need to get out of my house, right now. Everyone needs to cool the fuck down."

Amryn hesitates, his eyes moving back to me. "Are you OK?" He asks me.

Lordain turns on him. "Who are you to speak to her?"

Amryn's eyes flash to him for only a second before he looks back at me. "Are you OK?" He asks me again.

152

I nod. "Are you?"

"What is going on here?" Lordain demands.

"I'm asking a member of my clan if they're OK after they died in front of me!" I clutch a hand to my stomach as the memory overwhelms me, and I feel the sobs bubbling up again. "What is wrong with you?" I shake my head as I look at Lordain. "Why are you so hateful?"

"OK, Dad, out." Finn says, pushing his father towards the door. "Amryn, go get some rest. You're still recovering, and flying probably didn't help. Everyone, out. It's enough for tonight."

Lordain grabs Morgan's arm and glares at me. "You'll be in council tomorrow morning." He says, his finger darting in my direction. They leave the house without another word.

Amryn is still standing there, watching us.

"Go get some rest, Amryn." Finn says again, gesturing towards the door. "We'll talk in the morning."

Amryn's eyes meet mine for a moment, and they say everything he can't. He bows his head, and leaves, disappearing into the night.

Come back. I want to say it. I can't.

Finn presses a kiss to my temple. "I'm so glad you're OK." He says with a sigh. "My god, I thought I was going to lose my mind."

I don't want him to touch me. I want Amryn. I hang my head in my hands. "I'm tired." I murmur. "I want to get this blood off me."

"Of course you do," Finn says, putting his arm around me, leading me out of the kitchen and down the hallway to the bathroom. "Come on, let's get you cleaned up." He's being so kind and concerned, but it's still meaningless. The ache in my chest has been replaced by something else, something new.

We get to the bathroom and Finn moves to pull my t-shirt off over my head, and I clasp my arms around myself. "Please just leave me alone," I say. I look up at him, and his eyes flash with pain.

"Babe, I -"

"I just want to be alone." My fingers dig into the fabric of my shirt, pulling it tight around myself, like a security blanket.

His brow crinkles. He doesn't understand. He's happy I'm alive, and that I'm safe, and I'm not returning it. Please just get out. He gives a short nod and pulls the door closed behind him.

I turn on the water, and strip out of my bloody clothes. My blood, Amryn's, Heath's. I throw the clothes into the corner of the bathroom, and decide to burn them later. The metallic smell is nauseating. I step under the water, and press my hands against the wall. The water turns red as it washes over me. There's blood under my fucking fingernails, caked inside my goddamn ears. It's just everywhere.

Something snaps inside me, a sudden release, and violent sobs shake my shoulders. I put my forehead against the cold tiles, my fingers flexing against them. I just want to feel him. He's alive, he's here. And I can't touch him. I can't be with him.

I laugh through my tears, remembering my dream - the baby, our baby, the black curls and the big green eyes. Amryn smiling at me, at us, at me and our child. He's alive, and we'll still never have that. I'm back, and I'm still trapped. I still belong to Finn.

I sink onto the shower floor, and wrap my arms around my legs. The tears won't stop. My heart is calling for him, every inch of me is screaming for him.

And he's out there in the night. Alone. Always alone.

Finn is waiting in the hallway when I get out, leaning against the wall. He still looks hurt. "Babe, I don't know what happened there, but -"

"I was terrified, I thought I was going to die, and then someone tried to rape me." I reply, storming past him towards our bedroom. "And I finally got rescued, got back here, and your Dad tried to hit me. I think that sums up my past few days pretty well."

He hurries after me. "My Dad's a dick," he says. "I'm sorry, he's just worried that this is going to start a war."

"It should start a war!" I'm seething. I pull a pair of shorts and tank top out of the closet, pulling them on, and shaking out my wet hair. "It should start a war because someone kidnapped and tried to assault his daughter-in-law, not because I defended myself." I shake my head, sneering at him. "I know y'all don't value women but this is some next level bullshit, Finn."

"Hey." He snaps, and his face darkens. "I do value you. I'm here, trying to comfort you, and you're pushing me away."

"I wonder why that would be."

Finn throws his hands up in exasperation. "Are you ever going to let this go?"

"Let what go, Finn?" I ask, crossing my arms over my chest. "The fact that you raped me?"

He sticks a finger in my face. "I didn't fucking rape you, don't you dare say that I did. That's disgusting."

"So what does it mean to you when a woman tells you to stop and you don't?"

"I told you, I couldn't stop!" He cries.

"And we're back to that." I turn away from him, but he reaches out and grabs my arm.

"Cora, we can't have a marriage like this, you have to let it go," he says. "What was I supposed to do, huh?"

"You know, you're lucky," I say, sneering up at him, "because if I'd reacted the same way to you that I did to Heath, you'd be in tiny little pieces all over the fucking Great Hall."

I don't even see his hand, it moves so fast, but he hits me hard enough to send me into the cupboard door, and searing pain shoots across my forehead. I suck in a breath through gritted teeth. My mouth drops open as I look back at him. "What the fuck is wrong with you?"

He moves towards me, his lips trembling. "Oh my god, babe, I'm so sorry, you just -" He inhales sharply. "You just made me so angry."

I push against his chest. "Get the fuck out of this room, and don't you dare fucking come anywhere near me again."

156

His eyes shine with tears. "Babe, I'm so sorry, please, I don't want to leave you, I just spent two days thinking you were dead."

"Get out or so help me I will fucking burn you alive." I say, turning away from him, putting a hand to my head that won't stop throbbing. "I am sick of you and your fucking family and getting hurt all the time. You can sleep in the other room for a while."

"Babe, please."

"Fuck off!"

He backs out, helplessly, limply. He stands in the hallway, his eyes pleading with me. He's pathetic.

I slam the door in his face.

I leave the bedside lamp on as I lie down in the bed, pulling the blankets around me tightly. I don't know if I'll be able to sleep. Realisation washes over me, paralysing me, and all I can do is cry into my pillow. My tears fall freely as the ache in my chest takes my breath away.

Amryn's alive. He's alive. My body contracts in on itself as I sob. He's alive.

Please come and find me, Amryn. Come and find me, and get me out of here. Please.

9
Amryn

didn't sleep last night. Every time I closed my eyes, all I saw was her face, her eyes as she looked at me and realised I was still alive. My hands hurt, because all I want to do is touch her, to remind myself that I'm alive, to know that she's alive. My need for her, it's a physical ache, lodged deep in my chest. It's like fucking dying all over again.

I can't believe Lordain has summoned her to a fucking council this morning, the sadistic bastard.

I dress quickly and hurry across the yard towards the Table, eager to see her, to make sure she's still OK. It's still early, and mist is swirling across the ground. People are starting to come out of their tents, cooking breakfast over open fires, trying to make the best of all this. Kids run around playing in the dewy grass. The sky above us is turning pink and gold.

Vale and some of the others are waiting outside the building, the porch of which has been partially burnt away. He nods as I approach.

"Crazy day yesterday, huh?" He says, exhaling heavily. "I can't believe they just let her go."

"If she hadn't killed that fucker then they probably wouldn't have." I make a mental note to find out where they buried Heath so I can go piss on his fucking grave.

Vale shrugs. "I guess so. Just so weird." He points in the direction of the approaching car. "Here's your biggest fan."

My shoulders tense as Lordain gets out of his fancy fucking car, and the gaze he gives me as he approaches is laced with pure poison. Fucker. I should have set his whole arm on fire when he tried to hit Cora, not just singed his fucking shirt.

"Morgan not coming today?" I ask.

Lordain purses his lips. "No. She was tired from all the stress."

I suck on my teeth. "Oh that's too bad, I hope she can get some rest." I look past him. "Cora's not here yet, is she?" I look back at him, and I can see the old bastard wants to beat the shit out of me.

"She'll be here in a moment, I'm sure." Lordain replies, before pushing past me and heading into the building.

Vale grimaces at me. "You really are asking for a beatdown, aren't you?"

I square my shoulders. "Let him fucking try." I'd pulverise the old man into sand.

"You gotta be careful." Vale says quietly. "He's got his eye on you, and he's just looking for an excuse, man."

Finn's truck pulls up, and he jumps out of it. He looks tired, nervous, his fingers throwing the car keys back and forth quickly as he approaches the building. He stops halfway to the porch to turn and look back at the truck. "Cora?" He calls, and starts to walk back when there isn't any movement.

The passenger door opens, and Cora climbs down, her hair tied up in a high pony tail. She's in black leggings and a long red t-shirt. She has her head down as she approaches the building. Something's wrong.

As she gets closer, I narrow my eyes. She has a shadow on her face, but it's not from her hair, that's tied up. Then I see the purple and blue and yellow snaking along her temple, and I realise what I'm looking at. And it wasn't there when she got back yesterday.

Finn eyes Vale and I nervously as he puts an arm around Cora's shoulders, a half smile on his face. "Morning." He nods.

Cora's eyes meet mine, and my blood freezes in my veins. Her beautiful green eyes look out at me from amidst the fresh bruises, filled with tears.

"What happened?" I ask. I can feel my hands glowing. She hesitates, and her eyes flash, for just a second, to Finn. That was her sign. That was her telling me.

She shakes her head. "Heath. He beat me up pretty good. Guess the bruises just took a while to show up."

Finn laughs, the shakiest fucking laugh a coward can make. "Funny how that happens huh?"

160

I exhale heavily through my nose. "Fucking son of a bitch." I look at Finn and shake my head. "Good thing he's dead, huh?"

"What do you mean?" Finn asks.

I gesture to Cora's bruised face. "Well, we'd go and kill him ourselves right now, for doing this to her, right?" I meet her eyes, and I want to cry or scream or tear Finn's lungs out. "What kind of a fucker does this to a woman? I'd tear his fucking arms off and stab him to death with his own fucking bones, and boy, I would really enjoy that." I look back at Finn again. "I would fucking tear that son of a bitch into tiny little pieces and feed them to his mother."

Finn swallows hard, and nods. "Ok, that's enough man, you're scaring Cora." He ushers her inside. Her head stays down.

Vale and I follow them in, and we all assemble around the Table. Except this time, we sit at the opposite end, Finn in the Alpha's place, and Cora beside him. I sit beside Finn, Vale beside me, and the rest of the council around us. Lordain and Roche sit where we sat just a few weeks ago. It feels like a lifetime ago now.

"This meeting has been called as we need to ascertain exactly what occurred these past few days and decide how much damage has been done." Roche begins. "Obviously we're all relieved the Queen is safe, but there's a lot to be considered."

"The Queen's actions mean a war is imminent," Lordain says.

Cora scoffs. "My actions?" She asks. "I didn't act. I reacted. I was being assaulted."

"You killed the son of an alpha." Lordain replies, his hands clasped over his chest. "That's a serious offence."

"He kidnapped Cora and tried to rape her." I interject. I can't take this shit anymore. "I think that's a pretty serious fucking offence, don't you?"

"No one asked you." Lordain hisses at me.

"Am I the fucking Draw or am I just a lapdog?" I ask. "Because you told me over and over how important this role is. I've never seen you talk to Roche like this."

"You don't speak over the Alpha." Lordain says.

"I'm not, I'm speaking over you." I glare at him.

Finn clears his throat. "OK, that's enough." He looks at Cora. "Babe, why don't you tell us what happened? What did they say to you while you were there?"

Cora shifts in her seat. "They barely said anything to me. They left me alone in a room for two days, and then Heath came along."

"And what did he say?" Roche asks.

Cora shakes her head. "He said they were preparing for war, building tech, and that they'd made alliances that were useful since you cast them out of the mountains." She looks at Lordain. "He seemed real cut up about it, bitter. And he commented on my flames."

"What about them?" Finn asks.

"Their colour."

I watch Roche and Lordain exchange a brief side glance. "What about their colour?" Roche asks, leaning on his elbows on the table.

Cora holds up her arm, and the veins are glowing, irridescent white. "They're white. No one else has white flames. Just me." She flexes her fingers, and small white flames erupt from her fingertips. "He also seemed to be very eager to remind me I'm the daughter of an Alpha. He said this made me powerful, and he wanted more power."

Lordain scoffs. "Being the daughter of an alpha makes you no more powerful than any other woman."

"The angel called her the Shadow Queen." I interrupt.

Roche laughs. "The angel is a fool. We haven't had a Shadow Queen in centuries."

Lordain shakes his head, and gestures to Cora to continue speaking. "Go on."

Cora sighs, and balls her hand into a first, extinguishing the flames. "Who was the Shadow Queen?" She asks.

"I'm not conducting a history lesson here, I want to know what happened while you were kidnapped." Lordain says, and his jaw flexes menacingly.

"I told you last night," Cora says, leaning back in her chair, eyeing him with something akin to boredom. "I should ask the right people what happened to my father."

"You killed Ragnar's son," Lordain says, "you practically tore him open, how did you do that?"

Cora's hand shoots up and it's flaming. "I don't know, should I try and show you?" She points the flames in his direction. "What happened to my father?"

Lordain throws his hands up. "He died, he was killed because his Draw and his Striker failed in their duties." His eyes move to me. "Unfortunately rotten fruit begets more rotten fruit."

Sparks shower across the Table, and Lordain is thrown backwards in his chair as Cora's flames hit him. Finn jumps up, and grabs Cora, crying out as her flames touch his skin. "Fuck!" He holds his burned hand, his eyes wild as he looks around at us all.

Cora turns to Lordain, who is struggling to his feet, peering over the table, and she points at him again. "Do you want me to show you, Lordain?" She asks again. "Do you want me to try and do to you what I did to Heath?" Her face is almost vacant, and Roche is starting to move towards her.

I can see this is going to get bad real fast. She may be the Queen, but Roche is still bound by blood to protect Lordain. I spring out of my chair and rush at her.

"Amryn, stop!" Vale says behind me.

I grab Cora's arms, spinning her away from Lordain, clutching her hands against my chest. She gasps as I touch her, startled, her eyes full of pain as she seems to come out of some sort of trance.

"It's OK," I murmur, holding her gaze. "You just look at me, OK? You're OK. Just look at me now."

"How - how is he not burning?" I hear Vale ask.

Cora's eyes fill with tears, and her flames die down, just a little. "You're alive." She whispers. Her fingers wrap around mine.

"Just look at me." I say again. "I'm here."

"Amryn," she whispers. "I felt you die."

164

"I know," I say, quickly swallowing the words I really want to say, "but I'm here now. Just keep your eyes on me." Her flames extinguish under my hands. "Just look at me. I'm here."

The room around us has fallen into silence, and I can just feel Lordain's eyes boring into me. Cora's head drops against my chest, and sweetness and bitterness tear through me, the urge to take her into my arms overwhelming.

"Ok that's enough." Finn moves between us, pulling Cora away from me. He puts his arms around her and eyes me suspiciously. "I don't know what you two have going on, but -"

"What happened to my Father?" Cora asks again, turning back to Lordain.

"Go fuck yourself," he mutters, slumping back down into his chair.

"I'm your Queen, and you'll answer the fucking question." Cora says.

"Your father was weak!" Lordain spits across the table. "Weak, and stupid. He was reckless. He didn't think about the welfare of his clan, just the glory of the Old Ways. He put himself and his council and his clan in danger, and he paid the price."

Cora shakes her head. "I don't believe you. Tell me who killed him."

"I don't have time for this." Lordain rises from his chair, darting his finger in Finn's direction. "Get your Queen in order or we'll have bigger problems." He gestures to Cora's face. "A few more of those probably wouldn't hurt." He turns on his heel and stalks out of the room.

Finn's eyes move to me. "I'm going to take her home," he says. "She's had a tough day."

"And night." I want him to know I know.

Cora puts her hand in her pocket and pulls out a tissue, wiping the tears from her eyes. She looks up at me, and smiles. "Thank you for standing up for me." She extends her hand to me, and I take it.

Something presses into my palm.

I close my hand, carefully, put it in my pocket, and give her a nod. "Anytime." I straighten up and look at Finn, nodding. "You two go rest, it's been a lot."

Finn ushers her out of the building without a backward glance, and I let out a heavy breath, trying to release the tension in my shoulders.

Roche approaches me slowly, his hands behind his back. "Amryn, can we walk for a while?" He asks me.

There's no point in saying no. I nod, and follow him out of the building. Roche turns left at the bottom of the porch steps, and we're heading towards the lake. The morning sky is pale blue, and a breeze has sprung up, moving the trees gently overhead.

Roche exhales heavily as the lake comes into view. "Now, son -"

"I'm not your son." I say quickly.

Roche sighs, exasperated. "Fine. I apologise." He stops walking and turns to look at me. "Now, Amryn, I can see there's something - untoward going on here."

166

"I don't know what you mean."

"Don't act stupid, it doesn't suit you." He says, raising his eyebrows. "I know you two grew up together, you were always close. You trust each other, and you've trained together. And she's very beautiful, of course."

"You wanted to talk to me about Cora being beautiful?"

Roche sucks on his teeth. "Believe me, young man, I know what it means, loving someone you can't have. I understand that better than anyone else in this compound."

I cross my arms over my chest. "Do you have a point?"

"I'm trying to help you."

I laugh bitterly. "Yes, you're all eager to help me around here, aren't you?" I narrow my eyes at him. "You ever get called runt, Roche?"

"No." He replies.

"You ever get beaten up for touching a girl?"

"No."

I take a step closer to him. "You ever get accused of having a thing for Morgan when you were just doing your duty and protecting her and Lordain?"

Roche sighs. "No."

"So I don't really see just how you've done anything to help me. In fact, it seems to me that you've all made my life as hard as you possibly fucking can since the Fates decided I was the Draw."

"To be the Draw you have to be tough." Roche points out.

"Yeah, tough. Not fucking beaten down and degraded and made to feel like you're worthless." I glare at him. "I haven't forgotten what you did."

"What did I do?"

I lean a little closer, and grit my teeth. "I still remember you dragging me away from my mother's body. I was a little boy, and I was crying for her, and do you remember what you said to me?"

Roche shakes his head. "It was a long time ago."

I'm right in his face now. "You told me she did it because of me."

Roche swallows, his Adam's apple racing up and down his throat. He shifts on his feet. "I don't think I said that."

"That's exactly what you fucking said. And then you told me I'd be alone forever."

Roche gives a short, nervous laugh, and takes a step back from me. "I'm certain I'd never say anything like that, you must be remembering it wrong."

I grab his collar, and he looks up at me with frightened eyes. "I was 8 years old and I'd just found my mother dead in the bathtub and not one of you fuckers comforted me. The only person, the only one who looked at me, was Cora. She was the only friend I had. And you stand here and accuse me of, what, fucking her behind Finn's back?"

Roche struggles in my grasp. "Amryn, I understand it was hard for you all when the clan in Ocario fell apart."

"And you didn't make it any fucking easier." I let him go, pushing him away. "None of you."

He straightens himself up. "We did everything we could to take you all on, and look after you as best we could."

I scoff. "You keep telling yourself that."

I stalk off towards the lake. I'm done talking. Tears prick at my eyes. I haven't talked about this, ever, and the memories come flooding back. My Mother, floating in red water, that just kept dripping down the side of the bathtub. I'd touched her hand. It was cold. Her eyes, hazel like mine, just staring. Looking at me, but not seeing anymore. I clutch my hands to my face. I don't want to think about this anymore.

I take a deep, shuddering breath, and remember what's in my pocket. I pull out the piece of paper Cora slipped to me when she took my hand. It's been torn from a book, inky fingerprints left behind from when she hurriedly scrawled the words, smudged with tears.

Finn's not sleeping in the bedroom. I'll leave the window open. Please come tonight. I love you.

The wind is howling through the trees. Clouds race across the sky, and I wonder if a storm is blowing in. The waning moon shines brightly overhead. I walk slowly away from my tent, trying to look nonchalant. It's windy, it's noisy. I simply can't sleep. Just going for a walk. Nothing unusual.

I sidle along the lit walkway near Cora and Finn's house, my hands in my pockets, and kick a stone along the path. There's guards everywhere, armed to the teeth. Everyone is on high alert since the ambush. I wonder if I'm walking straight into a bad decision. But she needs me.

"Hey Amryn." One of the guards spots me and walks over. "Everything OK?"

I nod. "Yeah, just can't sleep real well these days." I give him a small smile and shrug. "Since the ambush, you know."

"Yeah, same here. I lost my brother."

"Shit. Sorry, man."

He sighs. "Yeah, it sucks." He looks up at Cora's house. "I heard the Queen killed one of them."

"She did."

"Good." He spits. "They say it'll start a war now, but I gotta tell you, I'd love me a fucking war right now, take out some of those fuckers myself."

"Revenge sure can feel good." I agree.

"Yeah." The guard adjusts his grip on his weapon, and gives me a quick nod. "Anyhow, I gotta keep patrolling, you stay safe and, uh, I hope you can get some rest soon." He looks up at the trees as they bend and sway in the wind. "This wind sure is crazy."

"Yeah it is, must be a big storm blowing in." I give him a wave as I walk away. "Take care."

"You too." He turns his back and heads back towards the training yard.

170

I walk along the side of Finn and Cora's house, trying to keep my pace even. Don't rush. Don't draw attention. I turn around, as though to gaze up to check on the bending trees, and cast a glance around at the guards. No one is looking in this direction. I slip down the back of the house, and edge along in the darkness. Her window is the third one. I see it standing out from the walls, cracked open for me.

I stand underneath it and hesitate. What if Finn's in there after all? What if he refused to leave, insisted on staying in there with her? I'm possibly about to make a huge mistake and get myself killed.

I give myself a shake, and hoist myself up the wall, gripping the window frame. I push the window open, the wood creaking softly as it gives way. I swing my legs into the room, and land on the floor. My eyes adjust slowly to the darkness, and I hear a soft whimper coming from the bed.

I take a step closer, and there's movement. My chest is icy for a moment, and then I realise it's Cora, rising to her knees.

"You came." She whispers.

I move towards the bed, as quickly as I can without making too much noise. "Of course I did." I reply. I reach the bed, and she leaps across it, throwing her arms around me, pulling me down onto the bed with her.

"You're alive." She sobs into my neck. "You're here and you're alive."

I crush her against me, my hands in her hair, holding her close, my lips moving over her face, kissing every inch

171

of it, drinking her in. "Oh my god," I murmur, "I thought I'd never see you again."

"You died in my arms." She wraps her legs around my waist. "I felt you die and I wanted to die too."

I look down at her in the dark, stroking her cheek, my eyes finally finding her features in the moonlight. "I'm here, and I'm not leaving you again."

"I love you." She whispers.

"I love you too."

She gives a small, choked sob, and pulls me down to her, her lips opening under mine. Oh fuck she's so sweet, and I can taste the salt of her tears and I feel like I'm about to split open.

"I love you." I say it again. "I love you and I was so afraid I'd never be able to tell you, that you'd never know."

"I've always known," she murmurs, brushing her lips against my jaw, "I've always known it, I just wanted to you to say it. I just wanted to hear you say it."

"I was a fucking fool." My eyes close as her warm lips press into my neck, her fingers raking through my hair. "I should have told you every day, every chance I got. I'm so sorry."

"Don't be sorry." She starts to paw at my clothes, trying to pull my shirt off. "Oh god, Amryn, I need to feel you. I need you, please."

"Baby, we gotta be quiet." I'm sure this is a very bad idea, but I can't say no. I can never say no to her. Even when Finn is one wall and an unlocked door away.

172

"We always have to be quiet." She starts to shuffle her shorts down, and then her hands move to the waistline of my pants. I reach down to undo them, and my need to feel her, to have her under me and around me makes my head spin.

She tears the shirt off over my head and I slip it down my arms. My hands going under her tank top, moving over her breasts, and she gasps. She shuffles it up over her head, and then we're against each other, warmth and skin and hot breath mingling between us.

She opens her legs for me, and I push my mouth against her shoulder, suppressing my groan as I slide my cock inside her. She stretches for me, sweetly, perfectly, and her back arches underneath me.

Fuck, for the hundredth, the millionth time I thought I'd never be with her again, that I'd never feel her against me again, that the ache I feel for her would just go on forever. But I'm in her arms, I'm inside her, she's mine, this is only for me.

"I can't live without you." She says with a sigh, holding my face in her hands, pressing her forehead to mine. "I wanted to die with you."

"I never want to be away from you." I move inside her gently, savouring every moment. "You're everything." Everything. She feels like heaven. She's hot and searing around me. Her veins glow white in the darkness. I put my mouth to hers, just tasting her, lapping up her moans as they escape her throat.

The door flies open and the overhead lights snap on. "What the fuck is this?"

173

Cora's eyes widen as she looks up at me. She shakes her head, her lips quivering. I rise off her and turn to the door, pushing her behind me to shield her with my body. She clings on to my shoulders, her hands shaking violently. "Oh god," she murmurs.

Finn is in the doorway, two guards standing right behind him. One of them is the guard I spoke to outside.

"What the fuck is this?" Finn asks again, storming into the room. His eyes are wild as he looks at us in the bed. "You, and him?" He asks incredulously.

"I knew you were acting weird," the guard says to me, shaking his head.

Finn stands at the foot of the bed, aghast. A disbelieving scoff drops from his mouth. "I can't believe this."

I hold up a hand. "Finn -"

"Don't you fucking speak." He hisses. "Don't you dare say a fucking word."

"Finn, please -" Cora whimpers behind me. "You don't understand."

"You won't fuck me, but you'll fuck the fucking Runt?" He screams. "How long has this been going on?"

There's movement in the hallway, and the guards step aside. Lordain appears at the door. His gaze moves from Finn, to me and Cora on the bed, and he narrows his eyes, nodding. "I fucking knew it."

"I should have listened to you, Dad." Finn rubs the back of his neck, shaking his head.

Cora starts crying. "Finn, please."

"You keep your filthy mouth shut, you fucking whore." Lordain says.

"Hey." I bark at him. "Don't talk to her like that."

"Get up and put your clothes on." Finn says to me.

Cora's sobbing behind me. "Finn -"

"I said get off of my wife and put your fucking clothes on!" He screams at me.

Cora's fingers dig into my shoulders. "No." She sobs. "Don't hurt him."

Finn gestures to the guards. "Get him out of here. Lock him up."

I get up from the bed and pull my pants on, and the guards rush me, seizing my arms.

"No!" Cora cries, and she lifts her hands, her flames ready to fire. "Let him go."

"Cora, put your flames down." I tell her, twisting in the guard's grip. "Baby, look at me, you're going to -"

"What the fuck did you just call her?" Finn asks, flying at me, his hands around my neck.

"Get away from him!" Cora yells. "Don't you touch him!"

"What the fuck did you just call her?" Finn asks me again, squeezing my neck tight in his hands. "What did you just call my wife?"

"Cora put your flames down!" I call again, my voice failing as Finn squeezes harder. I can see her flames burning out of the corner of my eye. "Cora!"

"Finn, let him go!" Cora cries. "I swear, I'll burn this whole place to the ground!"

Finn's head swivels around to look at her. "You want him?" He shouts. "You really want him over me?"

"Let him go!" She pleads. I see her flames leap higher, and a shower of sparks flies across the room. "Finn, I swear I'll do it!"

Finn flinches as the sparks blow across him, and we all duck as a gunshot rings across the room. Finn's grasp on my neck drops away, and I look around, trying to place where the shot came from. I look at the doorway, and Lordain has the gun pointed out in front of him. And it's pointed at Cora.

I wrench around in the guards' grip to look at the bed, and see Cora kneeling, eyes wide, looking down at the wound in her shoulder, blood running down her arm, dripping on to the bed.

"No!" I cry, fighting against the guards, freeing myself from their grip, racing to the bed. Cora buckles as I reach her, her brow furrowing. "Baby, oh my god, it's OK, it's OK."

"Get him out of here." I hear Lordain say.

Cora's looking at me, confused. "I don't -" She shakes her head. "I won't let them hurt you."

Guards flood the room, their hands on me, trying to drag me away. "Get the fuck off me!" I cry, fighting them off with one arm as I try to hold on to Cora.

"I said get him out of here!" Lordain commands, and the guards pull me away, on to the floor. They start landing blows on me, kicking me with their boots.

176

"Don't hurt him." Cora calls weakly. "Leave - leave him alone."

A guard's boot shoots out towards me, and I grab it, twisting his foot, and he cries out as his ankle snaps. Another one steps forward, and points a gun right in my face.

"Enough!" Finn's voice booms across the room. "Get him out of here."

I sit up, pushing the barrel of the gun away, and try to get to my feet. "She needs help!"

"I said get him the fuck out of here!" Finn says again.

"Finn. She's going to bleed out!" I fight against the hands of the guards as they begin to drag me on my knees towards the door. "Finn! She needs help!"

Finn stands in the centre of the room, watching them drag me out.

"Cora!" They have me nearly at the door. "Cora! Someone help her!" She's lying on the bed, her hand hanging to the floor, blood dripping from her fingers. She's looking at me, pleading. "Finn! You have to fucking help her!"

"Enough of this." Lordain says. Something hits me hard in the back of the head, and everything goes black.

10
Cora

I stare out the window as the healer puts a patch over the stitches in my shoulder. "The bullet didn't pass through." The doctor says. "But you'll probably feel ill with the silver nitrate in your system for a few days. And it will weaken your powers, of course."

I don't say anything. I don't look at him. I don't want to acknowledge anyone's even in the room. I know Finn's standing in the corner, watching. He's refused for me to be healed, just for the sake of it. Just to cause me more pain. I didn't give him the satisfaction of reacting to a single stitch. If he wants to torture me, then so be it.

"Well, that should do it." The healer says as he packs up his things. "I'll come and check on you tomorrow." I hear him cross the room, and the door closes. I almost think Finn went with him, as the room is so still.

"How long?" Finn's voice is cold.

I turn to look at him. "How long what?"

His gaze is steely, his arms crossed over his chest. His hands still have my blood on them. "How long were you fucking him?"

"About five minutes before you burst in."

He lunges at me, towering over me. "Bitch, I asked you how long? How long have you been fucking him behind my back?"

"Years." I reply dryly. "It's been going on for years."

"How many?"

"Five."

His eyes widen, and he laughs in disbelief. "You're a fucking whore."

I turn back to look out the window. "Whatever you say, Finn."

He grabs my chin and turns my face back to his. "When was the last time before last night?"

"Why does it matter?" I ask.

"When?" He's hysterical.

"The night of my party." I reply, pushing his hand away from my face. "When he got back from Isolation."

Finn shakes his head. "The night he was dragged in front of my father, when my father suspected you two of having something going on, and I fucking defended you both." He laughs bitterly. "Bet you both had a great laugh over me after that huh?"

"It wasn't like that." I reply with a sigh. "It wasn't about hurting you. It wasn't about anyone else. It was just -" I put a hand to my forehead. I feel light-headed from the blood loss. "It was about us."

"Did you fuck him before or after my father dragged him away from you?"

I suppress the urge to roll my eyes. "After, of course. He'd just gotten back. It wasn't - it wasn't..." I trail off, unsure of what else to say.

He shakes his head, smirking. "I can't believe this. You fucking whore."

"What are you going to do to him?" I ask.

"Where did you fuck him?"

I sigh. "That doesn't matter."

"Yes it does." Finn's eyes darken. "I want to know where you fucked my Draw."

"Everywhere, Finn!" I cry, throwing up the hand I can use without pain. "Everywhere, OK? At his place, in my bedroom at my Mom's house, in our bathroom, in his bed."

"Our bathroom?" His nostrils flare. "In *our* fucking bathroom, in this house? *I* haven't even fucked you in this house."

"Finn-"

"When?" He demands. "When did you fuck him in this house?"

"You want me to give you a list of all the times and dates and places we fucked? Will it make you feel better, knowing that?"

"You told me you were a virgin."

"No I didn't," I say, shaking my head, "you assumed I was."

"Why?" His face crumples a little, and his voice cracks. "Why him?"

"Because I love him." I reply, my chest heaving as pain shoots through my shoulders. "I love him, and he loves me. And we tried, god, we tried, for years, to stop." Tears prick my eyes. "We said it was the last time, so many times. We knew we couldn't be together. But I love him, and he loves me. and I can't stay away from him."

"He can't have you." Finn says, leaning over me. "You're mine."

I glare at him. "Just because you say it doesn't make it true."

"Oh but you are mine, babe, remember?" His lips peel back in a grin. "You're mine, and he knows that because he watched me fuck you and claim you." He leans right into my face, his eyes locked on mine. "Bet that drove him insane."

"You're a fucking monster." I whisper as a tear strays down my cheek.

"I'm going to pump you full of cum every fucking night until you're pregnant," Finn says, stroking my cheek, "and then I'll have you, and your child, and I will fucking own you."

"Try it." I say through gritted teeth. "Touch me and see what happens."

He scoffs. "What you going to do, Cora?"

"You saw Heath." I feel a jolt of satisfaction as his eyes widen a little, just a little. "You saw what I did to him. I dare you to put that pathetic soft dick of yours anywhere near me. See what fucking happens."

He grabs me by the throat and slams me back against the window so hard the glass pane cracks, his eyes wild as he stares down at me. "I'm going to kill him, you know that right?" He smiles when he sees my face falter. "Oh yeah, I'm going to whip him, and then I'm going to cut his fucking throat, Cora."

"Don't you touch him." I hiss through my tears. "I swear to god, I will -" I raise my hand, my veins glowing.

Finn slams my arm down, and pain shoots through my shoulder. He grimaces as the heat from my arm sears against his hand, but he keeps holding me down. "I'm going to kill him. And you're going to get to watch." He looks down at my glowing veins. "Remember what the healer said, babe. You're weak right now." He tuts and shakes his head as his eyes meet mine. "No powers. So you'll watch him bleed, and you'll watch him die, and you won't be able to do a thing about it."

There's a knock on the door.

"What?" Finn barks.

The door opens slowly, and my mother peers into the room. "Is everything OK?" She asks.

Finn laughs bitterly. "Just discussing your daughter whoring herself around." He gets to his feet and looks over at my mother, whose face is tense with worry. "Come on in, Anya. Maybe you'd like to hear about all the places your daughter's been spreading her legs for my Draw?"

My mother frowns as she walks into the room, looking at my shoulder. "Why hasn't a healer been to see her?" Her voice is small, and she regards Finn with trepidation. "Why is she being sewn up like a human? She's your Queen."

"I thought maybe she could learn a valuable lesson." Finn says. "I'll leave you ladies alone, maybe you can talk some sense into her." He leers at me one more time, and storms out of the room, slamming the door behind him.

My mother rushes to my side, sitting on the window seat beside me. She inspects the patch on my arm, the bruising around it, the haphazard pattern of dark purple veins from the silver nitrate poisoning my bloodstream. "Oh honey." She says with a sigh. Her eyes are full of pain as they meet mine. "Why?"

"Because I love him." I say simply, feeling tears in my eyes. "I've always loved him."

She takes my hand, stroking it gently. "I know you and Amryn understand each other, I know you've always had a close bond. But it can't be this. It just can't be."

"But it is." I shake my head. "I've tried, Mom. I've tried. I told myself we had to stop, we had to stay away from each other. But I can't. I just -" Sobs shake my shoulders, and my mother puts her arms around me.

"I remember walking into your room once," she says to me, "when you were about 15. Amryn used to sneak into your room, and I found you both sleeping, just holding each other."

I nod, swallowing hard. "He used to have nightmares. He hated being alone." I cry harder. Amryn, the one fated to be alone, was always afraid of being alone.

My mother strokes my hair. "I remember thinking, this is going to be a problem. I could see from the way you were lying there." She sighs heavily. "I knew it was love. But, Cora -" She lifts my face gently with her hands to look into my eyes. "It can't be. You're Finn's wife, you promised yourself to him, and you're going to have a family with him. And you'll need to get over this."

I push her hands away from my face, shuffling away from her on the window seat. "I won't get over it."

"Now, Cora, don't be childish."

"Childish?" My chest hurts, the betrayal tearing me apart. "You saw what Finn did to me! You stood there and watched him rape your child!"

Her face crumples a little. "It wasn't easy to watch, but -"

"That's what you want for me? A man who does that to me?" I get to my feet, holding on to the window frame as the floor tips away from me. "Dad wouldn't have stood there, he would have stopped it. I wanted -" I gasp, putting a hand to my chest. "I was lying there, and I was begging Amryn to stop it. To rescue me from it."

"I had to stop him," my mother says, far too casually. "Luckily I did, or they would have killed him."

"You stopped him?" I clench my eyes shut. Of course someone had to stop him. He would have torn Finn into pieces.

"Honey, come on now."

184

"How did Dad die?" I ask suddenly.

My mother splutters for a moment, and I turn around to look at her. "Cora, what has this got to do with anything?"

"The angel who abducted me, Zadkiel, he called me the Shadow Queen." I watch her face closely. It doesn't even twitch, she remains completely neutral. "He told me I'm the Shadow Queen, and he said it was important to ask the right people about my father, and what happened to him."

"Your father was killed in battle." My mother replies flatly. Her eyes seem to have glazed over. "His Striker failed to save him."

"Where was his Draw?" I ask.

My mother looks at me and blinks. "I - I don't - Your father didn't have a Draw."

"Every Alpha has a Draw." I reply. She's acting strange. Her eyes move rapidly, and she closes them for a moment, and I see her eyeballs continue to roll back and forth under her eyelids. Like she's trying to remember, desperately. I sit down beside her and take her hand. "Mom. Where was Dad's Draw?"

"I - I don't know." She says. "I think - I think she died."

I lean in closer. "She?" I've never heard of a female Draw before.

My mother nods, putting a hand to her forehead. "I - I don't remember." Suddenly her eyes open a little wider. "Astrid."

"Who is Astrid?"

"She was your father's Draw." My mother's head trembles, and she puts a hand to her nose. Blood starts dripping out of it. "Oh dear."

"Mom, oh my god." I look into her face, and her eyes are glazed over again. I rush to grab a tissue from the side table, and press it gently to her nose.

She looks me over, and reaches out to touch my curls. "Such pretty hair," she says quietly, "just like hers."

"Whose, Mom?"

She shakes her head, and more blood streams from her nose. "Oh dear." She murmurs. "I wonder what's wrong with me."

"Mom, what did you call me when I was little?" I ask. Something I heard, something someone said to me, echoes in my head.

Would you come and look at your daughter?

She raises her eyebrows, and she looks almost drunk. "Honey. Honey, because you were their little bee."

My chest constricts. "Whose?" I clasp her hand.

The door flies open, and Morgan is standing there. "Sorry to break this up, ladies, but it's time for Cora to have her special little drink." She holds up a glass containing a viscous green liquid, which sloshes sickeningly as she swirls the glass in her manicured hands.

I wrinkle my nose. "What the fuck is that?"

She sidles into the room. "Just something to ward off any unfortunate side effects of last night's little transgression." She laughs when I merely look at her. "Oh sweetie, you really are innocent. See, you've started your bleeding now, and that means you can have a baby."

"I know that." I reply, eyeing the glass in her hand. She's going to poison me, isn't she?

Morgan sighs, smiling angelically. "Sweetie, you had a man inside you last night, and I'm not in the mood for my daughter-in-law to carry his child. So -" She holds up the glass, tossing her red hair over her shoulder. "This will ensure that any little mutts that may intend on taking hold get flushed away, just like their Daddy will today." She makes a swishing sound, her eyes almost maniacal as she looks at me. "Down the river he goes, bye bye."

My throat constricts. "You're all sick."

Morgan throws her head back and laughs. "Oh sweetie." Her smile drops as she looks back at me, shoving the glass at me. "Drink."

"He didn't even finish," I reply, pushing the glass away. "As far as I know that needs to happen for a baby to appear."

Morgan shoves it in my face again. "I said, drink. Or I'll force it down your throat, you little slut."

I merely glare at her, and she seizes my face, her long red fingernails digging into my cheeks. "Open your fucking mouth." She hisses.

I flail against it, reaching out to my mother, who is still just sitting there, staring into nothing. "Get the fuck off me!" I cry. Some of the bitter liquid runs between my lips, and I gag, spitting it up over Morgan's hand.

Her eyes widen and she springs back from me. "You fucking little bitch." The back of her hand slams across my face.

"Your family has a real anger problem, you know that?" I feel blood pooling in my mouth, and spit it at her feet. "Go fuck yourself, Morgan."

She points a finger in my face. "Just you wait, you'll watch him die today. And I will love seeing it." She spins on her heel, and storms out of the room.

I look at my mother, who blinks rapidly, and her eyes clear as they turn to me. "I'm sorry, honey, what were you saying?"

11
Amryn

The wall is cold but I lean against it anyway. My body aches from the beating the guards subjected me to, and my head is throbbing from whatever it was Lordain smashed into my skull to shut me up. My throat is raw from screaming. I called out asking if Cora was OK for two hours. No one answered.

I pull my knees up, resting my arms on them. I close my eyes and take a shuddering breath. I'm going to die today.

Amryn.

"What?"

Amryn.

I close my eyes, and she's there, in front of me. "What do you want?"

You know where to go.

"I don't know what you're talking about."

You know. You'll remember, Your wings will carry you here.

"I'm going to die today."

She shakes her head. *I'll be waiting for you.*

The bolt on the door slides back with a metallic scrape, and it falls open. Finn steps in, and smirks down at me. "And to think I trusted you."

I get to my feet. "Is she OK?"

"She's none of your concern." He replies icily.

"Just fucking tell me if she's OK."

"And if I don't?"

I summon a flame. "I can't take out all of you but I will burn as many of you as I fucking can if something's happened to her." I snarl. "Now tell me if she's alright."

Finn chuckles, and holds his hands up. "OK, OK. She's fine. Happy now?" He leers at me as I extinguish my flames. "And once you're dead, I'm going to really enjoy fucking her. Every single night." He leans against the wall, crossing his arms over his chest. "She tells me it's been going on since she was, what, 16?"

"Yeah." I reply. "And I've loved her a whole lot longer than that."

"Ah, that's sweet." He grins. "Bet it killed you, to have to watch me fucking what you thought was yours, huh?"

"You didn't fuck her, you raped her." I reply.

Finn's eyes blaze. "She loved every second of it."

"I should have fucking torn you to shreds that night." I say through gritted teeth.

190

"Yeah you should have, and you didn't, and now you get to die." He says, and I wonder if the maniacal gleam in his eyes was always there and I just never saw it before. "I'm going to whip you, and then I'm going to slice open your throat, Amryn. And then you'll be dead, and everyone will forget you even existed."

"Cora will never forgive you for this," I tell him. "She'll hate you forever."

Finn shrugs. "She'll get over it." He rubs his chin thoughtfully for a moment. "Something I'm curious abut though."

"And what's that?"

"How did you know where she was?" Finn asks. "How did you know she was in Sfayder?"

I scoff. "What does it matter?"

"I just want to know." He replies. "Was it a lucky guess, or did you have something to do with it all?"

I laugh bitterly. "Yeah, man, I organised the whole ambush, that got me a whole lot, didn't it?"

Finn's mouth twitches pensively. "No, that's true, you're too much of a fucking lap dog for that. But still, I'd like to know how you knew."

I shake my head. "Lucky guess."

"You're not going to tell me, are you?"

I meet his gaze. "You can go fuck yourself, Finn."

"Have it your way." He tilts his head towards the door and whistles. "We gotta get the prisoner ready." He looks back at me, and his eyes widen as he grins. "For execution."

I feel hollow as the guards come in, tying my hair up so my back is exposed for Finn's whip. I've died before, at the hand of that angel. That was painful, for a minute. But then it stopped hurting, and it was over. I just slipped away.

Maybe this won't be so bad. Maybe it'll be faster than I think.

I think of the vision I had, of the baby, of Cora smiling at me. I was never going to have that life. It was just a nice dream. That was never destined for me.

Fated to be alone. Always.

And now I'm going to die alone, bleeding out on some podium while they all watch.

OK. Let's get it over with. I don't want to live without her anyway.

12
Cora

It's raining.

There's a podium set up in the clearing, with an a-frame in the middle of it, thick ropes dangling down each side.

I don't even feel sick anymore. I'm beyond terror. I can't believe this is happening. Tears burn in my eyes. This is my fault. I should never have called Amryn to my bedroom. I was stupid and selfish and now he's going to die because of me.

Lordain and Roche sit on either side of me, silently. My hands are bound to the chair I sit in, and it's all so ridiculous. Where would I run to? The rest of the clan is gathered behind us, hushed conversations going on about the whore of a Queen who betrayed the Alpha with the Draw.

I suppress a sob as Amryn is hauled out into the clearing by the guards, his hands bound in front of him. He keeps his head down. Please look at me. Please just look at me one last time. One last time. Ice runs through my veins. I had to watch him die once before, and now I have to watch it again.

The guards raise his hands and hook them into the ropes on the podium, tying them securely. He's facing the crowd. His eyes stay on the floor. Please, please just look at me.

Finn sidles across the clearing, his veins glowing red, a long black whip in his hands.

"Lordain," I turn to him. "This doesn't need to happen."

"Shut up Cora." His eyes stay fixed on the podium.

"Please." My voice cracks. "You don't have to kill him. Just send him away."

"He will always find a way back to you." He turns to me, his eyes cold. "And we can't have that."

I look back at the podium, and Finn is circling Amryn, leering at him triumphantly. "You're charged with betraying me, your Alpha, with my Queen. Do you admit to these charges?"

Amryn keeps his eyes on the ground. "Yes."

"You admit you fucked my Queen?" Finn says.

"Yes."

"You admit that you're a traitor."

Amryn takes a deep breath. "Yes."

"And do you repent?"

Amryn's eyes move from the floor, up to meet mine. Rain runs down his face. His jaw flexes. "No."

194

The crowd behind me murmurs, and Finn's face drops a little. "I asked you if you repent." He says.

Amryn turns to look at Finn. "No. Never."

"It'll only be 10 lashes if you repent."

Amryn scoffs. "10, 50, 100. I don't care." His eyes move back to me, and I see him brace himself. "I don't regret it. I'd do it again. And I will never repent."

Finn lunges forward and grabs Amryn's hair, yanking his head back. "It'll be 50 lashes, bitch."

"So get it over with, you fucker." Amryn replies through gritted teeth.

Finn releases Amryn's head, and steps back, swinging the whip back and forth. Amryn's eyes are fixed on me, and then there's a loud crack, and his hands grip the rope as the whip snaps across his back.

Pain shoots through my shoulder as I turn to Lordain. "Please, don't do this." I struggle against the bonds tying me down as Finn's whip cracks again. "Lordain, please. I'll stay here, I'll stay with Finn, I'll have his babies, I promise. Please, just let him go."

Lordain turns and sneers at me. "You'll do those things anyway, sweetheart."

"Please." The whip cracks again. "Please. Please let him go. Please don't kill him."

Lordain's hand reaches out to grip my shoulder, squeezing his fingers into the bullet wound. I cry out, trying to wrench myself away from him. "He's going to die today, and you're going to watch." Lordain hisses in my face.

Roche jumps out of his seat, his flames rising from his hands, and I turn to look back at the podium. Amryn's arms are on fire, and the rope binding him down is burning away, sizzling and snapping in the rain. His eyes are still on me.

Finn whips him again, the impact sending Amryn stumbling forward on to all fours as the burnt ropes give way.

"Finn!" Roche calls, aiming his flames at Amryn. "Stand back!"

But Finn isn't listening, and lunges after Amryn, grabbing on to his hair and pulling a knife from his waistband. "You wanna burn me?" He shouts. "You wanna fucking burn me? You can't fucking hurt me!"

"Finn!" Roche calls again. "Get away from him!"

I watch as Finn brandishes the knife in front of Amryn, laughing maniacally. Panic swells in my chest, and heat, unbearable heat runs through my arms and legs.

"Finn, no!" I shout. My arms are glowing, and the feeling in my chest thumps at my ribcage, like something is trying to claw its way out of me. "Finn, please!"

Finn puts the knife to Amryn's throat, and leers at me. "You ready?"

I scream.

13
Amryn

Roche's flames are aimed at me, and he's telling Finn to get back. To get away from me. My flames are going to burn him. But Finn wants this kill. He wants to cut my fucking throat.

"Ready to die, fucker?" His breath stinks of alcohol. He holds the knife up in front of me, and I can hear Cora begging him to stop, pleading to stop.

I look over at her, one last time. Her arms are glowing. Her eyes are fixed on me, crying, pleading.

They're turning white. I can see it from here.

"You ready?" Finn shouts beside me.

And then I see Roche turn to look down at her.

Cora screams.

And everything explodes.

There's nothing but white light, and a shockwave. Finn is thrown sideways, the knife clattering onto the wooden podium. I look up, the shockwave washing over me. I have no idea what the fuck just happened, and I can't see Cora for smoke and flames. Fuck. What was that?

I crawl across the podium, rising to my feet, but a hand shoots out and pulls my foot out from under me, sending me tumbling down on to the grass. Finn throws himself down on me with a roar, his flames snaking up his arms.

"Where the fuck do you think you're going, huh?" His teeth are lined with blood as he bares them at me, his hands burning my skin as he puts them around my neck. I ignite my flames, and Finn laughs maniacally. "You're my Draw, you can't hurt me!" He says, leering down at me.

His eyes widen as my flames hit him in the chest, and he gasps heavily, his hands falling away from my neck as he throws himself off me, onto the grass beside me. He stares at me, shaking his head.

"What the fuck?" His hands are shaking as he clutches the burn on his chest. "You can't hurt me."

"I'm not your fucking Draw," I snarl as I get to my feet. "I never fucking was."

"I - I own you," he stammers, the red raw wound on his chest shimmering as he sucks in one shallow breath after another.

I stand over him as he rolls onto his back, and summon a fireball in my hand. "You don't own shit."

Just as I prepare to fire at him, I hear Cora screaming. I leave Finn writhing on the ground, and follow the sounds of Cora's cries. "Cora!" I can't see anything, just smoke and flames. "Cora!"

The smoke clears enough for me to see. She's scrambling backwards on her hands, her eyes looking down at her body, which is covered in all that's left of Roche. Flesh and blood and a charred arm.

Lordain lies a few feet away, face down, unmoving. Everyone else is running away, their terrified screams going with them.

I skid to my knees beside her, and she shakes her head, her eyes wide and filled with terror. And green again. "Cora, we have to move." I say to her, pulling her to her feet.

"I - I don't know what happened," she stutters, her hand gripping mine.

A flash of purple flies between us, and Morgan is advancing on us, her hands illuminated, her eyes glowing violet as she roars at us.

Witch.

She's a witch.

"Oh god," Cora says.

"We gotta run!" I pull her along behind me.

Another purple flash flies past us, and Cora's whole body glows white as she turns back.

"You can't escape, Cora!" Morgan screams.

Cora's hands fly up, and white lightning bolts fly towards Morgan. All we hear is a strangled scream in the flash of white.

Fly! The voice is screaming in my ear. *Fly! Now! Before they can track you!*

"Cora, we have to fly!" I say to her.

She looks at me, desperation in her face, and shakes her head. "I don't know how anymore!"

I scoop her up in my arms, my wings unfurling through the lashes in my back. "Hold on to me," I say to her, and she wraps her arms around my neck, shaking violently.

I swoop my wings and my feet leave the ground. We fly away, over the mountains, over the trees, leaving Nilau far behind. And I hope the voice was right, and that I know where to go.

I don't know how long we've been flying, or where we are, but I'm feeling weak and we need to land or we'll crash. I'm not in the mood to fucking die again after the week I've had. Something, I don't know what - instinct? - tells me I've flown far enough.

We touch down on a soft mossy forest bed, amongst towering pine trees. It's warm and humid, the air heavy with the promise of a storm. A stream bubbles over rocks nearby, and birds sing overhead. The contrast of this peaceful place to the compound we just fled from is almost jarring.

"Amryn?" Cora looks like she's about to hyperventilate. She's been quiet, in shocked silence almost the entire time we flew, but now she's broken, and her breath comes in panicked puffs. She puts her hands on my chest, shaking her head. "They were going to kill you, and I - I don't know what I did, I don't know how -"

200

I wrap her in my arms. "Baby, it's OK. It's OK. Breathe. Breathe. We're safe." I take several deep breaths, feeling her still against me, her trembling finally easing. After a while, she looks up at me, with tears in her eyes.

"I'm so sorry." She says with a sob. "I should never have asked you to come, and they nearly killed you, and -"

"Hey, no, no, come on." I take her face in my hands. "You didn't do anything wrong."

"I should have stopped them."

"Baby, you just went nuclear and blew up half the council." I say to her, and it's so insane that we both laugh. We're out of the compound. We're free. It feels strange. I almost feel lost. I look down at her hands, the veins under her skin still glowing white. "So you have no idea how you do that? None at all?"

"None at all." She shakes her head. "It just, it just happened. It happened when Heath was trying to - to. Yeah." She looks down at herself, and balks. "Oh fuck."

"Yeah, I think that's mostly Roche right there."

Her eyes flash up to mine. "I killed him, didn't I?"

"He killed himself. He saw what was happening and threw himself on you to stop it." I take her hand and pull her towards the stream. "Come on, let's wash that off."

Cora scoops water from the stream into her hands and splashes her face, then looks around at the trees. "Where are we?" She asks, rubbing water over her arms.

I look around. "I don't know. But I feel like I've been here before." Thunder is rumbling now, in the distance.

"How's your back?" Cora asks me, moving behind me to inspect the wounds from Finn's whip. I hear her gasp. "Oh my god, Amryn."

"It's OK." I say, even though they sting real bad. "I heal quick."

She sobs again. "I should have set them all on fire."

I turn around and take her in my arms. "Stop that now, you saved me." My eyes move down to the patch on her shoulder, and it's seeping blood. "Fuck. You're bleeding again. What did they do to you?"

"Finn refused to get me a healer." She tells me flatly. "Said I needed to be taught a lesson. And Morgan tried to force me to drink some fucking abortion juice."

What? My eyes widen, and my heart leaps into my throat. "You're -"

"Oh no, no," she shakes her head quickly. "She just thought, with you, and if I was and -" She sighs heavily. "Amryn, what is this?" She lifts her hands. "Something is happening to me, and I can't explain it. I glow, all the time now. It never goes away. And then the feelings I'm having, and -" Her fingers claw into my chest. "I don't think my Mom is my Mom."

"What?" My brow furrows.

"She said something about my Dad, and his Draw. And I had a weird - I dunno, like a flashback? In Sfayder. I heard my Dad, and he called someone over, saying to come look at her daughter, and a woman called out to me and called me a name, Pcholka? And it wasn't my Mom."

"Something like that has been happening to me too." I tell her.

202

Cora's eyes widen as we both hear footsteps, and movement rustling through the trees. We both summon our flames, standing back to back as we look around the clearing, waiting for someone to appear. The movement stops, but I can feel eyes on us.

"Who's there?" A man's voice calls. The footsteps start again, and I can hear more than one voice moving towards us.

"Ey, all is well!" Another man calls, and suddenly someone breaks through the tree line. A middle-aged man in brown leather pants and a white t-shirt emerges, running a hand through his wet blonde hair as the leaves brush over him. "It's Keenan's boy!"

"Amryn!" The voice stops my heart. It sounds like my mother. "Amryn!" A woman breaks through the tree line, pelting past the blonde man. Her long black hair flails out behind her as she runs towards me. She bursts into tears as she sees me, and runs faster. "Amryn!" I extinguish my flames, and she reaches me, throwing her arms around me. "My little boy!" She sobs into my neck. "Oh my baby boy, you're here!" She pulls back, and her eyes crinkle as she smiles at me through her tears.

I stare at her face. She looks so much like my mother. "I know you." I say. "You spoke to me."

She nods. "My baby. You're here." She hugs me to her again, and I put my arms around her. "I was so afraid. I thought they'd hurt you."

"They nearly did." I tell her. "But Cora saved me." I let the woman go, and turn to Cora, who is eyeing us uncertainly.

The woman wipes the tears from her eyes with the sleeve of her sweater, and throws her arms around Cora. "Oh honey, you're here. I knew it. I knew you'd make it." She turns and calls over her shoulder. "Ebony! She's here!"

A woman with curly hair, like Cora's, just smattered with grey, emerges from the trees, a bow on her back. She smiles widely, and hurries across the stream towards us. "You made it!"

It feels like a family reunion, but I have no idea who anybody is. I turn to the woman with the black hair as the curly-haired woman embraces Cora. "I know you all, and I know this place, but - I don't remember anything."

The black-haired woman sighs, and puts a hand to my cheek. "I know, sweetheart. It's going to be a lot to take in. I'm your aunt, Elise. And this -" She gestures to the curly-haired woman, "is Ebony, Cora's aunt."

"My aunt?" Cora asks, as her hand flies to her mouth. "You're Ceili's mother?"

Ebony nods, and even though she's smiling, her eyes are filled with pain. "Yes, honey. I am." She gestures to the blonde man, who's hanging back near the stream. "And this is Liall. Ceili's father."

"We were told you died," Cora says, and she rushes towards Liall, who opens his arms as she approaches. "I remember you." Cora says to him, and wraps her arms around his waist.

"Oh honey," he says, stroking her hair gently. "I'm so glad you're back."

204

"Come on, we gotta move!" The first man's voice sounds from beyond the trees. "They might have trackers out." He emerges from the trees, his black hair hanging down over his shoulder, a long streak of white running through it from his left temple. He has a curved scimitar on his back. He eyes me carefully, and nods. "Glad you made it."

"This is Tallesaign." Elise says to me, and looks at me with a smile. "Your brother."

Cora looks at Tallesaign, then back at me, her hands over her mouth. I can't speak. Tallesaign and I stare at each other for a moment. It's like looking into my own face, like looking into the future, me in a decade. His brow furrows and his eyes break away. "Come on, I said we have to move." He disappears into the trees, and we all follow.

Lightning flashes as we move through the thick forest, thunder rumbling closer now. My head is roaring, everything is familiar and my brain is trying to place it all. I know this place. I know these people.

I have a brother. A *brother*.

We make our way through the trees, then follow a path at the base of a craggy cliff line which rises into the pewter sky above us. The path takes a sharp turn to the right, and we pick our way down jagged stone steps, slippery with moss and rain. Cora grips my hand, and her hand is warm as it continues to glow.

"It's not much further," Liall assures us. Tallesaign is leading the way, wordlessly, pushing ahead without looking back. Thunder rumbles loudly overhead as we reach the bottom of the stone steps, and we move through more thick trees, a series of streams snaking their way between the enormous roots in the ground.

We reach the edge of the trees, and there's a village in front of us. Mudstone houses with terracotta roofs are dotted in the lush valley. Beyond them lie fields of wheat, swaying back and forth in the breeze as the storm rolls in. An enormous round hall stands in the centre of the village, a metal dragon before it, with flames burning inside.

"This is home." Cora says beside me. "I remember it." She looks up at me. "Amryn, do you remember?"

Something is tugging at me, in the back of my mind. Hot summers in those wheat fields, twinkling lights in the snow. "I remember. This is Ocario." Our home. The one we were told was destroyed in the last war.

"Come on," Elise says, taking my arm. "You two need some medicine, and to get warm and clean and fed."

I wince as Elise applies ointment to the wounds on my back, and she tuts gently. "I'm going to tear that fucker's head off if I get the chance." She says, and I can't help but laugh.

"You'll be getting in line," I tell her. I look over at the fireplace, where Cora is sitting curled up on a leather armchair, her knees pulled up to her chest, staring at the fire. Her face is shiny from the ointment Ebony applied to the bruises Morgan and Finn left her with, and her wet hair hangs over her shoulders, finally free of blood. "You OK?" I ask her.

She looks over at me and nods, sighing. "Just overwhelmed."

"I bet you are," Elise says. "This is a lot to take in."

Ebony walks in from the kitchen with two steaming bowls in her hands. "Come on you two, you need some good food in you." She hands one bowl to Cora, who inhales with her eyes closed, and Ebony chuckles. "A good stew is what you both need." She hands me the other bowl, and sits down in the armchair beside Cora, looking at her adoringly. "I can't believe you're both here. I thought I'd never see you kids again." Her voice cracks, and she puts a hand over her mouth, shaking her head. She turns to look at me with tears in her eyes. "Is Ceili alright?"

I nod. "Yeah, she's fine. She's great."

"They - they just took her." Ebony exhales heavily. "I had no idea what happened to her, who had her, if she was OK."

"She lived with us," Cora says, "with me and Mom and Amryn, we grew up together."

Ebony nods. "Good, that's good." Her lips quiver as she tries to smile. She rises to her feet. "Anyway, there'll be plenty of time for all that later, and to tell you everything you need to know. I'll go and get a room ready for you. You must exhausted." She hurries out of the cabin, into the pouring rain.

Elise sighs. "Poor Ebony." She sits back from me. "OK, well they're already starting to heal, so the marigold will help the last little bit."

I turn around and look at her. "Were you and my mother twins?" I ask.

She nods. "We were. Not identical, but very similar, as you can see."

"We were told Ocario was destroyed, and that you all died." Cora says.

"Of course you were, because Lordain lied, and had his witch cast spells on you all." Elise replies. "You forgot everything."

"I have a brother." I say quietly, and Elise gives me a sad smile.

"You do, sweetheart. He's - he's been through a lot. He was there the day your father died, he saw it all. And then he saw them take you and his mother away."

"He's older than me, by a lot, right?" I can't believe I don't remember my own brother.

"12 years," Elise confirms. "You were the surprise baby. And oh he adored you." Her face crumples a little. "It's been hard for him. And then when the blood bond came back, between us, well, he - he struggled with that. He wanted to see you, but when I told you were in danger -" She reaches out and takes my hand. "I think he was afraid to lose you all over again."

"What's the blood bond?" Cora asks.

"After I died, when Zadkiel killed me, I started having visions." I tell her, and her face falters a little. "I guess it broke the spell. I started hearing Elise's voice. She told me -" I look back at Elise. "You told me to listen for Cora, that I'd be able to hear her."

208

Elise nods. "You're her Draw."

Cora looks back and forth between us, her mouth open a little. "What?"

I look back at her and shake my head, giving her a smile. "I have a lot to tell you, I guess."

Elise rises to her feet. "Come on, you two. It's been a lot for you, and you need to rest. We'll talk more later. I know you probably want to hear it all right now, but you need some sleep, and then we can discuss it all later."

We put down our empty bowls and follow her outside, across a small courtyard to a neighbouring cabin. Thunder rumbles loudly overhead, and rain is pelting down. We cross onto a covered porch, and Elise pushes open a wooden door set with a green glass window, and we walk into a cosy lounge room, a fire crackling in the hearth. A patchwork sofa stands in front of the fireplace, and a table with two chairs stands beyond it.

"You can sleep in here," she says, leading the way into a bedroom off the lounge room. There's a big bed made up with a thick comforter and several pillows. "The bathroom's off the kitchen," she says, pointing over our shoulders. "And we're all just across the courtyard if you need us."

"They can't find us here, can they?" Cora asks tentatively.

Elise takes her hand. "No, honey. You're safe here, I promise." She gives us both a smile. "Now, get some rest. We'll talk in the morning." She closes the door behind her, and Cora and I are alone.

We eye each other for a second before rushing into each other's arms. I push my mouth down over hers, and fucking hell, being alive feels amazing right now. She kisses me back urgently, then whimpers. "Are you OK?" I ask her. "Did I hurt your shoulder?"

She nods. "It's not just the stitches. Lordain shot me with silver nitrate."

"Fucker." I brush my fingers gently over her arm, over the dark purple veins that trace underneath her skin. "I hope he died too." My eyes move back to hers. "I should have killed Finn when I had the chance. But I had to get to you. I didn't know - I didn't know if you'd survived what happened."

She puts a hand to her chest. "I don't know what's happening to me. It felt like - like fire. But not flames. More like, heat. Panic. And then -" She shakes her head. "I don't know how to control it."

"Hey." I put my hand over hers on her chest. "We'll figure it out, OK?"

"OK." She leans her forehead against me and takes a deep breath. "Let's go get some sleep." She takes off her clothes and climbs into the bed.

"You sleep naked?" I ask, and suddenly I'm gripped by some weird realisation, and I can't breathe.

"Not all the time," she says with a shrug, her eyes filling with alarm as they settle on me. "Amryn? What's wrong?"

I gasp in a breath and shake my head. "I'm OK. It's just -" I let out a short laugh, and my eyes burn with tears. "Just - this is normal. So normal. Us getting into bed, and I don't know how you sleep, and now I do, and I just..." I swallow hard, willing the lump in my throat to fucking dissolve.

"Come here." She extends a hand out to me.

I strip off my clothes and climb into bed next to her. I lie on my side, and she snuggles back against me. She's warm and soft, and we're naked next to each other, with no sense of urgency, no sense that our time is running through our fingers. I can just feel her. I can just lie here with her. I can reach across the bed and pull her to me.

"I don't always sleep naked," she says finally.

I can't help but chuckle. "Well I hope you do from now on, because if I get to feel this every night I'll be pretty happy."

She looks over her shoulder at me. "How do you sleep? Do you sleep naked?"

"Depends on how much I'm thinking about you," I say, and she laughs out loud.

"Well we don't have to worry about that now," she whispers, her hand stroking my arm. "We have time, baby."

"I love you."

"I love you too." I can feel her heartbeat under my hand. Her heart. My heart.

We have time.

14
Cora

or just a split second I forget where I am as my eyes open, and why I'm in bed with someone else, but then I remember it's Amryn, and we're in Ocario. We're home. We're safe.

I press myself back against him, and he's so warm and his muscular arms are around me and it's bliss. We've never been able to do this. It was always just stolen moments, whenever we could have them. But now we're here and it's just us, and it's quiet and cosy.

He inhales, and his arms tense around me as he wakes up and stretches. "Morning, baby." He mutters, pressing his lips against the back of my neck.

"How does your back feel?" I ask.

He shifts a little. "It feels fine. Your shoulder?"

I lift my arm, and wince. "Still hurts."

He gently pulls his arms out from around me and sits up, looking down at the patch on my arm. He peels it back, and I grit my teeth. The skin around it feels like it's torn up. I look at the spot where the hole was, the stitches eating through my skin. It's black and seeping.

"We'll need Elise to look at this," Amryn says, "maybe she has something for it. It doesn't look good." He puts his hand over it, and the veins in his hands ignite instantly, glowing bright orange. "What the fuck?" His eyes dart to mine. "Does that hurt?"

"No." I say, shaking my head. "It - it feels better."

We both stare at his hand on my shoulder, as the dark purple veins pull back on themselves. My own veins glow brighter, and suddenly there's no more pain in my shoulder. Amryn lifts his hand, and the sickening hole is gone, the stitches lying on my skin, caked in black blood.

"What was that?" I ask him.

"I don't know." He replies. "I mean, I healed you. I've never done that before."

"Elise said something yesterday, that you're my Draw?"

"I never told you." He eyes me carefully. "When I went up to into Isolation, I had to do that ritual, with the Fidelis Stone, right?"

"Yeah, I remember."

"So, when you give the blood and hair offering, the stone throws up a flame, and the flame is the colour of your Alpha's flame. Well, when I did it -" He strokes my cheek. "It threw up white flames. Your flames."

"You're joking." I say with a gasp. "And you didn't tell me?"

"I didn't think anything of it," he says, "it seemed so strange to me, and I kind of just put it down to thinking

213

about you too much or something, I don't know. It didn't even occur to me to think of being your Draw, of you being Queen. But then Elise, when she started talking to me, she said I'm your Draw, and it all made sense." He shakes his head. "And then she told me to listen for you, while you were in Sfayder. She said I would be able to find you."

"And you did," I reply. "You found me. You told them where to find me."

"It was like I was there with you," he says, his brow furrowing as he remembers. "I felt the floor under you, and I could smell the ocean, and I heard you whisper my name. And I knew, I knew where you were."

"I didn't feel you." I whisper, and clutch my hands to my face as tears start falling again. "I didn't feel you, and I thought you were dead."

Amryn wraps me in his arms, kissing my forehead. "Hey, it's OK, I'm here."

"I had this dream," I say between sobs, "I had this dream, and I think it must have been Elise, and she was with us, and she was carrying this little baby, and I knew it was our baby." I look up at him. "And all I could think of was that we were never going to have that."

"I saw it too." He says, stroking my cheek. "I saw that baby too. Our baby."

I nuzzle into him, wrapping my arms around him. "What does this all mean?"

He draws back a little, putting a hand on my chest. "We're connected. That's what it means. This -" His fingers splay out over my chest, over my heart beat, "is mine. And

214

this -" He takes my hand and puts it on his own chest, "is yours." He brings his mouth down on mine. Yes, yes, I'm yours. My heart is your heart. I can't live without you. I don't want to live without you.

I wrap my legs around him, drawing him towards me. "I need you." I breathe against his lips.

He pushes himself inside me, and my fingers claw into his chest.

"Oh god," I sigh, "I missed you so much." I thought this would never happen again.

He moves slowly, languidly, smiling against my mouth as I moan. He's taking his time, like he always wanted to. He feels so good. This is his, and only his. No one else's. And now we never have to worry about anyone stopping us ever again.

He withdraws from me gently, and I whimper, grinding myself against him, not wanting him to stop, but his hands grip my hips, holding me still. His lips trail down my chest, his tongue playing over my nipples, sending electric shivers down my spine. His mouth continues down, over my stomach, and he moves down between my legs, pushing his shoulders under my thighs.

His lips graze over my skin, between my thighs, and my whole body tingles with anticipation, my hands in his hair. His tongue trails over my clit, slowly at first. His hands trace up my body, catching my nipples between his fingers.

I sigh, closing my eyes, surrendering completely to this feeling. His tongue probes harder, his lips exploring me.

Rippling heat courses over my skin, and I suck in a breath, my back arching under his hands.

Oh god, I'm going to come already, and it's crazy I don't want to, I want this feeling to go on and on. Just him and me.

My thighs start to shake, and I look down at him, his hazel eyes gazing up at me as he keeps licking and sucking, watching me tremble as my orgasm rises against his mouth. I throw my hands back, gripping the headboard, clawing into it. "Amryn," I moan, "oh god."

My very core becomes hot, aching and yearning for him, and I can't help but cry out as my climax grips me. I don't have to be quiet. I can let him know just how good he feels. I close my eyes, tipping my head back on the pillow, breathless as my trembling body subsides.

I feel him climb back over me, and he slides his cock into me easily, I'm so wet. His hand holds my face, and he thrusts into me, my stomach quivering against him, my climax still pulsating around him. I press my mouth up against his, and I can taste myself on his lips.

"Open your eyes, baby," he murmurs against my mouth. He gazes at me, desire hooding his eyes. "You're so fucking beautiful."

I turn my face into his hand, nuzzling his palm, moaning into it as he drives himself into me. "Oh fuck," he groans, his mouth against my neck. I wrap my legs around him, and he's buried right inside me. I'm going to come again, he feels so fucking good. I arch under him, and the heat between my thighs breaks, sliding between us, throbbing so hard around Amryn's cock my eyes roll back in my head.

216

Amryn groans loudly, his shoulders tensed over me, and then with a shudder, he comes inside me. He breathes heavily against my neck, his thumb stroking gently over my lips as I try to catch my breath and clear my head of the haze of euphoria.

His body jerks gently as he starts to laugh, and I turn to look at him. "Why are you laughing?"

He kisses me, and rolls off me, lying on his back. "Just thinking, what a way to get to know our family again." He looks over at me grinning. "You, screaming in here like a banshee."

I swat at his chest with the back of my hand. "Hey, you were making plenty of noise too."

"Yes I was." He gazes at the ceiling, moving his hand over to me, stroking my chest with the backs of his fingers. "It was fucking magical."

"We should probably get ourselves presentable and go see everyone," I say, rolling over under his arm, feeling his hot body against my skin.

He presses a kiss against my temple. "You're right. I think it's going to be a big day." He tucks a hand behind his head, and sighs. "I can't believe I have a brother."

I prop myself up on my elbow and touch his cheek. "This must all be - I don't even know."

"All these years I thought I was alone, and -" He exhales heavily, and gives me a small smile. "I mean, I wasn't alone. But-"

"I know what you mean." I assure him. "I know. It's different. Instead of it just being you and me against all of them, it's us and a family." A family. The word almost feels strange to say, especially now I don't even know if I can trust that Anya is my mother.

Amryn eyes me thoughtfully. "You OK?"

"Yeah," I say with a shrug, "just preparing myself for finding out how much of my life has been a lie."

Elise is sitting on her porch with a mug in her hand as we approach. She smiles wistfully at us. "Oh, you two," she says, "seeing you both here, it makes my heart happy."

"Good morning," I say, "sorry we slept in."

"Don't be silly, honey," she says, waving her hand dismissively. "You both needed a rest. For what you went through." She rises to her feet. "And for what's still to come."

Footsteps sound, and Tallesaign rounds the corner of the porch. His eyes settle on Amryn, and I see his brow crinkle for just a moment, a flash of pain in his eyes. He's just as beautiful as Amryn, the same hazel eyes and silky black hair. But he has a weariness about him that makes my heart hurt. His eyes fix on the floor, and he clear his throat. "Hope you two slept well." He says, putting his hands in his pockets.

"We did, thanks." Amryn says.

"You can call me Tal, by the way." Tal's eyes look back up at us, and he gives me a crooked grin. "Tallesaign is a stupid name, it's too long. That's why -" He straightens his shoulders, and shakes his head. "That's why I picked a better name for you, brother."

218

Amryn grips my hand a little harder. "You picked out my name?"

Tal leans against the post of the porch, and smiles. "Yeah. I got to do that. I was so -" His voice cracks, and he shakes his head, heading past us into the cabin.

Elise watches him, and turns to us, sighing. "He's struggling." She puts a hand on our shoulders. "Give him time. Now come on, let's go inside."

Liall and Ebony are waiting for us as we walk in, sitting at the long kitchen table. Tal is standing by the fire, his hands still jammed in his pockets, and he doesn't look up.

"Come and sit," Liall says, gesturing to the chairs opposite them. "Can I get you some breakfast?"

"Uh no, thankyou." I reply. "I'm feeling a little - I don't know."

Ebony nods. "Of course you are." She leans back in her chair and throws her hands up, smiling. "I don't even know where to begin."

I clasp my hands in my lap, and remember Zadkiel's words. "What happened to my father?"

Liall and Ebony look at each other.

"He was murdered by Lordain." Tal says.

My blood runs cold. "What?"

Tal looks over his shoulder at me. "Your father, and your mother too."

Amryn's hand reaches over to take mine, and I struggle to breathe. I look at Ebony, and she nods. "It's true." She sucks in a breath. "Anya isn't your mother."

I want to ask questions, but I can't. I can't speak. I put my hand to my forehead. My mother. She's not my mother. The woman who held me when I was sick, who comforted me when I was scared - she wasn't my mother, even though she's the only mother I remember.

"Sorry." Tal says, moving to the end of the table. He looks down at me and shakes his head. "I probably shouldn't have led with that."

"No, no, it's OK." I assure him, clutching on to Amryn's hand.

"Who was Anya then?" Amryn asks.

"Cora's nanny." Liall replies. "Her real mother was Astrid, Rodelth's Draw."

Elise sits down at the other end of the table and raises her hand for silence. "This is pointless, we need to start at the beginning." She looks at me and sighs. "I'm sorry, but you need to understand everything, because it's all connected."

"It's OK." My voice is wavering. "Please, I want to know. Everything."

Elise nods. "Before the clans divided, we were all one clan, united, under one leader."

"The Shadow Queen." Amryn says.

"Exactly." Elise says, nodding. "She's the conduit for the Old God to the Earth Realm, and without her presence the Earth fell into - well, it became choatic. Clans started to split off into their own groups, leaders declaring themselves Alphas, creating barbaric ceremonies to sate their need for power."

220

"But how did they do that?" I ask. "The Old God, why didn't he stop it?"

"When the angels cast us out of the Halls, their mutiny weakened him," Liall tells me, leaning on his elbows. His brow furrows, the light from the lamp overhead casting shadows over his face, making him look older, and tired. "And that in turn weakened the Line, our connection to him, to each other. It made the Line vulnerable. And then the witches came."

Amryn and I look at each other. "Morgan." Amryn says. He looks over at Elise. "Morgan, Lordain's wife, she's one of them."

Tal makes a sound like a growl, low in his throat, and I turn to look at him. He avoids my eyes, staring at the table.

"Yes, she is." Elise says, pulling her long black braid over her shoulder, fidgeting with the end of it. "She's evil."

"The witches corrupted the old magic," Ebony says. "They twisted the Line and gave the alphas power they shouldn't have had. And the angels kept the Old God weak, because without him, they had supreme power over the Earth Realm."

"Zadkiel, he was with the demons when they attacked Nilau." I say. "But he said he's on our side."

Ebony nods, a small smile spreading across her lips. "Zadkiel is a tricky one, but he's an ally. He hates the other archangels, ever since he saved that crazy man's kid up on that mountain. They all make fun of him." She shakes her head and sighs. "Zadkiel loves the Earth

Realm, and he loves humans, and demons, though he'd never admit it."

"So why did he ally himself with the Hjoldep clan?" Amryn asks, and his hand rubs over his chest, the spot where the dart hit him. My stomach lurches, and I grasp his hand tighter.

"He didn't. It was a trick." Liall tells us. "He needed to remove Cora from the clan in Nilau, without arousing suspicion. It had to look like he was working against her."

Amryn shakes his head. "Yeah, and killing me sure was good cover."

"It was the only way to break the spell, sweetie." Elise says, and her eyes flash to Tal for a moment. "We were all terrified. We didn't know if it would work, even though Zadkiel assured us the blood magic wouldn't kill you, not permanently at least. We needed you both free of the spell, and we needed Cora to come into her power. The Ascension activated it, but because of the Line being corrupted, it will take more."

My head is spinning, and I put my head down, taking a deep breath. "So why did Lordain kill my parents?"

"They knew you were the Shadow Queen, honey." Ebony says. "They knew, the moment you were born, when they saw your white veins, they knew."

"We all felt it." Tal says suddenly, and I look up at him. "It was like - the air became heavier the day you were born. Something important had happened."

"And the other clan leaders, they didn't want that." Liall shakes his head, running a hand through his hair. "Much like the angels, they now had reason to not want

222

the Old God to regain his power. There was no way they would relinquish all the power they'd been granted, all the control they now had over what they called Fate."

"There was a night," Ebony says, clasping her hands together tightly, "where they sent assassins to kill you. You would have been no more than 3 years old."

"Heath mentioned it to me when I was in Sfayder." Even though I knew already, hearing it again sends nausea coursing through me.

"Tallesaign killed them." Elise says, looking up at him.

My eyes flash to him, and Tal shifts on his feet. He gives me a brief smile. "You and Amryn were in there, I had to protect you both."

"How old were you?" Amryn asks.

"Seventeen." He replies, and his eyes go back to the table.

I can't stand this. I jump out of my seat and put my arms around Tal, hugging him close to me. I feel him tense for a second, and then his arms go around me tentatively. He feels familiar, like Amryn, but different. I clench my eyes shut, and I remember something, faintly, a teenage boy watching me fly, laughing, waving.

I let him go and look up at him, and his hazel eyes gaze at me sadly. He raises a hand to my cheek. I feel a deep ache in my chest, an old and distant echo, and I know I loved him deeply as a child. The adoring big brother. The one who slept on the porch to protect us. The one who taught us how to fly.

Elise sobs quietly, and the sound tears me from my memories. Tal laughs softly, self-consciously, and takes a step back from me. "There's - there's a lot there." He says to me.

Amryn looks at me as I sit down, and I can see the pain in his face. So much loss. So much time, gone. I put my hand back in his, and smile at him. He nods and pulls me close, putting an arm around me and pressing his lips to my forehead.

"So why did Lordain take us?" I ask. "Why didn't they just kill us like the other clan leaders intended to?"

"Power." Ebony replies.

"It was Roche's idea," Liall says, shaking his head. "There'd been a meeting, and the other clan leaders had heard about Cora, and about you, Amryn."

"Me?" Amryn asks.

Liall nods. "They knew about the bond between the two of you. The Line had been corrupted, but the Witches couldn't control everything. And the Line between the two of you, it was obvious, to everyone."

Amryn scoffs, laughing bitterly. "He fucking knew." He turns to me, his brow furrowed with pain. "When my Mom died, he said I would always be alone. That was years before the Council told us our Fate. He fucking -" Amryn breaks off, his shoulders heaving. "He fucking knew."

I hear Tal suck in a breath as I clutch Amryn to me. "I'm so sorry." I murmur.

Amryn shakes his head. "OK, so what then? How did Lordain get the support of the other clans?"

Ebony shrugs. "He didn't. He defied the other clan leaders and claimed you for himself. He's a power hungry bastard. And he thought that if he abused you long enough, beat you both down, he'd be able to control you, to keep you for his own ends. To -" She takes a deep breath, her hands balling into fists onto the table. "To - to breed Cora with his own useless offspring, to create some sort of private army."

"They kidnapped half the clan, to increase their numbers, to make themselves the largest clan, to take our power for themselves." Liall frowns for a moment. "They tore children from their parents, as many as they could take. Including -" He looks at Ebony, who has gone pale, her eyes unfocused. "Including our girl."

"I got back to the cabin, and Anya and Elspeth were gone," Ebony says, and her shoulders heave for a moment, "and so were you kids."

"I tried to stop them." Tal says, and his face crumples. He sucks in a breath through gritted teeth. "Rodelth, and Astrid, and me and Dad. We tried to stop them. And then that fucking witch, she hit me with something, some blood magic, and I was frozen. All I could do was watch." He looks at Amryn. "Dad took the first hit, shielding us. He died instantly."

Amryn pushes himself away from the table, putting his hands on his knees, his eyes closed. "I - I remember. I remember - something. You calling out to me."

Tal nods briefly. "Yeah. I was telling you to run. To fly. But you were so little, and you were scared. You and Cora and Ceili, you were crying." He clears his throat, and walks back to the fireplace.

225

"Astrid fell next." Ebony says to me, and she wipes a tear from her cheek. "She had the drop on the witch, had a knife to her throat. And then Lordain, he - he hit her with his flames. Your father -" she raises her tear-filled eyes to me, "I've never heard anyone make a sound like that. I'll never forget his face."

My lips tremble, and I clasp my hands to my mouth. My mother. My father. They had tried to rescue us. Amryn gets out of his chair, and kneels beside me, holding me to him.

"And then Lordain killed Rodelth." Liall says.

"How?" I ask. There's silence, and I raise my head to look at them all. "How?"

"Honey," Elise says hesitantly, "I don't know if you want to hear this."

"I'm going to kill him, and I want to know how to kill him when I do." I say through my tears. "I want to make him suffer the way my father suffered."

"He burned his head from his body." Tal says. "He put his hands around his neck, and hit him with his flames, until -" He turns around, walking back to the table, and leans on his balled fists, looking into my eyes. "I'll be there when you kill him. We both will be, right, brother?"

Amryn looks at him and nods. "We sure fucking will."

"We need to get ready to fight." Tal says, looking around the table at our family.

Our family.

"Cora isn't ready yet," Liall says, "she needs to harness the Inera first."

226

"The Inera?" I ask.

Liall nods. "The power you have, what killed Roche, and Ragnar's son. That's the Inera. Your core power. You'll be able to flatten cities one day, if you want to. But you need to learn how to control it first."

"How?" I ask. "I don't even know how it starts, and -" I shake my head. "I'm afraid of it."

"We'll find a way." Amryn says to me.

Tal looks down at Amryn. "Her flames can't hurt you, and neither can the Inera." He gestures at me. "You're her Draw." He smirks and looks at me. "You can use him for target practice."

We all chuckle, and the tension in the room dissipates. I look at Amryn, and he gives me a crooked grin. "We'll figure it out. Then we'll go back to Nilau, and we'll fucking destroy them. And we'll bring our clan back here, back home."

15
Amryn

I roll over again, punching my pillow for the fourteenth time, hoping that now it'll be comfortable enough for me to drift off. But it's no use.

Cora has been sleeping peacefully beside me for an hour, soft and warm, but every time I close my eyes, I see smoke and flames and I hear my brother calling out for me. I tried holding her, hoping her sweet scent would help unfurl the knots in my stomach, but I'm too tense. Maybe I should wake her up and fuck her to try and release what I'm feeling, but I roll my eyes at myself. Fucking juvenile.

I get up out of the bed, and pull my clothes on. I pause in the lounge room of the cabin, looking around, unsure of what to do. I can't focus. I need to move. I need fresh air.

Out on the porch, the rain rings across the tin roof above me. I inhale deeply, and the rain smells different here. Warmer. Fresher. Maybe it's just because this is home.

A light at the far end of the porch draws my attention, dim, glowing orange. As it dies away, I realise it's a cigarette. My eyes adjust to the darkness, and I see it's Tal standing there, leaning against the wall, his head down.

I approach him slowly, and his head stays down. "Hey." I say quietly when I reach him, leaning against the wall beside him.

His hand moves out in front of me, and he's offering me a cigarette. I accept it, and he raises his hand, a small orange flame coming from his palm, and I lean over it, lighting the cigarette. It doesn't taste like regular tobacco, somehow sweeter, the smoke rising white in the darkness.

"I'm sorry." Tal says.

"For what?" I ask.

"Not fighting harder to get you." He flicks his cigarette, and shifts on his feet.

"You weren't to blame, she hit you with blood magic, man. There's no fighting that."

Tal scoffs, and sucks on his cigarette, the orange glow illuminating his furrowed brow. "I'm still sorry. I thought about coming to get you, so many times, over the years. I could - I could feel that you were alone." He looks over at me. "We had informants over the years, Aevens. Shifters, I guess you'd call them. They'd fly over Nilau in their crow form, and they'd report back to us."

I inhale on the cigarette, waiting for him to continue, just wanting to keep hearing his voice. He sounds like my father, a little. Like me. My brother. My family. Just keep talking.

He scratches his cheek. "One of them reported back to say that you and Cora, they'd spotted you sleeping in a bed together. And I just, I don't know." He shrugs. "I know this probably sounds weird, but I'm proud of you for, you know, starting the thing with Cora. It's good. Knowing you weren't alone. It's good."

"I love her." I say simply. "All those years I was sure that I would have to let her go, because I was the Draw, and the Draw wasn't allowed to have anyone."

Tal scoffs. "It's bullshit. The new clans made that shit up, more power plays. Cora's parents were Alpha and Draw." He throws his cigarette into a water-filled bucket beside him, where it goes out with a hiss. "The point was to isolate you, to make sure you were alone, so you and Cora would never know that you were bound to each other. Because with her, your powers grow, and with you, she's untouchable."

"It still doesn't even make sense to me why Lordain would keep us together at all."

"Lordain's fucking stupid." Tal replies. "He probably saw it as an asset for his useless fucking kid, to have a more powerful Draw. But that's his downfall, he doesn't understand shit. He's blinded, and his witch doesn't help. She drives it."

I suck on the cigarette, feeling the tension release out of my back as the sweet smoke plays across my tongue.

"She killed Mom." Tal says quietly.

My head snaps towards him. "What?"

Tal nods. "I felt it happen. She drugged her, gave her some fucking poison, said it would help her relax. Mom was totally immobile. She had to lie there and watch this fucking witch slice open her arms. She was -" Tal's chest heaves, and he pulls his shoulders up. "She was crying for you, because you were asleep in the next room. She knew you'd find her."

I lurch forward, the cigarette falling from my hands. I lean on the post of the porch, sucking in the humid night air. Tears burn my eyes as I remember, walking into the bathroom. My Mom's hand hanging over the edge of the bath, blood dripping from her fingers, pooling on the floor. Her skin ice cold. I press a fist to my eye, trying to stop the tears, but suddenly Tal has grabbed me in a bear hug, and I gasp.

"I'm so sorry," he says again, his voice gruff. "I'm so sorry, little brother."

A breathless sob escapes me, and I clench my eyes shut. I remember him. I remember him carrying me on his back, through the woods, pointing at butterflies, knowing I liked the blue ones best. Teaching me to swim, in the pond with the waterfall. Showing me how to fly. A face like mine, smiling back at me.

"I remember you." I say, and Tal exhales shakily. I pull back from him and look at his face, my face, just older, weary. "I remember."

"The spell's breaking," he says, nodding. "It'll take a while. It's easier to make kids forget. But it'll come back. It'll all come back." He steps back from me, and sighs. "We have to help Cora. She has to get ready for what's to come."

"What is coming?" I ask.

"Michael's back." Tal replies. "He can feel that the Shadow Queen is awakening, and he'll do anything he can to stop it, because if she comes to her full power, that means his little angel mutiny was unsuccessful. He and Gabriel buried the last Shadow Queen, and he'll want to do the same to Cora."

"Is that why they're allying themselves with the demons?"

Tal nods. "The other clans are on the wrong side now. The side that cast us out of the Halls in the first place, to weaken the Old God and have free reign over the Halls and Earth." He puts a hand on my shoulder. "You know what to do. You're a warrior. You know how to train her."

"I don't know the first thing about the Inera," I tell him.

"You will." He nods, and steps back from me. "Go and get some sleep, brother. It's late."

I watch him retreat into the darkness, and my shoulders relax. Even with what's coming, even with the dangers that are imminent, I feel good. I feel better. Maybe it is being home. Maybe it's whatever was in that fucking cigarette, sweet and heady. Either way, I feel better now. Like something has released.

I head back into the cabin quietly, hoping Cora is still asleep, that she hasn't woken in a panic to find me gone. I sneak into the bedroom, pulling off my clothes and climbing into the warm bed beside her.

Instantly, she turns over, and her mouth is on me, her arms pulling me closer. I don't hesitate for a second, the thrill of having her to come to bed to, to climb into bed with, is so fucking sweet. I want to taste her, I want her on

232

my mouth, and I pull her up towards me, pressing against her thighs and guiding her up over my shoulders.

"Wait, wait," she says, turning herself the other way, so she's facing my feet.

I pull her down onto my face hungrily, licking and sucking on her clit, her taste making my head spin. I feel her lean forward, and then her mouth is on my cock, and I moan into her pussy. Her tongue swirls over me as my tongue works her clit, and fuck this feeling is incredible.

Her hand fists the base of my cock, and she takes more of me into her mouth, taking me down, down, further, and everything is wet and hot. Her hand slides up and down my shaft along with her tongue and her sweet fucking lips, and my own mouth probes her harder. She draws me further into her throat, moaning as she does, her lips and tongue vibrating around my cock, and I groan with a mouthful of clit.

She's moving up and down my cock faster now, and I follow her lead, licking and sucking her harder. I grip her thighs, holding her to me, determined to make her come first, but her fingers slide over the head of my cock, her lips pressing against the shaft as she kisses me, her tongue playing over my skin.

Her mouth moves back over me, and as she slides even more of me into her throat, she puts her other hand around my balls, rolling them gently in her hands. My stomach constricts as a wave of heat washes over me, and I explode in her mouth, her head bobbing up and down lightly as she swallows every last drop of my release.

I keep licking through my climax, my head swimming with sheer fucking arousal, and she releases my cock, sitting up on my face. I push my mouth against her, feeling her thighs shaking, her back elongating. She moans loudly, her hands gripping mine on her thighs. Her movements become smaller, and she's gasping in little breaths, and then her whole body shakes, her veins glowing bright white in the darkness, her head thrown back as she cries out.

I keep licking as she subsides, until she whimpers and pulls herself away from me, convulsing gently on the bed, her breath shaky against me.

"Why does everyone say a 69 is no fun?" She asks breathlessly. "Because that was definitely fun."

I chuckle, my hand straying over her legs curled up beside me. "Maybe they're just bad at it."

She sighs heavily, and stretches out on the bed. "Starting to come with your cock in my mouth, that was, that was something alright." She runs a hand over her face and laughs. "I liked that a lot." She sits up, and her veins are still glowing. She runs a hand over my stomach. "You're glowing too." She says quietly.

I raise my hand, and my veins are orange. "Must have been really good then." I say.

"I'm scared." She says suddenly. "What if I can't control it?"

I sit up and take her face in my hands. "Baby, you can. We'll do it. OK? I promise."

"But what if I can't -"

"You can." I insist. "You can, and you will. We just need to find the way. I swear to you, we'll figure this out."

She sighs heavily. "OK. I trust you."

"We'll start tomorrow." I pull her down onto the bed with me, tucking her under my arm, holding her close. "You'll see. It'll be OK."

"OK. Again." I say, holding up my hands.

Cora rolls her head on her shoulders, an exasperated sigh escaping her. "Fuck this."

"Come on, again."

She shakes her head. "Amryn, I can't. I can't fucking do this."

"Yes you can." I assure her. "Come on, you just need to focus."

She eyes me cynically, then closes her eyes again. The warm summer breeze blows across the field we're standing on, catching her hair, straying curls across her face. I see her exhale through her pursed lips, and she pushes her hands out in front of her, sending a shower of sparks dancing across the swaying grass.

"Fuck!" She sends a fireball into the ground, clawing her hands through her hair. "I can't fucking do this!"

"Baby, come on," I say, walking to her side, putting a hand to her cheek. "You can do it."

"No, I fucking can't," she spits back, "we've been out here for hours, and I can't summon more than a fucking spark and it's not the same thing."

"You just need to remember the feeling when it happened last time," I tell her gently, "focus on that, and draw it out -"

"Fuck you!" She pushes back against my chest hard, her green eyes blazing. "You want me to go back to those places? That's what you want me to draw on? One time I had a fucking drugged up demon on top of me trying to rape me, and then the other time I was watching you get whipped and thought you were about to have your throat slit open!"

Fuck. I'm an idiot. I move towards her to take her into my arms. "Baby. I'm sorry -"

"No!" She pushes me away again, shaking her head. "Fuck you, Amryn! And fuck this stupid power! If that's what it takes to summon it, if I have to go to that place every single time, I don't want it. It'll destroy me. I can't relive all of that, every single fucking time, I can't - I can't - " She breaks off, turning away from me and clutching her hands to her stomach. "I can't fucking do this."

I approach her from behind, putting my hands gently on her shoulders as they heave, as she tries to breathe. "I'm so sorry. I'm a fucking idiot." I say to her softly.

"Yes, you are." She retorts, pushing her hair out of her face with the back of her hand.

"You're right. It can't come from a place of fear." I turn her around to face me, and her eyes avoid mine. "Look at me." She won't. "Baby, look at me. Please."

With a sigh, her eyes meet mine. "What?"

"You can do this." I hold on to her as she sighs with exasperation and turns to leave. "Just not now. It's enough

236

for today." I pull her close to me, and kiss the top of her head, feeling her relax against me. "Come on, it's hot. Let's go cool off." I take her hand and pull her across the meadow, down the hill.

"Where are we going?" She asks as we approach the tree line.

I grin over my shoulder at her. "You don't remember this place?"

She looks beyond me, and her eyes narrow as she takes in her surroundings. "The water hole?" She asks suddenly. We can hear water flowing as we approach, and as we move through the trees it gets louder and louder.

We come to a clearing, and a waterfall thunders over the rocks, down the short distance into the water hole below. The water is clear and blue, sand and pebbles glistening in the sunlight.

Cora's eyes light up as she looks at me. "This is where we learned to swim!" She cries. With a joyous laugh she tears the shirt off over her head and shuffles her shorts down her legs, running naked into the water. I strip off quickly and run after her, seizing her in my arms. She squeals loudly as I plunge her into the cool water. "You asshole!" She cries, laughing as she grabs on to me, pulling me under with her.

She wraps herself around me, and I stand up, my hands under her ass, and carry her over to the waterfall. "You want a soaking, I'll give you one." I say, and I laugh as she clings to me, the falls pouring over us as we go through them to the pond just behind them.

Cora pushes her wet hair out of her face, and looks up at the roof of the cave we're in, which is bright with craggy crystals, reflecting the sunlight that dances through the veil of water. "This place is beautiful."

"Yes it is." I reply, and she turns to me to see I'm looking right at her. "Really beautiful."

Cora smiles, and wraps her arms around me tighter, putting her lips against my neck. "I love you." She whispers.

"I love you too." I reply. My heart still swells every time I say it.

She pulls back a little and looks into my eyes, a sheepish smile on her face. "Can I ask you something?"

"Of course."

"When you were with Ceili -"

"Oh fuck, Cora, come on." I don't want to talk about this.

She climbs down off me. "I mean, did you - did she - did she do anything that I don't do?"

"No, baby, she didn't. We were both really drunk, and that was it."

"So," Cora goes on, fidgeting with her fingers, "you didn't do anything different with her, that you'd want to do again?"

My stomach drops a little, and I don't want to lie to her, but I also don't want to have this conversation. "Baby, it was just sex. Nothing more. That was all. She was horny and drunk and I was horny and drunk and I wanted you, and -" I shake my head.

"So what did you do?"

"You want to know how I fucked your cousin?" I ask incredulously. "Baby, come on, you don't actually want to know."

"Yes I do." Her eyes flash with defiance. "I do."

"Why?"

"Because -" She breaks off.

"Because you're jealous." I finish her sentence for her. That's all this is. "You're jealous and you're insecure about it."

"Why won't you just tell me?"

"Because it doesn't matter!"

She shakes her head. "It does matter!

"Cora, this is ridiculous, and I'm not telling you which positions I fucked your cousin in." I push through the water, out of the cave and under the falls, back out into the sunlight.

"Just tell me!" She calls, splashing through the water after me. "If it didn't mean anything, you could just tell me!"

"It'll mean something if I tell you," I call without turning around, heading for the sandy shore. "It'll mean you're upset because you know something you don't need to."

She reaches me and grabs on to my arm, forcing me to turn towards her. "Just tell me!"

"No."

"Why not?" Her eyes flash with fury.

"Because it's none of your fucking business!" I retort. "Have I ever asked you once, one fucking time, whether you and Finn did anything?"

Her eyes widen. "I can't believe you just said that."

"Well?" I raise my eyebrows. "Have I?"

"That's not even close to the same thing!"

"No? Why? Because you were married to him?" I'm losing patience for this.

"Because you know I never did, that's why."

"Never?" I lean closer to her, and her face darkens. "You never made out with him, no fumblings in the back of his car, anything to avoid actual sex but doing just enough to make him feel like a big man and keep the lie going?" I know I'm being cruel now, and my own jealousy is rearing its ugly head.

Her veins glow brighter. "Just fucking tell me what you and Ceili did and stop being a fucking jerk!"

"Fine!" I shout. "She sucked my cock, and then I fucked her from behind, and she wanted me to fuck her in the ass, so I did, and she loved it, OK?"

Cora's mouth drops open. "You did what?"

I take a deep breath. Shit. This isn't how this conversation was supposed to go. "I told you, you didn't want to know."

She crosses her arms over her chest. "And then?"

"What and then?" I ask.

"She said you went back to your place and kept going."

"Oh my god, Cora." I laugh, because this conversation is becoming more absurd by the second. "You cannot be - "

"Tell me!" She cries, and her eyes are shining with tears.

"Why?"

"Because she had what was mine and I want to know why!" She buries her face in her hands.

I run a hand over my face, and step forward to pull her close. "Baby, it was sex. That was all. It was nothing more than that, and Ceili and I both knew that. I didn't do it because I love her or because I want her more than you or anything, it was just drunken sex, and I was hurting, and that was all." I tilt her face up to mine. "You are who I want. And sex with you is a fucking drug, I can't get enough of it. OK?"

Her mouth is pulled down into a frown, and she sniffs, trying not to cry. "It killed me knowing that you'd done that. I know that makes me selfish and horrible."

"No it doesn't," I tell her.

"I hated you." Her face crumples. "I was so angry. I was so jealous. And then, then I thought I'd lost you, and you died in my arms, and the last words we'd spoken to each other were in anger, and -" She buries her face in my chest.

I simply hold her for a while, because there's nothing else to say. She's hurting. She's scared. She's overwhelmed. I know it. And we don't know what the coming days or weeks will bring.

Cora pulls back and looks at me, and her nose is all red from crying and she's pouting and she looks so sweet and sad. "I'm an asshole." She says.

I chuckle and plant a kiss on the tip of her nose. "No you're not. You're just a regular old jealous girlfriend. I love you, and I want to have sex with you, no one else, OK?"

She nods. "I'm sorry."

"Don't apologise," I reply. "I'm sorry I told you."

"I can't believe I'm going off on you like this when we have bigger things to worry about." She says with a laugh. "Hey, the world could be ending, but also did you have fun with my cousin." She shakes her head. "I'm an idiot."

"Enough." I hold her face in my hands, and kiss her, long, slow, and deep. Her skin is cool from the springwater, her lips warming under mine. "You're perfect," I murmur against her mouth. "You're perfect and I love you."

"I love you too." She bites her lip. "Finn and I never did anything beyond kissing. He tried to, a few times, but it never went beyond groping over clothes. I promise."

"You don't owe me an explanation. It was a weird situation." I hate the part of myself that's relieved he never had her, never got to take her willingly, never got to have what I have.

"Let's go for a swim before we head back," she says, and takes my hand, pulling me back towards the thundering waterfall. She pulls me under the water's surface, pressing herself against me, and I'm pretty sure that this is what heaven must feel like.

242

If I die again, I hope it feels like this.

Cora blinks at me in the morning light, smiling. "Good morning."

I run a hand down her naked back. "Morning, baby." I trail kisses down her shoulder, pushing her hair aside to kiss the back of her neck. "I had an idea."

Her brow furrows as she frowns at me. "What idea?"

"Come here." I sit up and pull her on top of me, so she's straddling me. I lean back on one hand, and she looks down at my swollen cock, then back at me with a crooked grin.

"This was your idea?" She chuckles. "I mean, I'm not saying I mind, but..."

"Look, just trust me, OK?" I grip her hip with one hand, lifting her on to me.

Her hands dig into my shoulder as she sinks down on to me, and she gasps. "So what is this in aid of?" She asks. She rolls her hips on me, and bites her lip. "Or did you just want to come up with a new creative way to get laid?"

Her movements make my head swim for a moment, and I dig my hand into her hip. "So," I say with a sigh, "I wanted you to think about how this feels."

"Mmm." Cora keeps rolling her hips over my cock. "It feels good."

I breathe in deeply, trying to stay focused, even though she's riding me and she's hot and wet and her breasts are bouncing right in front of me and - fuck. Concentrate.

243

"Now, when the Inera starts, where do you feel it first?" I put my hand on her chest. "Show me."

She gasps a little as she keeps riding me, pushing my hand lower, to just below her ribcage. She leans back, and I have to grit my teeth to concentrate. Focus. Fucking *focus*. "And what does it feel like?"

"Hot." She moans. "It's just hot."

"Like fire?" Fuck she's so wet. "Burning?"

She shakes her head, her hips working me harder. "Like a fever."

"And where does it go then?" I ask.

She pushes my hand onto her thigh. "My legs." She pushes herself back further, her hands against my chest. "And my arms. And it's, oh, it's so hot." Her head tips back, and her hips roll harder, and she feels so fucking perfect.

I almost lose concentration for a second, aching to flip her over and grind myself into her, fuck her until she's screaming my name. Her veins are glowing, brighter and brighter, my own starting to match hers, glowing orange.

Oh fuck. Focus. Focus. "And what happens then?"

She's moving harder now, her hips undulating, and she tips her face towards me, her eyes fixing on me. They're completely white. "Then my whole body," she gasps, "it's like the fever."

I dig my fingernails into my palm, to distract myself, to stop myself coming. "And where -" Oh fuck. "And then where does it go?"

She moves my hand to between her breasts. "Here." She moans loudly, and the glow of her veins is so intense now the room is flooded with light. I can feel her pussy becoming tighter, and she's about to come. She's riding me hard now, her whole body is hot, searingly hot, and it makes me sweat, I can feel it running down my back.

"And then?" I pant, my hand digging into the bedsheets, gripping them as I feel my own climax rising.

With a loud cry, she comes, and there's an explosion of light in the room, the ground beneath us shaking as the shockwave bursts through the cabin. I clasp her to me as my own climax releases inside her, groaning against her illuminated skin.

"Oh my god," she gasps, breathing heavily. "Oh fuck."

"Was that it?" I ask, panting against her chest.

"Yes." She covers her face with her hand. "Oh fuck. Yes. That was it."

"Amryn!" There's frantic banging and shouting outside the cabin. "Cora! Amryn! Are you both OK?" It's Liall's voice.

We look at each other and burst into breathless laughter. "We're fine!" I call out. "Just trying something!"

"Sorry!" Cora calls, and wraps her arms around my neck, clutching me to her chest, which is shaking as she continues to laugh.

"OK, well, breakfast is ready if you two are done blowing up the village!" Liall says, and I swear I hear him chuckle.

"So was that your idea?" Cora asks, running her hands through my hair. "Did you achieve what you set out to do?"

"I sure did." I look into her eyes. "Something you said yesterday got me thinking."

"And what was that?"

My fingers trace over her shoulders, over the white veins that are starting to dim. "About the Inera coming from a place of fear. You're right. It would destroy you. It would be coming from a place of instability. It's not the way to harness your power."

"So you thought you'd introduce it into the bedroom?" She asks with a grin.

"I wanted it to come from a place of control, of security." I tell her, stroking her cheek. "I wanted it be something you summon from a place of love, of feeling good, not fear or sadness or anger."

"Well I think it worked." Cora says, and looks around the room. "I didn't blow the cabin up luckily."

"Only a minor earthquake." I agree, chuckling.

"Guess it gives a new meaning to the term earth-shattering orgasm." She jokes as she climbs off me. She throws herself down on the bed, gazing at me, her fingers tracing over my shoulders, my veins still glowing orange. "You're getting more powerful too. I can feel it."

"Well, I have to, if I'm going to protect you, baby." I push a stray curl out of her face. "And if there's a war coming -" I sigh, breaking off. I don't want to think about it, even though I know we have to. The thought that we could lose each other now makes my chest ache.

246

Cora's eyeing me uncertainly, so I smile at her and pull her off the bed. "Come on, breakfast. They're all waiting for us." I don't want her to know I'm worried. I don't want to scare her anymore than she already is.

Tal is sitting outside Ebony's cabin with a mug in his hands, and he shakes his head as we approach, a grin on his face. "Maybe some warning next time you two decide to set off any landmines, huh?"

Cora covers her face with her hands. "Oh god."

"Yeah him too, no doubt," Tal says, chuckling. He gestures for us to follow as he opens the door to Ebony's cabin. "Come on, breakfast. You two need your strength."

Ebony is setting out fruit and bread on the table as we walk in, and she meets us with a wide smile. "Good morning!" She says. "How's summoning the Inera going?"

Tal bursts out laughing, and I suppress a chuckle as I look down at Cora's face, which has gone bright red. "It's, uh, it's going great." I reply. Tal walks past me and digs me in the ribs, shaking his head, his shoulders still shaking as he laughs quietly.

Ebony's brow crinkles in confusion, but she merely shrugs and goes back to setting the table.

The door opens behind us, and a young man I haven't met before walks in, wearing a black hooded cloak. He gives me a quick nod, and hurries over to Ebony, who regards him with a stern look. He leans down to speak to her quietly, and Ebony waves her hands, gesturing to us, "Oh Yassin, it's OK," she says, "you can speak freely in front of them."

The young man pushes the hood off his head to reveal rust-coloured hair, and a large scar on his left cheek, dark against his brown skin. He nods to me again. "I meant no disrespect."

"No, none taken."

"We've spotted some movement, on the roads and in the skies," he says to us, looking at each of us in turn, "the Hjoldep clan have mobilised, and moved to Nilau."

"Son of a bitch," Tal mutters, sinking down into a chair by the table. "Ragnar's teaming up with his old enemy."

"That's not all," Yassin says, "it would appear Michael is there too."

Fuck. Tal's eyes meet mine. This isn't good.

"Michael?" Cora asks in a small voice. "As in -"

"Yes, the archangel," Yassin says.

"What does he have to do with all this?" Cora asks.

"He's sensed you're waking up," I tell her, turning to her and putting my hands on her shoulders. "He destroyed the last Shadow Queen, and now he's sensed there's a new one."

Her eyebrows shoot up. "And you knew this?" She asks, and scoffs. "You knew he would want to come and kill me?"

"Cora, I -" I try to take her face in my hands, but she slaps me away.

"You all knew this?" She backs away from me, looking around the room. "You all knew this wasn't about just defeating the clans, just about making it so the Old God could come back? Now it's about an archangel wanting to kill me?"

Ebony clasps her hands to her chest and moves around the table. "Honey, the world needs you, without you, the chaos will continue."

"I can't defeat an archangel!" Cora shakes her head.

"With the Inera, you can," Ebony assures her.

Cora scoffs. "I can barely summon it much less control it, and now - now there's a fucking archangel out to try and kill me?

"Cora, come on." I step forward, my hands reaching out to her.

"I don't want this!" Cora cries, pushing me away. "I don't want any of this! I never did! And now I have an even bigger target on my back, and -" She breaks off, her breath catching in her throat.

"Baby, come on, we'll do this together."

"There is no We in this, Amryn!" She cries, her eyes darkening as she looks at me. "There is no Us, there is no Team. This is on me. I'm the fucking Shadow Queen and if I don't succeed, if I can't control this power, what then?" She runs a hand through her hair. "Fuck this." She storms out of the cabin, slamming the door behind her.

I go to follow her, but a hand stops me.

"I'll go, brother." Tal says to me.

"She's scared," I tell him, "she's scared she won't be able to do it."

Tal nods. "I know. I get it. Just, let me go." He walks out of the cabin after her, and thunder begins to rumble in the distance.

16
Cora

"Stop following me." I call, hearing the footsteps keep pace behind me. "I know you're there." I'm headed for the tree line, for the craggy grey cliffs that tower above them. Dark clouds are pulling together on the horizon, the hot summer breeze blowing in a storm. The footsteps continue. "Fuck off!" I don't turn around.

"You fuck off." Tal says, chuckling.

"I want to be alone." I stomp through a stream, sending water splashing, soaking my pants, but I don't care.

"And I think you need to just chill out for a second." Tal says.

I spin on my heel, rushing right up against him. "I didn't want this." I hiss at him.

"I know that." His hazel eyes are kind and warm as he looks down at me. "It fucking sucks."

"My whole life, my whole fucking life, what I wanted didn't matter." I tell him, poking him in the chest. "I wasn't allowed to love who I wanted, fuck who I wanted -"

"Well, you did though," Tal points out.

I throw my hands up and walk away from him. "Yeah, in secret, and knowing that if we ever got caught he'd be dead."

"But you still did it. Amryn, he still did it."

I turn to look at him, frowning. "What's your point?" I ask. "That we're stupid and irresponsible?"

"No, it's that you do what you want," he says with a shrug. "It doesn't matter what Fate dictates, or what anyone else thinks. You do what you want. And if you want to run away, and forget all of this and just say, fuck it, then do that."

"That's not what I meant." I sigh. "That's not what I want to do. I don't want to just leave, not when it's this important."

"So what do you mean?" Tal asks me, fixing me with an earnest gaze. "What do you want?"

I pull a spindly branch from the tree beside me and whip it across the tree trunk. "I - I want Amryn. I want to marry him. I want - I want a home. For us. And babies. A family. All the things we thought we'd never have. All the things we thought we'd never have together."

"So, have that." Tal says to me. "Being Shadow Queen doesn't mean you can't be you."

"We have a war to fight, Tal," I say with exasperation. "A fucking war. Where we might all die. And I don't - I don't want -" I inhale deeply, trying to suppress the sobs that want to escape me. I don't want to die. I don't want Amryn to die. I don't want any of them to die, and the thought that now we have to fight a war and maybe lose it

252

all, it's too much. I press my hands to my face, and I don't want to cry anymore because it's exhausting, but I do.

I feel Tal put his arms around me, and I lean into his chest. "I'm scared," I say, almost hiccuping as the sobs steal my breath. "I'm scared. I'm not a warrior."

"You're a fucking hardass though," Tal says with a laugh.

"But what if we all die?" I ask, looking up at him.

He smiles at me, stroking my cheek gently with his rough fingers. "Darlin, all we can do is hope. That's all we have. Hope, and right now. There's nothing beyond that."

I sniff. "That's kind of depressing."

"It's how the world is." He says. "Depressing, beautiful, tragic, magical, unfair. It's all of it. But if we keep hoping, and we keep trying, we keep telling ourselves that we can have what we want, no matter what, no matter how unlikely it seems, then maybe we can. Just like you and Amryn did, all these years."

I relax against Tal and breathe him in, a faint scent of sweet tobacco, wood and leather. He's warm, and familiar. "I loved you a lot, didn't I?" I ask.

"You sure did, Darlin." He responds. "Your little face would light up whenever you saw me. Our little bee."

My eyes snap up to his. "Little Bee?"

"It's what we all called you." He looks up at the canopy, the light fading as the storm rolls in. "Your Mom, she called you something, I can't remember it now, but it meant little Bee in Russian."

I wipe my eyes with the back of my hand. "My Mom was Russian?"

"She grew up over there, with a large clan. When their Alpha died, they were invited to come here, to Ocario. She didn't speak much Russian anymore, but she had these sweet little names for you and your Dad."

I sigh. "I think mine was Pcholka."

He looks at me with a smile. "Yeah, that's it. I remember now." He holds me tighter, and I close my eyes, feeling incredibly safe with him. "I love you, kiddo." He says quietly. "I'm sorry I couldn't protect you back then. But I will now. With my life."

"I love you too." I whisper, my fingers clasping on to the lapel of his jacket. "I feel safe with you." Thunder rumbles loudly. "Why little Bee?" I ask.

"Because you could fly before you could walk," Tal says with a chuckle. "Caused us all kinds of trouble. Getting up into trees and on rooftops."

Will you come look at your daughter? I clench my eyes shut at the memory.

"I wonder what they'd say now," I say, looking up into Tal's hazel eyes. "I can't fly at all anymore. I forgot how. Lordain wouldn't let us, said it was too dangerous."

Tal gives me a wide grin. "Well now that we can fix easy." He takes my hand and pulls me along the path behind him. "Come on, time for me to teach you some shit."

We pick our way along the path at the base of the cliffs, and it starts to rain as we walk. We reach a break in the rock wall, a chasm leading upwards. Tal starts climbing
254

ahead of me, swinging himself up easily and deftly. I follow him, my fingers gripping the slippery rocks, my feet propelling me up the cliff face.

By the time we reach the top I'm bathed in sweat, and I tip my head up to the falling rain, trying to catch my breath.

"Good climbing," Tal says with a grin, stripping his jacket and shirt off. He has a large scar running from his right shoulder, just under his collarbone, across his chest, ending under his ribcage. He sees me looking at it, and sweeps his long black hair away from his face. "Blood magic. It leaves some nasty shit behind."

"Tal, that must have hurt."

"Yeah, it did, but it doesn't anymore." He says with a smile. "Now, let's get you flying." He unfurls his wings behind him, rising from his back like wisps of black smoke. "OK, that's step one."

"I don't even remember how to do that." I say with a sigh.

"Think of it like, you're just opening your arms." He says to me. "Just imagine you're stretching out a part of yourself, a part you know is there."

I close my eyes, and try to imagine my wings, just being there, just being a part of me. Like opening my arms. Like extending a hand. And I feel - nothing. "Fuck." I say, kicking a stone off the edge of the cliff.

Tal laughs. "You're impatient, you know that?"

I roll my eyes at him. "I hate not being able to do things everyone else can do."

"But you can do it, and you will do it. You were flying before Amryn and he's 2 years older than you. You just have to remember it."

"Like riding a bike, right?" I ask, laughing cynically.

"Exactly like that." He grins, and he looks so much like Amryn.

"You never got married?" I ask him, and his face drops a little, surprised by the question.

He rubs the back of his neck and looks out over the valley sprawling beneath us. "Uh, no, I guess I just never found someone."

"That's too bad," I say, "you'd be a good husband. And a good dad."

He shrugs, and crosses his arms over his chest. "After I lost everyone, I guess - I dunno. I guess I didn't want there to be more people for me to lose."

"Oh Tal." I say with a sigh.

"Hey, no, it's OK," he says, shaking his head emphatically. "I'm fine. I got you all back now, and well, who knows, right?" He takes a deep breath and gestures to the sky. "Come on, we're here to fly."

"Right." I look up at the sky, willing my wings to extend, to carry me up into the falling rain. I close my eyes, and breathe out, and I feel - "Fuck. " I rub my forehead with my fingertips.

Tal laughs. "Ok, well, we have a method for teaching real impatient kids real quick." He says.

I look at him questioningly. "And that is?"

256

"Sink or swim, Darlin." He seizes me around the stomach, lifting me off my feet, and darts across the cliff top with me in his arms. I don't even have time to cry out as he hurls me off the cliff edge.

Air rushes past my ears, and blind panic fills me as I watch the ground hurtle towards me. I hold my breath, waiting for the impact. He's killed me. The fucker's killed me. I'm not going to swim, I'm going to sink.

Suddenly I hear Tal laughing and whooping, and I realise the ground isn't getting any closer. My back tingles with electricity, and I look over my shoulder to see glowing white smoke behind me, my wings waving back and forth as I hover over the trees.

Tal swoops down beside me, laughing. "White wings, nice!"

"You fucking asshole," I say to him, "you could have killed me."

"I was right behind you," he says with a roll of his eyes. "God, you're so dramatic."

"You threw me off a fucking cliff, Tal! Who's dramatic?"

"Hey, it worked didn't it?" He crosses his arms over his chest, still grinning. "You just had to believe in yourself like I do."

I shoot a fireball at him, missing him on purpose. "Fucker."

He throws his head back, laughing. "You're a feisty little bitch, you know that?"

I fly after him, summoning my flames. "Say that again!"

With a swoop of his wings he heads back towards the village. "Feisty little bitch!" He calls over his shoulder.

I shoot sparks at him, and he laughs, and I look down at the ground as it blurs under me. I'm flying. I'm flying. This feels amazing. I spiral up into the sky, feeling the rain drops racing to meet me, and I laugh as thunder rumbles overhead.

We fly back into the village, touching down outside the Great Hall, and Amryn's waiting for us, shaking his head and grinning. Elise rushes out of the hall and laughs when she sees us. "I see flying lessons went well." She says.

"You could say that." Tal says, grabbing me in a headlock and roughing up my hair.

"Ey!" I protest, pushing him away. "He threw me off a cliff!"

"She deserved it!" Tal says, pointing a finger at me. "And she threw a fireball at me!"

"I missed!"

"Only because you're a bad shot!" Tal jumps, yelping as I send sparks shooting around his feet.

Elise is laughing so hard tears are running down her cheeks, and Amryn looks like his grin is going to break his face. Tal and I pull our wings back in, and they disappear under our skin.

"That was fun, huh?" He says to me, putting an arm around my shoulders and looking down at me proudly. "You're a good kid." He presses a kiss to my temple. "Elise, I think we should break out some of that fine whiskey tonight."

"Oh yes!" She says, clapping her hands together. "Let's have a party, huh?" She puts her arm around Amryn and gazes up at him. "We have so much to celebrate." She looks around at us all, and she bites her lip. "So much to celebrate."

"I still have these things," Elise says, hauling a bag out of her closet. "They belonged to your mother."

I sit on her bed, wrapped in a towel after my shower, and watch her pull out a small green velvet satchel, and some clothes. I open the satchel and pull out a gold chain with a medallion hanging from it, a peridot in the centre, along with some gold rings and a pair of large gold hoop earrings. There's a black dress with a tight bodice, thin straps and a long skirt in amongst the clothing. I stand up and hold it up to myself in the mirror.

"Oh yes," Elise says, sitting down on the bed, smiling at my reflection. "That's very pretty."

"Thankyou for all this," I say.

"Oh honey, these are your mother's things -"

"No, I mean -" I sit down beside her on the bed, and take her hand. "I mean, everything. All of this. It's the first time I've felt like I had a proper family in a really long time."

Elise smiles and claps my hand in hers. "It's so wonderful to have you back here, you and Amryn. Now we just need to go get Ceili and the others, and everything will be perfect."

"Yes it will be," I say with a nod. "Can I ask you something?"

"Sure, honey, anything."

I take a deep breath. "Why did you all leave us there so long?" I meet her eyes hesitantly, not wanting to cause her any pain. "I mean, why didn't you just come and bust us out, immediately?" Elise sighs heavily, and I feel bad that I've ruined the mood. "It's OK, you don't have to answer, I'm sorry."

She grips my hand and shakes her head. "No, please, don't feel bad. You have a right to ask that. At first, it was simply because we didn't have the numbers, and we didn't even know where you'd been taken. As we recovered and tried to rebuild, we slowly had information filter back to us, so we finally knew where you'd gone." She stops speaking, gazing out the window.

"And then?" I ask tentatively.

She gazes back at me, and her eyes shine with tears. "The decision was made that as long as you and Amryn weren't going to be hurt, we wouldn't intervene. We knew Lordain wouldn't hurt either of you, because he wanted you for your power." She strokes my hand gently with the back of hers. "You were safe there, and we knew we weren't going to be able to protect you, not properly. It took us years to gain our strength back." She inhales heavily. "I'm sorry. Everything you and Amryn went through, so desperate to be together, and thinking you couldn't be."

"It's OK," I assure her, giving her a smile. "We're here now."

"Yes, and soon Ebony and Liall will have their daughter back too, home, where she should be. With everyone else." She reaches up and gently strokes my cheek. "Anya, too. She's still your Momma, in a way."

I try to ignore the pang in my stomach. I'm not going to think about what that's going to take, what it means to try and get everyone back here, safe, home. Not tonight. We deserve to have a little fun.

Elise leaves me to get ready, and I pull on my mother's dress, which fits me almost perfectly, except it's a tiny bit long. I guess my Mom was taller than me. I look in the mirror, and I wonder if I look like her. I look like Ebony, so maybe I do. I have to ask if someone has a photograph of her. I want to see her face. I can only remember flashes.

I put the gold hoops in my ears and hang the medallion around my neck, and head out into the cabin. Tal and Amryn are sitting at the table, glasses of whiskey in hand, and Tal's eyes land on me first. He gives a low whistle, and nudges Amryn.

His eyes widen a little. "Wow."

"Do I look pretty?" I ask, giving a little twirl.

"You look incredible." He replies.

"Ready to party, huh?" Tal says, and takes a sip of his drink.

Liall comes out of the kitchen and hands me a beer. "Maybe leave the hard liquor to these knuckleheads at this early stage of the night," he says, shaking his head and smiling.

"Are you saying I can't hold my drink?" Tal says, pretending to be insulted. "Rude."

261

Amryn looks at me meaningfully for a moment, then taps Tal on the arm. "Brother, I need you to do something for me?"

Tal nods. "And what's that?"

"Your flames can burn me, right?"

Tal's brow furrows. "Uh, yeah, sure. Can I ask why?"

Amryn turns over his arm, the mark of the Draw tattooed on his forearm now facing up. "I want this fucking thing gone." He says. "And I want you to be the one to get rid of it."

"Amryn -" I say, but stop when I see the determination in his eyes.

Tal's mouth sets in a hard line, and he nods. "Gladly." His eyes flick up to Amryn's. "I don't need to tell you this is going to hurt like a bitch, do I?"

Amryn shakes his head, and Liall rushes out of the kitchen behind them "I'll go and let Elise know you boneheads are setting each other on fire." He hurries out of the cabin.

Tal raises a hand, which glows orange, heat shimmering across the surface of his palm. He raises his eyebrows as he looks at Amryn. "Ready?"

Amryn steels himself, looking over at me, and nods. "Do it."

Tal inhales through his nose, and puts his glowing hand down on Amryn's arm, covering the tattoo. Amryn's hand balls into a fist, and he exhales through gritted teeth.

"Fuck, that stings," he says, taking another swig of whiskey. "Holy fuck."

Tal frowns as he looks down at Amryn's arm, and I clutch my hand to my face as I watch the steam and smoke rise, the smell of burning flesh filling my nose. The door flies open and Elise rushes in.

"What in hell's name are you doing?" She asks, rushing to the table.

"He wants his mark gone," Tal says simply, keeping his eyes on Amryn. "He wants to be free of their bullshit."

"Oh." Elise's face relaxes nods and puts a hand on Amryn's shoulder. "Of course you do, baby boy. Good. I'll have this healed in no time."

Amryn pounds his fist on the table. "Holy shitting fuck." He clenches his eyes closed and a laugh escapes from between his gritted teeth. "Freedom sure comes with a fucking price."

I realise I've been frozen to the spot, and give myself a shake, rushing to stand behind his chair. I put my hand over his fist on the table.

"OK," Tal says, lifting his hand from Amryn's arm. "That oughta do it."

"Ah," Amryn says, sucking in another breath through his grimace, "finally."

Elise puts her hands over the shiny red wound on Amryn's arm, and his head tips back against me. I put my hands on his face, and he looks up at me, smiling. "Well, now that's done, we can party, huh?"

Elise chuckles. "I'd tell you to stay off the whiskey after being healed, but I'm pretty sure you won't be taking that advice tonight."

Tal leans over and raises his glass to Amryn, who picks up his own and clinks against it. "Thanks, Tal." Amryn says.

"Any time," Tal says with a smile, and takes a swig.

Music starts playing outside, and Liall comes back into the cabin. "The party's starting without you," he says, waving his hand in front of him as the scent of burned flesh hits his face. "Holy shit, that smells bad."

We all laugh, and Elise sits back, looking down at Amryn's healed arm. "There now, like it was never there to begin with." She says.

"Good," Amryn says, taking my hand and kissing my palm. "I'm done with that place. Come on, let's go have some fun."

Amryn takes my hand as we walk outside, and there's people everywhere, everyone is happy and smiling and laughing and drinking. The whole village. Our village. Our people.

Music is blaring from the great hall, and despite the rain people are staying outside. Fires burn in pits dotted around the square, the lights flooding from the homes illuminating the village as night falls. Thunder rumbles and someone cheers, and then I see flames go up. Three men, emerge from the hall, their flames burning red and yellow on their arms. They approach me and bow.

"The Queen is home!" One of them calls, and everyone cheers.

"The Queen is here!" The next one says, and everyone cheers again.

264

"And the Old God sees us!" The last one says, and they shoot their flames into the sky, where they are met with a bolt of lightning. The village goes wild, sending their flames up to meet the sky as thunder booms overhead. Amryn and I step forward to join them, my white flames mingling with his orange ones as they travel into the navy blue clouds above.

Amryn looks at me, smiling. "The Queen is home." He says quietly, and brushes a kiss against my lips.

"I want to marry you." I say suddenly.

Amryn's eyes widen as he looks at me. "What?"

"I want you to be my husband," I say, not sure where this idea is coming from. It's being at home, I'm sure of it. I feel safe. It feels right. I want him to be mine. I want to be his. Of course I do. This was how it was always meant to be.

"Are you proposing to me?" He asks with a laugh. "You want me to be your husband?"

I nod. "Yep. I am. I do. Obviously."

He pulls me into his arms and crushes my lips with his. The rain continues to pelt down on us, and I wrap my arms around his neck. "Well, then I accept." He says to me when we part.

"Good." I pull him back to me and kiss him again. He's mine. Mine alone. No one else's.

We walk around and talk to the others, mingling and drinking more, and finally a whiskey glass finds its way into my hand. I know I'll regret it but I drink it anyway. I feel amazing, and every time Amryn's eyes meet mine my stomach does a little flip, because he's beautiful and he's mine and I love him.

The music gets louder, and the night is getting hotter despite the rain that won't let up, and we find ourselves dancing in the crush of the crowd outside the hall. It's wet and hot and muddy and perfect.

Amryn's behind me, his arms around my waist, his mouth on my neck, and this is how it's meant to feel, electric and hazy and delirious. I grind against him as the music booms around us, and my arm curls behind me, around his neck. I turn my head to meet his mouth, my lips opening for his, for his tongue. The whiskey is making me feel so hot, and now I just want him so badly.

I turn around and put my arms around his neck. "Take me somewhere and fuck me." I murmur into his ear. My feet are off the ground as he scoops me up against him, his mouth on mine, his teeth catching my lower lip. We move through the crowd, through the darkness to our cabin. He pushes the door open, and we stumble in, entangled, our mouths on each other.

I'm stopped as I back into the couch, and Amryn seizes me in his arms, turning me around, pressing himself against my back. He pushes down the top of my soaking wet dress, his hands over my breasts, my nipples hard from the cool rain. His mouth is on my neck as my body warms under his hands. I reach down behind me, my hands moving over his cock, swelling inside his pants.

He pushes my dress right down, onto the floor, and I undo his pants, feeling them drop as well. He tears his shirt off over his head, and then he's against me, naked, hot, urgent. The whiskey is making us both crazy. He puts

266

his hand on the back of my neck and pushes me down over the back of the couch.

"You want me to fuck you, baby?" He asks, his fingers straying over my back, moving down, between my thighs.

"Yes," I whimper, my fingers clawing into the cushions as he pushes two fingers inside me.

"How do you want me to fuck you?" He pulls his fingers out, then plunges them back in again. "You want it slow?" He moves his hand up, his wet fingers moving over my clit.

I moan loudly. "Oh god."

"Slow?" He pushes his fingers back inside me, my heat meeting him, growing and growing with every move he makes. "I need you to tell me, baby."

I shake my head, flooded with delirious pleasure. "No."

"You want it fast, do you?" His fingers swirl around my clit.

I nod. "Fuck me hard," I gasp, pressing my ass back against him, my hips rolling against his hand. "Please, oh god."

He leans over me, his hot breath on my neck. His hips push against me, and he groans as his cock slides inside me.

"Oh fuck," I breathe, my back arching as his thrusts stretch me around him. He's so hot and hard, and he's pounding into me, his hand in my hair. My body is throbbing, just for him, the whiskey and heat and haze making me feel as though I'm floating, as though we're suspended somewhere. There's just us, nothing else.

267

I put a hand between my legs, and my clit is swollen and aching as my fingers move over it, circling myself as Amryn keeps thrusting, his fingers digging into my hip. His hand moves from the back of my head to my throat, turning my mouth to meet his, bouncing me on his cock.

"You're heaven," he says with a gasp. "You were fucking made for me."

"No one's had what you have." I can barely speak. "No one ever will."

I'm moaning loudly, my fingers and his cock and his hands and his mouth sending every nerve in my body into overdrive, shimmering heat dancing across my skin as my veins glow bright white. I feel the sweat breaking out over his skin, our bodies sliding against each other.

Amryn groans as I tighten around him, and I clench my eyes shut as I begin to shake and quiver. "Oh god." I breathe, and the hot pressure between my thighs explodes, dripping over Amryn's cock. I can't breathe for a second, my body so consumed by my climax and the sweet feeling of Amryn's sweat on my skin.

He thrusts into me harder, and clutches me to him, tensing with his mouth pressed to my cheek, then shuddering deliciously as his cock pumps inside me.

My head tips back against his shoulder, and we stand there, in the light of my glowing veins, trying to catch our breath as we subside together. How is every time with him perfect, always better than the last, always leaving me feeling like I'm going to split in two?

"I love you." I gasp, entwining my fingers with his across my belly.

268

"I love you too," he says against the back of my neck. "More than anything." I turn around, perching on the back of the couch, and gaze up at him. His eyes glow in the white light, and he takes my face in his hands. "I'd die for you." He says. "I'll protect you with my life. I swear it."

"Stop it." I say, pressing my cheek against his shoulder.

"No." He tilts my face back up to look at him. "You're everything. You're my heart, and my life. And no matter what happens, I will protect you. Always."

I wrap my arms around his waist, and just breathe him in. I don't want to think about it. Not tonight. "Take me to bed." I say, and he scoops me up in his arms, carrying me to the bedroom, where I know we won't be sleeping, not for many, many hours.

17

Amryn

Cora frowns as I kiss her shoulder, burying her head under the pillow. "Uh-uh." She mutters.

I chuckle, tracing a finger down her arm. "Ok , you stay in bed," I say.

We haven't slept much, but I'm feeling a little wired. The thrill of being able to go back to Cora again and again, have her pull me to her over and over all night, has me in some weird state of euphoria. She was insatiable last night, begging for more every time it was over. My muscles ache in the best fucking way.

I go for a quick shower, then dress in jeans and a t-shirt and head outside. I need to stretch before I head back to bed and maybe fuck my fiancee some more.

Fiancee. The word makes me smile. Is it stupid to be excited about something that was inevitable? I don't care.

The village is quiet, mist rolling around the surrounding mountains. The party went on for hours, so everyone's still asleep no doubt. I walk past Ebony and Liall's cabin, and there's a knock on the kitchen window. Ebony is smiling widely at me and beckoning me to come inside.

"Good morning," she says quietly as I walk in. Tal is sleeping on the couch in front of the fire, one leg slung over the back of the couch, and an arm hanging to the floor as he snores. "He had a bit too much whiskey." Ebony says with a chuckle.

I shake my head, grinning. "Yeah I think we probably all did."

She holds a basket up. "I was going to go and pick berries for breakfast, did you want to join me?"

"Sure."

We walk through the quiet village, and Ebony links her arm through mine.

"You and Cora had fun last night?" She asks me.

"Yeah, we did." I smile down at her. "She asked me to marry her."

Ebony's eyes widen as she smiles back at me. "Oh sweetheart, that's adorable! I'm assuming you said yes."

"I did, I did." I say with a nod. "I mean, of course I did, right?"

"Well, congratulations." She hugs my arm tighter and leans her head against me. "When this is all over, we'll have a wedding to look forward to."

If we all survive it. Fuck, don't think like that. "Yeah, we sure will."

"Your parents would all be so thrilled." Ebony says wistfully as we head down the hill towards the road. "I just wish they could be here to see it."

"Yeah me too." I hesitate for a second. "I was wondering, could you tell me more about my father?"

Ebony glances up at me. "Your father?"

"Yeah. I just, I don't remember much about him, and I'd like to know a bit more."

"This is probably a conversation you should have with Tal," Ebony says.

I shrug. "I don't know if I want to... I don't know. He went through so much and I don't want to bring up bad memories for him."

"Oh sweetheart, you're a good man." She frowns down at her basket, "Your father was a decent man, loyal, strong. He adored your mother. Just worshipped her."

I keep looking down at her, but she won't go on. "I feel like there's a But somewhere in there, Ebony." I say after a while.

She shakes her head, but still won't meet my eyes. "I don't want to speak ill of your father."

"Is there something ill to tell me?"

Her eyes dart up to mine. "Oh sweetheart no, like I said, he was a decent man. He really was. He loved you all, so much. He died for you."

"I still feel like there's a But waiting to come out here." My stomach tenses a little.

She stops walking, and looks at me uncertainly. "Your father was hard on Tal," she says finally. "He was real tough, from the time Tal was old enough to train. You got a much gentler father than Tal did, and it was hard to watch sometimes. Seeing Tal sleep on the porch to protect you and Cora because Keenan told him that he was responsible -" She breaks off, shaking her head.

"I can't imagine what that would have done to Tal, when he watched them all die." I say, and feel a lump in my throat as I think back on the few memories I have of that day. Tal remembers it all. In full.

Ebony nods. "He was so young, and he was so badly hurt, we thought he was going to die. That blood magic..." Her eyes become unfocused as she loses herself in the memory. "It clings on to you, claws in to you. It poisoned him for a long time. It left behind an enormous scar. In many ways." She gives herself a shake and smiles up at me. "Sorry. I don't want you to think I didn't like your father. I did, I loved him."

"It's OK," I assure her, putting a hand on her shoulder. "People are complicated."

"They sure are." She links her arm back into mine, and we continue along the road. "There's a mass of blackberries down here, I saw them last week and they weren't quite ripe, but today they should be."

A flock of ravens fly up from the forest as we pass into the tree line, the road shadowed as we walk along it. It's incredibly quiet, even out here. The wind is completely still, the only sound our footsteps on the gravelled road.

"Here," Ebony says, stopping at a blackberry bramble, its spiky vines snaking along in the underbrush beside the

273

road. "Look at them all!" She grins at me triumphantly, and starts plucking the shiny black berries from the brush. I join in, and within minutes our fingers are stained purple.

I see movement out of the corner of my eye, and look up the road. It's a little darker, the sun passing behind a cloud, and I squint. There's someone up there, moving in the clearing of the road ahead. I expect a deer, but it's upright.

A slim figure, with pale hair.

I stand up, taking a few steps out and away from the shadows to get a better view. The figure is hugging themselves, turning around in frantic circles, as though lost.

Ebony stops picking and looks up at me. "Is everything OK?"

"There's someone there," I say, pointing down the road. The figure touches their face, and moves a little closer. That long pale hair... Oh fuck. *FUCK*. "Ceili!" I call, breaking into a run.

I hear Ebony give out a strangled cry, and she flies past me. "CEILI!" She cries.

Ceili looks in our direction, and as I get closer I see the panic in her face. She turns suddenly, looking up the hill, holding her hands out towards us, as though telling us to stop. I follow her gaze, and I can't see anything, but when I look back at her she's shaking her head wildly.

"CEILI!" Ebony cries again. "My baby!"

There's movement in the trees, and I can hear voices, yelling a sharp command. A green light glows. I stop short. "Ebony!" I call. It's a trap. Trap. Trick. "Ebony, *stop*!"
274

The green light flashes, and something hits Ceili in the side, sending her sideways to land with a heavy thud on the ground. Ebony screams, knocked off her feet. I duck into a crouch, and look up the hillside, where there is no more movement. Ebony is crawling along the floor towards Ceili, and I stay low as I run after her.

"Oh, my baby." Ebony is crying as I reach them. Ceili is in her arms, staring up at her mother wide-eyed.

"Momma?" She whispers, tears in her eyes. "Momma?"

"I'm here, my sweetheart," Ebony says, rocking her daughter gently in her arms, "it's OK, I'm here. I've got you."

It's then that I see the wound in Ceili's side. She's torn open, the flesh ripped from her ribcage, blood oozing and bubbling with every strangled breath she takes. Fuck. Fuck. Her eyes move to me.

"I'm sorry, Amryn," she gasps. "I'm so sorry. They said they'd kill Anya."

I shake my head. "No, don't be sorry, it's OK. You're going to be OK." I'm lying to her, and she can see it.

Ceili's gaze moves back to her mother. "Momma, I'm sorry. I'm sorry." Tears run down the side of her face.

"Baby, it's OK." Ebony says. "Momma's here, I've got you, you're going to be OK." She strokes Ceili's cheeks with her fingers. "Baby, it's OK, I'm here, you're with me again, I've got you."

Ceili's eyes stare at Ebony, and I see the light leave them. The sickening, bubbling flow of blood from her side stops, and she slumps against Ebony's chest.

Fuck.

No no no.

"Ceili," Ebony says urgently, shaking her daughter. "Baby? Baby?"

Ceili lies limp in her mother's arms.

Ebony howls like a wounded animal, clutching on to her daughter's dead body. My chest constricts. Ceili's dead. She's dead. They fucking killed her. I reach out and touch her hand. Fuck fuck *fuck*.

I look up around the hillsides. They're here. They've found us.

"Ebony," I grasp her shoulders, shaking her as she screams . "Ebony! I need you to listen to me now!"

"My baby," she sobs, her tear-stained face tipped to the sky.

"Ebony, they're here," I say to her, and her eyes snap open to look at me. "They're here." I say again. "You need to hide, and then you need to go back to Ocario and warn them. Do you hear me?"

"But Amryn -"

"Do you hear me?" I ask again, grasping her shoulders tighter. "You need to warn them."

"Where are you going?" She asks me, panic gripping her voice.

"I need to lead them away," I say. "I need to try and stop them. You need to hide, now."

"Amryn, they'll kill you!" Ebony grabs my hand, and I quickly shake her off.

"Go and warn them." I cast one more glance down at Ceili, and push myself off the ground.

I run up the hillside before Ebony can say anything else. I summon my flames, ready to strike. There's another green flash which hits the tree above me, sending down a shower of sparks and wood splinters.

A demon jumps up from the brush, and sends a red flame straight at me. I dodge it and send my own flames back at him, which hit him square in the chest, and he flies backwards against a tree.

There's movement up ahead, more shouting, and I push myself to move faster, run faster, tear the fuckers who just murdered Ceili limb from limb.

I run between two trees, and I'm stopped short as the burn of acid ropes itself around me. I try to cry out, but it's strangling me, and no sound comes out. I try to summon more flames, but the flames cling to my skin, like they're bound to me. I let out a strangled groan as my skin blisters.

I push back against the acid bonds holding me still, but I can't move a fucking inch. I'm suspended between the two trees. Fuck fuck fuck.

Cora. I try to reach out to her, throwing my shields down, beating against hers. She's asleep, maybe I can wake her. Maybe I can let her know. *Cora, baby. They've got me. You have to stay safe.*

Nothing. She's still sleeping.

I clench my eyes shut. *I love you.* It's all I can think, the only thing I can think to leave for her. In case... Just in case....

No, fuck that. I'm not dying out here, not now, not today. I fight against the bonds again, gritting my teeth as the acid bites into my skin. I ball my hands into fists, pulling with all my strength even as it feels like my flesh is about to be torn from my bones.

"Now, now, calm down, young lad," a voice says behind me in a thick Scottish accent. "No point in getting yourself all worked up. You'll only hurt yourself."

A man appears before me, his grey hair tucked under a green felt cap. His hands are clasped behind his back, and he's regarding me with amusement. "Hello there, Amryn." He says amicably. "Last I saw you, you were a sullen teenager. Now look at you."

Who the fuck are you? I want to ask. But I can't make any sound.

"I'm Ragnar," he says, as though sensing my question. "And I'm here to finish what Lordain was too stupid to finish all those years ago."

18
Cora

"Cora. Cora. Sweetheart."

The light before me shimmers grey, and my mother steps out of it. Not Anya. Astrid. My mother. She smiles at me, the light bouncing off her shiny golden curls.

"Hello Sweetheart." She extends a hand to me. She is taller than me, just a little. Her grey eyes twinkle. "I've missed you."

"Mom?" I take her hand, and it's cold.

"Yes, Pcholka. I'm here." She looks so much like me. I look so much like her.

"Is this a dream?" I ask, not wanting to take my eyes off her in case she melts away. Please don't wake up yet.

She shakes her head. "No. But I don't have much time." She steps closer and her face becomes earnest. "You need to be brave, sweetheart."

"I'm frightened."

"I know," she says with a soft smile, "but you have it within you to defeat them."

"I don't know what to do."

"Yes you do, and you will when the time comes." She clutches my hand tight. "My medallion. Wear it. It will protect you."

"How?"

She starts to fade, her hand feeling like vapour wrapped around mine. "Wear the medallion. When the time comes, you'll know."

"Mom." I try to grab on to her hand, even as I feel it dissipate in my grasp. Tears sting my eyes. I need more time. Please, just a few more minutes. "Mom, please."

"Keep them both close." The words echo around me.

I sit up in bed with a start. Something's wrong. I can feel it. The hairs on my arms are standing on end. The air feels charged.

The bed beside me is empty, and I remember Amryn getting out of it earlier, leaving me to sleep. Where is he? My anxiety spirals so violently I almost throw up.

I love you. The words float through my mind. Amryn's words, Amryn's voice. I have this sensation of more, floating out of reach. A warning, words on the tip of my tongue, that I just can't quite remember.

Something's wrong.

I jump out of the bed and pull on some clothes. I rush out of the cabin to find Tal and Liall standing in the courtyard, laughing as they each smoke a cigarette. They eye me with surprise as I storm towards them.

"Cora?" Tal takes a step towards me. "Is everything OK?"

280

I shake my head. "No. Something's wrong."

"What is it, honey?" Liall asks, concern furrowing his brow.

"Where's Amryn?" I ask. My stomach is in knots. I feel the echo of Amryn's mind beating against my shields. Shit shit shit.

"He went berry picking with Ebony," Liall says, gesturing towards the hills. "They've been gone a while. They should be back soon."

"Hey," Tal says, taking my shoulders and looking into my eyes, "what's going on?"

"I - I don't know," I stammer, and I feel sweat break out on my back. "Amryn, he - he tried to reach out to me, through the blood bond. Something's wrong, Tal, something's really wrong."

And then we hear it.

Screaming. Spine-chilling, guttural screaming.

"Oh shit," Tal says.

We eye each other for a split second before breaking into a run, headed for the screaming. Liall is faster than us, sprinting across the village on light feet. The screaming continues. Gets louder.

"It's Ebony!" Liall calls over his shoulder. "Ebony! Where are you?"

Fuck. Fuck. What's happened?

We run between two houses, Liall just ahead of us, and I hear him bellowing.

"No!"

Ebony keeps screaming.

As she comes in to view, I see she's stumbling towards the village, carrying something - someone - in her arms. I'm gripped by sheer terror. I can see blonde hair spilling down over Ebony's arm.

No.

No no no.

It can't be.

It can't be.

"No!" Liall bellows again. "No! Oh no!"

Ebony collapses to the ground, clutching the inert figure to her chest, her mouth torn open in a scream that just won't stop. "My baby!"

No. Oh god. No no no no no no.

Ceili's beautiful blue eyes are open, staring upwards as I throw myself down beside Ebony and Liall. Liall takes Ceili from Ebony's arms and holds her to him, her arms limp, her head lolling back.

"No, no no no!" He cries, sobbing into Ceili's hair. "My baby girl."

Ebony doubles over, clawing at the ground. "They killed my baby!" She screams into the earth. "They killed her!"

Tears burn my eyes, and Tal is beside me, clutching my hand.

Ceili's dead.

"Baby, look at me," Liall pleads, stroking Ceili's cheek. "Baby girl, wake up, it's OK, Daddy's here, you're safe

282

now, please, baby, wake up." He holds the back of her head tenderly, laying his forehead against hers, his eyes clenched shut as tears roll down his cheeks. "Daddy's here, sweetheart. Come on, wake up, please."

I reach out and touch Ceili's arm. Warmth lingers on her skin. Ceili. My sweet cousin. She was innocent, she had nothing to do with any of this. It can't be. I turn and collapse against Tal, gasping for air. His arms lock around me.

"Where's Amryn?" He asks. "Ebony, where's Amryn?"

Ebony pushes herself off the ground, sobs shaking her shoulders as she looks at Liall cradling Ceili in his arms. "He led them away," Ebony says breathlessly, "he told me to hide and he led them away, and they killed my baby." She clutches her fists to her forehead, hammering at her skull. "They killed my baby, oh god they killed my baby." A scream tears from her again.

I look up at Tal, and he frowns back at me. "They've got him," he says quietly, "they set a trap, and they caught him."

I clutch at Tal's shirt. "No." I shake my head. "No, Tal, oh god." I turn back to look at Liall and Ebony as they hold each other, their dead daughter between them.

It's started. They've brought the war to us.

They're trying to draw me out.

We sit silently around Elise's kitchen table, me, Tal, Elise and Yassin. Liall and Ebony are with Ceili in one of the bedrooms, lying with her. We can hear a sob every now and then. My heart hurts, and yet I'm overcome with a strange numbness. This can't be real.

"They've captured Amryn," Tal says suddenly, his voice low. "They've taken him to Nilau, and they're going to use him to lure Cora in to them."

"Well it's going to work." I reply, and everyone looks at me. "I'm going in to get him."

Elise reaches across the table to me. "Sweetheart, I know you want to go and save him, but that's exactly what they want you to do. They'll have traps set for you."

"I'm not leaving Amryn to die," I say, shaking my head.

"Of course not," Yassin says quickly, "but they won't kill Amryn, they'll want him alive to get you."

"No, they'll just torture him," I counter cynically.

"Honey," Elise says sternly, "if they are trying to lure you back to Nilau then there's a reason for it. They have something in place that they're sure will overpower you. We need to know what that is before we make any moves to rescuing Amryn. You're too important."

"Amryn is important." My throat is threatening to close up. "Amryn is important. He's my Draw, and I love him, and I need him. I - I need him." I break off, my fingers clawing into the table. I need him. I love him.

There's a loud rush of air outside the cabin, and footsteps on the porch. The door is pushed open, and I leap to my feet, grabbing Elise's dagger from the table.

"What the fuck are you doing here?" I yell, brandishing the dagger.

Zadkiel holds his hands up and smiles warmly at me. "Now, now, Majesty, I come in peace."

"You sure about that?" I yell, poking the dagger in his direction. "Because the last time I saw you -"

Tal is at my side. "Honey, it's OK." He says soothingly, putting a hand on mine, the one holding the dagger. "He's a friend."

I look at Tal and shake my head. "He's a slippery fuck, I don't believe him for a second."

Zadkiel takes a step forward, his head almost touching the roof of the cabin. "Majesty, you have every reason to distrust me, I understand. But I am here to help, to assist you, I swear it"

"Swear on what?" I hiss.

"On my own life."

I spit at his feet. "Worthless. Try again."

Zadkiel laughs and looks around the cabin at the rest of them. "And you said she was nervous?"

"Swear on what?" I roar, pressing the tip of the dagger into his chest.

He holds out a hand, opening it for me. My mother's medallion is lying in it. "She trusted me." He says, and gestures for me to take the medallion.

I snatch it from his hands. "Sneaking into my cabin to try and trick me, huh?"

"No, my dear. I was a close ally of your mother's. I gave her that medallion, to protect her from blood magic."

"Where the fuck were you when Lordain burned her alive?" My voice falters in my throat. "Huh? Where were you when my father's head was torn from his body? Huh? Where were you then? You useless, useless fucking -" I can't breathe suddenly, my lungs constricting as the loss and the anger and the injustice of my beautiful, innocent cousin lying dead in the next room weigh on me. My legs buckle out from under me, and Tal puts his arm around my waist.

"Honey, come on," he says quietly.

I collapse into a chair, and watch as Zadkiel moves to perch his enormous frame in the chair at the end of the table.

"I'm sorry I wasn't there when she needed me," Zadkiel says sadly. "I truly am."

"Who was she to you?" I ask weakly.

"A friend. A dear friend." Zadkiel says, clasping his hands over his lap. "I rescued your mother's clan from rivals when she was just a child, brought them here, to Ocario. I knew she was special, there was something about her." His black eyes gaze past me, out the window, and his face softens. "She had a light within her, everyone saw it. It had been a long time since I'd met someone like her. I had no idea at the time that she'd be the mother of the next Shadow Queen."

"And you gave her this medallion?" I ask, holding it up, the round pendant swinging back and forth.

"I did." Zadkiel nods. "I have few protections to offer, but this one I could give her."

I reach over and tear up Tal's shirt, revealing the scar on his chest. "And this?" I ask, my anger returning. "It never occurred to you to try and protect anyone else in this clan?"

Zadkiel lifts his hands. "Cora, I'm sorry."

"No, I am fucking tired of you angels always being sorry." I get out of my chair. "We got cast out of the Halls for being barbarians, for being too like the humans, for not being holy enough. We came down here, to try and protect humanity, while your brothers ran rampant, and you just stood by, and now you're just sorry, sorry. Sorry is *worthless.*"

"You're right." Zadkiel says, the volume of his voice rising slightly. "And I apologise. I let my brothers rule me for too long, and instead of helping you, and the humans, I simply stood by and watched. I'm -" He breaks off as he sees my eyes flash at him. "It wasn't good enough, and I hope I can make up for it now by helping you regain your full power, and defeat the evil seeking to remove you from your throne."

I regard him critically, then Ebony begins to wail again from the other room. Elise hurries out, and I grit my teeth. I want revenge. I have to get Amryn. And if Zadkiel can help me then so be it.

"Fine," I say, collapsing back into the chair. "What do I need to know? What do I need to do?"

Zadkiel leans forward on the table, his long, taloned fingers clasped before him. "The last Shadow Queen was destroyed, thousands of years ago now, by Michael and Gabriel. She was the last connection of the Old God to the Earth Realm, and without her, he lost his way down here, his ability to oversee all of humanity. The angels were free to run rampant on the Earth, with no consequences for their actions."

"Yes, I know," I say, spinning the tip of the dagger on the kitchen table, "and now I'm here, can the Old God see Earth again?"

"He's getting flashes, impressions," Zadkiel says, "but your powers aren't fully awakened yet."

"So when does that happen?" I ask.

"The next Blood Moon." He says with a nod. "Therefore, until then must we wait."

I jump out of my chair, and it tips back with a bang onto the floor. "The next Blood Moon isn't for another month." They cannot ask me to leave Amryn there for a month. They'll torture him to death. He'll die before I can get to him. My hand clutches to my chest. No.

Tal springs up beside me. "It's the only way, Cora," he says, "if you go in there now, they'll kill you. They'll kill Amryn. It'll all be over, instantly. We can't overpower Michael, not how we are now. And who knows what other traps they'll have set."

"A month, Tal," I say, tears burning my cheeks, "an entire fucking month, where they'll torture him and abuse him and god knows what else. I can't do that to him."

Tal grips my arms. "Cora, listen to me." His eyes darken. "I get it, OK? It's hell. Amryn's my brother, and I want to go in there and get him too. But they did this on

288

purpose. They want to draw you out now. They won't kill him until they have you, and if you're not at your full power when you go in there, *you will die.*"

"They will try and get him to call to you," Zadkiel warns gently, "you must ignore it if he does, as painful as it will be."

Tal shakes his head. "Amryn won't do that, believe me. He'll have those shields up."

I push Tal away, and suddenly the room is tiny and I can't breathe. Everything blurs around me, and my chest is tight. "I can't - I can't do this." I put a hand to my head. "I can't, I can't fucking do this."

A hand takes mine, and I look up, flinching when I realise it's Zadkiel. He towers over me, and smiles warmly. "Cora, you can, and you will. I will help you. I will be there for you in the way I should have been there for your mother. I swear it."

"Swear on what?" I hiss cynically.

He lowers his face to my ear. "The little curly-haired baby? The one smiling in the sunshine at his father?"

I gasp, and tears spill down my cheeks.

"I swear to you, that will be your future. I've seen it." He puts a hand on my shoulder, his impossibly long fingers curling over me. "It will be alright, I promise. It will be."

The flames of the funeral pyre leap into the inky night sky. Tal has his arm around me. I can't even cry. My tears have dried up. Ebony and Liall stand nearby, clutching on to each other, watching their only child, the daughter they hadn't seen in 17 years, turn to ash.

"They're torturing him." I say to Tal, my eyes staying on the burning flames. "I can feel it. I can sense that he's in pain."

Tal exhales heavily. "Yeah. Me too."

"Is he going to survive a month there?" I ask.

Tal shifts on his feet. "Amryn's a warrior." That's all he says. Because there is no answer. We simply don't know. I huddle in under Tal's arm.

The moon rises above us, silver and swollen.

All we have is hope. Hope, and right now.

19
Amryn

"Wake up, runt." The boot connects with my face, and sends my head snapping backwards. I can taste blood in my mouth. That's all I taste these days. Ragnar leans over me, leering at me. "How are we on this lovely day, huh?"

I struggle to my feet. I'm not going to let him see how weak I feel. How much pain I'm in.

"Room service could be better." I say, crossing my arms over my chest.

Ragnar laughs. "You think you're very tough, don't you?" He looks me over, sneering. "You pretty boys with your tattoos and your long hair, you think so much of yourselves. You're not real warriors though. Although I do hold you in slightly higher regard than, say, Lordain's moronic offspring."

"I suppose I should be flattered." I reply.

"Oh you should be, son. I respect a man who's willing to die just for some sweet little cunt." He raises his eyebrows, leaning back against the stone wall of the cell. "And she looks like she has a really sweet little cunt too. Was she good?"

"Yeah, real good."

Ragnar's eyebrows waggle as his lip curls into a grin. "Well, then I hope she's worth all of this."

"I love her." I reply. "I'd gladly die for her."

"Oh, Romeo, you are romantic." Ragnar jeers.

"Well some of us have to be," I retort, "a lesson that might have saved your son from having his guts blown out of his body."

Ragnar's face drops. "Don't you talk about my son, you fucking degenerate."

"Why not?" I'm not afraid of challenging them. What else can they possibly do to me that they haven't done these past two weeks? "Or is being a rapist something that runs in the family?"

His fist flies through the air, connecting with my jaw, and I stumble sideways. "I told Lordain to kill you," he spits, straightening up, his whole body tensing as rage courses through him. "I told that fool to kill you, and that fucking little bitch, back when you were still in nappies and crying for your mams."

I suck on my teeth, and spit out blood. "Damn, must be frustrating when no one listens to you, huh?"

"Well, Lordain has the result of it now." His lips pull back into a sneer. "I had expected Cora to come and get you before now, I do have to wonder what's keeping her. Maybe she's moved on? Decided it wasn't worth all the trouble?"

I scoff. "Yeah, maybe."

"I am told you have a brother who looks very much like you." Ragnar says, sidling towards me. "Perhaps Cora has just decided which brother she actually wants, ey?"

"Yeah, sure."

"I do wonder," he stands in front of me, his hands clasped behind his back, "maybe she's out there opening those pretty legs for him now, ey? Letting him put his cock in that sweet little cunt. While you're in here," he gestures around us, "rotting away."

"Blow me, Ragnar."

He throws his head back and laughs. "Now now, remember not to summon those flames, or you'll get burned again." He looks down at my arms, and tuts. "Such a shame for all those lovely tattoos to get ruined, ey?"

The fucking blood magic bonds around my arms burn all the time. I can't summon my flames at all, or they turn back on me. And that really fucking hurts.

"Now," Ragnar says, "I want you to call out to your lady and urge her to come and get you. I'm sick of waiting."

I laugh. "You think I'm going to call her here, to be killed by you?"

"I'm not going to kill her," Ragnar says. "Someone else has already claimed that honour."

The door to the cell opens, and an angel walks in, bent over so as to fit through the door. I'm sure his wings are meant to be white, but they're grimy and grey. The edge of one wing is a rusty brown, as though it was once dipped in blood. The angel's hair hangs over his forehead in messy copper curls, and his eyes when they look up at me are an almost neon purple. He grins, revealing yellowed teeth, sharp like Zadkiel's. .

"Hello Amryn," he drawls, "I'm Michael. Nice to meet you." His tongue runs over his lips as he looks at me. "Oh, you *are* cute though. No wonder Cora likes you."

"Thanks," I say flatly. "You look like you need a dentist."

Michael chuckles, running a hand through his oily hair. "They said you were a little fierce." He comes closer, his movements almost serpentine. "But honestly it's the fierce ones who are even more fun. I love a good -" He inhales deeply, his eyes fluttering closed. "A good fight. Oh, and you smell good, even dirty as you are. They should let you have a bath." His hand reaches out, and he takes my hair in his fingers, sniffing it. "Yeah, you smell real good under all this dirt." He puts a hand on the wall beside me, and his fetid breath washes over my face as his lips pull back in a grin. "Shall I tell them to be nice to you? Hmm? Would you like a bath? A proper meal?"

I'm backed right into the wall, trying to get as far away from him as possible. "You do whatever you want."

Michael looks over his shoulder. "I want this gorgeous specimen to have a bath, and I want him to have a good meal, something proper." His eyes move back to mine. "Something for the appetite of a man." Disgust turns my stomach as he smiles down at me. His finger drags down my chin, the sharp talon scratching my skin. "Oh Amryn, once you're all clean and fed, we'll talk again, OK?" He purses his lips together, blowing me a kiss, and sweeps out of the room.

Ragnar is laughing and shakes his head. "Those angels sure have strange taste." He walks to the door, pausing with his hand on the frame. "Someone will be along to get you for your bath soon, majesty. We'll make you all pretty for your date." His laughter disappears down the hallway.

I lean my head back against the cell wall, and I want to think of Cora, but I block that out quickly. Don't call to her. She'll come if you do. And she can't, not yet, or she would have. She wouldn't leave you here. Not without good reason.

.... Would she?

The cell door opens and I'm surprised to see Finn walk in.

"Michael said he wanted you bathed and fed," he says impatiently, his eyes blazing.

I can't help the laugh that escapes me. "They got you running errands now, huh?" I ask him, getting to my feet. "Oh how the mighty alpha has fallen." I gesture to his chest. "How'd the burn heal up?"

"Shut up, Amryn," Finn says through gritted teeth, gesturing to the door. "Come on, we got a cabin ready for you."

"How nice of you, thanks Finn." I walk out into the corridor, and Finn presses a sharp blade into my back.

"Don't even think of trying anything," he hisses into my ear.

"I just want that bath, man," I say, holding my hands up. He shoves me along the corridor, the guards looking at me critically as we pass.

The sunlight surprises me as Finn pushes me outside, and my eyes begin to water. "Keep moving," Finn commands, pushing me on. We're out in the yard, in Nilau, and it's familiar and foreign at the same time. How long since we fled? Since I was strapped to that podium, being whipped? It hasn't been that long.

Where are you, Cora?

No. I clench my teeth together. Stop it. Don't. She can't sense your distress. It's too dangerous. Stop it.

Finn pushes me into one of the smaller houses next to Anya's house, surrounded by Ragnar's guards in their pathetic military uniforms. "The bathroom's through here," he says, pointing down a hallway by the kitchen.

"I know," I say, walking ahead of him. "This is like Cora's house."

"Yeah and you knew her house real well, didn't you?" Finn spits after me.

"Sure did." I say over my shoulder. "Every inch of it."

I walk into the bathroom, and close the door behind me. I allow myself to falter for a second, just for a second. Fuck, everything hurts. I look in the mirror, and my face is a mass of bruises, trailing from my temple down my neck and across my chest. My lip is swollen, and my right eyebrow is split. My ribs ache and my back hurts from their beatings. My arms are blistered from my flames, from the fucking self-own blood magic they cast on me. Fuck this.

I turn on the shower, and strip out of the clothes I've been in for the past two weeks. They're so caked with dirt and blood that they're stiff, the colours unrecognisable.

I wince as the hot water runs over my body, catching every cut and burn and gash on my skin. I lean against the tiled walls, breathing deeply, watching the water turn rusty brown as it washes away the filth and blood I'm covered in. I put my hair under the water, and as I try to wash it, I feel a huge cut on my scalp, at the back of my head, and it fucking burns.

Hopelessness overwhelms me for a second. Right now, I'm warm and getting clean and I'm not locked in a cell. But in a few minutes, I will be again. I'll be locked up and beaten again. I just want to get out of here.

I straighten myself up. Come on. You can do this. Just get through it. She'll be here soon. They all will be. They just need to get Cora ready.

Imagine her opening her pretty legs for your brother.

I clench my eyes shut. No. Don't let them fuck with your head. That's what they want. They want to make you think they're not coming. They want to poison your mind. They want to make you desperate enough to call for her, to bring her here. They want to weaken you. Don't give up now. Don't give in to their bullshit.

The bathroom door opens and Finn walks in, a pile of fresh clothes in his hands. "Michael wants you to look nice," he says, his voice dripping with sarcasm. "Sent some clean clothes for you. And I guess someone's cooking you a steak somewhere. So, lucky you." He throws the clothes on the floor, and looks me up and down, naked in the shower.

"See anything you like, Finn?" I ask. He shakes his head and slams the door. I can't help but chuckle. I have to take the wins where I can right now.

Once I'm dressed and back out in the corridor, Finn leads me out of the cabin. Morgan and Lordain are standing outside, and they both regard me with disgust.

"Ah, the runt," Lordain says leeringly. "I see Michael has taken a liking to you."

"He's going to be so very nice to you," Morgan purrs, lifitng a cigarette to her lips.

"I sure hope so," I reply.

Lordain shakes his head. "You really don't have any shame, do you?"

"What do I have to be ashamed of?" I ask, shrugging.

"Fucking another man's wife for a start."

"The wife he raped in front of the whole clan in the name of tradition, that wife?" I scoff, and shake my head. "I don't think you're in any position to lecture me on shame, Lordain, when you let shit like that go on in your own home." Lordain lifts his fist and I tut him. "Michael just got me this new shirt and if you get blood on it, I don't think he'll be too happy."

298

Lordain's face darkens, and he spins on his heel, stalking away across the yard. Morgan turns to me, blowing out a puff of smoke which glows in the afternoon light. "Nice to see you again, Amryn," she says, reaching out and tracing a hand down my chest, frowning when I flinch out of her reach. "I'll be seeing you soon." She throws the cigarette down on the ground, stamping it out with her red heels, and follows her husband across the grass.

"Come on," Finn says, shoving me in the direction of the Great Hall. "Michael wants to talk to you while you eat. Romantic, huh?"

I snort, his antagonism is so pathetic. "Great. I'm famished."

"Bet you've had a great time fucking my wife since you took her away." He says in a low voice.

"She's not your wife," I reply.

Finn turns on me, seizing me by the collar. "She is my fucking wife, and when she comes here to get you I'm going to fuck her in front of you, again."

I laugh in his face. "You think she's going to let you do that to her?"

"I got blood magic," Finn says, his eyes wild, "I can bind her down and fuck her as many times as I want, while you have to watch."

"I'm really going to enjoy watching her blow you to pieces then, fucker." I sneer back.

"Hey." We both turn, and Vale is standing nearby, gesturing towards the Great Hall. "Michael's waiting for him."

"We're just discussing what's going to happen when my wife gets back," Finn says to him, releasing me with a shove. He looks back at me and grins. "It was Vale's idea, you know, to send Ceili in. He knew you'd trust her, react to her. Good thinking, huh?"

Vale's shifting on his feet, avoiding my eyes. "They killed her," I say to him. "You know that, right? They blew a hole into her side and she died in her mother's arms."

Vale clears his throat, and looks at me with a shrug. "Sacrifices have to be made in a war."

"Even innocent girls like Ceili, huh?" I can feel the skin on my arms getting hot. I have to calm down. "You're a real piece of work, Vale."

"Shut up, runt." He walks away from me quickly, his head down.

Finn grabs my arm. "Come on, Michael's waiting." We continue to the Great Hall, the afternoon light around us glowing gold in the summer haze.

I look around the compound, and I wonder where Anya is, tempted to ask for a moment. I don't know if they know that she's not Cora's mother yet, and I wonder what they're doing to her if they do know. Ceili said they had threatened to kill her if she didn't - I swallow hard, quashing the thought, trying to push the image of Ceili's broken body out of my head.

I don't even want to think about what happened in Ocario after Ebony got back, after Liall and Cora found out Ceili was dead. I inhale deeply. Fuck. Poor Ceili. I decide not to ask about Anya - they don't need another target. They don't need any more sadistic ideas.

300

We reach the Great Hall, surrounded by yet more of Ragnar's guards, and Finn releases my arm, pointing in the doors. "He's waiting for you."

"Yeah, thanks." I straighten my shoulders, and open the door.

"I got fond memories of this place," Finn says behind me. "First time I got to fuck Cora."

I say nothing, and walk into the Hall. The space is dimly illuminated by flickering candlelight. There's a table set up in the middle, piled with food, and Michael is sitting in a chair, a silver goblet dwarfed in his enormous hand. He leers at me as I approach, swirling the goblet round and round.

"Hello handsome," he says, gesturing to the chair opposite him. "Care to join me? You must be starving."

My stomach is churning, but the smell of the food is pretty intoxicating after being starved on nothing but dry bread for two weeks. My mouth begins to water, but I try to keep my expression neutral. I don't want to give them an inch.

"Yeah, I could eat." I reply, sitting down in the carved wooden chair.

"Allow me," Michael purrs, taking the plate from in front of me, and serving meat, fish and fruit on to my plate, along with two slices of crusty bread. "Here, sweetie. You need your strength." He places the food down in front of me, and watches me with sheer delight as I eat. "Oh, you poor thing, they really have been so cruel to you."

"I think that's kind of the point of torture," I reply between mouthfuls. My stomach hurts as the food lands in it, and I slow myself down. I'll make myself sick. I lean back in my chair and pick up the goblet, taking a large gulp of wine, which is probably a very bad idea, but my throat is burning with thirst.

Michael sighs wistfully. "I do admire how you're handling all of this though," he says. "You're so strong and brave, doing all of this for the woman you love." He sniggers into his goblet. "Too bad it'll all be for nothing."

I look at him with a raised eyebrow. "All for nothing?"

"Oh yes." He grins at me. "My brother and I destroyed the last Shadow Queen, and I can destroy this one too. So easily." He snaps his fingers. "It's like child's play. She doesn't stand a chance."

I wipe my mouth with a napkin and chuckle. "If that were true, you would have done it already."

Michael's purple eyes falter a little, his laugh not quite as self-assured as before. "Maybe I just enjoy the game."

"Or maybe," I say, leaning on my elbows on the table, "you're all just full of shit."

"Do you doubt me, demon?" Michael asks.

"Yeah I do." I say with a nod. "You need to draw her out here, why? You obviously know where she is. Why not just go and attack, right now?"

"Ocario is a sacred ground," Michael replies, "I can't go there, none of us can. Besides, I don't like a, oh what do the humans call it?" He snaps his fingers as he thinks. "Ah. Yes. A home game advantage." He chuckles softly. "I have to say I am very surprised she's left you here for this long. Her true love. Her Draw, no less. Hmmm." He shakes his head, his eyes becoming brighter. "It does make

302

me question what's keeping her. Surely you've called for her, in the depths of the night, in your despair, begging her to come and save you."

"No." I reply flatly.

Michael's eyebrows shoot up. "No?"

"No. I'm not going to do that over a few beatings."

"Well, in that case perhaps we need to come up with something a little more creative." Michael tips his head to the side, gazing up at the ceiling. "Since you're such a big, strong man, maybe it's time to move on to some extrinsic motivation." He runs his fingers back and forth along the edge of the table. "I understand Cora has so little family left now, with the unfortunate passing of her cousin." He grimaces and sucks on his teeth, and I start to feel deeply uneasy as his eyes fix back on me. "The bond between a mother and a child, it is just so strong. Something I have always admired in humans."

Anxiety prickles at my lips, the hairs on the back of my neck standing up. "I don't know what you mean."

He clasps his fingers together, his eyes narrowing as he looks at me. "I understand you were the one who found your mother's dead body, is that right?" He sighs when I don't answer, his eyes rolling pensively to the ceiling. "That must have left some scars. Such a small child, not understanding, wondering why their Momma just won't wake up."

I swallow hard, a lump threatening to form in my throat. "Is there a point to all this?"

He gives me a sly grin as his eyes turn back to me. "There's a point to everything, handsome. We angels are such deliberate creatures. We do everything with..." His lips twitch. "Purpose."

"So what's your purpose now?"

He puts his hands on the table, tapping his talons rhythmically. "That you surely wouldn't want your lover to have to go through the same thing?"

My stomach drops. And then I hear it. Sobbing, pleading.

"Bring her in." Michael calls over his shoulder.

I jump to my feet as two guards haul in Anya, her hands bound in front of her, a filthy rag tied across her mouth. Her eyes are wild as they dart around the room, from me to Michael and back again. One of the guards tears the gag from her mouth, and they shove her forward, where she falls hard onto her bound hands.

She pushes herself up and looks at me, terrified, hopeful. "Amryn?" She croaks, stretching her hands out to me. Blood is running down her temple, from a gash along her hairline.

I take a step forward, and Michael extends his hand towards me. "Aht, aht, no. You stay right there, young man." He looks down at Anya, stroking her face with his fingers. She's shaking. "Now, I think despite what we now know about our Shadow Queen's parentage, she still wouldn't want the woman who rocked her to sleep and cared for her all those years to die, would she?"

"Please," Anya murmurs, her voice trembling. "Please, don't hurt me."

"Michael," I say, "let her go. She's got nothing to do with this."

304

"But she has *everything* to do with this," Michael says, continuing to stroke Anya's cheek. "Cora is a gentle, sweet soul. She loves this woman, even though she's not really her mother."

Anya's brow furrows, and her eyes flash to me. "What? What is he talking about?" She looks back at Michael, shaking her head. "Cora's my child, my daughter, I gave birth to her, I remember it."

"Morgan really is spectacular," Michael says, looking over his shoulder at me. "Her ability to control the mind of the weak, it's truly incredible. What a gift."

Anya starts to cry. "No, no, she's mine, she's my baby, I remember, I do. I fed her from my own body, and I rocked her to sleep in my arms, she's mine."

"Oh, my dear," Michael says, helping Anya to her feet. "It must be so terrible for you." He stands beside her, putting an arm around her shoulders, and looks over at me. "Imagine, finding out everything you knew, your entire life, all your memories, it was all just a lie." He bursts out laughing, tapping himself in the forehead with his fingertips. "Who am I talking to? Silly me! Of course you know what that's like, Amryn."

I hold out my hand. "Just leave her alone," I say, edging closer to them. "She's innocent, hurting her won't help."

Michael's lips peel back into a sickly grin. "Are you sure about that?" Anya cries out as Michael seizes her, and a dagger flashes in his hands. He holds the blade to her throat, the grin pasted to his face, his purple eyes glowing unnaturally. "In fact, I understand this good woman was like a mother to you as well, is that right?"

"Yes!" Anya gasps, her pleading eyes fixed on me. "I was, I cared for you, Amryn, didn't I?'

Michael sniggers. "See? The least you could do to repay her kindness is to end her suffering, don't you think?"

"Let her go," I say, "this won't help anyone."

"Amryn, please." She whimpers.

"Call out to Cora," Michael commands, "go on. Call out to her, and let her know just how desperately you need her." He looks down at Anya. "Let her know how much her mother needs her."

"Amryn." Anya is crying, her bound hands clasping on to Michael's arm. "Please."

I shake my head, holding out both hands. "Don't do this."

"Call out to Cora." Michael says again. "Or poor Anya here dies."

Anya struggles in Michael's grip. "I don't want to die!" She sobs. "Please, Amryn, please, call her."

"I'm not doing that," I say, my chest tight. I can't. I can't call Cora. She'll come, I know she will. She won't leave us here if she knows this is happening. "Michael, let her go. This won't help."

"Call out to Cora!" Michael's eyes widen, mad, insane. He presses the dagger to Anya's throat. "You think I won't do it?"

"Amryn!" Anya's voice cracks as she screams. "Please! She's strong, she can save us!"

306

"I'm not doing that!" I cry back, stepping closer. "Michael, come on, let her go -"

"You want Cora to know you killed her mother?" Michael sneers. "You're willing to face her and tell her you let this poor, sweet woman who raised her die a horrible death?"

"Amryn!" Anya pleads.

I shake my head. "I won't." I look at Anya. "I'm sorry, Anya."

"Amryn, please." Her voice is hoarse, the hope leaving her face.

"Call out to Cora!" Michael calls, and Anya cries out as the dagger bites into her skin. "You think I won't do it?"

"Just let her go!" I cry. Please just let her go. "I'm sorry, Anya." I don't know what else to say. Because I am. I'm so sorry. "Michael, please -"

"Amryn!" Anya screams one last time. She can see I won't do it. She knows I won't.

"Oh I've had enough of this." Michael says. He pulls the dagger across Anya's throat, and her eyes widen, her mouth falling open.

"No!" My hands clench into fists. "Fuck! No!"

Michael hurls Anya towards me, and she stumbles forwards, clasping her bound hands to her throat, blood pouring from the wound. I rush forward and take her in my arms, collapsing to the floor with her as she gurgles, struggling to breathe as she chokes on her own blood. She convulses in my arms, her mouth opening and closing sickeningly, gasping for air like a fish on land. Fuck. Fuck.

"I'm sorry, Anya," I say, holding her as everything becomes wet with blood, hot, sick, sticky. "I'm so sorry." Fuck. I'm sorry. I'm sorry. She begins to go still, her eyes fluttering closed as the last fight leaves her body. She slumps against me, and the blood pools on the ground around us. She's not moving. I clutch her to me. I'm sorry. I'm so sorry.

Michael walks around us. "Tsk, tsk." He says, shaking his head. "Look what you made me do, Amryn. It would have been so easy to save her."

"You fucking monster," I growl.

Michael laughs heartily. "Oh yes, blame it all on me."

"You didn't have to do this."

Michael turns and bends over us. "Yes, I did. And make no mistake, Amryn, we will break you."

"Fuck you," I spit at him.

Michael seizes my hair, his lips pulled back from his pointed teeth. "You will call out to your lady love before the Blood Moon, mark my fucking words." The Blood Moon. Michael seems to catch himself as he looks at me, straightening up and clearing his throat. He snaps his fingers, and two guards rush forth. "Take him back to his cell."

I'm hauled away from Anya's body, her blood soaked into my clothes, my hands sticky with it. I feel sick. The guards smash my head into the door frame as we go, sending pain through my skull. Blood runs down my forehead.

The moon is rising above us in the dusk as I'm hauled back to my cell. Half-full. It's half-full. Only two more
308

weeks. The Blood Moon is important. That's what they're waiting for. That's what they want to beat. I only have to hold out another 2 weeks.

I can do this. Even as the guards throw me into my cell and lay their boots into me, kicking me until I throw up, I know I can do this. Even as one of them kicks me in the head and the room goes black, I know I can wait that long.

I can do this.

They'll come for me soon.

"Hey, runt." Finn's voice sounds above me.

One of my eyes is swollen shut, and he's blurry even through the other one. "What the fuck do you want?" I can barely raise my head.

"Poor Anya, huh?" He walks around me, his footsteps heavy on the stone floor. "Imagine how Cora's going to react when she finds out her Mom died because of you."

"Fuck you, Finn."

He looks down at me, sneering. "You look like shit, pretty boy."

"Yeah well I'll heal," I reply, "you look like that all the time."

Finn's face drops, and his boot connects with my jaw, sending my head snapping to the side. I laugh as the taste of blood fills my mouth.

"What's wrong, Finn?" I ask, my voice thick.

He kneels down next to me, his face contorting with fury. "You know, coming inside Cora, that was quite something. Her pussy is just, wow, it's something else, huh?"

"Sure is," I reply.

"I mean, she was so fucking tight," he says, and growls low in his throat, "it was like she really was a virgin."

"Are you trying to piss me off or make me horny?" I turn my head, spitting blood across the floor.

"Does it piss you off?" He asks, leaning over me. "Does it piss you off that I was inside the love of your life? That I fucking came inside her?"

"Does it piss you off that I was there first?" I ask, my shoulders shaking against the floor as I laugh. "Oh man, my eighteenth birthday was a fucking blast."

Finn's face darkens. "You fucked her then, huh? That was the first time."

"Sure was." I look at him with my one good eye. "Do you want details or are you here for something else?"

He grabs my hair, yanking my head off the floor. "You'll fucking call out to her now, or I'll -"

"What?" I'm challenging him. I don't fucking care anymore. "If you were gonna kill me, you'd have done it already."

"Maybe I should just cut off one of your fucking legs?" Finn says.

"Go ahead." I grit my teeth. "You wanna fucking maim me, fucking do it. But you won't, because you're all fucking talk. You're pathetic, and you're a coward, and

310

you're nothing." I spit blood in his face, and he lets my head fall as he stumbles back, his hands frantically rubbing the blood out of his eyes. "You're insignificant. You're *nothing*."

"You're nothing!" He screams, and he lunges at me, grabbing my head and smashing it into the stone floor. "You're nothing! You're pathetic! Your own mother couldn't even stand to be around you! She'd rather die than fucking be around you!" His fists rain down on my face. "I'm the Alpha! And Cora's my Queen, and I'm going to fuck her in front of you for a week before I finally cut your fucking throat!" He leans over me, spit dripping from his lips. "The last thing you hear will be Cora screaming my name."

I look up at him and grin, through the pain, through the haze settling over me. "The last thing you hear will be Cora tell you that you're nothing."

One more week.

I think my arm is broken. It hurts when I move.

I lie on the floor of my cell, and I'm pretty sure I fucking pissed myself the last time they beat me, it stinks and my skin burns. I can't feel anything anymore, and yet I feel everything. Everything hurts. Nothing works anymore.

I can see the light of the moon grow brighter through the cracks in the shutter above me. Not long now. I can do this. I can last this long.

One more week. Just one more week.

"Amryn?"

Cora's voice whispers to me in the dark.

My eyes open slowly, the room illuminated by bright moonlight.

A hand touches my face, and I flinch, pain shooting through my body as I do.

"Baby, it's me." She whispers, her voice tight with tears. I feel her hair spill over me. She's sobbing. "Oh god, what have they done to you?"

I lift my arm, the one that's not aching, not broken, and touch her. She's here. Oh god she's finally here. I feel tears burning my eyes.

"You came," I murmur. My voice doesn't sound like mine.

"Of course I did." She lays her head on my chest.

"I'm dreaming aren't I?" I ask, holding her close.

She climbs on top of me. "No, baby, it's real. It's over."

What is she doing? "Cora, we have to go."

Her hand moves over my cock, and I'm swelling even though my body is screaming. What the fuck is she doing? My relief gives way to confusion, and I try to find my bearings.

"I missed you so much," she says, and through the haze of my pain I feel her lower herself on to me.

My hand digs into her thigh. I'm dreaming, I must be. This isn't really happening. But my back aches as she rides me, pain shooting through my whole body. I wince. "Cora, stop."

"I need you." She sighs. "I've missed you so much."

My body doesn't feel like mine, but I can feel myself rising all the same. What the fuck is happening?

"Cora, stop." I say again, gripping her thigh and trying to push her off. "Baby, just get me out of here."

"Don't you want me?" She sighs.

Fuck. I'm going to come. I don't want to. It's all wrong. I'm not dreaming. Her dark curls bounce in the moonlight, her long fingernails digging into my chest.

"Cora, please stop." The heat in my groin is growing, and it hurts. I don't want this.

She leans over me, pressing her mouth to mine, and she tastes like smoke. Like cigarettes.

Cigarettes.

Long nails.

"Get the fuck off me!" I cry, adrenaline coursing through me as I push against Morgan's thigh.

She cackles, throwing her head back as she rides me harder. Fuck. Fuck. I'm going to come.

"Stop!" I cry again, but it's too late, my aching body shuddering as I release inside the fucking witch who can't stop laughing on top of me. Fuck. Nausea washes over me. My lungs are drained of air. My stomach quivers and convulses.

"Oh Amryn," Morgan sighs, and she trembles, moaning loudly as her nails dig into my chest. She's breathing heavily, and I see her teeth glint in the moonlight as she leers down at me. "Now I know what all the fuss is about, you really are quite something."

"Get the fuck off me," I cry again, trying to buck her off, even as pain shoots through my back.

She climbs off me with a giggle, and moves back, sitting down. My stomach lurches as I watch her dip her fingers inside herself, withdrawing them, and raising them to her mouth. "Mmmmm," she moans as she licks them, "you're delicious, Amryn."

"Get the fuck away from me," I say, shuffling across the floor, just wanting to get away from her despite the pain that's screaming at me to stay still. "What the fuck are you doing?"

"What do you mean, sweetheart? I just wanted to show you a good time,"

The fuck you did. "What did you just do to me?"

She crawls towards me, leaning over me, stroking my cheek. "Cora really wants a baby, doesn't she?" She traces a finger over my lips, and I shake my head to get her hands off me. She grabs my hair, putting her mouth to my ear. "And so do you, don't you, Amryn?"

"What did you do?" I ask again. "What did you fucking do to me?"

"Stealing someone's fertility is so easy, so very easy," she whispers into my ear.

Fuck. My stomach drops, and I can't breathe. Fuck. Fuck. Panic overwhelms me.

"You think you can escape Fate, Amryn?" She hisses into my ear, her hands pulling my hair. "You think you can just decide what you want, and have it? Fate always wins. We always win."

I push her away, scrambling towards the wall, crying out as I put weight on my broken arm. Fuck. Fuck.

"We own you, Amryn," Morgan says triumphantly, rising to her feet. "We broke you once and we can do it again."

"Fuck you!" My voice cracks.

"Cora won't want you now, no one will." Morgan giggles. "You lived your whole life alone, and unwanted, and now you'll live out the rest of it the same way. You will die, all alone, and no one will remember who you were."

"You fucking witch," I hiss. "You fucking monstrous evil fucking witch."

Morgan laughs. "Your whole family, pathetic. You should have heard your mother, simpering and whining in that tub, so worried about her poor precious little baby in the next room. 'Don't let him find me, please, Morgan'." She raises her voice into a sing-song tone, mocking. "It was sickening. She was better off dead."

"I'm going to kill you," I say, backing against the stone wall. "I'm going to tear your throat out."

"I'd like to see you try," Morgan says. She knocks on the door, and it opens, light pouring into the room. "Have a good sleep, Runt. Thanks for the orgasm."

The door slams shut, and a shutter rolls closed over the window above me. I watch the moon disappear as it does.

It's almost full.

I clutch my hand to my stomach as I curl into a ball on the floor. For the first time, I wish I would just die. I want the feeling of Morgan's skin on me to go away. Endless waves of nausea wash over me. Tears prick at my eyes.

Stealing someone's fertility is so easy.

If anything is going to break me, it's this. I can't deal with it. I clutch my hand to my face and howl, pain and grief tearing through me. I can't fucking do it. If anything ends me, it'll be this. They've done it. They're going to break me. I can't do this anymore.

Cora. Cora, please. I reach a hand out, putting my shields down. I can feel her, the threads between us furling towards me in the darkness.

Amryn?

No. I grit my teeth, my chest heaving as I try to breathe. I throw the shields back up, cutting her off before she can reach me, before she can sense my pain and the hollow grief that won't stop reverberating through my broken body.

Make yourself pass out. You have to pass out. Do it now.

The guards watching me via the camera in the ceiling yell and bang on the door as I summon my flames, telling me stop, telling me I'll kill myself. It's agony, my skin searing and blistering as the blood magic binds the flames to my skin.

I hear myself scream, and the pain pulsates through my arms, through my chest, over my shoulders, wave after toxic wave washing over me.

316

The smell of burning flesh is the last thing my mind registers, as darkness pulls at the edges of my vision. My eyes close, and I hear the guards, distant, as though they're in another room, talking about me.

"What the fuck did he do that for?"

20
Cora

I watch the Blood Moon rising above us, and I expect to feel some rush, some acknowledgement of the change that's taking place within me right now. It doesn't come. My veins glow, are they a little brighter? I raise my hands to my face, turning them back and forth in front of me. Maybe I'm just imagining it.

Nothing else happens.

Shooting stars dash across the sky.

Maybe Zadkiel lied. Maybe he's working with the other clans, with Michael, to destroy me. I shouldn't have trusted him.

Amryn's still alive. I can feel him, even through the shields he's put up. He won't let me feel his pain, but I know they've hurt him. They've tortured him. He's weak.

Tal sits down beside me, and I don't look at him, my eyes fixed on the sky.

"So, how do you feel?" He asks.

"No different." I reply.

"Maybe it takes a while," he says.

"Maybe Zadkiel lied." I reply. "Maybe nothing's going to happen, and Amryn was just tortured for a month for nothing."

"Hey, come on," Tal says, putting an arm around me. "You're strong now, so much stronger than you were."

I push him away. I feel hollow. "It's all meaningless if I don't come into my power."

"You will," Tal assures me, his eyes meeting mine. "You will, I can feel it."

I get up, walking past the fire I was sitting at, past the houses, light streaming from their windows. Thunder rumbles in the distance, and lightning flashes on the horizon. I don't hear footsteps following me, and I'm grateful Tal is giving me space. I want to be alone.

I close my eyes, and reach out to Amryn. I imagine his eyes looking into mine, his smile, his black hair hanging over his shoulder. I edge against something and flinch, feeling the depths of the pain he's in. And then his shield goes up, and he blocks me out. He doesn't want me to know, he's still trying to protect me.

I'm coming, I tell him. I'll be there soon, Ascension or not. If we die, then at least we die together. I don't even care anymore.

"You should."

I spin around, the unfamiliar voice of a man coming from the darkness. I squint, only able to make out a tall, shaded figure walking towards me.

"Who are you?" I ask, summoning a flame and holding it out in front of me to be able to see better.

It's a ghost. It must be. He's translucent. I can almost see right through him. His eyes glint silver in the firelight. He smiles at me.

"Cora." He steps towards me. "Oh Cora, look at you."

"Who are you?" I ask again. I'm beyond terror at this point. I barely feel anything.

"I am so proud of you," he says, stepping closer. I can't see through him anymore, but he's still shimmering. The moon rises higher above us. "Don't lose hope now, you are close, so very close."

"Amryn's suffered," I reply flatly, "and I don't know if we can win. I don't know if I'm strong enough."

"You've harnessed the Inera, I can feel it." He puts a hand to his chest, underneath the black beard that hangs almost to his navel, and a light begins to glow. "It is within you now, dear one."

The Old God. He's come back. I gasp, and for the first time in weeks I feel something, a small spark, igniting in my soul. "How are you here?" I ask. Tears prick my eyes.

"Because of you." He smiles and walks towards me, right up to me. "Your powers have transcended beyond anything I could have ever hoped for, dear one." Thunder rumbles overhead. "I know you don't feel it yet, but it has happened. The most extraordinary things are sometimes those that we do not even notice at first."

"I don't know if I can do this," I say.

"Of course you can." He puts his heavy hands on my shoulders. "You are Cora, Shadow Queen of the Earth Realm."

"What if I can't?" My head drops, my chin to my chest as I sob, and a wave of emotion crashes over me. Everything I have suppressed and ignored for the past 4 weeks floods my limbs, my chest, and I clasp my hands to my face as I weep.

"You must only believe you can," the Old God says. "For what you believe, you can do."

"Cora!" I hear Zadkiel calling to me. "Cora! Where are you?"

The hands disappear from my shoulders, and I look up. The Old God is gone, like a whisp of smoke caught in a breeze.

Zadkiel emerges from the village, his black wings glowing blue in the moonlight. "What are you doing out here, child?" He asks me. "Come now, we must discuss what is to be done next."

"The Old God's back." I tell him, and his eyes widen. "He was just here."

"Then you have ascended, my dear." Zadkiel says proudly. "I expected some fireworks or something at least, but I suppose the Old God showing up works too." Lightning flashes and thunder rumbles in the dark clouds above us, and Zadkiel rolls his eyes. "Yes, *ALRIGHT*." He says, looking up at the sky. "I heard you." He shakes his head as he looks at me, and extends a hand, gesturing for me to follow him. "Come now, we must convene."

The Great Hall is full, the murmur of the crowd dissipating as Zadkiel and I walk in. All the warriors of Ocario are gathered here, to support us, to go to war, to destroy Nilau and the rival clans, and Michael. The elders, including Elise, Ebony and Liall, sit at the front of the hall, and I go to join them. The hollow ache in my chest returns. I'm afraid. I sit down beside Tal, whose eyes I don't meet.

"We leave for Nilau just before dawn," Liall says, his gaze moving around the room. "We will fly together, and swarm them, which should give us an advantage on the first attack."

"They have blood magic," a warrior at the front says. "How do we defeat that?" Murmurs of agreement echo around the hall.

"I will ward off what I can," Zadkiel says, "I am able to enchant against blood magic, and my span is quite great."

"Good," Elise says, and looks back at the warriors. "I will need some soldiers with me to find Amryn once we arrive. I need to heal him and bring him to Cora, as quickly as possible."

"He's hurt badly," I say flatly, not meeting anyone's eyes. "I don't know if one healer will be able to do it."

"I can go with her," Yassin says, rising from the crowd. "My healing abilities are not as strong as Elise's, but together we might just be able to do it."

Liall nods. "Good."

"How do we defeat Michael?" I ask, even though I've asked this question a million times over the past four weeks, and have heard the answer a million and one. I need to hear it again. I need to hear that it's even possible.

"The Inera will weaken him," Liall says, "and when he is weakened, our flames can hurt him, not to mention what the Inera itself will do to him in that state. If you strike him again, you'll take him out."

"It's that simple?" I ask. "Why couldn't the last Shadow Queen defeat him?"

The Hall goes silent for a moment, as though the warriors are all holding their breath.

"The last Shadow Queen was overpowered because she faced both Michael and Gabriel," Zadkiel says to me, "and she was weakened. She'd been badly hurt, abandoned by her Draw, and hit with blood magic. But you have your medallion, and that will protect you."

I pull the medallion out of my shirt, watching as it dangles from my fingers, spinning back and forth, glinting in the light. "And you're sure it will work?"

"Oh yes," Zadkiel assures me. "It will."

"So, we protect Cora, we fight them off, and we take out Michael," Liall says, rising to his feet. "Understood?"

The warriors all acknowledge the command, and one by one they shuffle out of the hall. Rain has started falling outside, thunder rumbling loudly.

I look at the clock. It's 10pm. We fly in 6 hours.

Hold on, Amryn. I'm coming. I'm coming to rescue you.

Tal turns to me, and gives me a weak smile. "It's going to be OK, you know."

I nod, not quite believing it. "Sure."

"Hey, kiddo," Tal says, putting a hand under my chin. "Really. It'll be alright."

"Sure." I'm coming, Amryn.

"Baby." He kisses my nose.

I shift in the bed, keeping my eyes closed. "This is a dream." I murmur.

His arms move around me, and I can smell him. I can feel him. He's so warm. "So what if it is?" He asks, stroking my hair. "Does it matter?"

I shake my head against his chest. "No."

"I miss you."

I feel a lump rising in my throat. "I'm coming to get you." I whisper, holding on to him, feeling his skin under my fingertips, and it's real, so real. If I wish hard enough, if I keep my eyes closed long enough, he'll be here, even when I wake up. "I'm coming to get you."

"I'll be waiting."

I open my eyes. The sheets beside me are cold. The moon is still high in the sky. It was just a dream. Dawn is a couple of hours away. It's time to go.

I swing my legs over the edge of the bed, looking at the leather clothing they fashioned for me. Like armour. Not that I need it. I put a hand to my chest. I can summon the Inera now, though I still need to learn how to harness it.

But I'm strong now, more powerful. Powerful enough to save Amryn.

I'm coming to get you.

I put my mother's medallion around my neck, clutching it in my hands for a moment. If I ever needed you to be with me, Mom, today is that day. Please be with me. Please fight at my side. She was a fierce warrior, a Draw. Maybe a part of that resides in me. Maybe it's just waiting to come out.

I pull on my leathers, and they're tight but flexible, moulding to my body.

I walk into the lounge room, and Tal is waiting for me, dressed in his leathers. His hair is braided, drawn back from his face, his scimitar on his back. He looks me up and down and nods his approval. "You look good, Kiddo." He walks over to me, giving me a small smile as he adjusts the buckles on my shoulder armour. "Now, this is how this is going to go." He fixes me with an earnest look. "You keep your eyes ahead of yourself. I'm your eyes in the back, and I will not leave you, not for a second, do you understand?"

I nod.

"Until Elise and Yassin can find Amryn, heal him and bring him to you, you're vulnerable, and they're going to know that." He goes on. "Amryn will be able to take any strikes thrown your way, he can shield you. And he'll be able to heal you faster than any of us will be able to, OK?"

"Ok." I reply. I don't think I'm breathing anymore. I'm just existing in one moment to the next.

"Now," he takes my hand in his, "if you have a shot at Michael, and one of us is in the way, you take it." He clasps my hand as I begin to protest. "Kiddo, you need to take that shot. The Inera is the only thing that can weaken him enough for us to take him out. And one of us being in the way isn't reason enough to stop that."

"I'm not sacrificing anyone." I say quietly. "No family dies today."

"Cora, we might not have a choice."

"Sure you do," I say, mustering a small smile. "Just stay the hell out of my way."

Tal chuckles, and puts his arm around me, squeezing me to him tightly for a moment. "It's going to be OK, honey. We're bringing him home today. We're bringing them all home."

We walk outside, and the edge of the horizon shows a mere whisper of light. Dawn is coming. The warriors are assembled outside the Great Hall, armed with swords and round golden shields, some with bows and arrows slung across their backs. They all stop and bow their heads as Tal and I approach, and I remind myself they're bowing to me, not to him.

I'm their Queen.

Liall raises his hands, and calls for attention. "We fly together, and swarm the guards," he announces. "You," he points to a group of four warriors, "go with Yassin and Elise, and ward off any attacks while they seek out the Draw and heal him." The warriors nod. "Everyone else, protect the Queen, destroy the opposing clans, and make

326

sure we all get home safely." He raises a fist into the air, alight with flames. "The Queen is home!" He calls.

The warriors raise their fists in response, their flames lighting up the village. "The Queen is here!"

"And the Old God sees us!" Liall calls in response, and the warriors roar and cheer. "We fly!" Liall's smoky grey wings unfurl behind him. He lifts off into the sky, Ebony following close behind. The warriors take off after them.

Zadkiel is standing beside me, and he gives me a warm smile. "Ready?" He asks.

No. No. "Yes." I say, feeling my wings unfurl behind me. Like opening my arms. My feet leave the ground, and Zadkiel and Tal fly either side of me, Zadkiel's feathered wings cutting through the air audibly as we fly higher and higher.

I don't feel prepared. I don't feel ready. I still have a million questions, a thousand scenarios rolling through my head as I wonder what will happen when we arrive in Nilau. It all seems so simple, and yet so unknown. Defeat the enemy, blow the place to pieces. But how? What awaits us there? What if they can't find Amryn?

We fly and fly, the sky becoming slowly brighter around us, the landscape beneath us warming from the dark of the night, hills and trees and mountains beginning to glow ethereally below. I look over at Tal, and he looks so young as he focuses ahead of him. He said he won't leave my side. I'm glad he'll be there. But I'm scared to hurt anyone, for anyone to be caught in my line of fire. I've lost too many people I love to lose anyone else today.

The warriors ahead of us begin to fly lower, and we follow suit. The towering trees just below our feet are familiar, and I know we're near Nilau. It smells like home. No, not home. Nilau. It smells like that place, the place of enforced Fate and lies and rape and despair. It's not my home, not anymore.

I feel a pain in my chest, and I cry out, clutching my hand to my heart. My wings falter for a second, and a hand grips my arm, steadying me in the air. I see it's Zadkiel's hand around my arm, his brow furrowed as he looks at me.

"What's wrong?" Tal asks urgently.

"She can feel him." Zadkiel says sadly.

I try to catch my breath, let the pain subside. It's Amryn. He's close.

Suddenly, there's a flash of green up ahead, and the warriors disperse in the sky. They're firing on us.

"That's my cue," Zadkiel says, and with a loud rush he swoops towards the green light, a shimmering red field emanating from him as he flies ahead..

"Cora, come on." Tal says, pointing to the south side of the compound. "We'll stay under the tree cover.

Something drops on me, something heavy, and I hear Tal call out as I hurtle to the ground with arms and legs wrapped around me. I hear wings, and I know it's an angel. I wrench around in their grasp, fixing them with my eyes. Their eyes widen in terror, and I know my eyes have gone the ghostly white that signifies the Inera. "Big mistake." I say, and there's a flash of white light. The angel blows apart right in front me, their wings flinging off, catching the air and sailing away into the glowing dawn.

Tal swoops down beside me. "Are you OK?"

I nod, wiping the blood from my face with the back of my hand. "Just needed some war paint." I reply.

Tal allows himself a quick grin, then gestures for me to follow him to the tree line at the south side. Flashes of green continue to go off in the sky, and then a fireball is detonated, and I hear screaming as someone - many someones - down in the compound are incinerated.

We touch down just inside the fence line, and quickly there are two guards running at us, dressed up in the stupid military uniform I recognise from the warehouse in Sfayder. Tal brandishes his scimitar in one hand, and a flame in the other, slicing one demon across the chest, and hitting the other one with his flame.

The demon with the chest wound raises a gun in my direction, and Tal swings his scimitar, swiping the demon's head clean off his body. It rolls across the grass, coming to rest against the fence. I suppress a gasp. I'm going to be seeing a lot of this today.

In a low crouch we run along the fence line for one of the guard towers. I can see demons up there, firing on our warriors, up into the sky with the neon green canons that must be new tech or blood magic or something else Ragnar dragged up here with him to equip his old enemy.

I wave Tal away with my hand, back towards the fence. I focus on that feeling, that feeling that's now familiar to me, and the feverish heat beats at my ribcage, clawing its way out of me. With an explosion of light the tower topples to the Inera, taking the guards with it. It lies in a pile of flaming rubble, and the green canons go silent.

Tal moves back to my side, and gives me a smile. "Nice one, kiddo."

We keep running, taking cover behind one of the log houses near the perimeter. Tal peers around the corner, then ducks back down. "There's a group of demons there," he says quietly, gesturing to the left, in front of the house.

I step out and edge down the side of the house, and as I round the corner, one of the group looks up, and it's Vale, staring right at me. His brow crinkles with confusion, then he sees the white glow bursting from my hands. His eyes barely have time to widen, and I hit them, taking them all out, leaving only burnt ground behind.

Bye, Vale, you piece of shit.

Tal is chuckling quietly behind me. "You really are a weapon, kid."

A gunshot hits the house beside us, and we scurry for cover.

"Come out!" A voice demands. "Come the fuck out!"

"That's Finn." I say to Tal. He grips his scimitar and rises to his feet, but I stop him. "No. He's mine." I say, summoning a flame. I step out from the cover of the house, my white flames licking up my arm.

Finn stares at me in disbelief. "You're back?" He says incredulously, lowering the gun. "You came back?"

I shake my head. "Nope, just stopping by."

Finn scoffs. "To get him, right? The fucking Runt."

"I wouldn't call him that if I were you." We're circling each other, moving slowly.

Finn sneers at me, bitterness twisting his features. "Well, don't hold out much hope for what you're getting back. He's a wreck. He's nothing but a broken, twisted fucking wreck. You'll be begging to come back to me."

I laugh and shake my head. "You think I'd want you over him? He's a million times the man you'll ever be."

"I loved you," Finn says. "I really did."

"No you didn't." I say, brandishing the flame in my hand, making it dance. "You wanted to be Alpha, and I was just the means to an end. And you raped me so you could claim your Alpha status, and you were going to kill the man I love to prove a point."

"It was fate, Cora!" He says, dropping the gun and holding his hands up. "Babe, we're meant to be together, remember? I'm the one for you, not Amryn. Fate says so."

I point my flames at him."Fuck fate then." I fire at him, and he cries out, thrown onto his back. I walk towards him, and he lies on the ground, gasping for air, his skin burned and blistered. His eyes are wide as he looks up at me.

"Cora." He can barely get the words out, his throat raw and gleaming.

"What is it Finn?" I ask, standing over him. "Does it hurt?" I lean down over him. "Do you want it to stop?"

"Cora, I'm sorry." He gasps.

"You're nothing, Finn." I sneer. "You're nothing." His eyes widen as my flames wash over him, and reduce him to ash within seconds.

Tal cheers from behind me. I look up, and I can't see any angels around. This isn't right. They're waiting for something. They haven't launched a full attack yet.

"They're biding their time." I say to Tal as we both scan the sky above us.

"As long as we have time to get Amryn healed, I don't care," Tal says, retreating back to our shelter. "They can take all the time they want."

21
Amryn

The eerie silence that settled over the compound a couple of hours ago - or was it minutes? - is interrupted by the fire of cannons, guns, yelling. The ground beneath me shakes as explosions go off.

When was the Blood Moon? That's tonight, isn't it? No. Tomorrow. I blink, trying to remember. I've lost track of time. Stupid.

I pull myself into a sitting position, creeping slowly up the wall, and just this action costs me every ounce of strength I have. I cry out as I lean on my arm, the blisters and seared flesh sending black spots in to my vision. The pain turns my stomach, but I have nothing in there to vomit up. I retch dryly on the floor.

There's gunfire right outside the building, and yelling. Flashes of green light illuminates the cracks in the ceiling. They're using blood magic. That acid shit that's bound around my arms.

There's more shouts in the corridor outside my cell, and then gunfire, followed by an explosion. The door is blasted open, and I press myself back against the wall as air rushes past me.

"Amryn." Someone's hands are on me, holding my face. "Amryn, sweetheart, it's me."

I open my eyes and look at her. "Mom?" I ask. It's another one of Morgan's fucking spells. "You're not real." I shake my head, trying to push her away, closing my eyes. "Not again. Leave me alone. Don't touch me."

"Amryn, it's me, it's Elise." She says. "Baby boy, it's OK."

Panic swells in my chest, and I ignite my flames, screaming as they burn my arms. "Get away from me!"

"Shit." I hear a man's voice say. There's cool hands on my arms. "Amryn, come on, stop now."

I open my eyes, and it's Elise's face in front of me. "It's another spell." I mutter,

"No, baby boy, it's me." Her hands press against my chest, and my skin glows under her touch. "Amryn, it's me, and I'm here to heal you."

I shake my head. "No, no, you're her, you're her." Nausea overcomes me again as I feel her hands push on my chest, and my jaw trembles. "Please, don't. Not again."

"Baby boy," she says, "Cora's here. She needs you." A gentle yellow glow begins to come from her arms. "Amryn, it's me." Warmth begins to flood my body. "This will hurt a little. But it'll be over, just let it take over. Yassin, look at his arms."

334

Strong hands lay themselves on my blistered skin, and they're cool. I close my eyes, the relief at the acid bonds falling away so strong I feel tears in my eyes. The maddening feeling of bugs eating away at my skin shrinks away. I exhale heavily.

"He's hurt bad," the man says. "I've never seen anything like the shit on his arms."

Elise's hands stay on my chest, and I suck in a sharp breath through gritted teeth as bones knit back together, as torn muscles repair. I feel all of it now. The warmth is giving way to a feeling of a million steel traps going off in my joints.

An explosion goes off right outside the building, and Elise cowers against me as rubble showers down from the ceiling. "Tell those warriors to keep that shit away from us!" She yells at the man. My ears are ringing. A searing pain burns through my skull, and I throw my head back, bellowing as my vision goes black. My head's going to shatter, it's going to split apart.

"Amryn, stay with me," Elise says, her hands on either side of my face. "Amryn, this is the worst part, it's nearly over, come on, stay with me." I try to claw at my head, to stop the embers that are burning through my brain, but Elise holds me down. "Amryn, it's OK. Come on, stay with me, I'm here, I'm here."

Images flash through my head, the torture I've endured, the pain they've subjected me to. I feel like I'm suffocating. I gasp for air, and a throbbing pain thumps at my temple. Someone screams, and I'm pretty sure it's me. Then everything is light, and warm, and I'm in the water, with Cora, her arms around me. I panic for a moment -

am I dying again? - but air fills my lungs, and even though it's thick and sticky, it's air.

I can breathe. I'm alive, and I can breathe.

Something snaps inside me, and I slump to the ground. I stretch my hands across the stone floor, and I can feel it, properly. Not muted through the bonds on my arms. I ignite a flame, and it doesn't hurt. My body doesn't ache anymore. I can move my arm again.

I sit up against the wall, and Elise is eyeing me anxiously. I give her a smile. "I'm fucking glad to see you."

Her face is flooded with relief. "You're OK," she breathes, putting her arms around me.

"I guess I am." I reply, hugging her back. "I feel like I am, so that's a good start."

"You really do heal quick," she says, pulling back and getting to her feet. She unhooks a satchel from around her shoulders, and pulls out clothes for me. Ones that aren't caked in blood and sweat and filth. "Come on, we gotta get out there."

I stand up, flooded with relief as nothing hurts, and I pull on the black pants and long sleeved black shirt. They feel like light-weight armour, the fabric flexible but hard to the touch.

Yassin rushes back into the room, and he gives me a nod. "Glad to see you're back on your feet, my friend. You had us worried for a minute."

"Thanks. What's it look like out there?"

"A load of demons, and not too many angels." He replies.

"They're hiding somewhere," Elise says, "they're waiting for something. Probably protecting Michael and they'll come out when he finally decides to attack."

"Where's Cora?" I ask.

"She's with Tal, I'm not sure where." Elise replies.

"I have to find her." I say.

Yassin heads out into the corridor, looking back and forth, his flames at the ready. He motions for us to follow him, and together we creep along the wall, the morning light streaming in through the open door at the end of the building. I can see flames and smoke rising outside. The sky is darkening, as though a storm is rolling in.

Something like a trumpet sounds, and Yassin turns around to look at us. "Oh fuck." He mutters.

"What's that?" I ask.

"That's a battle cry," he says, "the angels are coming."

I have to find Cora. *Where are you?* I put my hand on my chest. *Where are you?* Fire burns, and something hard is at my back. A wall. Wood. A steel fence opposite. She's covered in blood. Fuck. Fuck.

"Come on," I say, and we head outside. The compound is burning around us as we dash across the yard, keeping low, our eyes on the skies above us. It darkens further, clouds drawing together in a dramatic display above us, silver and grey and navy blue. The trumpet sounds again.

She's close. I can feel her. The thread between us pulls taut, drawing us closer.

I throw my arms up as there's a violent flash of green, and Yassin flies sideways. Elise cries out, and I turn to see Yassin clawing into the ground. His back is torn open, bleeding, half his spine exposed, flesh glistening with blood in the light of the flames around us.

"Yassin!" Elise goes to him, crouching beside him, but he waves her off urgently.

"Go," he gasps, "go now."

Elise and I break into a run as another green light flashes beside us, and Elise sends a fireball in the direction from which it came. Something screams. Good. I hope it was one of them.

I see the log cabin ahead, and I'm sure that's where they are. "Cora!" I call out. "Cora, where are you?"

Tal rounds the corner, his flames ready, his eyes fixed behind us. "Here!" He calls.

Elise and I take cover along the side of the house, and Cora's there, her face covered in blood, dried on her clothes. Her eyes widen as she sees me.

"Amryn." It's all she says before she stumbles into my arms.

I take her face in my hands, looking her over. My veins start to glow as I touch her. "Are you hurt?" I ask.

She shakes her head. "No, it's not my blood. It's OK." She takes a deep breath, and touches my cheek with trembling fingers. We both know there's not much time.

There's a rushing sound above us, like a flock of birds flying low, and we look up to see a swarm of angels pass over us.

"They're here," Tal says.

Cora and I look at each other, and she grasps my hand.

"You ready?" I ask.

She hesitates for only a second, before nodding, and straightening herself up. She glows bright white as she walks past the edge of the house, out into the open. I follow her, my flames ready.

I see her hands curl into fists as she spreads her arms, and there's a scream, followed by a shockwave, reducing the first line of angels in the yard to ash. Beyond that there's flurries of movement, as those in the furthest scramble to escape.

Several of them turn on us, and Tal is suddenly at my side, brandishing his flames and his scimitar. An angel tears open their mouth and throws itself at Cora. She sends a bolt of lightning straight into its face, its skull flying apart in mid-air.

The remaining angels break into a run, swarming at us. We send our flames into them, taking out a few but the rest leap into the air, swooping over us.

"Amryn watch out!" Tal cries, swinging his scimitar as one of the angels screams, brandishing a dagger as it bears down on me.

The angel lands on me, the dagger inches from my throat. It screams in my face, like a banshee, and I push back, igniting my flames. The shimmering red shield comes up, absorbing my fire, and the angel cackles.

I can hear Tal and Cora calling out to me, angels standing between me and them.

"Ready to die?" The angel sneers, pushing the dagger closer to my skin.

"Not today, bitch." The voice comes from my right, and suddenly the angel is hit in the throat with a bright yellow bolt. It rears up, screaming, clutching at the black blood that seeps from the wound. I kick it away from me, and it flails, looking to where the strike came from.

Elise stands a few feet away, her yellow flames licking up her arms. The angel launches itself at her, and Elise's flames hit it square in the face, and it collapses into a heap on the ground.

"No one hurts my baby boy," Elise says as I get to my feet.

I don't have time to respond, as another wave of angels moves towards us. Cora steps forward, Tal at her back, his scimitar flying as angels fall either side of him. White lightning crackles up Cora's arms as she summons another wave of the Inera. I turn and throw myself over Elise as the shockwave explodes, the angels shrieking as they fly away. The Inera seizes some of them in its grip, electricity coursing over their skin, strangling them slowly.

Cora's eyes meet mine, and she smiles, blood smeared across her face.

"You're fucking lethal," I tell her.

She shrugs. "I had some training while you were gone."

"I can see that."

"Elise!" Liall's voice sounds across the compound. "Elise, we need a healer!"

Elise breaks into a run, into the smoke, Tal right behind her, and as we go to follow her, there's a flash of green from our left. I throw up my flames, shielding Cora. The green shot dissipates into sparks on the ground, where it turns into shards of glass.

"Just give up, Cora!" Someone calls, and Lordain is approaching us through the flames, Ragnar right behind him. They both have their flames at the ready.

"I think you're probably the one who needs to give up." Cora replies, her hands iridescent as she turns to them. "Unless you want to end up like your useless sons."

"You think we're scared of you?" Ragnar spits, and sends a flame in her direction. Cora waves her hand, a streak of light forming in the air before her, and Ragnar's flame is deflected, up into the trees. Ragnar laughs, advancing closer. "Ooh, scary. We've got more than fancy tricks up our sleeves, lass." He produces a silver dart, like the one Zadkiel threw at me. "I believe you've seen one of these before?" He laughs maniacally, using his flames to propel the dart straight at Cora.

I push her out of the way, throwing up a shield, bracing myself for the impact of that fucking thing, but it hits my shield and turns to ash in mid-air.

"What the fuck is this?" Ragnar cries.

"You're a fool!" I reply, the roaring of the flames around us getting louder all the time as the compound burns to the ground. "You still don't fucking understand anything. You think you can take on the Shadow Queen?"

Ragnar runs at us with a bellow, leaping at us with his flames, and I seize him mid-air, my hand around his throat.

"Who's a useless pretty boy now?" I ask.

"You. Fucking. Little Shit." His voice is garbled, spittle foaming at his lips.

"Say hi to your son for me." I snarl in his face. He gasps for air, one last time, and I ignite my flames, engulfing his head in a wild, snapping roar. He screams and gurgles, and I throw him to the ground, where his skull cracks apart, distorting his face into a wide-eyed grimace.

Cora and I turn to Lordain, who regards us with gritted teeth, his shoulders heaving.

"You killed my parents," Cora says to him, stalking closer.

"You're violating what the Fates decided!" He cries, his voice breaking. He's fucking terrified.

"The Fates have no hold over me," Cora replies in a voice I've never heard her use before. Low. Venomous. "They never have. And neither do you."

"I should have listened to Ragnar!" Lordain says, throwing his arms around, fanning his flames to make them look larger, wildly grasping at anything to intimidate us. He knows he's dead. "I should have killed you both when you were kids."

"Yes, you should have," Cora agrees, "but you're stupid."

Lordain sends a flame at her, which Cora waves away easily. "You think you can defeat Michael?" He sneers, breathing heavily. "You think you can win this war? You think they'll just let another Shadow Queen rise?" He laughs, maniacally, clawing his hands along his thighs. "You know what they did to the last one, right? They're going to put you in the ground, Cora. Deep underground where you'll spend an eternity suffocating, wishing they'd just killed you."

Cora points her hands at him. "I'd like to see them try." Cora rushes him, and before he can react, her hands are around his neck, his mouth lolling open in panic. "Tell me, Lordain, how did you kill my father again?" He gurgles in her grasp. "Was it something like this?"

Lordain screams as Cora's hands melt away his flesh, his muscles. I smell ash as his bones burn, and then his body slumps away, leaving his molten head in Cora's hands, distended and blistered, the mouth still torn open. Cora spits in what's left of his face, and then hurls the smoking mass across the yard.

"Fucker," she says. She turns to look at me, and smiles at my expression. "What?"

"You're a fucking badass," I say with a grin.

She shrugs, and turns to step forward into the yard.

A flash of green bursts towards us, and Cora is thrown backwards, landing with a thud on her side, facing away from me.

"Cora!" I cry out, putting up a shield as I rush to her, turning her over.

She's gasping for air, but as soon as I'm at her side she sits up. "I'm OK, I'm OK." She assures me, wincing. "It just knocked the wind out of me, that's all. I'm OK."

"That was blood magic, how did you -"

She pulls a medallion from her clothing. "My Mom's. A gift from Zadkiel." She grasps my hand, and I help her up. "Come on, let's finish this."

"Cora!" A woman's voice sounds across the yard, and Cora looks around frantically.

"That's Mom," she says urgently. "That's Anya, where is she?" Morgan. She's playing games. Cora breaks into a run. "Mom?" She calls.

I rush after her. "Cora, stop, it's a trap!"

"Cora!" The voice is desperate, pleading.

"Mom!" Cora calls again. "Where are you?"

"Cora, it's a trap!"

I see her hesitate, turning back to look at me, but then there's a scream, and she runs towards it. "Mom!"

Fuck. Don't fall for it. But she's running ahead and I'm running after her and she's faster than me and this witch is luring her in. I hear footsteps thudding into the ground behind me.

"What's she doing?" Tal calls out to me.

"It's the witch!" I call over my shoulder.

We clear a wall of flames, and Michael is standing with Morgan in his grasp. Except it doesn't look like Morgan, it looks like Anya, and she's crying and pleading and clawing at his arm.

344

"Let her go!" Cora cries, holding out her flames.

"You wouldn't kill your own mother, would you?" Michael says, baring his pointy yellow teeth. "If you strike now, she'll die."

"Cora," Morgan whimpers, tears streaming down her face. "Please, sweetheart, help me."

"Cora, that's not your mother!" I call. "That's not Anya!"

Her face turns to me, twisted with anguish. "How do you know?"

"Because Anya's dead."

Cora's face crumples. "She's what?"

"He's lying, sweetheart!" Morgan calls out.

I turn back in time to see Morgan step out of Michael's grasp, summoning a purple light in her hands. Tal and I must see it at the same time, and we fire our flames at her, too late. The purple light hits Cora, winding itself around her ,and she drops to her knees, her eyes wide.

Michael disappears into the skies before our flames hit Morgan, and she cries out as she's thrown sideways. Tal strides over to her while I go to Cora, who is straining against the purple bolts that are wrapping around her stomach, around her neck, pressing the air out of her body.

I put my hand on them, and they send electric shocks up my arm. I grit my teeth, but I get a hold of the tail end of one, and pull it off her body, unwrapping it, and it's stiff like wire. I unfurl it, bit by bit, and it writhes on the ground like a dying snake. Cora gasps for air, grasping on to my shoulders. My hands glow as I hold her, and she quickly starts to breathe normally.

I look over my shoulder, and Tal has seized Morgan by her hair, dragging her towards us. "Got a bone to pick with you, witch." He says as he hurls her to the ground, pointing his scimitar at her. "You killed my Mom. You stole my family from me. And now you're going to die."

Morgan hisses, and sends a purple bolt flying at him. Tal tries to dodge it, but it strikes him across the cheek. "You're all dead," she says, clawing her fingers into the earth. "You're all fucking dead."

"No, you're all dead," Cora says, rising to her feet. "Your husband. Your son. They're ash now. And you're about to join them."

"You won't win, Cora," Morgan says, grinning. "If you think this is the end, you're very, very wrong."

"Enough," Tal says, blood pouring from the wound on his cheek. He puts the blade of his scimitar under Morgan's chin. "Little brother," he says to me, his eyes staying on Morgan, "how are we going to kill her?"

I tower over Morgan. "Well, I did have an idea," I say.

Tal steps aside. "Go ahead. I'd really like to see what you've come up with." He sneers down at Morgan. "I fucking hope it's painful."

Morgan's face falters as I lean down over her, and she whimpers, her eyes blinking rapidly. "Please, don't hurt me, Amryn, please. Not after what we shared in the cell that night. That was special."

I push her down onto the ground, my glowing hand burning her flesh. She cries out, her eyes wild as she looks up at me.

"Amryn, please."

"I told you I'd tear your throat out, didn't I?" I put a hand to her throat.

"Amryn -"

My fingers claw through the skin of her neck, and I feel sinewy fibres give way as I grasp onto her windpipe. She gurgles wildly, her arms and legs flailing. Her eyes roll back in her head, and then with one hard jolt I pull everything loose. There's a rush of blood, and Morgan's body lies arched on the ground, fingers clawed into the dirt.

I stand up, beside Tal, and he spits on Morgan's body.

"Fucking witch." He growls, then claps me on the shoulder. "Nicely done, brother."

22
Cora

I watch Amryn tear Morgan's throat out with a rush of satisfaction, marred only by what he told me before - Anya is dead. I almost fell for it. I almost got us killed. I give myself a shake. I can't think about this now.

"We have to find Michael," I say.

"Oh but he's already found you." The voice sounds behind us, and the three of us turn to face him. He regards us with amusement, rubbing his hands together. "What a sight, the Queen and her Draws."

"Tal, run." I say, feeling the Inera clawing at my chest. I can't control it yet, not how I need to, not to do a targeted attack like this, and I don't want to hurt him. Only Amryn can survive the Inera.

Tal is in a lunge beside me, his scimitar and flames drawn. "I'm not going anywhere," he says. "I told you, we're in this til the end. You do what you need to do." He and Amryn flank me, and I advance on Michael.

Michael throws his head back, laughing. "What do you think you're going to do, Shadow Queen? Blow up an archangel? You know we put the last -"

"Yeah I know, you put her in the ground, you angels are so fucking proud of yourselves for it," I say impatiently. "You really need to come up with a new fucking story to tell, you boring ass fuck."

Michael chuckles. "You really are rather fiery, aren't you, dear?" He points at my hands and slaps his thigh. "Get it? Fiery?"

"You're hilarious." I respond. "And yes, I will blow you up."

Michael spreads his arms wide, grinning at me. "Go ahead, then."

I release the Inera with a rush, the ground quaking below us. Michael's arms fly into the air as the shockwave hits him, and Tal and Amryn fire on him, their orange flames combining into a flash in front of us. Michael stumbles backwards, and he cackles, clutching his chest.

"Nice!" He cries, holding out a hand to us. "Well done!"

It should have hurt him more than this. It's barely weakened him.

I step closer. "Hurts a bit, huh?" I ask.

"I could do with some more."

Tal runs at him with a roar, his scimitar swinging, and Amryn rushes from the other side. Michael backs away, summoning a ball of green lightning in his hands, but he underestimates Tal's speed. His scimitar swings into

349

Michael's wing, slicing into cartilage, and Michael cries out.

As he buckles over, Amryn grabs him from the other side, his flames lighting up Michael's face. Michael cries out, and throws the green lightning blindly, and it hits Tal square in the torso.

"Tal!" I run to his side, kneeling beside him where he landed in the dirt.

"I'm OK." He assures me, gritting his teeth. A red shield shimmers and dances across his body, and we both look up to see Zadkiel swooping overhead.

"Stay away from the green stuff!" Zadkiel calls, as a wave of small black creatures pursues him through the sky.

Michael is trying desperately to shake off Amryn, who has a hold on his wings. I see Amryn's eyes turn bright orange, glowing like embers in his face. He bares his teeth, and with a loud roar he tears one of Michael's wings clean off.

Michael screams, throwing out his arms, a green pulse moving through his limbs. Amryn is sent flying, hitting a tree with a sickening thud. Panic rises in my chest for only a moment, because he's back on his feet, recovered, and rushing at Michael again.

I step forward and send another wave of the Inera into Michael, who's trying to claw at his bleeding back, at the gaping wound where his wing once was. He's thrown back, stumbling, and Amryn seizes his head, igniting his flames again, and I see Michael's ear melt away. He flings Amryn away, towards us, and he lands in a lunge a few feet from Tal and I.

"He's not dying fast enough," I say. "The Inera, it should weaken him more than this."

Amryn shakes his head. "What else do we do?"

Michael looks over at us, visibly shaking, but still smiling his sickening smile, teeth glinting in the firelight. "Out of ideas already?"

"Not even close." I spit back.

Michael leers at me. "Probably needs a closer range attack, majesty."

Tal grabs my arm. "Cora, don't."

"It's fine," I assure him, rising to my feet. "I was born for this."

I run at Michael, taking a leap, and I land on him, knocking him backwards. His remaining wing snaps as he lands on the ground. He's half-cackling, half-babbling. "Oh that's the spirit, majesty!"

"Close enough for you yet?" I sneer.

"You can't win," he says through gritted teeth, stained with black blood. "You'll face your end just like the last Shadow Queen, it doesn't matter what you do."

"Is that so?" I claw my hands either side of his head, and his eyes widen as I look down at him, the glow from my body illuminating the whites of his eyes. "You don't get to put me in the ground." I roar, and I unleash the Inera straight into his skull.

The burst of the shockwave is so loud that I don't hear a sound he makes, but I can feel him screaming, his chest caving and contorting underneath me, his jaw stretched wide. Lightning flashes overhead, and when the light

351

begins to dim, I'm holding on to scorched flesh. Michael's yellow teeth are torn wide open, his last moments clearly painful. Good. Fucker.

"You don't get to put me in the ground. " I say again as I rise to my feet, kicking the charred skull from his body. I turn around to look at Tal and Amryn, and smile at them. They meet my eyes, relief in their faces.

Then their eyes stray down and their faces simultaneously distort with horror. Tal stumbles backwards, his hand flying to his mouth. Amryn cries out, and rushes towards me.

What's wrong?

I look down, and I see the hole in my chest, dripping green mingling with my blood. I look over my shoulder, down at Michael's hand. It's covered in my blood, and the menacing, sickly green glow of blood magic. My hand moves to my neck. The medallion is gone.

Amryn reaches me just as my legs give out.

23
Amryn

"Cora?" I catch her just as she falls, her face twisted with confusion. "Cora, oh my god, Cora?"

She shakes her head as she looks at me. "It doesn't even hurt." She murmurs. "I can't even feel it."

I put my hand over the hole, the gaping hole right there in her chest, seeping green and blood and my hands glow orange. "Where's your medallion?" I ask. It was meant to protect her. I look over my shoulder, and see Tal bending down to pick it from the ground, from the purple glass Morgan's spell left behind.

His eyes meet mine. Fucking witch. She knew. She fucking knew.

I look back down at Cora. Footsteps thunder towards us, and Elise is there, next to me on the ground, putting her hands on Cora as well, trying to help me heal her.

"Cora, it's OK," I say. She's bleeding, there's so much blood everywhere. I smile down at her, trying to reassure her. I'm her Draw. I can heal her. I can heal her. "It's OK, baby, you're going to be fine."

Blood runs out of her mouth, and she grits her teeth. "It's alright." She says. "We destroyed him, we won."

"Yes we did, baby," I say, pressing both hands on the wound. Close up. Fucking close up. Close the fuck up. Why isn't she healing? "You did so good, Cora. You were amazing."

Elise looks at me helplessly and shakes her head. "I can't heal this, I'm not strong enough."

"I can," I say, pressing harder. More blood rushes out of Cora's mouth. No. Come on. I'm the Draw. I'm meant to heal her. I can do this. "It's OK. This is what I'm here for, right Cora? I'm going to heal you, and we're going to go home. That was the plan, right?"

Cora puts a hand on mine. "Amryn, it's OK." She whispers.

I shake my head. No. No. It's not OK. "I can do this, Cora, I can do this, come on."

"Amryn."

I clench my eyes shut for a second as they burn. No. I'm not letting her go. "Stop it." I say to her. "It's OK, I can do this, I can."

Her hand raises to my cheek, and she turns my face so I'm looking at her. "It's OK." She says, her voice quivering. "I love you."

"Stop it." I say again, clenching my jaw, willing my hands to burn brighter to heal her faster. Come on. They glow and glow, and her wound keeps seeping blood, it just won't close up.

Ebony and Liall reach us at a run, throwing themselves down on the ground beside us. "Oh no," Ebony says, clutching a hand to her mouth. "Cora, oh my god."

"Shit." Liall says with a gasp. "Oh my god."

"She's OK," I insist. "She's OK, it's just taking me a second. She's going to be fine."

Liall reaches out and touches my arm. "Amryn, you're too weak, you can't heal this."

I shrug him off, tears stinging my eyes. I can feel her heartbeat slowing against my palm. "I can do it." I wipe my face against my shoulder, sweat and tears mingling in my eyes, blurring my vision. "Come on, baby, you have to live, come on, it's over now. You're not dying on me now. I won't let you."

"I love you," she says again, her voice weak. I look into her eyes, and she smiles. "I never cared what Fate decided. You were my choice. Every time."

"Don't do that," I say, shaking my head, "don't you dare talk like you're saying goodbye, we're not doing that, stop it."

"Take me home, OK?" She says. She puts her hand around the back of my neck, pulling me down weakly to her. "Maybe next time we can try again." She whispers, and presses her lips against mine.

I sob against her mouth, and I feel her go still, her heartbeat going quiet under my bloody hands. One final breath escapes her lips, and a dagger of ice runs through my heart as I feel her die. I clasp her face in my hands. "Cora, no, wake up, come on, I'm here. Wake up, baby, wake up, wake up."

Elise is crying. Ebony is crying, Liall swears and throws flames somewhere across the compound. No. No. She's not dead. Not now. Not after all this. No.

"Cora, wake up!" I shake her, her head hanging limply, her green eyes dull. "Cora, no, no wake up! Wake up!" I crush her to my chest, and my roar echoes around us, bouncing off the walls of flame. I bury my face in the crook of her neck, desperate to feel her pulse. She still smells like her. She's still warm. "Cora, please." Please don't leave me alone.

Tal kneels beside me, puts a hand on my shoulder. "Brother, let her go." He says quietly.

No, I won't. I lay her back on the ground, shaking Tal off and pressing my hands back on to the wound in her chest. "Fuck off!" I cry. "I can do this."

"Amryn, stop." Tal says, his voice strained. "She's gone."

"No, she's not, I'm the Draw, I can bring her back, this is what I'm here for, this is my purpose, I can do it."

"Amryn -"

"No, I can do it." I shake my head, pressing against Cora, looking at her face, willing the light to come back into those green eyes. Willing those lips to quiver and come to life and for a fucking breath to pass them. "Come on, baby, wake up."

"Amryn." Tal puts his hands over mine on Cora's chest. "Brother, look at me."

I don't want to. If I look at him, I have to admit she's gone. If I look at him, I've given up. If I look at him, Fate wins and I'm alone. I'm alone. I'm alone.

"Amryn, look at me," Tal says again gently.

I turn my eyes to his, and he shakes his head. "She's gone." He tries to lift my hands off her body, but he can't. I won't let her go. "Amryn, it's over."

"No." I shake my head. "No."

"Brother, come on."

"No!" I press harder. "I'm not letting her go." She can't be gone. She can't be. She has to live.

"Amryn -" Tal breaks off, and his hands tremble on top of mine. He's crying too. They've all given up. They've all fucking given up. Everyone except me.

But then the last thread of hope leaves me as I look down at Cora's face, her features swimming as my eyes fill with tears. She stares at the sky. Still. Silent.

She's gone.

A scream threatens to explode out of me, from the deepest, darkest place that didn't exist until she died. That didn't exist in a world with her in it.

And then there's a thump against my hand. Faint. But it's there.

Tal and I both look down, and our hands are glowing. Both of our hands. Both of us. Our eyes flash up to look at each other.

There's another thump. Then another. And another.

The wound in Cora's chest closes up under my hands. Under our hands. Elise gasps beside me. I look back down, and Cora's lips quiver as a breath passes through them. Shards of green glass dig into our hands as the magic dissolves.

Tal inhales sharply. "I can feel her heart," he says, his voice hoarse.

So can I. It's beating again. Slowly. Getting faster. Getting faster.

Cora sucks in a breath, and her green eyes glow as she looks up at me. Her chest heaves under our hands. "Amryn?" She whispers.

I gasp and put my forehead to hers. "I'm here, baby." I say to her, tears running down my cheeks. "I'm here, it's OK."

"What happened?" She murmurs.

"You were gone, but we brought you back." I tell her.

She breathes a sigh of relief. "Oh god." Her hands wind around my neck. "So it's over?"

I nod. "It's over, baby. It's over." I push my lips against hers, her beautiful, perfect mouth that's warm and alive. The millionth kiss I thought we'd never have. "Come on, let's get you up." I say when we part, helping her sit up.

Her eyes move to Tal, over his glowing orange hands. Her head snaps back to look at me, then back at Tal. "Both of you?" She asks.

Tal's face crumples as he nods. "Both of us. Guess you needed extra help." He leans forward, pressing a kiss to her forehead. "You scared us there, kiddo."

Cora looks down at her chest, and I reach out, putting my hands to the spot where the hole was, just a few minutes ago. All I can feel now is ribs and flesh and her heartbeat, her heart beating. Her heart. My heart. She puts her arms around me, and I pull her against me, nuzzling into the crook her neck and feeling her pulse and her breath and her warmth, and she's alive.

She's alive.

The sky begins to clear above us, the darkness lifting. The clouds part, and golden sunlight washes over us.

"Oh everything's OK?" I hear Zadkiels' voice as he approaches us.

"Yeah, no thanks to you," Tal says jokingly. "Where were you?"

"Got accosted by the sodding cherubs," he says, sighing heavily. "They're an absolute menace. They look so sweet but my god they're barbaric. Had me staked down with their little tridents, I was terrified." He looks down at Cora and I and smiles. "So you're alive then, ey?"

Cora laughs. "I sure am."

"What a relief." Zadkiel points to mine and Tal's hands, which continue to glow orange, his eyes darting from me back to Tal. "Oh my, so you're both -"

"The Queen's Draws, yes, so it would seem." Tal says, smiling at Cora.

Zadkiel clasps his hands to his chest and shakes his head, smiling. "Wonderful, how perfect. Good time to find that out too, ey?"

I help Cora to her feet, and she inhales deeply. "Being alive sure does feel nice." She says, squinting at me in the sunlight.

I pull her into my arms.

Yes. Yes it does.

"Take me home," she whispers. "Let's all go home."

Whatever you say, majesty. Whatever you say.

24
Cora

mryn cries out in his sleep, and I reach over to feel him bathed in sweat.

"Don't touch me!" He snarls, and rolls away from me, sitting up at the edge of the bed.

"Amryn, it's me." I say, kneeling behind him. "Baby, it's me, it's OK."

He leans on his hands, his chest heaving, his hair hanging over his face. "Fuck. It was - fuck." He gasps, running a hand through his hair. "I was back in that fucking cell, and she was -" He exhales heavily. "I - I don't know -"

I tentatively put a hand on his shoulder, and he doesn't flinch. I lean against his back, pressing my cheek against his skin, wrapping my arms around his waist. "It's OK." I whisper. "It's OK. You're here, with me, and you're safe."

"I can't breathe." He gasps.

"Yes you can, baby." I say. I take a deep breath. "We breathe together, remember?"

"Y-yeah." He takes a shuddering breath. Then another. And another.

We've been back in Ocario a month, and this is our routine, almost every night. The nightmares just won't stop. Amryn won't talk to me about what happened, about what they did to him while he was in that cell.

I've stopped asking him. It causes him pain, I can see it, and I'm helpless to stop it. I was so stupid to think we'd get back and everything would just return to normal. They tortured him for a month. The scars run deep.

He turns around and clutches me to him, pushing me down on the bed, kissing me hungrily. This is also part of our nightly routine now. First the nightmares, then recovery, then sex, sometimes two or three times a night.

I'm trying to be understanding, though sometimes I lie awake and wonder if life will ever be the same again. The look on his face when I started bleeding last month haunts me, and I don't know why. Another thing he wouldn't talk to me about, wouldn't explain.

Amryn pushes himself inside me with a groan, and I wrap my arms and legs around him, holding him close as he thrusts.

"Talk to me," he gasps, "let me know it's you."

"It's me, baby," I whisper, "I love you." I moan as his hips grind against me. "You feel so good."

"I'm yours," he murmurs into my ear, "I'm only yours."

Tears burn my eyes. I just want him to tell me what's wrong. Amryn stops suddenly, collapsing on me, holding me close. I feel his chest quivering as he starts to cry.

"Baby, what's wrong?" I ask him quietly. "Please, tell me what's going on?"

He rolls off me and covers his face with his hands. "I don't want to lose you."

I sit up and put a hand on his chest. "Amryn, why would you say that? You're not going to lose me."

He sits up, leaning back against the headboard, hanging his head. "Because something happened, and it's going to change everything, and I just don't know how to get past it." His voice cracks, and I can't bear it anymore.

"Amryn, please tell me what's going on," I plead, reaching out to take his hand. "We can get through anything, come on, it's you and me, right?" After everything we've gone through, what could tear us apart?

He sighs heavily, and clasps my fingers in his. "One night, in the cell," he begins, "Morgan glamoured herself. She crept in and I thought - I thought it was you."

Oh god. I stop myself from saying it, just keep holding his hand, and listening.

"I was weak, and in pain, and starved," he goes on, his other hand picking at the bedsheet, his face turned away from me in the moonlight. "I could barely move. And then she - she -"

My chest tightens. I suppress a gasp. I edge closer to him.

"She climbed on top of me, and I was so confused," he says, "I thought it was you. I thought it was you, coming to get me, and - and then she -"

I bite down on my lip, trying not to cry.

"She wouldn't get off me." Amryn says, and his chest shudders as he breathes. "I couldn't get her off me."

I can't stand it anymore, and press myself against him. "I'm so sorry." I whisper, holding on to him. His arms encircle me, and he buries his face in my hair.

"I tried," he says, his voice strained. "I really did."

I look at him, and the sadness in his face breaks my heart. "You don't have to justify it, she did that to you, it's not your fault." I take his face in my hands. "Baby, there is no reason for you to be ashamed, not at all. This was not your fault. They tortured you, and used everything they had at their disposal to do that. It was not your fault." I kiss him gently. "Why would you ever think you'd lose me over something like this?"

He gazes at me mournfully. "There's more."

I shake my head. "What more?"

"Morgan said that she - she made it so I couldn't have kids." His shoulders shake, and he inhales through gritted teeth. "She said it was so easy to take that, and that I couldn't escape my fate."

I clasp his face in my hands, looking into his eyes. "She was fucking with you, she was lying." Realisation dawns on me. "So when my bleeding started last month, and you got upset, it was because -"

"I know how much you want a baby, a family," he says, "and I wanted to give you that, I wanted a family with you, and now -" His eyes close and he pushes my hands away from his face. "And now, it might not be possible. She's taken that from me, from us." He gets up from the bed and walks to the window. "It doesn't matter what I do,

364

what I fucking do." He punches the window frame, running a hand through his hair. "Those fucking demons, that fucking place, they have me, they own me."

I follow him and turn him around to face me. "Hey, look at me," I say. "Look at me now." His eyes meet mine reluctantly. "They don't own you, they never did. We never let them own us. We defied them, every day, every time we looked at each other, every time we touched each other. Their Fate had no hold over us then, and it doesn't now."

"You don't think Morgan could do that to me?" Amryn asks. "She wiped our memories, our entire lives, from our minds."

I shake my head. "I don't believe her for a second, she was evil, and she was trying to break you. She went to the thing she knew would cause you the most pain."

"And what if she did do that to me?" Amryn asks. "What if now we can never have the family we wanted to have? What if you never get to hold our baby in your arms?"

"I want you," I insist, "*you*. We defied Fate all these years, fought against everything we were told was impossible, you risked death to be with me. You think I'm going to give up on all that now?"

"Cora -"

"No." I clutch him to me, my face tipped up to his. "I love you. You're everything. We're everything. And I will never give that up, ever." I wrap my arms around him, and press my cheek to his chest. "I love you. I love you so much."

His arms wrap around me, and he sighs. "I love you too. More than you'll ever know."

Zadkiel sidles across the yard towards me, his hands behind his back. He looks out over the fields and inhales deeply. "The change of seasons certainly has a scent to it this year," he says.

I look up from my gardening, out over the forest, dotted with trees turning red and gold. "Yes it does," I agree. I squint at him in the warm afternoon light. "Any news?" I ask.

"The last few remnants of the rival clans are scattered to the winds," he says, perching on the edge of the raised garden bed, "I doubt we'll be hearing from any of them ever again. They'll try their luck amongst the humans, and that will be that."

"Good." I stab my pitchfork into a pile of hay, lifting it and spreading it over the dark soil. "And the angels?"

"Azrael has allied himself to you," Zadkiel says, crossing his legs and wrapping his hands around his knee. "He's rather proud of you and Amryn, though he won't admit it."

"Excellent," I reply with a grin, "I always wanted a Grim Reaper on my side."

Zadkiel chuckles. "Indeed."

"And the others?" I ask, raising my eyebrows.

"With the exception of Gabriel, they've all agreed to stay in the Halls and leave the Earth Realm to you. The

Old God's power will never be what it was when we were all in the Halls, but he's stronger now, more than ever." Zadkiel plucks a pansy from the garden bed beside him, lifting it to his face and regarding it curiously. "You really enjoy all this, digging around in the dirt and planting things?"

"Yes, Zadkiel, it's very rewarding."

He scoffs, waving his hand over the pumpkin vine, and I watch as football sized pumpkins sprout. "I don't have the patience for it." He says, shrugging.

"Well thanks for the help," I say, putting my pitchfork down and sitting beside him, wiping my brow with the back of my hand. "So, what about Gabriel?" I look up at Zadkiel when he doesn't reply. "Is he going to be a problem?"

"Oh yes," Zadkiel says, looking out over the valley, avoiding my eyes. "I think he's going to be a big problem. He's not happy about the loss of his brother."

"But he's weak alone, right?"

"He's weak against you," Zadkiel says, casting a sideways glance down at me. "And now that the Line has been restored, he can no longer romp around the world without consequences. The Old God will be keeping an eye on him."

"So what do we do about him?"

Zadkiel shrugs. "Nothing. We drink mead and celebrate your wedding and do nothing."

"Nothing." I repeat with a nod. "Good."

"And how is your groom?" Zadkiel asks me.

"He's -" I break off, rubbing my hands back and forth to get the dirt off them. "He's struggling."

Zadkiel nods. "He suffered a great deal."

"I don't know what to do to help him." I say quietly, and I push back against the lump that forms in my throat. I don't want to cry anymore. I feel like I've cried enough for 20 lifetimes.

Zadkiel uncrosses his legs and rubs his enormous taloned hands along his thighs. "Well, there is something." He says. "It's a bit of old magic, but it might help him."

"What is it?"

He reaches into his pocket and withdraws a vial filled with a liquid that shimmers in the sunlight. "It's a healing elixir, angel's tears." He says to me with a soft smile. "The best thing for a broken heart, or a broken soul." He presses the vial into my hand, and I look down at it as the liquid undulates behind the glass.

"So I just sneak this into his water, or something?" I ask.

"Yes, exactly." Zadkiel nods. "And never tell him. Ever. Healing must come from within, and this is merely a way to help."

"Thank you." I sigh, and lean against Zadkiel. He chuckles abashedly, and his arm moves around my shoulders.

"This is nice," he says, "much nicer than having a dagger in my chest."

I laugh softly. "Yeah, sorry about that."

"No problem. I am a bit of a slippery fuck."

"Did you know?" I ask him.

"Know what, Cora?"

"About Tal. Being my other Draw." I ask, picking at stray pieces of hay stuck to my jeans.

Zadkiel exhales heavily. "Yes, I did. I've always known. Your mother knew too."

"Keep them both close." I say quietly.

"What's that?" Zadkiel asks.

I smile up at him. "My mother, she came to me, in a vision. She told me to keep them both close. To wear the medallion, and that I would know when the time came. And to keep them both close."

"The last Shadow Queen, she was tricked, you see." Zadkiel tells me. "She had dual Draws as well, that was the norm. And the enemy told her to kill one, her lover." He gives me a side glance. "That is also the norm, one is the lover, the other is - well." He chuckles. "I suppose sometimes both may be."

I giggle. "To each their own I guess."

"I suppose so, yes." Zadkiel shakes his head and squeezes my shoulders. "But that was the downfall of the last Shadow Queen. She believed that by killing her lover, using an enchantment, she would ensure his resurrection. Instead, it weakened her, and she was left vulnerable. Which meant Michael and Gabriel could put her in the ground."

"That's terrible." I shudder at the thought.

"It was indeed." Zadkiel agrees.

"Never tell Amryn you knew," I say to him, "if he finds out you kept that to yourself while I was dead on the ground, he'll set your wings on fire."

Zadkiel chuckles. "He most certainly would. And I would perhaps deserve it. It's not easy being an angel sometimes, you know?"

I cock my head. "Is that so?"

"Oh yes." He ruffles his wings. "Knowing things, but not being able to say anything. It's hard." He stops suddenly, his brow furrowing. "It's hard. Seeing people you care about die, knowing you can't stop it."

I nod. "My mother."

"Yes." He straightens his back and clears his throat. "I deeply regret not defying the order of things that day."

"She loved you."

"More than anyone else ever has." He smiles at me sadly. "She was extraordinary, Cora. You are so very much like her. She would be so, so proud of you."

"Thank you," I say, my voice wavering. I sigh as the breeze washes over us, starting to turn cool. "When does life go back to normal, Zadkiel?"

"What is a normal life, my dear?" He asks me, and looks down at me with a smile. "Is it gardening and waiting for pumpkins to grow? Is it going out and battling every rival clan that opposes you?"

I shrug. "I don't know anymore."

"How I see it, you have two options - one, is that you can wonder what if, and wonder what it all means, and never know peace because you're constantly wondering what will come next."

"And option 2?"

"You just - live." He hands me the pansy he picked. "You live and find joy in the small things, and accept that while things may change, some things never will. And those are the things that keep you steadfast, that keep you sane, and that make you happy."

I chuckle, and twirl the pansy between my fingers. "Thanks, Zadkiel. You're one hell of a philosopher."

I'm chopping up vegetables for dinner, the fire crackling away in the hearth behind me, a pot of soup bubbling away on the stove. Wind batters against the window, and I look out at the gathering clouds. It's gotten colder over the past few days, and though it's not yet winter, the sky is heavy and luminous with the promise of snow.

The door flies open, and hurried footsteps sound across the wooden floor of the cabin. "Hey baby," I call as I keep working on dinner. "How are you?"

The knife falls to the floor with a clatter as Amryn's arms go around my waist, his lips pressed urgently to my neck. One of his hands finds its way into my shirt, working my nipple between his fingers.

"Baby," I gasp, "what are you doing?" I giggle as he spins me around, pulling me to him, his mouth on mine, his tongue pushing my lips apart.

371

"I want you," he murmurs, and his hands are at the waistband of his pants, undoing them. I undo my jeans and push them down my legs, kicking them off, and then Amryn grabs me by the waist, putting me up on the kitchen counter.

I wrap my legs around him as he pushes his cock inside me, one hand bracing on the counter behind me, the other wrapped around his shoulders. He fucks me hard, grinding his hips against me. He doesn't ask me to talk, he doesn't need to know it's me, because he knows, it's just us.

He groans. "Oh fuck you feel good," he gasps, and grins at me. "You been thinking about me, huh? You're so wet."

I smile as I throw my head back, the delicious warmth from between my thighs growing. "Always." I whimper as I stretch around him.

"You like that?" He asks me, his hand in my hair, pulling my face to his.

"Yeah." I gasp. "Do it harder."

He growls. "Always wanting it harder, you're so greedy."

I moan as he slams into me. "Yeah," I say with a gasp, "like that."

"You better make plenty of noise for me when you come, baby." He says, his lips pressing against my quickening pulse.

He pulls me down off the counter, spinning me around and pressing himself to my back. I arch against him as his cock slides into me again. "Oh fuck." I moan.

His thrusts are slower now, and his hand moves between my legs, over my clit. He circles me as he savours me, as he drives me closer, closer to the edge. "You're so fucking tight," he groans.

I'm warm all over, and the pressure in my belly starts to unfurl, breaking loose, making my thighs shake as his finger swirls over my clit. I cover my mouth with my hand, and I don't know why, because I haven't had to do this for months now.

"I want to hear you, baby," he says breathlessly.

"Oh fuck," I cry, and I push back against him. I call out his name, and then my body goes straight over that edge, crashing right over it, and I'm pretty sure that scream is me, and my head is so flooded with delirious pleasure I can't see straight.

Amryn groans, and shudders against my back as he comes, his breathing heavy against my ear. "I've been wanting to do that all afternoon," he says, nibbling on my earlobe.

"I'm not opposed to a pre-dinner fuck," I say with a breathy laugh.

He puts a hand on my throat, turning my face to his, and kisses me, deep and sweet. "I don't know what's happened, but I feel like - like -"

I raise my eyebrows. "Like what?"

He withdraws from me, and I turn to put my arms around him. He shrugs and laughs. "I don't know. I just feel better. No more nightmares. And I'm not, I don't know." He smiles at me sheepishly. "I wanted to fuck you today, you know? Like how it used to be, just because I wanted to, because I love you, not because I was trying to push something away."

I lay my head against his chest and smile. "I'm glad you feel better." My eyes flicker to the empty glass vial on the top shelf, leaning up against a clay vase. I look up at him and smile. "And that was a lot of fun, even if I'm not sure if it's like how it used to be. All those stolen moments in bathrooms and on porches in the dark."

Amryn laughs. "That night, god, I was sure someone had heard us. You throwing me down on the fucking garden chair and riding me like that." He kisses the tip of my nose. "You're the reason angels all think we're depraved and sex-crazed."

I swat at his chest. "Asshole."

He laughs and wraps me in a hug. "I love you."

"I love you too."

25
Amryn

The sun illuminates the dust floating over the fields as it rises, and everything looks hazy and magical. I walk back and forth in front of the windows, looking out at the brightening dawn, the floor creaking softly under my bare feet.

Spring has given way to summer, and the surrounding hills are brilliant green. Dawn is a time of day I see a lot these days, and I don't even mind. I missed a month of sunrises in that cell, and I don't want to miss one more. Every single one is perfect.

I hear soft footsteps padding down the hallway, and Cora's standing in the doorway, leaning against the frame, smiling at me. "Good morning." She says quietly.

"Morning."

"He's asleep again." She says.

I look down at the tiny baby curled against my chest, his little mouth moving as he dreams of milk and warmth and his mother. "Yeah, he was out as soon as I picked him up." I reply, my hand gently stroking his black curls. "So I thought I'd just hold him for a bit." I gently kiss Phoenix's head, and he nuzzles in tighter against me.

My son. Our son. Every time I look at him, it's magic.

Cora walks over to me, and leans her head against my arm. "He's so perfect." She whispers, and her green eyes gaze up at me. I still get that same feeling, those same butterflies, the ones only she can give me. I know that will never change.

"Why don't you go back to bed?" I say. "You must be tired. I'll wake you if he gets hungry."

"I'm enjoying this too much," she says, putting an arm around my waist. "I could just watch you two, like this, forever."

The day she told me she was pregnant, I couldn't speak. I was so sure Morgan's spell had worked. Month after month, Cora bled, and the anguish was awful. We told ourselves it was fine, we were young, we weren't really trying, it was just something we hoped for. But the sneaking fear never went away.

Then, a year after Nilau crumbled, and Cora defeated Michael, six months after our wedding, she came running out across the field to find me, to tell me she was pregnant. To tell me I was going to be a father.

And six weeks ago, there he was. Our son. Perfect and tiny, with his mother's eyes. Hair as curly as hers, but as dark as mine.

Being told my whole life that I was fated to be alone has left its scars. I still wake up thinking I'm in that cell, or up on that mountain, or locked in my cabin desperate for Cora's touch, aching for her.

Some days I'm still afraid Fate will call in its debt, and tell me a mistake has been made, and take it all away. But then I reach across the bed and feel her right there beside me, and I remember it's all over, and she's here, and she's mine and I'm hers.

Fate can go fuck itself.

Elise wanders up ahead, Phoenix perched on her hip, his chubby fists clutching on to her blouse. He turns to look at Tal and I as we follow them, and he babbles something. Dadda, Bubba, Mum mum. Tal chuckles.

Cora walks alongside Elise, plucking poppies from the wheat field. She hands one to Phoenix, who tries to eat it, and we all laugh as Cora frantically plucks the petals from his mouth. She smiles over at me, the warm breeze catching her curls, straying them across her face, and she's still the most beautiful thing I've ever seen.

Elise looks over her shoulder at us and waves. "Come on then, you two! There's peaches over here that need picking!"

Cora tucks her hand under Phoenix's chin, tickling him, and he giggles. "Say, come on Daddy. Come on, Uncle Tal." Phoenix waves to us with a closed fist.

Tal puts a hand on my shoulder. "Life is good brother."

I nod. "It sure is."

I'm not alone.

I'm not alone.

I'll never be alone again.

Epilogue

The old man hears the footsteps behind him on the gravel, and he sighs.

"Never thought I'd see you again, Gabriel." He says.

"I'm full of surprises," Gabriel says, sitting down beside him. He looks out over the city sprawling below them, and shakes his head, his nose wrinkling with disgust. "Why do you even like the humans, hmm? They believe in versions of you that don't even exist."

The Old God shrugs. "It doesn't matter to me what they believe, I just want them to be happy."

"Blegh," Gabriel exclaims, grimacing. "You really are going soft."

The Old God chuckles. "Perhaps I am." He gives Gabriel a side-glance. "You've been trying to behave yourself I hope?"

"Why do you ask me like you don't know?" Gabriel says, crossing his arms over his chest and slumping down on the bench. "Now you're all-seeing again, thanks to your fucking Shadow Queen."

"I still like to know you're self-aware," the Old God says with a chuckle.

"Well, I am." Gabriel says, rising to go. "And don't worry, I'll be a very good boy."

"So the ground shaking hasn't got you wondering then."

Gabriel pauses. "I don't know what you're talking about."

"Oh, yes you do." The Old God looks up as two pigeons fly overhead. "You can feel it, can't you?"

"Feel what?"

He looks at Gabriel with raised eyebrows. "You really are the most terrible liar."

Gabriel shrugs. "So there have been some earthquakes, so what?"

"It does make you wonder," the Old God says, stroking his white beard thoughtfully, "how deep you have to bury something before you can be sure it will never come back to haunt you."

Gabriel snorts. "I don't have time for -"

"She's waking up," the Old God says pointedly, fixing his blue eyes on Gabriel. "She's waking up, and when she does, we'll want to hope she doesn't remember anything. Because if she does..." He trails off, tipping his face back as it starts to rain.

"I'm not afraid of her," Gabriel scoffs.

"You should be, my son." He rises to his feet, and puts a hand on Gabriel's shoulder. "You really should be."

Acknowledgments

Mark, my amazing husband and partner, thank you for listening to me, for letting me bounce ideas off you, for ferrying away children so I could work in peace, for letting me sleep in when I spent another night staying up until 3am writing. You googled formatting and watched endless Youtube videos on creating book covers. None of this would have been possible without your love and dedication.

Skye, my beautiful BFF, you listened to endless WhatsApp voicemails about this book, read every scrap I sent you and were always anxious for more. Your enthusiasm kept me going, and drove me to create this world and these characters.

Mum, who high-fived and cheered every milestone, who bragged to anyone who would listen that her daughter was writing real books, who even read the spicy scenes and graciously said nothing about them - thank you.

JR Korpa, you created the beautiful artwork that forms part of the cover for this book, thank you so much for giving me such a stunning face for this story.

Makenna, you read through my ramblings and wrote the blurbs I could never have written - thank you.

My incredible ARC readers , who wept and laughed and blushed, who told me this book is remarkable, a new favourite, your best read of this year - I will never be able to put into words what your love and support meant to me. I cannot thank you enough, and I hope to work with all of you again in the future. (Book 2 - who's ready?)

And finally, the BookTok community, who came through for me during a time when I was so low, when I was ready to give up - you lifted me up, gave me hope, cheered me on, and without all of you this project may never have happened. Thank you, thank you, thank you.

About the Author

R D Baker began writing stories with the encouragement of the amazing Mrs Shooter back in the First Grade. It began with poetry and short stories, growing into full-length novels later in life.

She has previously published a romance novella and two full-length romance novels. The Shadow and The Draw is her first foray into fantasy romance, and definitely not the last.

She lives in the Blue Mountains, Australia, with her family.

Made in United States
North Haven, CT
12 June 2023

37678538R00232